SUBURBAN SOULS: BOOK ONE

'I have always been a great reader of amatory literature and all books and novels relating to sexual matters, whether wilfully obscene or cunningly veiled. I often remarked that such tales were far from true to nature. Most of them are written by men who misjudge women, and when lady novelists write about love they seldom show us a woman as she really is. True tales of sensuality are thus rare, and I come forward to give you mine. It will hurt me, and drag open smarting, half-healed wounds, but I mean to do it and go through it as an expiation.

'I am at the top of the sinners' class and my only excuse is that somehow I manage to be intensely wicked on an honourable, chivalrous basis of my own. You shall find out my style of villainy as you read on ...'

Thus writes Jackie S. at the beginning of his remarkable 'minature drama of lust', the beautifully written, erotic masterpiece -- SUBURBAN SOULS

SUBURBAN SOULS
BOOK ONE

Anonymous

NEXUS

A Star Book
Published in 1982
by the Paperback Division of
W. H. Allen & Co. Plc
Sekforde House, 175/9 St. John Street, London EC1V 4LL

Reprinted 1985, 1989

Printed and bound in Great Britain by
Courier International Ltd, Tiptree, Essex

ISBN 0 352 31176 2

I

DEDICATE

THIS STORY OF SORDID SENSUALITY

TO

MY HEROINE

ONE OF THE WICKEDEST WOMEN IN THE WORLD

THIS HOMAGE IS DUE TO HER,
FOR HAS SHE NOT WRITTEN
A GREAT PART OF THE
BOOK HERSELF?

I

1

Her father loved me, oft invited me.

SHAKESPEARE.

HEART. Why did you not ravish her?

. . . .

CONST. Not I, truly; my talent lies to softer exercises.

SIR JOHN VANBRUGH.

My great fear in setting forth this simple adventure of love and passion is that I shall not be able to carry home to my reader's mind the feelings, the hopes, the doubts and fears that so long racked my soul and stirred up all that was good and bad in the heart and brain of the writer—a very ordinary man.

I have always been a great reader of amatory literature and all books and novels relating to sexual matters, whether wilfully obscene or cunningly veiled; whether written by medical authorities, novelists, or even issued from the secret presses of Belgium and Holland. I often remarked that such tales were far from true to nature. I do not speak of lewd works, where impossibilities are presented merely to augment the sale of the volumes, but of the few which impress us with an idea of truth, being incidents, which, although highly coloured, might perhaps have happened all the same. Such are some of the best French novels. But most of them are written by men who misjudge women, and when lady novelists write about love they seldom show us a woman as she really is, their sympathy for their own sex guiding their partial pens in spite of themselves. Really true tales of sensuality are thus rare, and I come forward to give you mine, where I have carefully endeavoured to keep my imagination within bounds and tell nothing but what did really happen.

It will hurt me, and drag open smarting, half-healed wounds, but I mean to do it and go through it as an expiation.

I am the hero. I cannot help smiling as I write that word. I guess my readers will think I am going to praise myself, and with excuses lead up to an eventual conversion. Do not be led away. I am not a good man. Some may call me vile. You must not put me down as a professional romance-writer. No, I am plain Jacky S—, of the Paris Bourse, writing plain facts, and if I were to see the error of my ways and retire to a monastery at the end of the story, it would be feeble-minded and contrary to human nature. So pity me, and do not crush me beneath the weight of your righteous self-satisfaction. Had I been my own maker, and had I, as a baby, possessed the knowledge of the world I have now, I should have been a good man, without voluptuous longings or abnormal passions, and I should not be writing this vicious book. I know some men get more pleasure out of one Sunday's church-going than I have ever done in a year's enjoyment of wine, women, and gambling. I know not how they do it. I should like to be as they are, but I cannot change my nature, and I shall go to my death as I was born.

Let all young men who read my story, and who will spit out their pitiable contempt for me, the unworthy author, wallowing in the slime of sensuality, take a scribbling diary and jot down their secret longings for a few months. Truthfully, mind you. At the end of a quarter's record, just hark back and see if the chronicle agrees or disagrees with my acts.

Why are we as we are? Hereditary influences, education, surroundings—Heaven knows what. Conclusion: some men are bad, a few are good, most of us are betwixt and between.

I am at the top of the sinners' class and my only excuse is

that somehow I manage to be intensely wicked on an honouraḃle, chivalrous basis of my own. You shall find out my style of villany as you read on.

I have spoken the prologue. Let me now try and introduce the actors in this miniature drama of lust.

Eric Arvel was a correspondent of the financial press. His duties brought him to the Bourse nearly every day, and he used to watch the market and send off long columns of criticism on the rise and fall of stocks and shares to newspapers in England, Germany, and Russia. He was a man of many languages and I never knew his precise nationality. I expect he was born of English and Continental parents and had been brought up in Great Britain. But his business and birth have very little to do with the present memoirs, although I often thought he was of Jewish extraction and the German strain seemed to predominate. Besides his financial elucubrations, he wrote letters of Parisian gossip for many newspapers, and had other strings to his bow. I think he was often employed by houses of business in London to travel and collect debts, or help to get evidence for solicitors in Great Britain. He journeyed greatly at one time all over Europe, and once had a mission that took him to China and Japan, returning from those countries with heaps of curiosities, such as quaint idols, dainty porcelain, and beautifully embroidered silk gowns, wherewith to delight the females of his household. I never troubled about his writings or his doings. It was no concern of mine what money he had or how he accumulated it. I had known him for years, how many I cannot now remember. I am 47, as I write now, and I am nearly sure we must have been acquainted twenty years before. I occupied a good position on the French Stock Exchange, and earned and spent money like water. When plying his avocation, he frequently fell across me and other members of my family, who were in the same line of business, and he knew all my parents at home. He was perfectly straightforward in all his monetary transactions, which is paying him a great compliment, as journalists are generally shifty paymasters. We seemed to have a little sympathy for each other, as we had many tastes in common, and so we got drawn together, although I think he was about twelve years my senior. I do not know his precise age, but we will say he is about sixty. He was fond of tales of scandal, liked gossiping about people, and was pleased to know how much money they possessed and if they were in good circumstances or not. I used to feed his curiosity and chop funny stories about all sorts and conditions of men with him. I would furnish him with what information I could for his articles, and he in return gave me a cunningly worded advertisement as often as possible. He liked reading as I do and I lent him books. One or two were of a spicy sort. I furnished him with reviews and magazines for years, sending him packets of papers twice and thrice a month. His tastes seemed to lead him towards lechery. I was always fond of women and so our conversation was often of the most lascivious kind. He was a great smoker and was seldom without the Englishman's briar in his mouth. I am also a votary of the weed, and we would swop tobaccos and have many a long chat together about the scandals of the Exchange, the amours of our circle of financiers and the latest echoes of the London clubs, for I am an Englishman, although my life has been passed in Paris. I never was much of a scandalmonger myself, being too indifferent to the wagging of the world, but I used to collect little stories to please my friend. I do not think he was very liberal-minded, nor very particular to a lie or two, especially when he fell to boasting about how he had succeeded in one thing or another, but I took good care never to contradict him. He possessed the usual vanity of ordinary middle-class folk, and gave his opinion on current topics boldly, albeit I could often see he had never studied the subject he was talking about. He was very fond of money, but careful and saving withal. One trait that always grated upon me was that he seemed pleased to hear of the downfall of anybody, even when the victim of circumstances was a perfect stranger to him and had never been in his way. So I suppose there was a little envy and a great deal of jealousy in his composition. In appearance, he was tall, corpulent, and a trifle weak at the knees. He was far from ill-looking and must have been handsome in his youth. He was fair, with a thick moustache and no beard; bald, with a fine-shaped Roman nose and open nostrils. He was shortsighted and wore a pince-nez. His eyes were blue and he bit his nails to the quick. Some ten years ago he had suffered from a mysterious malady, and he wasted to a skeleton, so that everybody thought he was not long for this world. He spoke vaguely of some kidney trouble, and then he rallied, miraculously as I thought, and grew quite stout.

During all these years I had only met him as one man of the world meets another and cared nothing about his private life. He had frequently begged me to come and see him at his suburban dwelling at Sonis-sur-Marne, which, as all the world knows, is about twenty minutes ride by train from the Eastern station of Paris, but I had always refused, or put him off on some specious pretext, as I was very diffident about making fresh acquaintances, and if there was one thing I hated more than another it was pushing myself into people's houses. But in 1895, having been bitten by a mania for possessing and rearing dogs, I happened to have a very fine litter of fox terriers, and I asked Mr. Arvel if he would care to accept a bitch six months old, who promised to make a nice animal. He seemed very pleased at the offer, telling me that he wanted a dog who would be watchful and give the alarm down in the country, and he asked me to come to lunch and bring the puppy, who I had christened Lili. Oddly enough, I found that my friend's house was called Villa Lilian, and this name was cut into the stone at the side of the gate. The name of Lilian or Lily is destined to play a great part in my life, as my mistress—for I have a mistress, as every Parisian has—was also named Lily. This latter lady plays but an insignificant part in this narrative, and so I pass her by for the present.

But the story is of my love and I will introduce her at once, as I am dying to write her description. My pen moved slowly as I tried to conjure up the heavy, sullen, dull figure of my host and now it runs fast; my pulse quickens and my heart beats, as I endeavour to give a faint idea of the lineaments and bearing of the girl who was destined to offer me a little pleasure and cause me plenty of pain.

And her name was Lilian too. She was a pronounced brunette, and at first sight you could scarcely call her handsome. But she was full of expression, and when pleased, and her face lighted up in the heat of conversation, was very pretty. Her visage might be compared to an unfinished sketch; the features were good, taken one by one, but they lacked completion and rounding off. Her eyes were beautiful, of a rich brown, large and liquid, like those of an intelligent hound, with long lashes, and symmetrical, bushy, black eyebrows overshadowed them. The sign of jealousy was unmistakeably there, for the brows met above the bridge of a sharply cut nose, which was perhaps a trifle too long. There was an air of decision about the pointed chin, but this singular young girl possessed a remarkable mouth, which could not fail to attract a masculine observer and which was in perfect harmony with her other features. It was long and large and the fleshy lips seemed to be never still. All her emotions, all the secret inward movements of her mind betrayed themselves by the ever-changing unrest of these two rosy cushions. Sometimes the corners rose up, unveiling a chaplet of pretty, white teeth, as pointed as those of a young wolf, and their pearly enamel contrasted with the brilliant carmine of the lips, which she was always biting and licking with the end of her tongue. Her sensual mouth resembled a brutal red wound across the dark olive tint of her face. Sometimes these strange lips pursed themselves together in a rapid pout; or half-opened, appeared to be drinking in a delightful draught of air, or better still, imploring the white heat of a lascivious lover's scalding kiss. When out of temper, she was positively ugly: two black circles appeared round the eyes, which became gloomy; a dull, bluish tinge overcast her skin and the mysterious lips turned positively violet. She possessed an admirable forest of splendid blue-black hair and needed but a blood rose behind her ear and a lace mantilla on her shapely head to be the living picture of a cigarmaker of Seville, and this was not to be wondered at, as she had Spanish blood in her veins. She was of middle height; thin, with no bust, and the lines of her figure were perfect, there being nothing angular about her. Her waist was naturally small, while her hips and the lower part of her frame were well developed. She was quick, deft in her manner, with a pleasing voice, and possessed the gift of being at ease in society, thus making those who approached her happy to be in her company. She spoke English with a slight accent, which

was an additional charm, and was fairly well educated, writing
both English and French with very few faults. She was domesticated, and knew how to sew, cut out and make dresses, and cook
a little, but thanks be to Heaven, she was no musician and although the Villa Lilian boasted a piano when I first knew her she
could only teaze it with one tapering finger. Her Papa had some
peculiar theories about the necessity for a young lady to be able to
earn her own living, and he had placed her for some years at
Myrio's, in the Rue de la Paix, a celebrated house for making
ladies' head-coverings. So Lilian was a milliner, and she made hats
and bonnets for the wealthy little bourgeoises of Sonis, and the
wives of the retired tradespeople, who inhabited the mansions and
châteaux in the sleepy village during the summer, so Lilian had
several workgirls in a kiosque in the garden, and was supposed to be
lucratively employed in her leisure hours until such time as the
proverbial Mr. Right should come along and take her away to bear
him a strictly limited number of children and become a staid married lady. But this was not to be.

On my first visit to the Villa Lilian, in the middle of May,
1895, I was received with great cordiality. The little bitch seemed
to please Monsieur, Madame, and Mademoiselle.

I must say at once that Mr. Arvel was not married and the
lady who was at the head of his household was not his wife. She
was a short, stout, little Frenchwoman, about 45 years of age, as
far as I could judge, with the fine eyes, black hair, and pearly teeth
that she had handed down to her daughter Lilian. She was very
vulgar and quite uneducated but was a fine specimen of the French
middle-class housewife, having all the qualities and faults of the
Gallic peasantess. She was very frugal, avaricious, a foe to dusty
corners and untidiness, and an excellent cook. I think Eric Arvel,
who was a tremendous eater, loved her for the dainty dishes she
used to set before him. Her greatest pleasure was to see him gorge
and all her guests were bound to overeat themselves to please her.
She seemed tolerably artful, cunning and hot-tempered. Besides
her daughter Lilian, there was a son, two years younger, Raoul, but
he was being brought up in England and I was not destined to
meet him until three years later.

I already had a slight bowing acquaintance with Madame Adèle, Arvel's mistress, and I knew he had lived with her as her husband for about sixteen or seventeen years when this story opens. He told me frankly of his position, and how everybody at Sonis believed them to be married, and I found that he had brought up the boy and girl, his mistress being left a widow only three years after the birth of the children, and they had lived together ever since. He intended to marry her eventually and although they quarrelled now and again, she was evidently fond of her lord and master, but he, very hasty, obstinate and despotic, did not seem to care much for her. He liked his house, his garden, his dogs, his pipe and his bicycle, and when his routine work was done, dashed off with sufficient facility, his pleasure consisted of a heavy meal, a pipe, and desultory reading.

His house was a pretty one, and had been bought cheaply with the economies of Madame, to whom it belonged. A year after I knew him, some adjoining ground being in the market, he bought it, enlarged the garden and improved the house. I must not forget that Adèle's mother occasionally appeared on the scene, but she was a silly old lady, slightly eccentric, inasmuch as she tried to doctor everybody with mysterious herb medicines and was a general nuisance. Eventually, Mr. Arvel pensioned her off, to stop her coming to the house. He was the breadwinner, and I could see that his mistress and the girl did all they could to make him a comfortable home, as they were entirely dependent on him. He spent plenty of money on the villa and garden, meaning it as a little piece of property for Adèle, if anything should happen to him.

After this first day spent with the family, I did not mean to return, as Arvel's boasting conversation was trite and commonplace, and the mother was a cypher, once away from her housework or the kitchen. But I fell in love with Lilian at first sight. When I say I fell in love with her, I hardly know how to analyse my own feelings. I can only say that I desired her. But she was 19, and I was 43, and I tried to put this new passion out of my mind. There was my Lily too, in a pretty little home I had put together for her, bit by bit, and I had an idea that it would be a scurvy trick to make love to the young lady, who I may call the stepdaughter of my host. I made myself agreeable to the two ladies and was invited down to their pleasant little country house over and over again. Sometimes my faithful companion, my dog Smike, was invited too, to be petted and made much of by Lilian, and so was his mate, the mother of the bitch Lili, good old Sally Brass. I never came empty-handed, and brought them presents of perfumery, flowers, sweets, and such trifles as please the female mind. Lilian took no particular notice of me, treating me with politeness and nothing more. The little bitch grew apace, and Papa, who was very hard to convince, got into his head that in-and-in breeding was good for fox terriers and borrowed its father to cover the daughter, Lili. He got a tolerable litter, but they were all more or less faulty. An outside cross was wanted, but they doted on their pets and kept several bitches of the litter, and one dog, Blackamoor, who became the special pet of Mademoiselle. They already had one dog, a tremendous Bordeaux hound, very good to his masters, but ferocious with strangers. All this brought me continually to the cottage and no doubt I pleased the women, or else they would have taken good care not to Have had me at their house so often.

I remember meeting Mr. and Mrs. Arvel, I speak of them as if they were legally married, at Le Treport, in August, 1896, quite by accident. I joked freely with Adèle, as French matrons are very fond of loose talk, being alone with her for a short time, and chaffed her about this trip with her husband to the seaside. Lilian was at home, with her Granny to look after her. It was quite a honeymoon, I said. She answered me quietly that Mr. Arvel was far from loving, and that she suffered greatly from his neglect, being rather sensual. This startled me a little, and I drew back and kept out of the way, as I was thinking of the daughter and not of the mother.

But it made me open my eyes and I began to think that perhaps I was rather too scrupulous and there might be a chance for me with Lilian. Mr. Arvel's conversations too were very lewd, but he particularly impressed upon me how innocent Lilian was. She knew nothing of the relations of the sexes and was very frivolous, not caring for any serious pleasures.

He complained that he could not get her to read a book and

so form her mind. In fact, he spoke against her and ran her down continually, and his mistress came in also for a share of his disdain. I was a long time victim of this peculiar mania of his, but I found out afterwards that such backbiting is a common fault with little-minded people, and occurs in many families. The more such parents love their children, wives or relations, the more they speak against them. The principal motive is jealousy, lest you should think too much of them, to the detriment of their own vanity, and they seem to get annoyed with themselves to find that the person they are trying to lower in your estimation should take up so much of their own thoughts or yours. But I could see that he was very fond of Lilian and was always talking about her. He would teaze her and call her "Scraggy," and pinch her calves as she passed him. She would shriek, putting out her tongue at him, and appealing to Mamma for help, and Adèle would scold both her and Papa.

I used to try to get alone with Lilian in corners, but she did not want me, and when she stroked Blackamoor, I would caress him too and attempt to get my hand on hers, but she never took heed.

I remember one day she was indisposed, as she seemed to suffer from stomach troubles, and, in her dressing-gown, she came and sat next to me on a sofa. Her father, as I call him to prevent useless reiteration, was seated opposite us. She was quite close to me and I could feel the warmth and pressure of her body through the light fabric of what was evidently her only garment. A thrill of sensual longing stirred me, but she felt nothing. I mentioned the circumstance to her a year later, but she confessed that she had no recollection of this trifling incident, which I always remember.

So things went on until the summer of 1897, when I made up my mind to gradually drop the Arvel family. I loved the girl, although I had never betrayed myself and I could see I was nothing to her. I dared not speak out, as I still had the sentiment of honesty, which told me that I must not take a mean advantage of my friend's hospitality, especially as he appeared to be very fond of the girl, and they were for ever together, when she invariably sided with her Pa against her Mamma.

When I was invited to Sonis, Lilian would often write to me in obedience to Papa's wishes, and I would answer her as prettily as I dared. I was quite surprised and delighted to find that in July or August, 1897, her letters seemed to get more cordial and one day she asked me to accompany her to the post-office alone. I went with great pleasure, especially as up to now Papa had always accompanied us, and the only liberty I had ever taken was a little mild chaff about marriage, when she would retort that she never intended to wed, but would always remain with her Papa. I was pleased to find that Lilian was as near as possible making love to me and I could see that I had very little work to do to make myself thoroughly liked.

The first few letters, which were merely invitations by her parents' orders, I have destroyed, but some of them now contained very gracious hints to encourage me to carry on what was fast growing into a real flirtation. We had many such walks and talks, but I was too flushed with my triumph to remember dates or take notes, and I must try to sum up all our conversations together and so get on rapidly, as I mean to endeavour to stick to plain facts, making my confessions as concise as possible. I have carefully avoided all reference to extraneous events (except in one or two notable instances), passing guests I met at Sonis, or indeed anything that has no bearing upon the loves of Jacky and Lilian.

Our talk began to run into very loose channels, as Lilian, in answer to an insidious question of mine, told me that one of her lady customers had made love to her, and much to her disgust had kissed her on the mouth. I explained that there was something masculine about her—she was wearing a boy's straw hat—and soon led her to talk about lovers. She told me that she had never had one, but had flirted a little. She did not like young fellows, but preferred men of mature age. Upon this I followed suit and put myself forward, to be, of course, agreeably received. This was our first important chat, as far as I can recollect, and I was soon in receipt of another note, begging me to come and spend the day and asking after the health of my dog Smike. She added that she sent a kiss to him, as she did not dare to offer one to his master, although she would dearly like to do so.

Our next interview, during another quiet ramble in the streets and lanes of Sonis, was more to the point. I took her hand in mine and caressed her bare neck as I made a bold declaration of love, but she spoke of danger. I explained that I was not a youth and that a man of the world like myself could give pleasure without fear of disagreeable consequences. I offered, in one word, caresses without danger.

"I should want more than that," she answered.

I thought immediately that she had already been in the arms of a real lover, and that she was alluding to the male's approach in its entirety, and resolved to let my pent-up desire have full vent. So I told her how I had long since yearned for her and reminded her of my little attempts to approach her. She quite understood that if I had returned to Sonis again and again, it was for her and her only. So I soon extracted from her a half-promise that she would come to me one day in Paris, and I was to correspond with her in a feigned lady's handwriting, as neither Papa nor Mamma tampered with her letters, as long as the envelopes seemed to betray. a female correspondent, who might be a customer. I then asked for the promised kiss, but explained that I did not want a silly, grand-motherly pressure of the lips.

"I want a real French kiss," I said.

She laughed. I guessed she understood.

I simply thought that here was a young person fresh from the workroom of a milliner of the Rue de la Paix, who probably had already been enjoyed by a man, without counting possible Lesbian approaches of her companions, and thus I grew bolder and bolder. We returned home, and nearing the kitchen, which was in the basement, we passed through a lobby where there was hardly any light.

"How dark it is here!" whispered Lilian, and I immediately turned round and clasped her in my arms. My lips were on her mouth at once—the mouth I had longed for two years and more —and to my delight I felt her cool and moist, pointed tongue slowly insert itself between my willing lips and join mine. It was an enchanting embrace. I felt such a shudder of longing lust rush through my veins as I have never felt before or since, and I believe I shall never forget Lilian's first kiss.

LILIAN TO JACKY.

Sonis-sur-Marne, October 20th. 1897.

My dear Mr. S . . . ,

You must think I am a little humbug by not having received an answer to your charming letter, but really it is no fault of mine.

I have much to do this week and in spite of my great desire, it has been impossible for me to get away for the whole of one afternoon.

When I meet you, I should wish to have enough time not to run away directly I arrive. I am certain that we shall have much to say to each other.

Will you let me come to you Thursday week? If yes, I shall be in Paris at 2:30. Do not wait for me at the Gare d l'Est, but tell me yourself the place where I am to find you. I am too ignorant to fix a rendezvous myself.

I hope to have a word from you shortly. Awaiting a reply, please accept the assurance of my most lively sympathy,

LILIAN.

LILIAN TO JACKY.

Sonis-sur-Marne, October 26th. 1897.

As I know my dear Marie is very amiable,* I ask her to kindly await me next Thursday, so that I shall not have to ask the concierge about . . . you?

I can see you smile, but what would you have? . . . I cannot surmount a certain feeling of timidity.

I have to go to London, Friday or Saturday, but this will not prevent me keeping the appointment, for—must I confess it?—I await next Thursday with immense impatience!

Soon I shall have the pleasure of teazing you and listening to all the silly things you talk about in your last note,

LILIAN.

Lilian was acquainted with a young woman about her own age, whose Christian name was Charlotte, and who was employed in a

---

* My letters, written in violet ink in a feminine hand on fancy note-paper, quite different from my own, were supposed to be from a female and I always signed them: "Marie."

firm of some importance in Paris. They sold lace, and Charlotte's uncle was at the head of the firm, I think. Anyhow, Charlotte occupied a certain position in the business, and as a person of confidence was required to visit London yearly in the autumn, it had been arranged that Lilian should accompany Charlotte and talk the necessary English. Lilian had already done this journey the year before and the two families were friendly. All Mademoiselle Arvel's expenses were defrayed, and she received one hundred francs for each week she stopped in London. It was generally a fortnight or three weeks until all the customers had been visited. Lilian was delighted, as she could thus see her brother Raoul, of whom she appeared to be very fond.

LILIAN TO JACKY.

Sonis-sur-Marne, Thursday, October 27th. 1897.

Here are all our, or so to speak more correctly, all my beautiful castles in the air demolished. I am really unlucky, I, who was full of such great joy at the idea of seeing you to-morrow, to be able to tell you, perhaps even to prove to you that a certain person not only seems to like you and interests herself in all you do, but that she really loves you.

But to return to the real reason of this letter. I am kept a prisoner by a severe cold.* Impossible to go out. If you will allow me and if it does not worry you, I will give you an appointment for next week, unless I have to go to London on Saturday. In that case, I will write immediately I return. It seems as if everything was against me just now. I hope you will think of the poor little invalid, who is always thinking of you.

LILIAN.

LILIAN TO JACKY.

London, November 2nd. 1897.

I am here since Saturday evening and I already wish to be back again. No, decidedly, I shall never get used to London! All is sad and dull. The women look like machines on springs and the men seem to

---

* Her monthly indisposition?

be running as if pursued. Nowhere is there to be seen the grace of true Parisienne. I hope you will not be vexed at my frankness. I ought not to say what I think of your fellow countrymen, and yet in my eyes you are so unlike most Englishmen. At any rate, you only have their qualities. Thus having all English and French qualities, you must consequently be perfect. Still I confess that my hope is that I shall not find you so. What a bore a man must be who possesses every virtue!

No, I really do not know what I ought to bring you back from London, but you have only to make a sign and if it will give you the least pleasure, I shall only be too happy to do it.

I hope to be at Sonis for the end of next week. It is useless for me to tell you that as soon as I am free I shall write to you to ask if you still have the same wish for me. I have not quite got over my cold. Thanks for kind advice.

This letter carries to you a kiss as soft and as sweet as you can possibly desire.

LILIAN.

Strange to say there was no address on this letter from London, so that I could not answer it.

LILIAN TO JACKY.

Sonis-sur-Marne, November 16th. 1897.

Once more I am near you. According to my promise, and for my own pleasure, I quickly write to you. I shall be free any day you like next week. To you, my dear confidant, I may tell the little trouble I had on the eve of my departure from London. I lost a five pound note. Am I not unlucky? But I weary you with all my stories, so I leave you, but expect a line in return.

Soon I hope to see you.

LILIAN.

I did not like this letter, and my growing passion, from fever heat fell to freezing point. Was this the missive to receive on the eve of a young girl's first appointment? It smacked of the professional. Did she want to sell herself? I resolved to have no more to do with her, and despite the agony of disillusion, I answered as follows:

Jacky to Lilian.

Paris, Thursday, November 18th. 1897.

My dear Lilian,

I am very pleased to hear you have safely returned from your journey and that you are in good health.

I was not able to answer your letter from London, for you forgot to give me your address.

You are very kind in letting me know that you can come and say "how d'ye do" to me next week, and I should like to fix a day, but unfortunately I am forced to go away on Monday, having something to do in another country.

I am very sorry to hear of your trouble, but I hope things will right themselves. We are neither of us very lucky.

Affectionate sympathy from your friend.

MARIE.

This last note crossed one from Papa, as follows:

Eric Arvel to Jacky.

Sonis-sur-Marne, November 18th. 1897.

Dear Jacky,

If you have nothing better to do, the ladies would be glad to see you to-morrow at eleven, to give your valued opinion as to the merits of a turbot fresh from England and a hen pheasant. I shall be at my office in the Rue Vissot until 10:15 to-morrow morning, and then I shall take the train for home.

Hoping you are all well at home, and asking you to remember me to everybody, believe me to remain,

Yours very truly,
ERIC ARVEL.

NOVEMBER 19, 1897.

I kept the appointment with Papa and he informed me that he had been in the North of England, but had passed a few days in London with Lilian, Charlotte, and the boy, Raoul, for whom, it appears, he had procured a situation in a big wine-merchants' establishment of the British metropolis. He was in a terrible rage against Charlotte for she and Raoul were engaged to be married, much to his disgust. Raoul was too young to think as yet of conjugal ties and Charlotte was very silly, and had no money, earning only a slight salary in her uncle's business. He was very angry to find she had captured the youth by her blandishments, and he hinted vaguely that the loving couple had stopped out late and left poor Lilian alone in the lodgings, which annoyed him very much. He swore that the erring girl should never darken his doors again or corrupt his daughter.

The day passed as usual, but Lilian was cold towards me. She had to go and see a lady from England, who stopped at a hotel in the Rue de Rivoli and who always bought a few hats of her, whenever she passed through Paris. I asked to be allowed to accompany Mademoiselle, as I too had an appointment for that afternoon, and Pa and Ma being nothing loth, we started off together.

In the railway carriage, I once more clasped my Lilian in my arms, and found to my great delight that she was what I should call a natural kisser, revelling in long-drawn-out caresses of the mouth. Her lips seemed to weld themselves to mine, and I am sure that my dove-like osculation and the touch of my tongue round her throat, ears, and eyes gave her as much pleasure as a girl could feel.

"Your kisses make me crazy!" or: "Your mouth drives me mad!" were two of her favourite phrases as, when shivering with lasciviousness, she would tear herself from my embrace, only to put up her brilliant mouth over and over again a moment afterwards.

There was no doubt that she had no physical repugnance to me, for it often occurs that a woman thinks she would like a man, and when he at last takes her in his arms, something about him, his odour, his skin, his manner of embracing, his breath, nay, the merest trifle, sometimes rudely dispels all the feminine illusion. Lilian freely yielded herself up to the delight of being clasped to my breast, and my lips pleased her as hers did me.

She asked me what I meant by my voyage for the following Monday. I replied that I had business at Amsterdam, which might or might not be done by letter, but that I really felt great remorse and shame at my dishonourable conduct in making clandestine love to a young lady under her parents' roof, and I said that I trembled to think what would happen if her mother and father found out how I was betraying the implicit confidence they had in me. She replied hotly that her so-called father was a lazy, selfish, bad-tempered man, who cared not a jot for her or her future. And her mother was wrapped up in him and herself. They forced her to contribute one hundred francs a month for her keep, whether she earned them or not, and she was not happy at home. She could not understand the change in my conduct. I took her tenderly in my arms and told her that all my scruples vanished now that I felt her clinging to me, and the kisses of her soft and voluptuous mouth made me forget duty, honour, everything, but the hope of making her mine.

My hands wandered all over her body, pressing her luxuriant posteriors, her thighs, which I found of proper size, her arms, hands and neck, and I exclaimed:

"I know that Lilian returns the love I have felt for her for two years, although I am twice her age. I am happy now and care for naught else!"

And it was true, I was drunk with love, desire, lust, passion, call it what you will.

I made her unfasten her jacket, and sought to press her breasts, but there were only two little, faintly-developed hillocks. Her cloth dress was closely fastened under her arm with hooks and eyes.

"You hurt me," she said, as I feverishly moulded her little bosom.

"I love to hurt you. I love to think that you are mine to do with as I choose, to make you suffer, if I so will it, and I'll squeeze your tiny breasts until you wince with pain."

"They are small," she retorted, laughingly, "but they are firm. Now I want to know what it was you asked me to bring you back from London?"

"I would have written in answer to your letter, but you forgot to give me your address. This is what I wanted you to carefully keep for me and bring back with you," and I pressed my hand between her swelling thighs, outside her dress.

She hid her face in my neck, whispering:

"It is yours. I am yours entirely!"

Luckily, we had arrived at the station, and I drove her to the hotel in the Rue de Rivoli. I had forgotten all about her letter. I was oblivious of everything and everybody. I could only clasp her to me and caress her and kiss her, and kiss her again, until her lips were on fire.

But I did not forget to give her an appointment for the 23rd. I was on good terms with the proprietress of a house in the Rue de Leipzig, where they let furnished apartments, and where there was a little *pavillon* at the bottom of the yard. Lilian had only to walk through, without speaking to the concierge, and come straight to me, who would be eagerly awaiting her arrival at half-past two. With a last luscious embrace, I saw her go into the hotel and I drove home.

NOVEMBER 23, 1897.

I have just left Lilian. The day was partially spoilt, but neither of us are to blame. I was punctually at my appointment and I had made the toilette of a bridegroom. I waited an hour, but there were no signs of her, so I left in a rage, pursued by the sardonic grin of the *bonne*. I returned home and took off my finery, when I received the following *petit bleu*:

LILIAN TO JACKY.

November 24th. 1897. 3:45 P.M.

Have just been to the Rue de L. I was one hour and a half late, but through no fault of mine. There has been an accident at the Gare de l'Est and all the trains are late.

I hope you will excuse me and believe that I am furious, especially when I was told that you had just gone.

I am longing to see you,

LILIAN.

I shall only take the 6:45, from the Gare de l'Est to-night.

Of course, I was at the station at the hour mentioned, and found that her story was true. There had been an accident and there was a thick fog. The entire service was disorganized. The station was full of a seething, roaring crowd, and Lilian telegraphed home, stating the case, saying she should go and dine with her grandmother, who lived near the Bourse, and return to the station later, or perhaps sleep with the old lady.

I drove her about in a cab for an hour, which was all the time I could spare, having disposed of my evening.

We were now thoroughly familiar, and in answer to my eager queries, she told me she was a virgin. I did not believe her for an instant, but I naturally said nothing. I told her how I had made an elaborate toilet in anticipation of full possession, and she confided to me that she was very fond of fine linen, and that she, too, had put on everything she had of the best, including a black satin petticoat she had made herself. I put my hand under her clothes to verify her statement, and she let me place my inquisitive fingers on her thigh above her knee, but she objected that my hands were like ice, and I desisted. But I took her hand and thrust it upon the rapidly rising sign of my virility, outside my trousers, and she offered no resistance. I told her, with many cunning periphrases, that my lips would kiss every part of her sweet little body and cause her ineffable delight.

"And I will give you back kiss for kiss. You must teach me to love you as you love me."

"You shall be my little slave of love. Everything I tell you, you must do. I shall exact obedience. And now you must tutoyer me."

"That I shall never dare to do. You must keep on saying your delicious tu to me, but I shall always be respectful to you."

"As you choose. Perhaps you are right. I am so much older than you. I will be your father, and you shall be my little daughter. You are my incestuous daughter. Do you like the idea of committing the infamous crime of incest with me?"

"Oh, yes! It is a very pretty idea. I love to hear you talk, and as you kiss, tell me what you are going to do to me. You shall be my Papa, my sweet Papa."

"Now let me ask you something. Has M. Arvel—do not be offended with what I am going to say—he is not your real father, but only your Mamma's lover, as he has told me himself. Has he ever taken liberties with you?"

"Oh no! He is very respectful to me and very severe in everything of that kind. The only time he ever said anything rude was after he had nursed me through a long illness, when I had inflammation of the bowels. He said, one day: 'Lily, what a big black forest you have got!' I was so angry!"

I forget now all the promises of voluptuous passion I poured into her willing ears, but I can well remember that she answered incessantly:

"Yes, yes! Tell me more! Tell me what you will do to me!"

And she sucked my mouth deliciously. I spoke vaguely of infinite delights, of unknown joys, but I was afraid to go too far. If she is a virgin, I thought, I may alarm her, and, if she is not, she knows already as much as I can tell her.

So I dropped her near her Granny's but not before we had made another appointment for the 26th.

She is profoundly vicious and deeply naïve, not knowing herself what she wants. If my diagnostic is wrong, then she is the most consummate actress ever seen, beating Sara Bernhardt and La Duse out of sight.

I had now begun to make a few notes in my diary concerning this bizarre maiden. The idea about her being a clever comedienne, I jotted down at the time. My souvenirs will now take a more tangible form, as nearly every date stated is correct, and I can manage to render an account of every important caress we ever gave or received. Her letters were generally in French, but a few are written in English, and others in both languages mixed. I have not altered a word, but have simply translated them as well as I could. I wrote in French. Papa's letters I also give, and in fact every scrap of documentary evidence bearing on the story. Some of my own letters I give in extenso, as I kept copies of a few. Unfortunately certain missives,—the best or the worst,—are in the hands of the heroine, and I can only give a brief summary when necessary, as memory serves, or omit them altogether. The greater part of this narrative was written day by day as the incidents occurred, especially the later portion, and events, serious to me, transpired, which in the hands of a craftsman ought perhaps to have modified earlier opinions, and caused a more harmonious resetting of the whole story. I prefer to leave my manuscript as it is. It may be full of faults and contradictions, but these defects will show the reader that this is not a novel composed on ordinary lines. It is a simple confession, where a man coldly performs the operation of vivisection on his own heart and brain, and my greatest reward will be if the reader, on finishing the memoir—supposing that he does finish it—exclaims: "I should think it is all true!" And if lady readers gibe bitterly at the author, and say it is a tissue of falsehood and utterly impossible, then my triumph will be complete.

NOVEMBER 26, 1897.

Everyone knows the feverish excitement experienced by an eager lover, when awaiting his mistress at the first appointment. I felt hot and excited, and gave a great sigh of relief, when Lilian slowly lifted the portière and advanced towards me in the tawdrily furnished bedroom of the mysterious pavillon of the Rue de Leipzig. I quickly bolted the door, and drew her to me, placing her on my knee, as I sat on the inevitable chaise-longue. She seemed worried and frightened, and told me that she had great trouble in getting away from home. There was a tremendous struggle to get her dress unfastened, and she studiously avoided looking towards the large curtained bed that occupied the middle of the room. She hoped I would not touch it, as if I did, people of the house would guess we had been using it! I tried by my kisses to warm her blood, and I think I succeeded, for she grew more and more bold, and I was able to undo her dress, and feast my eyes on her tiny breasts, which were like those of a girl of fifteen. Nevertheless, the size of the red and excited nipples proved her real rage. I sucked and nibbled them greedily, and her pretty ears and neck also came in for a share of attention from my eager lips and tongue. I begged her to let me take off all her garments, but she wanted me to be satisfied with her small, but beautifully made breast. I pretended to be deeply hurt and she excused herself. I must have patience. This was the first time. She would be more yielding when she knew me better. I replied by boldly throwing up her skirts, and after admir-

ng her legs, in their black stockings, and her coquettish be-rib-
boned drawers, I, at last, placed my hand on the mark of her sex.
It was fully covered with a thick, black undergrowth and quite
fleshy. The large outer lips were fatter and more developed than
we generally find them among the women of France. Her legs,
though slim, were well-made, and her thighs of fair proportions.
I began to explore the grotto.

"You hurt me," she murmured.

And as far as I could tell, she seemed to be intact, or at any
rate had not been often approached by a man. I could feel that
my caresses delighted her greatly and she gave way a little. At last,
I persuaded her to take off her petticoat and drawers. She consented, on condition that I would not look at her. I acquiesced
and she dropped her skirt and took off her bodice, standing before
me in her petticoat and stays. She wore a dainty cambric chemise,
tied with cherry ribbons, and I enjoyed the sight of my love thus
at last in my power. I gloated over her naked shoulders; the rosy
nipples, stiff, and glistening with my saliva; and the luxuriant black
tufts of hair beneath the armpits.

She consented now to drop her petticoat, and as I leant back
on the sofa, she placed one soft, cool hand over my eyes, and with
the other, undid everything, until she stood in her chemise. She
would not go near the bed and struggled to get away from me.
Indeed, she would not let me touch her, until I closed the window-
curtains. We were in the dark. I placed her on the chaise-longue,
and going on my knees, I tried to part her thighs and kiss her mossy
cleft. With both hands, she tried to push me away.

"You hurt me!" she said again, but I licked her as well as I
could, and feeling the warmth of my mouth, she opened her thighs
a little, and I managed to perform my task. It was difficult, as she
writhed about, uttered pretty little cries, and would not sufficiently
keep her legs apart. But I was not to be dislodged. I was not com-
fortably installed. My neck was wellnigh broken. The room too
was very hot; but I remained busily licking, sucking, perspiring,
and my member, bursting with desire, already let a few drops of the
masculine essence escape from its burning top. I am certain she
experienced a feeling of voluptuousness, by the shuddering of her
frame at one moment, and by the peculiar taste that I could not

mistake. At last, she thrust my head away. And I rose to my feet, greatly pleased at leaving the prison of her soft thighs. I got my handkerchief, wiped my mouth, and returning to her, as she still laid motionless and silent on the couch, I threw myself upon her without ceremony. I inserted the end of my turgescent weapon between the hairy lips of her lower mouth, and forgetting all prudence, I pushed on. She shrieks and dislodges me. I try to regain my position, but I cannot succeed. She was a virgin; there was no doubt about it.

Lilian is half-seated on the narrow sofa, and I have no way of getting to her, unless I pull her flat down on her back. I am tired too, and very hot. I have twisted my neck and it is painful. So I relent and give up active warfare for the present.

"Take it in your hand yourself," I say, "and do what you like with it."

She does so, and leaning over her, I find she lets the tip go a little way in. Now all was dry and far from agreeable. I suppose I had done wrong to suck her so long. She had no more feeling of lust. So I moved up to her face, as she reclined with her head on a cushion, and straddling across her, rubbed my arrow and the appendages gently on her face and mouth. She did not move. I took her hand and placed it on my staff of life. She started and roughly drew her hand away. Strange inconsistency. She had placed it herself at the entrance of her virgin cleft; she had allowed me to caress her lips and cheeks with it, but now she recoiled at the idea of grasping it.

So I resolved to overcome any disgust she might feel, and putting the end between her lips, I told her rather roughly to suck it at once. She tried to, timidly; I could see she did not know how.

"Tell me, show me, and I will do all you wish."

I took her hand, and sucked and licked one of her fingers by way of example.

She took to it readily, and I tried to excite her and keep her up to her work by talking to her as she sucked me awkwardly. But the soft warm caress of her capacious mouth and the clinging grasp of her luscious lips excited me to madness. I moved in and out, slowly, saying:

"Darling! Lilian! It is delicious! Not your teeth, Lily. You must not let your teeth touch it! So! Lick it nicely! Let me feel your tongue! Do not move! Do not go away. I am going to enjoy in your mouth, and you must remain as you are until I tell you."

With angelic docility, she continues the play of her lips and tongue, and to my great surprise and delight I feel her hands gently caressing my reservoirs. And the crisis comes too soon. The pleasure I had was beyond words. I had kept back the moment of joy as long as I could, but now the charge exploded with violence, and I could feel that a very large quantity gushed into her mouth. I thought I should never cease emitting. Lilian did not stir until I slowly withdrew, having exhausted the pleasure until there was not a throb left, and my organ had begun to soften. Then she sat up and uttered inarticulate cries.

I rushed to get her a pail or basin, and in the darkness, knocked down a screen. She empties her martyred mouth. I give her a glass of water, and she rinses her throat.

"What was that?" she asked, as I half-opened one of the window-curtains.

"Little babies," I replied. "Did you like me sucking you?"

I lit the lamp, kissed her, and we chatted as she dressed.

"Yes!"

"And when I spurted that stuff into your mouth—did you like that too?"

"Yes."

"I ought to have penetrated your pretty body. Why did you not let me? Has no one ever done so to you?"

"I am a virgin, I swear it!"

"Have you never given pleasure to yourself with your hand?"

"Never. It hurts. I don't like that. I love you. I shall never marry. I shall live for you. You seem to be vexed that I am a virgin? If I was not, why should I not say so? Tell me what you want."

"I can't tell to-day. My brain is in a whirl. Egotistically, I want to be inside my Lilian. With regard to your interests and future —I ought not to take your maidenhead. You must get married and your husband will do that for you."

"Yes. Mamma says a husband can always tell on the first night if his wife is a virgin or not."

"I have been too merciful to you. I ought to have fastened your hands with my trousers' strap."

"Why didn't you? You know you can do anything you like to me."

"Well, we will let things be until another day."

"You must not be angry if I have been silly or have not pleased you, as this is the first time, you know. I promise to be more obedient in future, and I will try not to struggle when you touch me."

"You are a little demi-vierge."

"I know what you mean. I have read that novel: *Les Demi-Vierges*."

"I think you like the idea of mutual caresses without the real approach of a man?"

"I think I do. Cannot we be happy like this?"

"Perhaps. There are other things we can do together. Do you know what we did just now?"

"Certainly I do. I am not going to pretend I don't. The girls at Myrio's often talked about it. It is called *mimi*. And it is very bad for the health, is it not?"

"Yes, if repeated too often."

I thought she was sensual but silly. Had she chosen me to gratify her curiosity, having confidence in me from my age, and probably Ma's and Pa's praise, as Lilian tells me they think a lot of Jacky? She promised to write to me shortly for another afternoon's fun, but she still refused to *tutoyer* me, and never did at all, during our *liaison*.

I drove her to the station, and in the *fiacre*, she was dull and ill at her ease. Her eyes had a faraway look in them. She seemed to be thinking deeply. About what?

At that time I believed she was reflecting on the novelty and obscenity of what we had done together.

But as I write nearly two years later, vile and horrible thoughts rise uppermost in my mind. Let the reader guess, or return to this chapter when he has finished the book.

2

. . . . . . Most merciful God
Thou hast revealed to me the agony
And bloody sweat of dire Gethsemane,
The scourging of the pillar, the crown of thorns,
The cracking, splitting nerves, and racked joints
Of three hours' crucifixion. Thine anguish
I here do feel, O God! bound, crucified.

GEORGE MOORE.

To my great surprise, I had no news of Lilian, but a few days before I saw her at the Rue de Leipzig, I had sent to Mr. Arvel a parcel of kippers, haddocks, and bloaters, which I had promised the household on my last visit. I had talked to Lilian about the packets of periodicals I sent her father, the little presents I gave her mother, and how I praised and flattered them in every way so as to be often invited and thus approach her. She urged me to continue, but I was to be very careful with her Papa, as he was of a most jealous nature. She told me that she always spoke against me, as if she were to appear pleased when I came, I should never be asked down to Sonis any more. They were all going to Nice shortly after New Year's Day for three weeks.

35

LILIAN TO JACKY.

Sonis-sur-Marne, December 2nd. 1897.

My dear Mr. S . . . ,

Papa was desirous of writing to you these last few days, but he could not get a moment to himself to do so. I take his place therefore, and thank you on behalf of everybody for your present. The fish were exquisite. There is only one fault; there were too many of them.

Mamma wants to know when you will do us the pleasure of lunching with us? The sooner the better, as we have not seen you for a century. It was Lili's birthday to-day and that of her three little ones yesterday. We await your visit to celebrate that event. All our darlings are well. A caress for your faithful Smike, and all your other spoilt pets.

In the hope of soon seeing you, I pray you to accept the assurance of my most devoted sentiments.

LILIAN ARVEL.

I found the note strange, cold, and mysterious. I suppose I wrote that any day would suit me, but I received no reply. So on the thirteenth, I sent the following ambiguous missive, supposed to be from the female friend, Marie.

JACKY TO LILIAN.

Paris, December 13, 1897.

My dear Lilian,

You know I do not like to trouble you, and I have always told you that although I feel great friendship for you, and you, I believe, have a little for me, I never intend to worry you. I know your time is occupied and that you are not always at liberty.

What does all this mean, you will say? Simply to tell you not to forget me the next time you come to Paris, and try to pay me a visit for a minute or two as you did before, that is to say if you have the desire to see me. That would give me the greatest pleasure.

At your last visit you let me hope that I should hear from you shortly.

Dare I add that I am a little grieved and wounded at your silence?

Come soon if you can, and later on if you cannot manage otherwise.

Anyhow, a word from you would rejoice the heart of your sincere friend,

MARIE.

This note crossed the following invitation:

LILIAN TO JACKY.

Sonis-sur-Marne, December 13th. 1897.

My dear Mr. S...,

You must think we are all dead. Such is happily not the case. If we have not written sooner to fix the day when we should have the pleasure of your company at lunch, it is because we have been very much troubled. Our three puppies have been grievously ill. We do not know if we can save the little bitch. The other two are better. My Blackamoor is luckily almost out of danger. Can you come next Thursday, the 16th? We count upon you to pass the day with us. Do not bring any of your dogs, not even your big treasure Smike. We find that the distemper is contagious and it would be a pity to make your pets ill. We hope you are in good health and that your new venture is successful.

Awaiting the pleasure of seeing you, we pray you to accept the assurance of our sincere friendship and believe me,

Your entirely devoted,
LILIAN ARVEL.

The above was typewritten, as Miss Arvel was very quick with her Papa's Remington, but there was a little piece of paper in the letter, bearing the following words, in her own handwriting:

The little girl will frankly tell her Papa the reason why she has not written to him, although she had the utmost desire to do so.

DECEMBER 16, 1897.

In spite of my most earnest efforts of memory, I can find nothing to remember of great importance during this visit to Sonis. I had lunch and did not stop to dinner. The girl kept out of my way. In the afternoon, Papa, Lilian, and I went for a walk together, and I can see myself now, strolling sadly along, my ungloved hands clasped behind me. Lilian, unseen by her father, placed her fingers in my palm for a moment.

I dropped back, and as her stepfather went on in front, I whispered to her: "Is it all over between us already?"

"Yes!" she answered, laughingly.

I quickly walked away from her. She trotted after me, saying: "No, no!"

At this moment, Papa joined us, and I was no more alone with her. When leaving for the station with my host, she came to bid me good bye, and called out with deep meaning:

"A bientôt!"

I thought her conduct passing strange. And I began to reflect about many things I had noticed. She seemed frightened of Mr. Arvel and yet very fond of him. He frequently told me the same stories two or three times over, and she would make fun of him behind his back. Yet when he laid down the law at table. I could see her eyes fixed upon him with enraptured attention. He was always talking about her and her future. She was lazy and quarrelsome and unable to earn her own living. Her bonnet-building scheme was a farce. And still he romped with her. I noticed too that the best bedrooms were on the first floor, where there was a long wooden balcony. The largest room in the front had two windows, and was Mr. and Mrs. Arvel's, with one big bed. This opened into a smaller bedroom at the back, where Lilian slept. The door of communication had been taken down and there were only two flimsy, looped-up curtains in the opening, not even a portière. I thought this was a peculiar arrangement for the bedroom of a young person of 21.

In fact, I began to fancy that there was something between Lilian and her mother's lover. It seemed to me that he looked upon her with the eyes of a satyr. He was always playing with her and pinching her. And she was so careful to tell me to befriend him in every way.

"I alone get on with him beautifully," she would say, "as his temper is awful at times, and Mamma will contradict him, but I flatter all his manias."

I sent him some enormous parcels of books, novels and light literature, and listened patiently to all his talk.

I felt very unhappy about Lilian and things in general were going very badly with me; the new law of 1893 on Stock Exchange operations had dealt a deathblow to my business. I scarcely ever went to the Bourse now, so that I no longer met Mr. Arvel, and I was busily engaged in putting on the market a new chemical product I had invented.

To add to my worries, my own devoted Lilian at home was very ill indeed, and I was her nurse. And I must digress and tell a rather sad story, which, however, has some slight bearing on this tale of vice.

As far back as 1880, I made the acquaintance of a young girl, aged sixteen and a half, who was taking lessons at the Conservatoire, with a view to adopting the stage as a profession. She was divinely handsome; fair, with light blue eyes; as upright as a dart, and she had a figure that sculptors begged her all her life to let them copy. I fell in love with her, my first Lilian, and as she innocently reciprocated my affection, I am ashamed to say I profited by the influence I felt I had over her, and brutally ravished her.

As I rose from the couch, where my love lay swooning, in great pain, unable to realise as yet the wrong I had done her, I mechanically went up to a looking-glass, and stared at my own reflection in the mirror. I did not know myself. My face was livid, my lips were white and cold, and my teeth chattered. I trembled all over and two big tears rolled down my cheeks, now that my animal desire was assuaged.

In truth, I felt like a murderer, and I registered a solemn vow that never more, if I lived a hundred years, would I take advantage of a virgin's yielding tenderness.

Now you know the principal reason why I respected my friend's daughter. This secret I have never divulged. I never told Miss Arvel. She does not know it now, nor will not, unless she reads this book.

My Lilian forgave me because she loved me, and our mutual affection grew, until it became perfectly plain that she could not live without me. There were no spoken protestations of affection on either side. Naturally we sought each other continually; and simply joined our hearts, souls, and bodies in God's union of the sexes. There was no question of money between us, to speak plainly. In fact, at that moment I had none. I was a gambler. When in luck I spent my gold, and when reverses came I cut down my expenses, and waited until the blind lady came my way again. This is one of my motives for having remained a bachelor. I often fancied myself allied to a young damsel of the commercial world, accustomed to the steady tradesmen of her family. I could see myself, after a winning settlement, buying her, for instance, a pair of diamond earrings, and perhaps the very next month pawning them out of dire necessity.

So when I seduced Lilian, I was down on my luck considerably. Her family was an illustrious one, but her father was a spendthrift, and he dilapidated the fortune, driving his wife into an early grave. This lady was a sainted victim and freely forgave her erring daughter, never depriving her of her maternal affection and advice. But she died a few years later.

One evening, Lilian came to me in great grief, and covered with wounds and contusions. Our intrigue was discovered, and her father had beaten her unmercifully, being drunk with absinthe. He had knocked her down, jumped upon her ribs, and bodily cast her out.

I took her to live with me. I shall never forget our initial attempts at house-keeping. We hired a small, unfurnished apartment, and our first acquisition was a mattress stuffed with dried seaweed. This cost five francs. It was laid upon the floor, and one end propped up by a travelling bag, served as a bolster and pillow all combined. But circumstances improved, and from odds and ends of furniture, picked up in the lowest salerooms, I was able in time to make a pretty little home for Lilian, full of quaint curios, fine, ancient furniture, and pictures, which I routed out of strange holes and corners in my travels.

Every summer, we went away on a pleasure trip. I took her to England, Italy, and Switzerland, where together we climbed mountains and explored glaciers. Her health then gradually failed her, and I became a sick nurse. She was alone in the world now. Her mother was dead. Her sisters and brothers did not recognize her. From time to time, her drunken, dissolute father cropped up, and begged some old clothes and a little silver. Times out of number, has she saved the unworthy author of her being from ruin, dishonour and starvation.

She had no one but me to look after her. I passed one whole winter at her bedside, when she went through the acute sufferings of articular rheumatism, and she knew no one half the time. She would take nothing, but from my hand, and for three months, I never let the fire go out by night or day. I was perfectly happy in nursing her. My own health was good; I had never been ill in my life.

But in the summer of 1895, she developed signs of heart disease, inherited from her mother, and was a confirmed invalid ever since. I could see her great beauty leaving her by degrees; all changed for the worst. Her temper became soured. I never complained. I hoped against the doctors who gave me no hope. I tried to nurse her, and pet her, and spoil her, and make her forget how ill she was.

Such was my life in the winter of 1897; business at a standstill, my devoted mistress suffering from a mortal malady, nearly always in bed, and I casting about, ready to try anything to make money, and hard at work on my new chemicals.

ERIC ARVEL TO JACKY.

Sonis-sur-Marne, December 23rd. 1897.

My dear Jacky,

I have been so busy writing Christmas letters, that I have not had time to write and thank you for your magnificent donation of books, the majority of which are new to me, and will be read with the greatest interest. Lilian promises herself a treat with them, when she gets to Nice, so you see you have given pleasure to more than one.

I am pleased to inform you that mercury in the shape of blue pill, cascara and podophyllin have proved admirable remedies for the canine species, and if you like, I will give you all the details, which will enable you to cure distemper with lightning-like celerity.

We want to know if you have any particular engagement on Saturday next? If not, will you come and spend the day with us, as we are anxious that you should sample the Christmas pudding. We should not, however, like to interfere with any family arrangements.

Again thanking you, believe me to remain with every good and seasonable wish for you and yours,

Yours very truly,
ERIC ARVEL.

No news from Lilian privately, only this invitation to their Christmas dinner. I resolved not to go, although I was perfectly free to do so, and I wrote a polite letter of excuse. They were off to Nice all three of them and I supposed I should never "have" Lilian again. As for the reason why she did not communicate with me that winter, after our first meeting, I have never known from that day to this, but I can make a shrewd guess now.

I made up my mind not to trouble the girl, but on the 30th. of December, I took a present for the mother and daughter to Arvel's bureau in the Rue Vissot, and sent Mamma the following letter. In preceding years, I had only given bonbons.

JACKY TO MADAME ARVEL.

Paris, December 30th. 1897.

My dear Madam,

Let me be the first, or at any rate one of the first, to come and wish you health, prosperity, and all you can desire of happiness for yourself and all those you love, during the coming year, without counting numberless years afterwards.

In gratitude for your frank hospitality and to prove that I have not forgotten your good, little (big) dinners, I take the liberty of offering you a slight present—a little umbrella.

Mademoiselle, your charming daughter, has always been so kind to me every time I visited your house, that I wish to show the esteem I hold her in, by begging her to accept a smelling-bottle, which will come in useful when she breaks the bank at Monte-Carlo.

And I wish her a happy new year too, and the realisation of all her wishes in 1898.

If I have badly selected my gifts, please excuse me in favour of the intention.

Now I am sure you will pardon me for not having come on Christmas Day, but we have the habit of making a family day of it at home in Paris.

I shake hands with Monsieur Arvel, and wish him all the compliments of the season also, without saying more, as he knows the feelings of sympathy I have for him.

I have sent the two little articles to his bureau, Rue Vissot.

Yours devotedly,
JOHN S. . . .

Please let me know Mr. Arvel's address and the date of your return, so that I may send him his papers and magazines to Nice.

But I have forgotten the dogs! How could I forget the blood of Smike and Sally Brass—my own flesh and blood—I have no heart!

Therefore, gravely, I wish a happy new year to Lili, Blackamoor and all the others, on my behalf and on the part of my own kennel. So be it!

LILIAN TO JACKY.

Sonis-sur-Marne, January 2nd. 1898.

My dear Mr. S . . . ,

Mamma and I are delighted with the two pretty presents you have had the kindness to send to us.

I hope to have to use my silver smelling-salts for the purpose for which you have given it to me. I do not believe it will be wanted in this way, I am not lucky enough for that, and besides, I am no gambler.

We thank you from the bottom of our hearts, and also for your good wishes. We form such a quantity for your happiness, that I will not even seek to enumerate them. It would be vain trouble; all this sheet of paper would not suffice. Papa begs me to tell you that he does not yet know where we shall put up, but as soon as we arrive in the sunny South, he will wire to you. As for our return, we will write as soon as the date is fixed. Mamma begs you to accept a slice of her famous Christmas pudding, which she sends you this day.

Our doggies are all restored to health. They have begun the New Year well. They send their caresses to you as well as to their parents, relations and all the others.

My dear Mr. S . . . , I pray you to receive the assurance of all my friendship,

Yours very devotedly,
LILIAN ARVEL.

Why not a word of love or passion? I never knew, I tried not to think of her and sought refuge in hard work. My days were spent during this dull winter, with manufacturers and patent agents, and my nights were passed in the sick room of my poor ailing Lily.

A worthy Dutch bookseller, Mynheer Vanderpunk, who had frequently procured old and curious works for me, now wrote from his dusty old shop at Rotterdam, and begged me to be kind enough to correct the text and revise the proofs of a voluptuous volume he intended to bring out under the rose, and which he called: "The Horn Book; or, the Girl's Guide to Knowledge." The manuscript was amusing and the task not a displeasing one for me.

I got very little rest in the long winter nights, being continually awakened to care for my sick mistress. She would settle down to sleep as early as possible and I, in an adjoining room, would read, or smoke, or try to change the current of my ideas in furbishing up this most lascivious text-book.

I remember well one chapter, which spoke of "pleasures of man alone, by the aid of woman, but without her reciprocal participation." One paragraph recommended a kind of false copulation, between the tightly closed thighs of a female.

I added: "This position can be recommended to all having to do with very young girls or half-virgins. . . . Incestuous Papas please note." (Dialogue V. Chap. II.)

And I had in my mind the lecherous old man and the passionate, dissembling girl of Sonis.

No news came from her until a fortnight had passed, when she suddenly took it into her shapely head to send me the following letter:

LILIAN TO JACKY.

Hôtel Joli-Site, Monaco. January 17, 1898.

My own darling,

You must really think I have forgotten all about you, yet such is not the case. Ever since our arrival here, the weather has been so fine that we have been out all day long.

Mamma being ill in bed with influenza, I am her nurse, so I am free for a little while. She is asleep and my very first letter is for you. How is my sweet Papa? Well and happy, I hope. Very naughty?

Since the last few days I am in a nervous state which I am unable to describe. I do not know what to attribute it to, unless it be the warm weather. It acts upon me like the coming of spring. If my little Papa was like that, I should be very much annoyed, for I have not the confidence in his chastity that I have in mine, and as I am absent the results would be disastrous.

I have got my smelling-bottle with me. It is on my toilet-table, and every morning as I dress, I tell to it a heap of things about my Papa. Oh! such pretty things!

I have not been out on my bicycle yet, but I have been several times to the pigeon shooting, and last Friday to Nice races. I have played roulette too. I have lost, then won, and after all I am just as well off as the day I started, being quits.

I expect a letter from you as soon as possible. You can address it to me like this, of course in your feigned handwriting: Mademoiselle L. Arvel, Hôtel Joli-Site, Monaco.

But I won't have "Marie" to write to me any more, or sign. I tear up your letters as soon as read, for my sake as well as yours, which you can well understand.

I fret about my dogs, yearning especially for my Blackamoor. Yours are happier, as they do not leave you. I know a certain person who would often like to be in the place of Smike. You know who I mean as well as I do.

I send you a big, long, and passionate kiss.

Yours lovingly,
LILY.

LILIAN TO JACKY.

Paris. Wednesday, January 23, 1898.

My dear little girl,

Your pretty letter made me very happy. I venture to think that you hoped for that result. It does me good to think that I possess a little bit of your heart and that you have truly some tender feeling for me. All the rest is very nice, doubtless very intoxicating, but without sincere feeling, it has but little value for me.

I tell you frankly that I began to doubt you slightly. I had good reasons. Since the 26th. of last November, you have treated me in rather a peculiar manner. But I will not darken my letter by scolding you. The first time that I shall be alone with you, I will explain in a few words what I mean, and which, by the way, is without importance now, for your letter completely effaces all my doubts. You will understand me if I say that you are not "business-like" enough. Even in love, you should try and realise what torturing thoughts come over us, as we wait for some sparse news of her who has said: "I love you!"

You owed me a word of tenderness; a pretty thought scribbled hastily; a telegram; no matter what to make he who was waiting far away take patience, my darling.

How you forget all those little things which nevertheless are important in life! You wrote to me on the eve of your departure, promising your address in the South. I have not had that wire. I could not therefore send the papers and magazines to Mr. Arvel. Tell him that you have done it, and next Sunday I will post him a packet.

My beautiful Lily, your Papa has had a strong attack of influenza, short, but not sweet, and at this moment I am worthless. I am flabby, feverish, and stupid. I am a rag, an empty sack, and I could look without emotion and see every sofa in the world burnt before my eyes.

I am pleased that you are in good health and that you are amused. Be a good girl, don't let yourself be cajoled.

Often I think of you. Since we . . . I think of you always, and I hope you will write to me all the pretty things you tell your smelling-bottle. I think that the ideas that gallop through your little brain are the same as those I also have when I think of my daughter. Do you know, my child, that we have such a lot of pretty, nice little things to practise together? You can have no idea of them.

But we'll see about that when you return. Good luck when you gamble! You know the hackneyed saying: "Unlucky at play, lucky in love!" Try and make the proverb lie, by being happy in both. I will attend to my part of the contract. Such is what I wish you.

If you should have bad news of your dogs—or especially of Black-amoor,—quick, send me a telegram and I will go to Sonis. They shall have the best of care, the same as mine. This is serious.

My dogs are fit. Smike fought big curs twice this month and he has been well bitten.

He is like his master, his bark is worse than his bite. He is very loving, cannot live without caresses, and the only thing he detests is neglect from those he loves.

Write to me soon and often. I think I deserve a few nice letters. You, wicked one, do not deserve a long letter, such as this is.

I think I love you too much. Thank you for your loving kiss. But it is only one. I send you a heap, placed where you like them best.

And now, do not be lazy. Do not be too long without writing to ask me if I am better.

I squeeze you tightly against me, sweet, and ask nothing better than to always be

Your own darling.

(Unsigned.)

LILIAN TO JACKY.

Cercle des Etrangers de Monaco.
Salon de Lecture. Monte-Carlo.
January 21st. 1898.

My dear Mr. S ...,

Just two words to give our address here: Arvel, Hôtel Joli-Site, Monaco.

We are all in good health and we hope you are the same.

We beg you to accept the assurance of our good friendship.

LILIAN ARVEL.

LILIAN TO JACKY.

Cercle des Etrangers de Monaco.
Salon de Lecture. Monte-Carlo.
January 21st. 1898.

Dearest,

You are not "business-like" in love, you tell me, in your long and good letter. I did not know that to please you I had to be "business-like," above all in love. In future I will be as you wish!

You had doubts, but what doubts could you possibly have? That is an enigma for me. Have I not been always very frank with you; have I not always told you everything, down to the smallest stupidities which other girls less—how shall I say it?—less foolish than me, would have hidden from you? Unless I receive from you very ample and fully detailed explanations, your daughter will be quite angry.

Make haste then to write, and unveil your heart until it is naked before my eyes.

If you would be a real darling, you will go to Sonis and pay a little visit to your grandchildren . . . the bow-wows. That will please me greatly, and in this way you will insinuate yourself still farther into the good graces of Mamma, which is quite indispensable.

We have received your papers, which are vastly appreciated by Papa and myself. I thank you.

We intend to pass a month at Nice from next week onwards. Until Sunday, you can write to me here. As soon as I know my new address, I will let you know.

You say your dogs are in good health? I am happy to hear it. I send a loving caress to all, and particularly to my fat Smike.

I leave you. They are waiting for me to have tea. Au revoir. A million kisses.

LILY.

MADAME ARVEL TO JACKY.

Hôtel Joli-Site, Monaco. February 1st. 1898.

My dear Mr. S . . .,

I wish to thank you for your kindness, but really when I spoke about you going to see my dogs during my absence, it was only a joke, and I should never have dared to give you that trouble. I am delighted nevertheless, as I am now quite reassured about them. It is not necessary to be in Paris to have the influenza, as my mother has told you. I have had it, and severely too, although I am in the land of the sun.

We intend to remain another three weeks here; we wished to go and live at Nice, but the Carnival is shortly about to begin and it will be too noisy for Mr. Arvel.

I am pleased to hear that my pudding had such success; had I known it, I should have sent you a bigger slice, but that will be for next year.

Mr. Arvel begs me to thank you for the very interesting newspapers you send him.

Lilian was very happy to hear you had seen Blackamoor and found him well. She charges me with her thanks, and says you must caress Smike and Sally Brass, and all the others for her.

We have magnificent weather here and yet I long to be home again; the hotel food is very bad.

We hope that on our return to Sonis, you will do us the pleasure

to come and see us often, and in the meantime I pray you to accept
the assurance of my good and sincere friendship.

ADÈLE ARVEL.

I remember visiting Sonis, reviewing the dogs, conversing with
the grandmother, whose acquaintance I made for the first time,
tipping the servant, hearing that Madame Arvel had the influenza,
and returning to Paris, when I wrote to Nice.

I also wrote to Lilian, and gave her to understand that I was
not an ordinary lover. I was not jealous, I put no check upon her
liberty, nor did I venture to criticise her conduct in any way. I
wished her to enjoy herself, to flirt, and do as she liked. I only
wanted her love, as long as she chose to bestow it on me. I suppose
I must have said that I was grieved by her long silence, and that I
did not require long letters, only a line now and again to show that
I was not forgotten.

Her allusions to her own frankness and stupidity I must now
explain.

Before what I venture to call my first possession of her body,
after a fashion, I had asked her who taught her to kiss so nicely.
She frankly told me that she had carried on a strictly platonic intrigue when she was apprentice at Myrio's, with a young law-
student, who she called Gaston, but more familiarly: "Baby." He
used to wait for her when she left the workroom in the evening,
and take the train with her to Sonis, going back to Paris alone. He
had kissed her lips, she said, and that was all. She added that he
was fond of talking very lewdly, and liked to tell her what he
wished to do to her if he could get her in his power—"just like
you," she added.

One evening, in the railway carriage, he suddenly seized her
by the two wrists, and throwing her skirts up to her waist, tried to
violate her. She struggled and got away from him, when he burst
out crying and begged her pardon.

He was always writing to her and I saw one of his letters.
Sometimes he wrote in very free terms. I have a distinct recollection of some long story, where he said his family were forcing him
to marry a rich woman, and he intended to get divorced and come

back to Lilian. It appears he had arrived at Sonis one night and made his way into the garden, intending to climb up to her window, but Papa had come out with a gun, and he had jumped over the wall and escaped.

All this seemed very strange and rather rambling, but I did not cross-examine her. I think she also added that "Baby" had sent his sister to negotiate a marriage, but she had turned traitor after a visit to Mr. Arvel, who frankly confessed that he had not a penny to give Lilian, and that her husband must take her in English fashion for better or worse.

How much of this story was false or true, I know not, but I wish to make an avowal at once which will show the reader what a perverted debauchee I was.

I loved to hear Lily tell me about her platonic lover, Gaston. Her story of the attempted rape acted upon my senses like an aphrodisiac, and I often made her repeat it.

I wanted all the details. I would ask her if he saw her sex, or only her drawers, and how high her skirts were up.

I felt that I should like to see her in the arms of a strange man, or I dreamt of causing her to be shamelessly exposed and outraged by a woman in my presence.

The idea that her mother's lover desired her, and I was sure he did, transported me with lust, and I used to watch them narrowly. I loved to see him romp with her, slap her posteriors outside her clothes, and putting his hand a little way up her petticoats, pinch her calves.

She always used to say she would never leave her Pa, and I used to agree with her in front of him, and tell her that she could not do better than to love and obey him blindly.

I knew that she would make a wonderful instrument of pleasure if properly attuned. I came to the conclusion that she had been caressed, handled and dandled, and mauled about, ever since her early infancy by her Papa and Gaston, without counting any other male and female playmates I knew not of, and that is why she so freely accepted all my ideas, and was not surprised at my retreat in front of the fortress of her virginity.

Although she excited my sensual longings to the fullest extent, I yet felt great tenderness for her. I took an interest in her, as I could see her mother was selfish and stupid, and that Mr. Arvel, for reasons best known to himself, was not giving her proper advice. I wanted to enjoy her artificial love, which was quite an enervating novelty for me, and yet teach her honesty, and I was always thinking of her interests and her future. I could not do much for her, but I wanted her to find a worthy husband and go to him a virgin. I told her so. I made her understand that on the day of her marriage I would retire from her life, and whatever I felt I would keep to myself. She always answered that I should be her lover. I also told her that without marriage she could always tell me frankly if she tired of our connection and I would go from her without a word. I tried to put her at her ease and above all not to lure her on with false promises or lying tales.

I said I was vile, but may I not timidly plead that I was honest in my lewd way?

LILY TO JACKY.

Sunday evening.
(No date. Received February 8, 1898.)

My beloved,

A word in haste on this wretched paper that I find by chance and with this atrocious pen. You demanded it, so much the worse for you!
I have hardly time to breathe here.
And see, now I must leave you. They are calling me!
I kiss you all over . . . madly!

LILY.

I was very busy and very ill. The sharp attack of influenza I had undergone, and which I caught from my Lily, who had it still very badly, had left me weak and depressed, and I felt pains in all my joints, such as I had never experienced before.

My mistress was dreadfully, dangerously ill. I shared her bed of agony, and her condition required that the heat of the room should be kept up over 70° F. We were at the fag-end of a disagreeable winter, and I often rose in the night to attend to her wants, and hurried into the other rooms, where the thermometer would be at freezing point.

I finished "The Horn Book," and sent the manuscript to my good friend Vanderpunk.

My new chemical invention was put on the market on the 9th. of February. I could scarcely stand, and it was all I could do to muffle myself up in a fur coat and go to my Lily's bedside.

After a night of torture, when I got up several times to do my duty as a nurse, with my aching limbs bathed in my own perspiration and that of my suffering companion, I got a little sleep in the small hours, but when I tried to leave the bed at eight o'clock in the morning, I found every limb locked; each joint racked, and I howled with pain. It must be remembered that up to then I did not know what bodily suffering was.

In my impotent rage, mad with the burning fever of rheumatism, I lost all manly feeling and so far forgot myself as to bitterly upbraid my poor sick Lily.

"I have sacrificed myself for you. You have had the best part of my life. I never refused you anything I could afford to give you, and now you have taken the only riches I had left—my health! I shall be a cripple, and then what will become of me? As long as I was hale and hearty, I never complained. I have endured fearful nights of unrest by your side, as you tossed your fevered body about, and I have tried to sleep bathed in your sweat, and rushed, reeking, suddenly into icy atmospheres, to fetch you your medicines, light fires, and attend to you as if you were a baby. Each night you found me with clockwork regularity at your bedside. And now I am a physical wreck! My health and strength gone from me by your fault! You have taken everything, even to my health! God knows how I shall come out of this hellish strait! And just when I wanted all my energies to retrieve my fallen fortunes!"

I am ashamed to write more of my ravings. I was mad. I cursed myself, I cursed the world and I cursed our bed, and spat upon the mattress and tumbled sheets all fuming with my sweat.

Poor Lily stood aghast in a corner, her eyes distended with horror, and convulsive sobs shaking her debilitated frame.

One day I will ask her forgiveness for what was delirious blasphemy. She will pardon me, for she always loved me and always will. She has proved her love. She possessed every quality we are supposed to find in a woman—tenderness, devotion, and truth.

Perhaps I have already asked her pardon? Who knows?

How I huddled on my clothes; how I crawled out, I cannot tell, but I managed to be hauled into a cab and drove to my aged mother's little cottage in the outskirts of Paris.

There I hung upon the railings until I was carried to bed; a helpless, groaning stiffened log, on the morning of February 10, 1898.

I now went through all the sufferings of muscular and articular rheumatism. I knew my malady well, as I had seen my mistress through it.

I felt my hands beginning to pain me, and made haste to scribble a few lines with a pencil, from my bed, to tell Lilian Arvel, at Monte-Carlo, how bad I was.

On the morning of the 20th. of February, I received the following undated letter.

My two hands were now attacked and they were shapeless, evil-smelling bundles of cotton wool. Nevertheless, I had Lilian's letter placed on my pillow, and waited until I was left alone. I took it between my two stumps, although it was untold agony to move my arms. With my teeth, I tore open the envelope, and read as follows:

LILIAN TO JACKY.

Friday. (No date or place.)

If my Papa would give great pleasure to his little daughter, he must send her two hundred francs by return of post. Figure to yourself that since I came here I have lost freely, so that I have not a halfpenny.

It is naturally impossible that I can remain like this, and I at once thought of you, knowing well that you would be delighted to render me this slight service, and by the same occasion prove to me that you really love me as much as you say you do.

For the last two days I have been very, very ill, and I pity you with all my heart being in bed, and suffering as you do lately. If I could only be near you, how happy I should be to care for you in every way, to pet you and thus be able to prove to you how much I love you.

I long to be back in Paris. I am horribly bored here. I am like those village girls who fret when they can no longer see the steeple of their village church. I am absolutely lost when I am so long away from my dear Paris.

Yes, I flirt, but out of patriotism; so you need not be jealous, for you alone possess my love.

You will ask how I manage to flirt patriotically, so I explain:

There is at this hotel a young German officer, who is absolutely, madly in love with me. I encourage him, and sometimes I laugh at him, just when he believes that I am beginning to let myself be persuaded. This plunges him into fits of melancholy, which it would be impossible to describe.

You see my darling Papa, how wicked your little daughter is!

But enough gossip, I shall finish by wearying you with all my stories. So I leave you, telling you that I await next month with impatience. You guess why?

LILY.

My head fell back on my pillow. I shut my eyes and groaned with mingled physical and moral pain.

3

. . . . Telle que la voilà
Sous les rideaux honteux de ce hideux repaire,
Dans cet infâme lit, elle donne à sa mère,
En rentrant au logis, ce qu'elle a gagné là.

ALFRED DE MUSSET.

BEL. . . . Sure it must feel very strange to go to bed
to a man!
LADY BRUTE.—Um, it does feel a little odd at first,
but it will soon grow easy to you.

SIR JOHN VANBRUGH.

The next day came an illustrated postcard, bearing a view of
the Château of Monte-Carlo, with the words: "Souvenir de
Monaco."

Lily had written thereon: "Best and affectionate remembrance."

It is needless to say that I did not answer her letter. I was too
ill and too much worried on all sides.

ERIC ARVEL TO JACKY.

Paris. 10, Rue Vissot. 4th. March 1898.

My dear Jacky,

You must excuse my not having written sooner to thank you for all
the pleasant hours you procured for me in the midst of my stay at

Monte-Carlo, where I think I nearly qualified for a hospital nurse, with the influenza, which thinned the company at dinner and filled up all my spare time.

I had some news of you all from Colonel B . . . , who was down at Monte-Carlo, not precisely "picking it up," I am sorry to say.

I hope your people are all quite well. Remember me to all your family.

I am still reading some of the books you gave me and when you have time and "envie," remember that the cook is not dead yet at the Villa Lilian, which is on the point of being done up and made beautiful for ever.

With every good wish, in which both the ladies join, and hoping that "Mord Emly" will, for the sake of Lilian, turn out all right and not a "Pall Mall Tribute," I remain, very truly yours,

ERIC ARVEL.

"Mord Emly" was the title of a serial story, detailing the adventures of a cockney girl, and then running in the pages of a weekly magazine which I sent him regularly. The allusion to the virtue of the heroine in the novel that Mr. and Miss Arvel were reading together struck me as far from delicate.

I still continued to suffer greatly and I had several relapses. My mistress was very ill as well.

ERIC ARVEL TO JACKY.

Sonis-sur-Marne. 11th. March 1898.

My dear Jacky,

I am very sorry indeed to learn from your letter that you have been called on to experience what a sad thing it is to be laid up. I do hope that the second convalescence will be more serious than the first and that when I call on you some day in the next week I shall find that you are right again.

Do not trouble to send me any books or papers. Wait until I call for them and see you at the same time.

I saw J— at the Bourse last Saturday, and I met your brother P— yesterday, and in answer to my enquiries they told me everyone was well and hearty.

Do not come too soon in this damp, nasty weather. Stop in until we have a change, and then you will perhaps come down and put in a week with the dogs, and try the cooking of our *chef*, roosting in one of the bedrooms upstairs, which shall be fitted up as you like.

Remember me very kindly to everybody at your house, and with every good wish from Madame and Mademoiselle, as well as from myself for your complete and speedy recovery, I remain, hoping that you will consider the invitation to stay down here, not as a compliment, but in the genuine manner in which it is meant,

Yours very truly,
ERIC ARVEL.

I had the visit of Papa, as announced, and I was able to thank him cordially for his kind invitation, which I could not accept, as though I got up for a few hours each day, I was not yet able to do more than hobble from the bed to the window. The doctor refused to let me leave my bedchamber at present, where I was carefully surrounded by screens, and I was even forbidden to go into the rest of the house.

Mr. Arvel came and talked. No one spoke but he, which I was very grateful for, as I was not in a fit state to carry on a conversation. I only remember that the Zola trial was discussed, and I discovered that my friend was a rabid enemy of Dreyfus. He refused to hear a word spoken against any man wearing the uniform of the French army, and as usual with him, I soon saw that he knew nothing at all about the case.

Just before he left, I was alone with him for a few moments and I begged him to remember me to Madame, and Mademoiselle Lilian.

To my surprise, he accepted the message curtly and sulkily. He frowned and his face grew dull.

I must not make myself out too clever. This change of countenance when I spoke of his daughter struck me as strange at the time, but I did not attach the importance to it that I do now. In fact, I am certain that all through the year 1898, I was not as perspicacious as before. I suppose my illness must have dulled my brain. I am perfectly sure that at any other time of my life I should not have been so patient as I was with Miss Arvel, nor should I have continued my *liaison* with her.

I am certain now that I was blinded by my great desire for

her, and that my ordinary power of reasoning had been shaken by the severe trial I had undergone.

I did hunger for the girl, in spite of her mercenary disposition and I fancied that she had some sort of love for me. I ventured to think that there was a little affection for me in her selfish soul.

LILY TO JACKY.

Tuesday. (No date or place.
Received April 26th. 1898.)

My dear little Papa,

Two of my letters with no reply from you. I do not understand it. That my last from Monaco did not get an answer, I allow, but how about my second? You have been ill and to prove to you that I have a little heart more tender than yours, I send you this note, but I swear it will be the last, if it is not more successful than the others. Then I shall understand that you wish to forget the end of the year 1897.

I have been bitten by Blackamoor in trying to prevent him killing another dog. As my right hand is damaged, I am obliged to use the machine to write to you.

I am anxious to have news of your health, which is only given to me very imperfectly by Papa, from what he hears of your people at the Bourse.

Therefore I pray you to answer me as quickly as possible, if you care to make me forget your gross rudeness.

I suppose you will honour us with your presence soon. Perhaps that is asking too much?

I count absolutely upon a scribble as soon as possible,

LILIAN.

JACKY TO LILY.

Wednesday, April 27th. 1898.

My dear little girl,

I had much pleasure in receiving news of your dear self. I have been thinking about you for a long time. In my thoughts you possess a double personality. Firstly, you are my sweet little woman with an intoxicating mouth and then you change into an amiable and demure young lady. I have been asking myself which you were going to be for me in the future?

I see that you have not forgotten the end of November, any more than I have.

The two last communications I received from you from Monaco, were a letter, to hand February 20th., and a souvenir postcard on the 21st. Since then I have two letters from Mr. Arvel and that is all. Have you posted me another letter which I never received? That is surprising.

Yes, I was angry, I confess, when I received your last letter from Monaco. Ill, exhausted by pain, I wrote you a few words in pencil from my bed. You answer me quite coolly, without saying a word about me or my health. I lost my temper and wrote to you no more. I will tell you about this when I see you.

Since the 10th. of February up to Good Friday, I have been in bed, then confined to my room, with lots of ups and downs—more of the latter—and now I get out, but not yet at night. I think it is all over.

I hope your bite will be nothing. I will teach you how to separate two fighting dogs. I pose as a cunning professor, but nevertheless, I was bitten myself last September, through tearing Smike away from a big hound. I never told anybody, not knowing the strange cur. But I am not frightened of going mad. I am perhaps mad already, who knows?

My poor Sally Brass, the mother of your Lili, died Saturday night last. She took cold. There was congestion of the lungs. Friday, they put her on a mustard plaster; then another Saturday night, and she dropped down dead. It was impossible to foresee this. I've had enough of dumb animals. Never again, after those I have are gone. Smike is wonderfully well. My two little bitches also, except Sally's daughter. She is unhappy. She keeps seeking for her mother.

The closing sentence of your letter ". . . honour us with your presence—that is perhaps asking too much," is a pretty little piece of impertinence, which I certainly do not deserve. Our private petty quarrels have nothing to do with my visits to Sonis, I think. Have I not always been correct? You deserve to be severely punished. If you want to be chastised, come quickly to Paris, one afternoon when it is fine,—will you?

Little Lily, do you feel naughty and wicked? Answer me quickly and fix a day for your coming, no matter when. I will await you, as on the last occasion, to kiss you all over and make you enjoy as much as I can. It will be very lovely. Come! I want you—entirely.

You see that I am not very bad and that my anger does not last long, especially with you, my daughter treasure.

My lips on yours,

Your PAPA.

I can see now as I write, that either by the effect of my illness itself, or possibly on account of the enormous quantity of salicylate of soda I had absorbed, I did not see things as clearly as I ought to have done.

For instance, I reproached Lilian with not having mentioned my malady in the letter where she asked for the two hundred francs. This was quite wrong on my part, as the reader will have seen.

At the same time, I ought to have been more impressed with her story of the letter which was mislaid. I have received hundreds of letters in Paris at various addresses, business missives, and love-letters, either at my dwelling, wherever it may have been, or even at post-offices, during the course of my various intrigues, and I cannot remember that one single one was ever lost.

I have not the slightest doubt that Lilian told a lie. She never wrote to me on her return from the South. If she had, she would have shown some anxiety for the ultimate fate of her letter, and would have been uneasy lest it should have fallen into the hands of some of my numerous relatives, who were daily at my bedside, or been stolen by a servant. I shall allude to the lost letter mania later on in my narrative. And when I tell her that I never received the epistle she mentions, she takes it as a matter of course, as the reader will see in the ensuing translation:

LILIAN TO JACKY.

No date or place. (Received April 28th. 1898.)

Beloved little Papa,

Your note has poured some balm into my heart, although it caused me to shed two big tears. Yes, I must confess that the death of Sally Brass made me weep, when I think she was neglected during your illness! If I had had the care of her, how different it would have been. Happily, my big darling Smike is well, but then you look after him yourself.

The reproach you make to me about my last letter from Monaco is unmerited. If you had read it properly you would have seen that on the contrary it was full of allusions to your health. The only thing that might have wounded your feelings was the demand I made, for naturally you have now classed me in the ranks of mercenary females.

And yet if you knew me well you would never have dreamt of such a thing. I was in a fix and worried. I supposed that I could tell you my troubles and even ask you to help me. I see that I made a mistake; let us say no more about it!

One of my letters has gone astray. I wrote to you immediately on my return home.

My health is good. I am slightly unwell at present, but that is nothing.

I can only see you in some little time from now. At present, I have no customers in Paris. I must therefore find a plausible excuse. But you will lose nothing by waiting.

I send you my best caresses, grumbling Papa!

LILY.

This letter was useful to me, as by reason of the mention of her slight indisposition, which I took to be her menstrual derangement, it fixed for me certain monthly dates.

It is impossible for me to remember how I answered her, as I have no copy or recollection, but it could not have pleased her very much, as the next communication is from her stepfather, nearly a month later.

ERIC ARVEL TO JACKY.

Sonis-sur-Marne. May 23rd. 1898.

My dear Jacky,

We have had a rare time here since you came down to see us last. We have been successively turned out of every room and even now we are reduced to the kitchen. We want to see you and show you what we have done up to the present, but it is only fair to say that we are still living in the kitchen, reviving old times, and all the upstairs rooms are encumbered with those odds and ends a housewife likes to collect around her.

Do you mind taking pot-luck in the kitchen on Wednesday next? I have a day free, and we can go over the garden without wooden shoes, unless it rains; but at all events come down in your heaviest of shooting-boots, or you will get your feet wet. If you are better engaged than visiting in the kitchen, let me know. I hope we shall see you fit and well and with a forty horse-power appetite. The ladies send their kindest regards and hope to see you.

With best and kindest regards to all your family,
Believe me to remain, yours very truly,

ERIC ARVEL.

MAY 25TH. 1898.

I think I was but a sorry sight as I dragged my aching limbs up the gravel path that led through the pretty garden of the Villa Lilian to the house, where my sweetheart and her mother greeted me warmly, thanked me for the usual peace-offerings I brought them, and soon put me at my ease, while the father, in the best of humours, did all he could to make me as comfortable as possible. While on the subject of their hospitality, I must render them justice once for all by saying that no one could be received more cordially or better treated than I was at Sonis-sur-Marne. Nothing was too good for me. My advice was asked on all sorts of subjects and I believe that they all had a kind of respect for me. I speak calmly and without vanity, but I really fancy that at one time they all liked me and looked up to me.

The house was greatly improved. The garden was double the original size, through the acquisition of the adjacent property, and there was a small house, with a little garden, to be sold exactly next door. Mr. Arvel begged me to buy it, but it was impossible for obvious reasons, despite Lilian seconding his proposition with meaning looks.

The dark passage near the kitchen where I had enjoyed Lilian's first kiss was gone, and in its place was a brand new dining-room, as yet unfinished, so the meals were served in the kitchen. I had lunch, and then they made me stop for dinner. This was, I think, the first time I had ever spent the whole day with them. It was my first outing after sunset since my illness.

Arch Lilian begged me to help her to lay the cloth for lunch and we were alone. Can my readers understand that I was so delighted at once more being near my love that I have now no recollection of what I said to her about her neglect of me since November, her request for money, and the missing (!) letter? I shrewdly suspect that in my convalescent condition, boiling over with lust for her, I said nothing at all. I was in the seventh heaven of delight. Whenever she touched me, purposely or by accident, the voluptuous effect made itself felt at once, and her influence over my sexual organs never failed all the time I knew her, until a certain moment which shall be described in due course.

She was sweetness itself all day long, and nothing could equal the grace and girlish abandon of her manner. Her caresses were frequent. Whenever we could get behind a door or on a staircase, no matter where, her lips were joined to mine, and she would shudder with delight as my hands wandered freely all over her lithe frame.

The great trouble in my mind was that I knew I did not see her often enough. I was certain that after a few times that she might have been with me, I could have done anything with her and bent her to my will.

I am not boastful and do not think much of myself—if I did, how could I write these cynical confessions?—but I could see that when I talked to her, her whole soul was mine, that she experienced the greatest pleasure a woman could have in being with me, in feeling me near her.

She made me sit next to her at meals and took care to keep my plate and glass replenished. Pa and Ma were beaming with joy. I knew instinctively that I was looked upon as an admirer of Lilian. The position was an enviable one, and I resolved to let things go on without recrimination, nor trouble at present about the future.

Ma's attack of influenza was alluded to. Lilian had had it too. I told the tale of my illness, but without mentioning the cause. I never spoke of my mistress, nor did they. It was well-known in Paris that my handsome Lily was always with me and what I may call my "conjugal" address was engraved on all my dogs' collars. But they never alluded to her, nor did Lilian Arvel.

With regard to Mamma's sickness at Monte-Carlo, Lilian, being alone with me for a few moments in the afternoon, casually let drop how she had been miserable down in the South. She never meant to travel again with her parents if she could help it. Papa always wanted to go to bed early. Mamma had to obey him, so there was no fun for her at night. I chaffed her about the German officer, but she said it was only a flirtation of the hotel-corridor type, and the epidemic had spoilt the whole trip. She had nursed her mother with the help of Papa. They had two bedrooms, one for her and one for her parents, but one night when Ma was very bad, Pa had come and *slept in her bed with her.*

I purposely refrained from taking any notice of this slip of her tongue, but I should have been as a blind man, if I had not noticed the visible desire of Mr. Arvel for my Lilian, the daughter of his mistress. And instead of feeling disgust or jealousy, I am bound to confess the truth: it excited my lust in the most terrible manner to think he loved her, and I seemed to breathe an atmosphere of incest that aroused my passions to the utmost extent.

Lilian was not well. She drank milk with her meals and had no appetite. Her mother tried to tempt her to eat, but she would refuse the heaped-up plateful and ask for smaller morsels, saying: "Tiny! Tiny!" This expression of hers became a catchword at the villa.

Raoul, her brother, was also talked about at table. He was doing well in his situation in London, but his infatuation for Charlotte, or Lolotte, as they called her, worried his mother greatly and sent Papa into fits of rage. Lilian took her part in some slight degree, but she could not forgive her for what looked suspiciously like the seduction of her handsome brother, of whom she seemed inordinately fond. When she first went to London with Charlotte, Raoul met the two girls at the station, and after dinner they went for a walk. On returning to their lodging, Lolotte let Lilian get into bed, and then said she was going out for a few minutes. She went off and slept with Raoul at a hotel that night, leaving Lilian to tremble and worry alone until the morning.

This story was openly told before me; and Papa, fulminating, narrated how he forbade Lolotte ever to come to his house again, or face him. But she was still friends with Mammá and Lilian; and, when Pa was away, would come and stop many a week-end down at Sonis and share Miss Arvel's bed, an arrangement which was known to the master of the house. These sidelights of suburbia delighted my vice. I enjoyed the study of this family, but most of all, of course, Lilian's love for me. It flattered my pride. I was 46; she was 22; she had chosen me as her lover. Could anything be more flattering for a debauchee verging upon 50?

I pressed her to come to Paris. She said that her mother was very strict and kept a vigilant eye upon her movements. I think she did look sharply after her and appeared to be very artful. I often had little conversations with her, but she would not be drawn out concerning her daughter. I gave her up in despair. The father was more communicative, and I felt that I had only to wait and listen to him, if I wanted to hear about Lilian.

I gathered that if she had work for Paris, or customers there to attend to, I might be able to possess her. Of course, it was easy to see that money would get her to come to me. I should have had to invent buyers for her hats and bonnets in the gay capital, pay for the things ordered, which would never have been made, or some like scheme.

But I had no money to spare. What little my purse contained was to pay for my poor mistress's comforts in her incurable illness.

Lilian showed me a small and very pretty watch her father had given her; and in his presence, she said she wanted a true lover's knot in various little precious stones to hang it on to the bosom of her dress. I said that I should be pleased to get it for her, if her father would let me do so.

He replied frankly enough: "Well, Jacky, as far as I am concerned, I shouldn't mind a bit, but her mother would never let her take it. She would be awfully offended and give it back to you at once. So you must not do it. We are English you know, but the 'missus' is French."

Some months later, when alluding to this, Lilian shrugged her shoulders, and said: "You should have given it to me all the same; they would not have minded, after the first growl."

When I left them late at night, with Lilian's promise to come to me soon and her parents' flattering compliments and hearty good wishes, I could not help thinking that Papa's pretty gift of the watch to Lilian was in return for some slight pleasure he had experienced by her side and in her virginal bed, while nursing Mamma through the influenza at Monte-Carlo. And a wave of concupiscence swept over me at the thought.

LILY TO JACKY.

No date or place. (Received May 29th. 1898.)

The little daughter is thinking deeply about her darling little father. She adores him and hopes to see him soon.

A long and soft kiss,

LILY.

I tried to get her some customers among my friends' mistresses, talking to them of a cheap little *modiste* I knew down in the country, who would not object to do up their old hats or work with their own materials. I was promised some orders, and I wrote and told her about my negotiations. I suppose by her answer, I must have written a very voluptuous letter, although for the life of me, I cannot remember now what I said.

LILY TO JACKY.

No date or place. (Received June 1st. 1898.)

My own beloved,

What a naughty, wicked, cheeky, and yet delicious letter! Truly only you can write like that. But what effrontery to class me as a little *modiste*.

Know then, my beloved Papa, that here I am considered as the best bonnet-builder of the locality and for miles round my fame has spread. I am the Virot of the village. It is a very grave thing to try and destroy my good reputation, so that you will get one kiss and one caress less. That is how I serve you for being so rude.

But let us speak seriously:

It is quite immaterial to me who I work for. I do not care if they are the sort of women you mention. They already form the majority of my customers. The only trouble is that they would take up a lot of my time, whereas if I could get an order from a wholesale house, as

I told you, I should only have to give the necessary orders to set my workgirls going, and then I could escape and be a whole afternoon with my adored little Papa. Which would be very naughty, but very agreeable. You, who have plenty of time on your hands, why do you not go among the wholesale people and try and find something for me to do?

If you don't find a way to make me come to Paris, I can't answer for my virtue, for since last Wednesday, after the day you passed at our house, I have no wish to be a good girl, quite the contrary.

So search and you will find. You will see that you won't regret your trouble, for your little daughter knows well how to reward you for all your efforts in her favour.

I love you,

LILY.

LILY TO JACKY.

No date or place. (Received June 23rd. 1898.)

My very dirty, but well-beloved Papa,

It is absolutely charming of you to think of your little daughter. She, on her part, does not forget you, which is quite natural, is it not? I await with impatience these famous lady customers you write to me about, for then my adored master will have all his work cut out to content me!

I am as naughty as can be at this moment in imagination only, naturally. From the idea of the action nevertheless, there is but one step, I think?

Your little daughter is unhappy just now; her mother is as hard and unjust as possible towards her. Mr. A. . . tells me that it is her change of life that is beginning to upset her, and that I must not pay attention to what she says or does, but I assure you that very often my patience gives out, and twice this week I have been on the point of leaving the house, as this sudden change in her conduct where I am concerned, afflicts me awfully and makes me miserable. I cry nearly every day. If I were with my dear little Papa, how different all this would be! I want you more than ever. I hunger for that warm affection you show for me. I am discouraged.

I love you madly,

LILY.

I had indeed noticed that Lilian and her mother were at loggerheads. It was not to be wondered at. Mr. Arvel's mistress was evidently jealous of the attention he paid to her daughter, and, I could see, did not like the way they played together. They always had sly jokes to crack together, on very lax subjects.

Papa would chaff Lilian about "going to the theatre." He would say: "You like going to the theatre, Lilian?" The girl would giggle, the mother frown, and my host laugh outright. I sat by like a fool, and had to wait my opportunity to ask Lilian what "the theatre" meant, especially as they were not playgoers. It appears they knew a gentleman who had stopped at their house some time and who hated the drama. He had said that playhouses were sinks of iniquity and that people only frequented them to indulge in sly caresses and pull each other about. So "going to the theatre," in the Arvel language, meant the action of a man and a woman touzling and libidinously romping. Lilian, it was easy to see, was on the road to become her stepfather's pleasure-tool, to say the least. And I liked to see the lickerish girl and the sensual old man together. I was thus able to come to the conclusion that neither Mr. or Mrs. Arvel were capable of giving proper advice to the brother or the sister. How they were to behave in life; the duties that they owed to themselves or society; the future of the woman; or the honesty and honour of the man; nothing touching on the proper way to live had ever been told to them. And why? The mother and he who stood in the position of father were absolutely incapable of instructing them. There were no sentiments at the Villa Lilian—only appetites. All they knew was that they should try and earn money and save a little; eat and drink; and when they found anybody less cunning than themselves—take advantage of them.

I could see no real affection in Arvel's house at present. He liked Lilian in a lustful way; Mrs. Arvel was fond of her man because he kept the house a-going, but they all spoke against each other, as each turned their backs. And when their appetites were satisfied they started quarrelling, I suppose, as they quarrelled before me without shame.

Papa had a rough, loud voice, and one masterbuilder, who was engaged on the house, refused to come any more, as he said he was not used to be bullied and holloaed at. Mrs. Arvel was a shrew, and could not keep a servant, and Lilian answered her mother impudently, because she felt that Papa was behind her.

Nevertheless, Mr. Arvel sometimes vented his wrath on saucy Lilian too. He had told her on my last visit that women were incapable of getting their living. She turned sullen, and the black cloud came over her face. Her lips were blue, as she answered: "I get mine. Don't I pay you for my board?"

"Yah!" snarled Arvel, "but you don't pay any rent or taxes!"

"That would be the last straw," snapped the damsel back at him, "ask me to give you money now for my rent and I'll be off!"

These rows generally took place just at the beginning of the meals, as all their nerves were unstrung by the pangs of hunger. As soon as they were warmed up by wine and meat, they all got amiable again, and Pa would pinch Lilian as she passed him, and bandy pet names with his mistress. I always sat by and said nothing, although Mrs. Arvel would appeal to me and say ironically: "Is he not polite?"

I often had the impression that I was lunching or dining in a pantry, and that the coachman and cook were having a tiff with their daughter, the lady's maid. But what cared I? I lusted for Lilian.

In answer to her missive, I told her to try and put up with her domestic troubles, as if she ventured to leave her home, she would be ruined for life. She could have no idea of the career of a young woman alone in the world. There was no possible happiness for her outside the pale of social conventions, and she must play the hypocrite in a good cause and put up with everything from her mother, who, after all, loved her and had brought her up and educated her. I tried to give her an idea of the position of women according to worldly notions, and that is how I saw that the young lady who wanted to be kept well in hand, had been allowed to drift into my arms, for the want of good advice. Why Arvel had never put her on the right road was obvious. He wanted her for himself, although perhaps at that time he did not know what he really desired, or was powerless to judge his own feelings. I fancy that could he have analysed the sensations that were springing up in his breast, he would have tried to curb what I felt was a fast-growing desire for his mistress's daughter. But he could not reason; he only knew that her contact warmed his sluggish blood; that he felt young again when he tickled her, or romped with her, and that was all he desired or cared about.

Her future, her interests, the ultimate end of such unnatural intercourse could never have occurred to him, or he would have behaved more decently and stopped low wrangling, besides refraining from discussing the mother's menopause with her. But he had gone still farther with the maiden, as she had told me in answer to a question as to whether Mr. Arvel loved her Mamma or not:

"Oh, not much! Ma tells me he never touches her now. He only proves his love now and again at rare irregular intervals."

I threw all scruples to the winds. If Lilian did not play with me, she would get somebody else and Papa will be sure to have his turn one of these fine days. I cannot save her.

I began to tell her that I should love her more if she would be very obedient to me. I wanted to be her master. She must submit to be my slave.

I could wait no longer. I wanted her, and the promised customers not coming forward as quickly as I wished, I, impatient to taste her sweet body once more, reflected, and thought that a little cash would facilitate matters. I wrote and asked her if it was possible for her to carry out this little comedy:

"Tell your people that you have heard of a bad debt—surely someone owes you a little bill?—and come up to Paris to fetch it. Meet me and I will give you a fifty-franc note. Go back and exhibit the money to your Mamma and give it to her if she wants it, saying that you have succeeded in getting that on account, and that you are promised the same amount again, to be given by the lady before she goes to the seaside. A fortnight later, up you come to Paris again and return home to your parents with a few louis more. Thus I buy the liberty of my slave from her mother!"

LILIAN TO JACKY.

Wednesday. (No date or place. Received June 15th. 1898.)

My only master,

This time I will try my hardest not to bore you with all my troubles; I will keep everything hidden in the very bottom of my heart and only when we shall be all alone, will I, in the costume of Mother Eve—since such is your will and pleasure—open the corner of my heart which holds all that causes my tears. Thank you for the promptitude with which you answered my last scrawl. I have found fresh strength in your good and long letter. As soon as mother begins to be unjust, I think of you, and I, who have no patience, find enough to let her do and say all she likes without answering, or saying what is on the tip of my tongue, which always brings on quarrels. It is very hard all the same, and in truth I must love you profoundly to restrain my temper as I do. Evidently you are right in all you tell me, and I have decided to follow your good advice.

Your idea is quite feasible, especially as I have a customer who owes me money and Papa knows it. There is only an "if" and a "but," however. The idea of accepting money from you is repugnant to me, since your feelings were wounded during my sojourn at Monte-Carlo.

I do not explain myself well, but you who understand me so well, will be able to read between the lines.

This customer I am telling you about is a certain Madame Helena Muller. She owes me nearly seven hundred francs and I shall never get a sou.

You must write me a word, telling me when I can see you. I will arrange to tell the story you suggest and all will be well.

I am free, excepting Friday, when I have got some ladies coming to try on some hats.

Soon I shall see, I hope, my too much beloved little Papa.

I send you no kisses; I keep them all for our next interview.

Your entirely submissive slave,

LILY.

ERIC ARVEL TO JACKY.

10, Rue Vissot. Paris, June 17th. 1898.

My dear Jacky,

You are overwhelming me. Many thanks for all your books. You are one of the best. Will you come and dine with us sans cérémonie on Monday night? M. is coming, and we can offer you a good dinner.

Remember me very kindly to your good parents and everybody else, and believe me to remain ever,

Yours very truly,
ERIC ARVEL.

LILIAN TO JACKY.

No date or place. (Received June 19th. 1898.)

Beloved Master,

To-morrow, Saturday, is the most busy day for me, as I have to send home all the work of the week, and as you can easily understand, I must be there in order to see that everything is properly finished off.

Monday, we have a gentleman coming to dinner and there is some talk of inviting a certain M. Jacky S . . . as well. I do not know him, but I want to make his acquaintance and as I wish to please him I must not go out that afternoon, or I shall not be pretty enough in the evening!

Miss Arvel will tell M. S . . . what day the little daughter can pass a few pleasant hours with her dear Papa.

In the meanwhile, I send you a long, long kiss and a thousand caresses each one sweeter than the other.

LILY.

JUNE 20, 1898.

Of the informal dinner-party, I have very little to say. I managed to get a few brief moments alone with my love and reminded her that I should expect and exact entire obedience from her. She would have to submit to the worst kind of caresses next time we met, and I should measure the depth of her love by the manner in which she put up with the most brutal conduct from me, if my caprices should lead me that way. She was mine and I could do as I chose with her body. It would be the height of voluptuousness to feel that she was in my power, that I was free to inflict pain upon her, and she was to support all suffering, buoying herself up with the thought that all she endured, however disagreeable, was conducive to her master's pleasure. So saying, I smartly slapped her face, and she positively cooed with delight like a turtledove.

"You hurt me!"

And emboldened, I pinched her arms. She longed to cry out, but dared not, as Papa was not far off, and murmuring: "Oh! You did hurt me!" melted away on my eager lips.

I explained to her again that although she was absolutely free in the eyes of the world and could get married to-morrow if she liked without a jealous word from me, when alone in *tête-à-tête* with me, she was to have no shame, and I intended to destroy in her all feelings of pudicity, by forcing her to do everything I wanted. I should teach her the pleasure of being humiliated and degraded by the man she loved, and she would gradually get to relish the idea of trampling on all laws of decency. The initial stage would produce a novel kind of peculiar pain and suffering that would heighten and prolong her sensual enjoyment, as the smarting hurt of my mischievous punishments would retard the moment of joy and these conflicting emotions plunge her finally into the wildest vortex of lubricity. She listened devoutly and said the idea pleased her greatly. I secretly resolved to make an expert whore of her. She should have no shame, and recoil from nothing a man's lechery could invent in the delirium of desire. I wanted— mad vision!—to fashion a harlot out of a virgin, and hand over to a husband a Messalina with a maidenhead. I knew that I could easily fashion her to my wishes.

Anybody can by hook or by crook get a girl to lie still and with the aid of a little force and fascination gradually establish complete connection, but moulding a virgin to one's wishes seemed to me something new, and soothing to the last few fragments of my tat- tered conscience. I hankered to enjoy the winsome lassie and I would at that moment have cut off my hand sooner than have harmed her, or dishonoured her. I thought, in my folly, that I was behaving honestly to her, and I took great credit to myself for my forbearance. How far was I right or wrong?

JUNE 22, 1898.

I hesitate before beginning to narrate how I at last was able to press my Lilian's unveiled form in my arms, because I have to make an avowal, which I am sure will not be fully understood by many of my readers.

I loved Lilian with all the strength of my black soul. I cannot help if my brain is incapable of jealousy. I had given her my heart. I thought of nothing but her night and day, but I cared not what she did or to whom she granted her favours, as long as she proved her love for me. Worse than all, I wanted her to have other adorers. I would have placed her myself in the arms of many men, if she only came back to me afterwards. And the idea that her mother's lover pursued her with his lascivious obsessions; that he was perhaps her real father, caused me to love her more. Am I not sufficiently vile? And yet at the same time—supreme contradiction, that I cannot understand myself, unless it was the remembrance of my first Lilian—I respected her virginal film. I looked upon her as a sacred trust, as something I must not harm or violate. She was to me an idol to be worshipped, that I venerated too much to shatter or spoil. Once for all, I must, since I have sworn to tell the truth, make a statement to which I shall not recur again.

Whenever I had an appointment with Lilian, I always took care to have had at least one emission, either the night before, or more frequently in the morning, as our meetings were in the afternoon, so as to be sufficiently cool and not too excited, thus remaining master of my passions and preventing myself being tempted to rob her of her virgin's crown.

My sweet girl came at last quite punctually. She sat by me, close to me, and chatted. She told me that an employé in the offices of the Gare de l'Est had been frequently pestering her with his attentions. He wanted to marry her. He had seen her father, who had bluntly told him that his daughter had no dowry, and that he would not give her to any man unless the suitor could prove that he possessed at least a fortune of ten thousand pounds. The poor clerk had retired crestfallen. If the story was true, it only proved that Mr. Arvel did not want her to be married. I hinted as much to her, but she laughed the matter off and kissed me passionately, and I returned her caresses, devouring her face and neck. And now she gave me a great deal of trouble. I could not get her clothes off or pull up her skirts. She struggled against me. I was vexed, tired, and hot. It was not a loving encounter, but a wrestling bout, and to every one of my efforts she kept on repeating:

"You hurt me! Oh! You hurt me!"

At last, I persuaded her to consent to undress and get into bed with me. After a deal of haggling and on condition that I closed the window curtains, she gave way. I think she saw I was getting disgusted at her prolonged resistance.

She made me undress first, go to bed, and await her. I agreed and soon afterwards she slipped under the coverlet by my side. I went to take her in my arms, when she pulled the sheet between us so that my body should not touch hers, and giggled hysterically. But I soon clasped her in my arms, and pulling up her chemise, enjoyed to the full the pleasure of feeling her flesh against my naked body.

I took her hand and put it on my member. She dragged her fingers away and turned her face from me. I asked her why she did so.

"Oh! I make such faces when I enjoy! You can't know how nervous I am!"

How did she know she was ugly in the moment of joy? Who had told her?

"You must take my thing in your hand, Lily!"

"No! No!" she exclaimed.

"But see, I touch you!" said I, as I deftly manipulated her little button.

"You hurt me!" she whined once more.

So I, out of temper, feeling inwardly that she was coquetting with me, grasped her round the waist, threw her light frame over on to her belly, and pulling down the sheets and blankets, fully exposed her posteriors. Her bottom was round, well-shaped, and larger than one would have expected from such a slightly made creature.

"You won't do what I want, will you? Well, I'll make you. I'll slap you until you obey me!"

Then, without sparing her, I held her tightly with my right arm, and my left hand rained down a succession of smart slaps on her buttocks.

She struggled, shrieked, and kept on her eternal complaint:

"You hurt me!"

I spanked her with all my strength, paying no heed to her cries, and I should think she suffered nearly five minutes; a long period when being punished.

At last, my fingers aching, and being out of breath, I was about to desist, when she gave in and begged for mercy, putting out her hand to caress my private parts. She was more tractable now and I masturbated her until she gave down her elixir, but she still complained of the pain my exploring finger caused her.

Perhaps I did go a little too far. Perhaps I wanted to see if the hymen had been ruptured between November and June. But no, she was still *virgo intacta*.

She was very wet with all these manœuvres, which I could see and feel she enjoyed. I got on top of her, made her open her thighs, and put the head of my instrument just beyond the outer lips of her grotto, which, by the way, were very large and hairy, and enclined to be fat. I did not intend to follow up my advantage, but I enjoyed the feeling that the clasp of her lower mouth gave to the tip of my acorn.

When I got too far, or pushed forward as if to begin the work of penetration, she continued her parrot-cry:

"You hurt me!"

I rolled off her body, she turned on her side, and her bottom was against my dart, as I clasped her to me. I placed the bursting, swollen weapon between the robust hemispheres. She liked this. I imitated her eternal, plaintive: "You hurt me!"

I asked her if she was happy and whether she would like me to suck her now.

"I want you first!" she murmured.

So I, being rampant, in spite of my efforts to keep back the emission, started plunging and pushing as if I would sodomize her, and I am almost sure that the tip of my organ of virility was in her anus. She was very hairy, and unlike women in general, had a slight growth all round the little wrinkled hole of her beautiful bottom.

I soon exploded my cartridge and she remained in bed. The closeness of her posterior charms prevented a drop escaping. I asked her if I had penetrated a little way in behind, but she denied it.

Then a little more play, and once more I made her spend with my finger, the while I sucked her large and fiery nipples. This time, she herself asked me to masturbate her. She thoroughly appreciated this last bout and wanted nothing more.

She had got some sort of an idea vaguely into her head that she could get married, and not let her husband penetrate her. She seemed to have horror at the idea of a man's perforator piercing her body. She kept telling me to be careful how I tickled her clitoris, as she had heard a story of a girl being violated by a young lover's middle finger! There was an impression I had, that real coition with a husband or a lover did not tempt her.

I began to talk cautiously to her about a friend I had in England. He was a lord and was married. Being much older than his wife, and being blest or cursed with the same tolerant ideas as I had, he allowed his better half to have lovers and I wanted Lily to send her brother, who was working hard in London, to the easy-going couple. She refused to communicate with him on the subject.

I offered her other women if she cared to try a little tribadism. But she would not entertain the idea for a moment. I soon found out that she really liked men and would not object to "fun" with two men at once. I asked her if she would lunch with me and my friend from London. She would certainly, but would not go to him when she went to England in the autumn.

After all was over and she was dressed, seeing that I was rather quiet and cool towards her, she crept up to me and apologised spontaneously and prettily for all her shortcomings.

"I meant to be your slave, and coming up in the train I re-hearsed all that I should do and how I would be quite unresisting in your arms. But when you took hold of me, I could not overcome my feelings of shame. Let me get used to you and I will really be your 'thing,' as devoted to you and even more obedient than Smike, but you don't know how difficult it is for me to summon up courage and come along this Rue de Leipzig to you."

And then she wanted to remake the bed, so that the people of the house should ignore that we had used it.

Her mixture of true or feigned innocence, with her natural perversity and coquetry, bewildered and delighted me. She aroused my lust completely, and I could not look at her without the most filthy ideas of refined enjoyment crowding into my mind.

We left the house, and I took her to a *café* where we had a pint bottle of dry champagne. While drinking it and talking on indifferent subjects I saw her eyes half closing, her nostrils began to quiver, and her carmine lips, all fiery from the recent touches of my moustache and teeth, were bedewed with saliva.

"Why, you're coming!" I exclaimed.

"Yes, darling, but how do you know?"

I explained the signs that had betrayed her, and asked her the reason.

"Only because I am seated here alone with you! Oh! I'm sopping!"

She would have returned to the Rue de Leipzig, but it was too late. I was fortunate enough, although it was the month of June, to secure a closed fiacre and was able, during the drive to the station, to verify the fact that she was really inundated.

I must not forget that I gave her a fifty-franc note, which she said she was bound to show to her Mamma, to account for her prolonged absence from home, and I regretfully left her, thinking on my way home of her handsome drawers, ornamented with lace, and the dainty chemise to match, with its little bows of pink ribbon, and I weaved new schemes of future orgies with her—my Lilian. I was in truth very far gone.

4

Trouver, dans une souffrance de degré très variable, tantôt
légère, tantôt grave ou d'un raffinement atroce, qu'on
fait infliger, qu'on voit infliger ou qu'on inflige enfin
soi-même à un être humain, la condition toujours néces-
saire, et parfois suffisante, de la jouissance sexuelle: telle
est la perversion de l'instinct génital qu'on désigne sous
le nom de *sadisme*.

L. THOINOT.

LILY TO JACKY.

No date or place. (Received June 24th. 1898.)

It is five o'clock in the morning, but as I cannot sleep, I get up
softly so as not to wake the slumbering household and quickly write a
line to my well-beloved master.

The most conflicting sentiments agitate me since yesterday. I feel
ashamed of my lewdness and yet I regret having been so reserved.

I adore you, the thought of you alone drives me absolutely mad. I
am eager to see you again. I thirst for you. I want to be yours, yours
entirely; to be your thing, your slave.

I have a prayer to offer up to you: Next time we meet, if now and
again, in spite of myself I refuse you the least favour, I must beg of you
only to repeat to me this simple sentence: "Do it to prove to me your
love!"

I know that I am very silly, but my dear and beloved little Papa, I only ask to learn, and I often say to myself that I am very foolish to reserve myself for some creature I shall certainly never love, since you alone possess my soul, my heart, my body.

How long the days will seem to me until the end of the month! And I fear already that I have wearied you by my ignorance and my timidity.

I remember your dear lips,

Your
LILY.

LILY TO JACKY.

Sunday. (No date. Received June 27th. 1898.)

Adored master,

Your little girl is suffering to-day. Have no fear. It is nothing serious; in three or four days it will be all over.

How good and generous you are! You possess the patience of an angel, but your little daughter will really become your slave in every sense of the word.

One of the reasons which as well as my wretched shame prevents me from being as submissive as I should wish, is that I do not esteem myself handsome enough for you. I have an awful fear lest I should dispel all your illusions, you who have known so many women. If I was formed like a real woman and not like a silly, awkward young girl, it would be quite different.

I am well-built, I know, but really too thin. I should like to be marvellously beautiful for you; for your sole joy and pleasure.

I have a heap of questions to put to you the next time I see you. There are certain things that I do not understand at all, and that I should dearly like to know!

When you want to see me, make a sign, and I'll fly to you, my love, but not until the end of the month as arranged.

I adore you,

Your
LILY.

Eric Arvel to Jacky.

Sonis-sur-Marne, 30th. June 1898.

My dear Jacky,

I am commissioned by Madame to tender you her very best thanks for the very handsome addition you have enabled her to make to her dressing-table. I cannot tell where you discovered such handsome cut-glass bottles, such as they do not make nowadays, and which I can assure you are highly appreciated. We cannot help looking at them and since they arrived last night they have been in our hands time after time. You are really too good, and you embitter our minds when we think how handsomely you are always inclined to recognise a hospitality which in your case it is to us a true pleasure to exercise. Can you come down on Saturday and spend a long day with us so that we may thank you personally for all your kindness? We will have some fresh fruit and vegetables, and with a bit of luck we can give you some peas such as you have rarely eaten. Give my very best wishes to all your good folks at home, who I trust are well.

Yours very truly,
Eric Arvel.

Lily to Jacky.

No date or place. (Received July 1st. 1898.)

My best beloved master,

Do come to-morrow, then we can settle about Monday if you wish. But I am longing to see your darling face.

Come as early as you can, and try to stay as late as possible if you wish to please your slave and make her very happy.

I should like to bite you,

Lily.

July 2, 1898.

This day was a long and happy one. The best part of the time I managed to be alone with my Lily. And she was mine then, if ever a woman was. She was quite changed, and I felt she was now entirely under my influence. She was sweet, tender, and confiding.

As before, she asked me to help her to lay the table for déjeuner and although Mamma kept coming in and out of the dining-room, we managed to exchange many a sly caress. Lily had pleasant touches of amiability peculiarly her own. One spontaneous approach of hers I shall never forget, as she never repeated it, and it happens that I do not remember any other woman having done the same thing to me. I was seated on a little sofa at the end of the room and she was busy at the table. I was supposed to assist her, but I never did anything but kiss her. She dropped the plate she held, and coming to me without a word, bent her head and placed her cheek against mine. I did not speak, neither did she. And there she remained for a moment. That is all.

I treated her with kindness, but I exacted obedience, and told her curtly to kiss me and touch me as my wayward fancy dictated, and being forced to be obedient to me pleased her greatly. She told me that she knew she had not a good temper, could not brook authority, and that neither her mother nor her father could get her to do what did not please her. And yet to me she willingly gave way.

What she wanted me to explain to her, according to her letter, was the entrancing mystery of manly erection. I told her briefly, and she said she thought that males were always stiff and hard. I asked her if she had never looked at her dogs. She replied that she did not like to, that she had never dared.

Papa had told me that Lilian hated reading books. He had tried to educate her mind a little by giving her a few healthy English novels to read. French romances, he would not have in his house. I thought of Les Demi-Vierges, but kept silent. I never spoke of the girl to him, never even mentioning her name; but we hardly ever conversed without he talked of her. I asked her if she cared for books and she confessed she adored reading. So I had brought with me "The Yellow Room," which I gave her, and she ran and hid it away

This story is thoroughly obscene and relates to flagellation and torture practised erotically on two young girls by the uncle of one of them.

During the day, in her impatience, she managed to slip away and peep into it, and in the evening told me that she thought she would like to read how the heroine suffered. I put her on her guard against the exaggerated cruelty therein described. I tried to make her understand the pleasure of subjecting a loved woman to one's most salacious desires, and that submission had its joys. I laid stress again on the enjoyment I should have in degrading and humiliating her when we were alone together, and she freely said that the efforts she would have to make, to curb her own disobedient nature for the sake of my despotic pleasure, would exercise a most extraordinary emotional effect on her sensuality.

I cannot tell how we kissed and fondled each other. I taught her to lick my face, neck, and ears, and I frequently made her feel my stiffened spear outside my trousers.

I would make her put her hand on it and note its softness. Then I joined her mouth to mine, and taking her fingers, placed them once more on the now hardened standard. This lesson of turgescent virility greatly delighted her.

I now come to the principal novel experience of the day. The last time I was at Sonis, I told her that when I came to visit at her house, I ordered her to tie a string or riband to the hair of her "pussy," and let the end peep out of her frock. The colour was to be assorted to the hue of the dress-fabric, so that I could pull at it now and then, unsuspected by anyone. By the slight smart the tug would give, I could thus feel that I was in intimate communication with the most secret part of her body, and could test her devotion to me by being able to inflict pain upon her whenever I chose.

She would prove her love by supporting this teazing inconvenience and therefore show that she loved me greatly by such humble submission to all my most weird and voluptuous caprices. She tried to laugh at the idea, but I could see she listened attentively and liked the originality of my strange whim. She found extraordinary delight in being the slave of a "very dirty Papa," as she called me, and when I mentioned the word "incest," as I did frequently, her eyes closed, her nostrils quivered, and her mouth literally watered, the moisture of her saliva bedewing her sensual and expressive lips.

Just before lunch, I said:

"You pretend you will obey me and yet you have not done what I told you on my last visit."

She knew at once what I meant, gave me an arch look and said she would obey.

In the course of the afternoon, Mamma went up to Paris to fetch another new servant. Papa asked me to go out with him and give the dogs an airing, but I objected, complaining of pains in my ankles. It is true they did hurt me, but not as much as I made out. He begged me to remain on a bench in the garden, and called his daughter from the kiosque, where she was at work with her assistants, to keep me company, while he went out alone, and there was no one in the house, but Lily, her workgirls, and me. Lily showed me the end of a piece of tape which peeped out of the pocket-hole of her dress behind, she having fastened it to the hair on the left side of her mount, and brought it round her hip through the slit of her petticoat. She sat by my side and I pulled it frequently. She would wince, tell me I hurt her, and kiss me furtively, as she kept a sharp lookout, so that the girls should not see her. I told her that I did not believe she had really fastened it where I wanted, and putting my hand in this opening, I got it round to where it was tied, verifying her statement, and tickling the top of her furrow a little. I told her she had placed it badly, and another time it must come out over the top of her belt or waistband. She told me that could be done.

I informed her that my doctor was sending me away to Lamalou, to go through a treatment lasting twenty-one days, to get out of my system the remaining vestiges of the malady that still made me suffer. I could hardly walk or close my hands, but the protracted illness had not dulled my masculine energies.

She arranged to meet me on the 5th. of August, at two P.M., and as usual, I told her what I intended to do to her. I should have a small riding whip with me, and no doubt after she had received a few cuts with it, to avoid further punishment, she would be very docile, and not struggle against me, and thus in time I should succeed in breaking down the barriers of her shame, which I allowed without hesitation was excusable and natural.

I informed her that I meant to kiss every part of her frame, which she would have to lewdly expose to my bold gaze, and I would even thrust my tongue between the cheeks of her bottom and command her to do the same to me.

"Yes, darling! And what else—tell me?"

I taught her to take my fingers in her mouth and lick them, and suck them, and then I did the same to her.

"Gaston used to kiss my hands," she said.

"But did he not kiss your lips?"

"Never!" she retorted, unblushingly. "You are the first man who has put his mouth on mine."

She forgot she had told me that "Baby" was the man who had taught her pigeon kisses.

After this, we were not alone together, until she went off just before dinner to gather some herbs for the salad. I went strolling behind her and saw the fatal cord trailing round her feet. It had fallen from her hip to the ground. I told her of it in a whisper, as Pa and Ma were not far off, seated at table, for we dined in the open air. She got confused, and turning awkwardly round, trod on it herself and the sudden jerk made her jump with pain.

When dinner was over, her stepfather, accompanied by Lilian, saw me to the station by a round-about road, so as to walk the dogs a little, and we spoke of her business as a bonnet-builder.

"I suppose," I said, "when you make out the bills, you add a few francs here and there when the customer is one of the silly sort?"

"Never," she answered, "I wouldn't cheat one of my own weak sex. Robbing men, I understand, but not women."

I never forgot this unguarded statement of hers.

Our conversation now turned upon marriage, and she once more said that she could not think of leaving her Papa and she nestled closely up to my host. I answered that I quite understood that and she was quite right to stop by his side, while he would be a fool to let her go. I added that he spoilt her, but a husband would exercise authority over her. I, for instance, believed in corporal punishment. Young women needed the whip, and if I had a giddy damsel to look after, daughter or wife, I should always have a small riding-whip handy and use it unsparingly. He agreed with me and I could see that he enjoyed my risky talk amazingly. His face grew serious, and then he laughed. A voluptuous feeling had crept over him, I am sure, by the peculiar look in his eyes and the general dull-ness of his physiognomy. Real sensual desire is a serious thing. Man is always serious and sulky-looking when his lechery is aroused, which is a sign of his dormant animality. Lilian laughed, with many a sly look at me. She knew what I meant. On nearing the station, she lagged behind, and signed to me that she had rectified her blunder, and got the end of the string above the waistband, in front of her dress. In the dark, I was able to approach her and pull it. I got a low, "Ah! it hurts!" and then a squeeze of her hand, a hasty kiss, and a sigh of pleasure in return. I was off, and the mother and father thought I left on the 5th., but I had arranged to devote that afternoon to Lily and depart the next day.

"The Horn Book" was now ready and I promised Mr. Arvel I would send it to him at once, as he was always pleased to read a smutty novelty. I despatched it to him a day or two afterwards. He said he would be careful to keep it out of Lily's way and would read it at his office. This remark struck me as quite unnecessary on his part, and during my little journey back to Paris I vaguely dreamt of Arvel and Adèle's daughter, reading "The Yellow Room" and "The Horn Book" together. I began to think that I could understand his talk in general much better if I believed the contrary of all he said, above all when he brought up Lilian's name.

I told her that Papa was going to have an obscene work from me, and that she should also read it on the sly when I returned to Paris. I told her I wanted him to have this naughty book so that he might be excited and perhaps violate her when I was away. In August, she would be alone at home with her Granny, as Pa and Ma were going to Germany for a short time.

With many cordial wishes for renewed good health by my baths at Lamalou, and a request that my first visit on my return should be for the Villa Lilian, I got into the train and shut my eyes to think of the delights in store for me before my departure.

JULY 2, 1898.

On my way to the Rue de Leipzig, where I was to meet Lily, I bought a light bamboo switch or riding-stick, preferring this to walking through the streets with a whip.

When she arrived, as she did punctually, and coquettishly dressed, showing that she had taken great trouble with her toilette, her first words were:

"Where is your whip?"

I showed her my switch:

"This is for you, Lily, and my dogs afterwards."

She had in her hand "The Yellow Room," which she had understood I wanted back at once. I told her she could keep it as long as she liked and not hurry through it. She had been reading it in the train. She said she liked it. It had made her "naughty," and she had been obliged to finish herself with her finger. I replied that I thought she had told me she never did that.

"I do not as a rule, but now and again I can't help myself."

I warned her to beware and not give way to the habit. When I went on to inform her that habitual masturbation deprives the sexual organs of women of their tone and elasticity, causing the secret slit to gape, and the inner lips to become elongated, she thanked me for the advice and told me she would resist the temptation, so as not to wither that pretty part of her body.

"I like my pussy," she said, "I like to look at the hair on it. I love to play with my hairs."

I informed her that she had a very pretty one and it would be a pity to spoil it. The two large outer lips should close themselves naturally, but if Lily gives way to onanism they will do so no longer.

I asked her to show me the paragraph which had brought about this crisis. She did so:

"He inserted his enormous affair in her burning c . . ., etc."

It was not exactly that sentence alone which so unduly excited her, but what lead up to this termination. She did not understand certain words, but guessed them from the context. She thought that the extreme and bloodthirsty, long-drawn-out cruelty, described in the volume, was impossible, but thoroughly appreciated the idea of man's domination over a woman, and to bend her to his lewd will, a little brutality appealed to her imagination. She wanted more books later on, but not tales of Lesbianism. Anything, simple lust or cruelty, as long as it took place between men and women. She thought that everything and anything was possible and agreeable, if a male and a female were fond of each other. This was far from bad philosophy, springing naturally from a virgin of 22. How changed she was now with me!

During our conversation, I had made her sit by my side on the sofa, with her clothes well up, as I wanted to see and feel her legs, calves, and knees. I made her open and close her thighs, and cross and recross her legs, as I chose to command.

I kissed her passionately. My lips wandered all over her face. I kissed her eyes, and licked and gently nibbled her ears. This last caress pleased her very much.

I made her stand up in front of me, and by threats of ill-usage and pinching the fat part of her arms, I got her, after a little resistance, to let me put my hands up her clothes, lift her chemise out of her drawers, and put my hand between her thighs, entirely grasping her centre of love. In this manner, my hand still gripping her plump, hairy lips, I walked her round the room, in spite of her blushes and protestations. It was an agreeable sensation for both of us. I had great enjoyment in feeling the movement of her soft thighs as she walked, my hand clasping her furry retreat. I halted in front of the looking-glass of the wardrobe, and forced her to look at the strange group we thus formed. She hid her face on my shoulder and I could feel she was now quite wet, heated, and ready for anything.

I asked her if she could take off her drawers without undressing. She replied in the affirmative.

"An English girl could not, but my drawers are fastened to my stays."

I reclined on the sofa and told her to take them off slowly, without sitting down. She did so with docility, and I enjoyed the sight of seeing her get her legs out of her beribboned undergarments. I called her to me, and stood her up again in front of me and close to me, as I sat on the *chaise-longue*, while my hands, up her clothes, now for the first time roved without hindrance over her belly, bottom, thighs and nature's orifice. It was a delicious moment for me. I put the left index as far as possible up her crisp fundament, gradually forcing it up with a corkscrew motion, as I felt her pleasure in front increasing, for I was masturbating her scientifically the while, with the middle finger of the left hand. I had great difficulty in piercing her anus, but to my astonishment, she did not complain of pain. She afterwards told me that she liked the feeling of my finger in the posterior aperture. The crisis came quickly for her and she could no longer stand upright, but soon sank gradually to her knees, all in a heap, sighing with satisfied lust, her head pillowed on my breast. I kissed her sweet neck and finished her as quickly as my wrist would let me, until she tore herself from my grasp.

Now I tell her to disrobe before me, until she is entirely naked. She refuses indignantly. The moment has now arrived for me to take hold of my cane, and as she still refuses, I give her two or three stinging cuts over biceps and shoulders, and, smarting with pain, she consents to undress until she is in her shift. I kiss and lick again all the charms of the upper part of her frame, which is now quite bare, and I teach her how to suck my lips, and tickle my cheeks and forehead with the point of her tongue, not forgetting my neck and ears.

Sufficiently excited, I order the chemise to be taken off.

"Never!" she exclaims.

I get my stick again, and show her how silly she is to refuse, as it is already nearly down to her navel. But she still will not consent, and I cut her, not too severely, over her back, shoulders and arms. I love to see the dark stripes raised by the whistling bamboo. She hardly winces at each blow. I am certain she likes the chastisement of the male. Suddenly, I twist her round and tell her to remain quiet, and take three cuts on her naked bottom. I pull up her shift, fully exposing her plump posteriors and she is quiet on her knees, leaning over the sofa. I do not hurry, but count slowly: "One, two, three!"

And the poor little bottom receives three severe cuts, stretching across both posteriors and equalling, although I do not tell her so, six stinging blows. I have tamed her, for she rises with a wry face, and drops the offending chemise to her feet. She is naked at last before me, in the full light of a sunny summer day. I kiss her and caress her again, admiring her flat belly and her splendid bush, as black as night.

She seems uneasy, but I soon bring a smile to her face again, by telling her that I will never do anything to her by surprise.

"I will always let you know beforehand, what I want, and if what I propose to do displeases you, tell me and I will then see if your master should give way or not."

And now I make her plainly understand what I intend to do to her:

"I shall lick you all over and then suck you, and you shall suck me until I discharge boldly and without reserve in your mouth. But I want to tell you something which is very important. The first time I had you, you expectorated my elixir. That is an insult to the man who is loved by a woman. You must swallow all to the very last drop, and remain with your mouth on the instrument until told to go. If you cannot perform the operation as I describe, it shows you do not love me, as nothing, however seemingly dirty, can cause disgust in you coming from me."

"But I can't. I shan't be able. I shall perhaps be sick?"

"You must try, and if you really love me, you will succeed."

I now stripped quite naked, and took her in my arms, as if she was a baby. She was as light as a feather. I lifted her up, until her body was on a level with my chin, and threw her from me on the bed with all the strength I could muster. It was a pretty sight to see her naked body tumble down all in a heap.

We were soon entwined together, outside the bedclothes, and I cannot describe our mutual kisses, caresses and pressures. I licked her face all over and sucked her neck, her nipples, and waggled my tongue under her arms, while her belly, navel, and thighs came in for their share of the kisses of my eager mouth. She uttered little shrieks of pleasure, and anon cooed like a turtle-dove, or purred like the rutting kitten she was. I turned her round on to her belly, and the nape of her neck, her shoulders, spine, loins and bottom were soon wetted by my saliva. I wished to get my tongue between her round posteriors but she would not consent. I was now too feverish and unnerved to press the point. It was a very hot day. So I laid over her, and started pretending to copulate and the end of my dagger went in a little.

"Oh! you hurt down there. On the top it is nice."

"Take hold of it yourself and put it where you like."

She placed the head just on her sensitive button, and I moved gently, the swollen tip rubbing against her clitoris. This she approved of. I told her that a woman could be enjoyed in the hole of her bottom. Would she let me? She answered me affirmatively without hesitation. I warned her that it hurt the first time.

"What a pity it is that everything hurts the first time!"

She turned her posteriors to me, freely offering them with a loving look.

"I must lick you there to make it wet."

"No! no!"

So I wetted my arrow with my saliva, and began to push between her rotund cheeks.

"You are not right!" she exclaimed.

"Guide it yourself, Lily."

She did so, and I thrust home.

"Oh!" she shrieked, piteously. "It hurts! You do hurt me so, Papa!"

At these words, a wave of pity broke over me. It would be a cowardly trick, I thought, to sodomize my confiding sweetheart. So I desisted, and my organ grew limp.

"Try again," she said. And she seized my weapon.

"Oh! you are not excited enough now!"

I did not tell her what had crossed my mind. And I never did. I often thought since of warning her against ever yielding up her anus to a man, but the idea to speak of this escaped my memory. I am afraid it will be too late when she reads this book.

I was hot, tired, and perspiring, but still full of desire. I rested and gave her a little lesson in the art of manuelisation, teaching her how to hold the manly staff, the way to move the wrist, slowly or quickly, and so on. She was an apt pupil.

Then she got up to arrange her hair and taking out the combs and pins, let her long black tresses escape in freedom. They fell below her tiny waist.

She seized my bamboo switch and began to teaze me as I laid on the bed, giving me slight blows with it. I jumped up to catch it, but the task was an impossible one. I chased her round the room and I must have looked a ridiculous sight with my semi-erection, and my testicles dangling as I ran. When I was about to seize her, she would spring on the bed, and landing on the other side, always get the couch between us. So, I, panting, lie down again and say coolly:

"It is disgusting to see a young lady jumping about a room stark naked. Lily, are you not ashamed?"

She took my words literally and rushed to huddle on her chemise.

"Of course, I'm naked! I forgot that!"

And she sat on the sofa trying to hide her pussy. I soon laughed her out of her chemise again and she was in my arms once more.

Then I gamahuched her seriously, reversed over her sideways, while she felt my spear, and stroked the appendages, masturbating me as I had just taught her. I did not ask her to touch me thus while I sucked her. She did it of her own accord. I opened the big lips of her little shaded slit, and looked well at it and inside it. It was small and pink, rather tight and thin inside, but seemingly little. The vagina was clearly closed up. She was a perfect virgin. She spent, and we rested awhile.

"Now you!" she said.

"How?"

"As you like!"

I opened my legs, and placed her on her knees between my outstretched thighs. She bent her head and engulphed her playfellow. After a few hints, she sucked me like a professional. Her large mouth and sensual thick lips proved that she was born to be a sucker of men's tools all her life. I took her cheeks in my two hands, and held her head still, as I moved slowly in and out of her mouth, telling that I was having connection with her in a vile, unnatural manner. I then took it out of her mouth, and made her suck the balls alone, and tickle the erect member up and down the shaft, with the pointed end of her tongue. While she was busily engaged on the little olives in their purse, I rubbed my organ, all wet as it was, on her flushed cheeks, and informed her I should emit one day on her face, and in her hair, and in fact all over her, until every part of her body had been sullied by me. She got very excited by listening to this filthy talk, as she performed her task, and worked fast and furiously. I put my thigh between her legs and rubbed it against her furrow. At last, I felt I could bear the touch of her tongue no longer. I held her head, and pushed up and down myself, talking to her in a most disgusting manner, as the storm burst, and she tickled my member with her tongue until I was forced to push her away.

She looked up, and talked to me very gravely and seriously.

"You see it is all gone!"

I praised her, and she asked me timidly to be allowed to drink a little water. That I graciously permitted, and the voluptuous vestal begged me to let her suck again! She liked doing it!

It was five o'clock. We had been in the room since a quarter to three. I was dead beat, and I had not yet packed up my things for my departure the next day. We kissed and said good bye effusively.

She showed great jealousy, and tried to get me to talk about other women, probably to hear about my mistress. She would not believe I was going alone to Lamalou. She told me that she would write to me every day to prevent me forgetting her. I was not to have any love-affair with a woman, but she allowed me a night with a female now and again, as she was sure I needed it. She did not care how many different women I had, but would brook no rival. She could not receive any answers to her letters at her house, as the postmark would betray her. So I arranged to reply under initials to the post-office, Rue de Strasbourg, next to the Gare de l'Est. She was not allowed to go to Paris alone without valid reasons, but often unawares her people sent her up to fetch something, but she had to return by the next train. On those occasions she could go to the post-office. She did not care much about the accommodation of the Rue de Leipzig. The little minx would have liked me to take a place of my own, where she could keep a peignoir, etc.

She was fully dressed again, and said that when she talked to me she got quite wet. I verified the fact. Inside the big lips, which were very large and hairy, there was an astonishing amount of moisture, but as they closed so perfectly, her cleft was dry outside.

I told her about French letters. She did not know what they were.

"Why don't you get some, and then you could have me entirely, without fear of getting me in the family way?"

"Why don't you . . ." was a favourite expression of Lily's, but I knew I could not rely upon it.

I made her feel outside my trousers how the knowledge that she was so wet excited me, and she wanted to get on the bed again.

I asked her if her stepfather looked like a man who might be reading "The Horn Book" on the sly? I told her I was certain that he was in love with her.

"Why do you think that?" she asked me, assuming a very innocent air.

"Because you are a girl, who must fatally excite men's lust, and I cannot understand how he can live under the same roof with you, and not want you, especially as I know he is of a very voluptuous nature and don't care much for your mother."

I watched her narrowly as I said this, but she did not turn a hair. There was no indignation, real or feigned, nor any disgust or astonishment.

"You should rub against him whenever you can, and let your cheek and hair touch his face while type-writing together, etc., and then look at his trousers and see if he is in erection. You will then know if he has the carnal desire for you that I suspect."

"The other day," she replied, "he came into my bedroom without knocking. I was in my chemise, doing my hair in front of the glass. He turned very red and looked so silly. He scolded me for not locking my door and I answered that he ought to have knocked."

But she forgot about the curtained opening between the two rooms.

She mentioned that her favourite Blackamoor had contracted the habit of getting on her chair behind her back, and sniffing under her armpits. I told her to wash that part frequently.

"I do, of course, every morning!"

"Then use a strongly perfumed toilet soap. Dogs hate perfumes of any kind."

"Mother says I must never use soap under my arms. It is very bad."

"If you want to catch the men by the odour of women; by all means do not use soap. But the advice of your mother is what might be given to a *cocotte*, not to a respectable girl, and surprises me very much. But I suppose she does not know."

And then I slipped the promised fifty francs into her hand, and put her in a fly. With many protestations of affection, she left me, quite an altered girl; loving, and all her shame gradually going from her. I thought that after a few more meetings like this one, I should have no more to teach her.

5

Heaven first taught letters for some wretch's aid,
Some banished lover, or some captive maid:
They live, they speak, they breathe what love inspires
Warm from the soul, and faithful to its fires.
The virgin's wish, without her fears, impart;
Excuse the blush, and pour out all the heart.

POPE.

The Right Honourable the Earl of Fontarcy was an old friend
of mine, and our acquaintanceship was of over fifteen years standing, as far as I can recollect. He was superior to me in every way, by
position, birth, wealth and education, and I looked up to him and
admired him, for he possessed all the solid qualities of the Anglo-
Saxon. He was a man of few words; undemonstrative, but strictly
honourable; shrewd, and farseeing. I was very proud of his friendship, and I tried to be as staunch as possible towards him. I never
cared to have friends who were beneath me in social position, nor
visit people of no education. If I could not go into the drawing-
room of the highest in the land, I preferred to stop away, or taste
the pleasures of solitude. Therefore, I felt proud and flattered that
Lord Fontarcy should seek my society. When I went to England,
he invited me to his mansion in London, or received me at his
castle in the country, and he never passed through Paris without

seeking me out. He is over 60 as I write, and is still active and energetic, masterful and born to command. He had the same unprejudiced ideas as I have, with regard to the relationships of the sexes, and, as two voluptuous men of the world, we had had some extraordinary adventures together, which, however, have no bearing on the little episode of my life that I am now narrating.

Lord Fontarcy was divorced from his wife, but he had formed a connection with a most charming lady, a distant relative of his, who he eventually married. His *liaison* was known and winked at, as is usual among the British aristocracy. When he was invited by friends to hunt or shoot, Lady Clara, as I shall call her, was always welcomed as well, and by strange hazards, their bedrooms, if they did not actually communicate, were never very far apart. And in the fashionable society papers, their names always jostled each other.

She was a very good woman, quiet, calm, and sensible; but she possessed an inward fire of passion, which did not obscure her sound judgment of men and things. She liked me and was very kind to me. I never made love to her, although I think had I desired her, Lord Fontarcy would have shut his eyes to any little escapade on her part with Jacky, but I did not wish to jeopardise our old friendship for the sake of a few moments of pleasure.

I had told my friends a few of my ideas concerning Lily, and they were very anxious to meet her. I promised them that I would introduce her, if I could get over her prejudice, and that we would have a little orgie, when my lord and my lady, and Jacky and Lily, should shamelessly empty together the loving cup of unrestrained lechery.

In the meantime, I asked Lady Clara to send me her opinion of Lily, and I offer it here as a curiosity. It is not often that one woman gives her unbiassed opinion of another. It must be noted that she had never seen her.

CLARA'S OPINION OF LILY.

"Your Lily is really a nice girl and carefully brought up, but she does not care to give herself away too easily.

"Clara thinks that when the opportunity occurs, that if a little force is used, after gentle persuasion, that Lily would be more pleased than offended.

"Clara thinks that Jacky should see more of Lily if possible, as he cannot expect her to be heart and soul with him, unless she feels his presence or caresses often. She thinks Lily is ready to love him, but is a little wavering, or not quite sure how it will end with her. Lily will be like herself, and give her whole being entirely to her lover, only feeling real pleasure when in his arms, making him take pleasure sheathed within her.

"Clara also thinks that although Lily's mother says 'No' to a present or two offered to the daughter, she does not mean what she says. Besides, every true woman likes gifts from the man she loves."

No better example of the nature of Lord Fontarcy's liberal ideas can be given than the following extract from one of Clara's letters to me:

". . . Perhaps Lily would be benefited by the experience Clara went through with an elderly admirer of hers. She met him at a country house and was left alone with him, her host returning to town in the evening. His feelings ran away with him, but servants coming into the room, kept his overflowing attentions in check.

"He asked her to meet him in town. An opportunity occured to take him to certain chambers, where Clara and another could have a little amusement out of him. Clara made up a little tale about an uncle having gone away and left his chambers to be looked after. The other (Lord Fontarcy) was locked in an inner room, with his eyes to a convenient hole to witness operations.

"Clara went out, met her senile suitor, and brought him to the rooms, feeling very loth to display herself before the one she loved with another man, but there was no drawing back, and she had to do violence to her own feelings.

"When he was in the room, he at once tried the locked door, and Clara had a fit in case he discovered who was inside.

"After his inspection of the premises, he produced a French letter and suggested that he should commence at once. He got on her, and pushed and poked about, but the more he did so, the smaller his affair began to get, when he thought that if Clara knelt up, he might do it by the back way—dog fashion—but alas! that did not succeed. Clara did not even feel the tip of his member.

"He then said the letter pinched all the stiffness out of him and that he was too excited. Finally, he got atop of her again, and working up his organ with his own hand, managed to spend all over Clara's new drawers, which she had put on for the occasion.

"At which she blessed him, and he went away with the idea that he had still a maidenhead to take on the morrow, when he suggested meeting again.

"Clara retired into the locked room, to find consolation, feeling as if she had taken part in a battle.

"Clara must end this long scrawl by saying that she hopes the reader will find in Lily all he wishes and would like to know his plans for her."

LILIAN TO JACKY.

No place or date. (Received at Lamalou, July 7th. 1898.)

My best beloved master,

I want you to have this scribble to-morrow evening when you arrive, but for that I should have to post it to-night and I cannot do so. Anyhow, you will get it on Thursday morning for certain, and I hope you will feel less lonely. It is true you have your good and faithful Smike, but that is not the same thing as if your Lily was with you.

I am so sad at the idea of your departure. It seems as if you will forget me during these three weeks.

I hate your doctor who separates us thus cruelly. How I should like to be near you! Thus I should prove to you that I could never be dull at your side, because I love you.

I care naught for the pleasures that you tell me are necessary at my age, for all that is false and superfluous. True happiness, after all, is to love and be loved and naturally give proofs of affection.

If you choose to try me, I venture to say in advance that you will be tired before I shall, although I would do all in my power to sweeten your life.

Would it not be delicious, say, my sweet Daddy, to be always together, never to part?

But I am mad, for I am not lucky enough to have the supreme joy to feel myself yours, entirely belonging to you and to be able to say to myself that nothing in this world could ever separate us again.

You find yourself too old for me, but do you not know, my well-beloved, that if you are proud to have inspired a passion like mine, I, on my part, am doubly proud to have been chosen by a man who knows what life is, and has been able to appreciate it as you have.

I am a little fool, but I only ask to know all, to learn all from you. How stupid I must appear to you!

I see that to be loved, a woman should never let the love she feels be seen, but some unknown force within me drives me to tell all that passes through my brain like the silly thing that I am.

Now all marriage with another becomes impossible. It would be a martyrdom of every instant for me. Never could I make up my mind to be even brushed against by any other man. There now, see what you have done, my dear and adored master.

I kiss you everywhere where it will please you the most.

Your slave,
LILY.

A caress for Smike.

LILY TO JACKY.

(Received July 8th. 1898.)

Only just a line to let my own darling know that his slave is continually thinking about him. How I envy Smike, he is always with you and can by a thousand little ways prove his love for you.

Besides, I am sure you really love him, whilst I am not quite so sure that you care for your naughty girl.

As you are away for your health, do not trouble to write too often; you must not tire yourself, but simply take life easy, and come back to your Lily quite strong, never to leave her any more.

I hope you found everything as you wished it to be at the hotel. Is everyone very kind to you?

How I should love to be down there, nursing and taking care of you!

I am anxiously looking forward to the end of the month, when you will be back again quite well and strong.

We have nice weather here; I trust you also have it fine. Hotel life is so trying, it would be dreadful if you had to keep to your room on account of the weather.

If you are not too tired to write, tell me all you do and how you like everything.

A most passionate kiss for my master and a caress for lucky Smike.

LILY.

Lily to Jacky.

(Received July 9th. 1898.)

My adored master,

I have not been able to go to Paris yet and nevertheless something tells me that there is a note awaiting me. I shall go to-morrow morning, for I have several little errands, and I shall profit by them to go and fetch what I am sure is there.

I am impatient to have news of you, to know what you are doing, if you are not too much bored and above all if your health is good.

In all my letters, I can only tell you and tell you again one simple thing: I am horribly wearied. At this moment, life is a burden; I feel so lonely and so sad. My existence is incomplete, something is wanting and that something is you.

We have beautiful weather still, a little stormy, which gives me very naughty ideas.

If my beloved little Papa were here, I know what his pet daughter would do to him.

I am dying to see your darling features again, your dear face that I dote to gaze upon, but I have still a long time to wait—nineteen interminable days. I think I shall devour you when we meet again.

Now I must leave you. My big Blackamoor is waiting to take his daily bath, and Father is calling.

I kiss you with mouth, tongue, and lips, as you love to be kissed.

LILY.

Lilian to Jacky.

Telegram, received July 10th. 1898.

Lily feels lovingly.

LILY.

Lilian to Jacky.

(Received July 11th. 1898.)

It is useless, well-beloved master, to try to dissuade me from the resolution I have taken with regard to marriage. After having seriously reflected on the consequences, I have taken this determination. If I get married, it will be with you and with no one else. Please note, however, that I do not wish in any way to make you think that it is your duty to marry me; my thoughts are quite different. I only want to make you understand once for all that any union where you are not concerned is impossible for me. Think what a martyrdom of every moment it would be, and then my nature is too loyal to allow me to play a part. In spite of myself, I always let my feelings be seen. Being thus, there is no remedy. One must take me or leave me. You, my only lover and adored Papa must decide my fate.

Now let us talk of less serious things. I thank you infinitely for your good letter that I found here yesterday. I am going to tell you all my adventures at the *poste restante*.

a) Sensational entrance, when I do not dare, before all the eyes that are fixed on me, to go at once to the grating. I buy some stamps.

b) Still fearing to go up to the department of the *bureau restant* I buy a letter-card and write, and post it to the Louvre about a little purchase there.

c) Still being the silly goose you know so well, I take a telegraph form, and write thereon the initials you know, for despite the desire I had to read your letter, I still had not the courage to ask for your missive out loud.

There you have the confession of a very stupid little girl.

Next time, however, I think I shall be bolder, for after all I am not the only female who has letters sent to a post-office, am I?

I am still more jealous than ever of my big Smike, who I love so well. He has every happiness, while I am like a poor, little, neglected one. He never leaves you, and can see you all day and even all night. All this is clearly very unjust. I am bored to death. Really, if my life does not soon change, I believe I shall go mad.

You must have lots of amorous intrigues to write from one till six. It is frightful to think about. I should like to be able to make you love me so much that you would not be able to do without me, which is at present my position with regard to you.

I have finished reading "The Yellow Room." The effect produced by this book upon me was terrible. Nevertheless, there is one thing that I found rather grotesque; it is the way in which the future betrothed makes love to Alice. It is quite in the modern style, is it not?

I cover you with kisses, literally all over, and each one is longer and more passionate than the other.

Your slave,
LILY.

LILIAN TO JACKY.

(Received July 12th. 1898.)

Another day gone by, and I am delighted, for 'tis one day less without you. What a pity that you should be away at this moment; Papa and Mamma are off to-morrow until Sunday and I shall then be alone. If you were here I should be full of joy, but in this case I shall only feel myself a little more lonely.

You can write to me here this week, if you like. I hope your health gets better every day. I am still very well; my heart makes me suffer, and that is your fault. Everything bores me, nothing interests me. Life seems to me empty and commonplace. If I had my master, it would be quite different.

Your newspapers were received Saturday evening. Thank you for "Our Dogs."

I have still not caught sight of the famous book that you lent to Papa. I think he keeps it at the Rue Vissot. And for a very good reason! . . .

I drink you slowly, softly, but passionately. To you go all my thoughts, all my desires.

LILY.

LILY TO JACKY.

Telegram, received July 13th. 1898.

Sweetest remembrance, love.

LILY.

LILIAN TO JACKY.

(Received July 14th. 1898.)

You know perfectly well I am jealous, and it is always very wicked, just like a naughty Papa that you are to teaze your daughter with that silly little Yvonne of yours; and although she is only eight, it is nevertheless a little of the love that is mine which she steals from me.

I am not pleased with you, nor with Smike, who lets himself be fondled by anybody. When blest with a Papa as dirty as mine is, one can never be easy, even when it is a question of a child only eight years old.

The master may want his slave to make him naughty from a

distance, but his slave is not going to excite you, for others might get the benefit.

Yes, I went and spent Sunday afternoon in Paris at the house of one of my lady friends, but accompanied by the servant-girl.

I want you to hear from me every day; that is why, when I can't write to you, I send you a wire.

You can tell me whatever you like about your "wretched fat belly." That will not prevent me from loving you. It is therefore useless to continue in that strain. You hurt my feelings.

I should like to be near you, so as to be able to rub you myself with Eau de Cologne, and to be able to kiss you all over, and suck you as you love to be sucked, making you thrill with pleasure.

You simply make my mouth water and something else too, when you tell me about the little drop that escapes you when you write to me. What shameful waste!

Yes, sweetheart, I like the idea of you doing mimi to me while I should suck you; I should think that must be simply delicious. I like everything you have done so far, and am looking forward to your idea of the paint brush. Shall I be able to do so to you also?

LILY.

I had been quite surprised by her matrimonial projects and I considered that she was getting too fond of me. Of my own feelings I will not speak, but I considered it was my duty to check her rising passion. So I began to write her coarse and disgusting letters. What I said, what I proposed, can be guessed by her answers. I painted myself in the blackest colours and impressed upon her that I was too old; a man of 46 could not marry a girl of 22. Besides, was I not an invalid, cursed with rheumatism, which might return at any moment, and slightly obese into the bargain? To my great stupor, the more brutally crude and lewd I was, the more she seemed to like me.

LILY TO JACKY.

(Received July 15th. 1898.)

Really, Papa, you are not serious. Fancy throwing away a letter I ought to have had! It shows how careful you are and how much you love your daughter. Your slave is very, very cross indeed, and if you go on in that shameful way, she will have to look about for a better master.

Your incestuous daughter has no preference for any tongue, but she would very much prefer yours. But, as she cannot have it, she must, for the moment, put up with French or English, as you choose to write.

I am very glad to think the treatment agrees with you and above all that it does not weaken you. I will do that when you return.

You can write to me here up to Sunday, but afterwards we must make shift with the *poste restante* of the Rue de Strasbourg.

Yes, I had your letter. I went expressly to Paris to fetch it. I should have been so sad if I had not got one. Smike is really too much spoilt, but I understand that you cannot bring it over your heart to punish him when he gets up to his tricks. I am just the same with Blackamoor. He is a darling, and I tell him everything that passes through my mind about my dirty Papa.

Good night, dear love, I run to put this note in the post, for I want you to have it to-morrow.

I desire you,

LILY.

LILY TO JACKY.

(Received July 16th. 1898.)

Do not write here any more, my adored one, as my parents arrive this evening. We must once more make use of the *poste restante*, which is,—my faith!—very convenient.

I also prefer the word "daughter" to that of *fille*; it sounds more intimate, does it not?

Do you know, dear master, that if I spoil you as you say so prettily, I am also spoiling myself.

You deserve to be very severely punished and you shall be when you return, and this is what I shall do to you: I shall suck you twice running, for having dared to write this sentence: "above all, at my age." Whatever do you mean? Verily, one would think that you take a pleasure in making yourself look older than you are in my eyes. I repeat to you once more, you can do whatever you like, I shall love you in spite of all.

You know very well that I shall not tell anybody what we do together and I do not wish to please any other man. I don't care a straw for anybody but you. You are the only one who will ever possess me, since you are the only one I love.

To be your footstool, lying under your writing table, with your booted feet upon me, and to serve as your chamber utensil, since you say you will make water on my naked body, are two ideas that are far from being commonplace. You know you can do whatever you like to me; oh, dirty and very disgusting Papa!

Smike is as cheeky as his master; I send him a sweet caress, and as for his proprietor, I bite him all over.

LILY.

LILY TO JACKY.

Telegram, received July 17th. 1898.

Soft kiss from your Lily.

LILY.

LILY TO JACKY.

Telegram, received July 18th. 1898.

Sweetest remembrance; love, kisses.

LILY.

LILY TO JACKY.

Telegram, received July 19th. 1898.

Many happy returns of the day, that we may love each other a long time yet.

LILY.

LILY TO JACKY.

Telegram, received July 20th. 1898.

I am very busy. Write here. Father away. Love.

LILY.

LILY TO JACKY.

Telegram, received July 21st. 1898.

Naughty darling. Best love.

LILY.

LILY TO JACKY.

(Received July 22nd. 1898.)

Papa, master,

Since you desire it, your slave submits, and although it is late, and she is very tired, she writes you a simple scrawl, for the sandman has passed and I can hardly keep my eyes open.

I have a deal of work just now, but in spite of that have a great desire to be very naughty. It is so nice, say, darling little Papa?

Women are bores. No, decidedly I love them not. My weakness is always for the strongest sex. Am I not right? See, how badly I write and what mistakes I make. No, really, I must leave you, my little bed awaits me. Nevertheless, I believe that if you were in it, I should not be long waking up, and your pussy, which is yours only, would be wetter than ever.

Your slave adores you and pines for you,

LILY.

A kiss for Smike.

LILY TO JACKY.

(Received July 23rd. 1898.)

It seems to me that you are neglecting me in no slight degree. It is probably the treatment that you follow, which by fatiguing you beyond measure, makes you lose all count. That is a pity, you know, for I do not love a dirty Papa who forgets his daughter. You are a real monster.

As I told you, Father is absent and Mother goes on Tuesday to join him. I shall never have the happiness to be able to go and join you. But also you do not make a move towards me and really one would think that you do not particularly care about me. If such is the case, you would be wrong to trouble about me. A little frankness and you shall soon be rid of me. I will never hang after you against your will, I assure you. Why should I do so? Forced love is ever worthless and I am too young to know all the tricks that certain women make use of to force men to adore them.

Once more, my very loved one, I say there is no tie that binds me to you, therefore you are quite free, especially as I won't go to the Rue de Leipzig any more, and if you do not think I am worth more than that, so much the worse.

You never informed me before you started that the doctor had told
you to rest and stop over Sunday, and I strongly suspect that this is only
a pretext to remain absent a little longer.

Lily is vexed.

LILY TO JACKY.

Telegram, received July 25th. 1898.

Just one kiss. Naughty.

LILY.

LILY TO JACKY.

Telegram, received July 26th. 1898. (Morning.)

Are you living?

LILY.

LILY TO JACKY.

Telegram, received July 26th. 1898. (Evening.)

Am ill through you.

LILY.

LILY TO JACKY.

Villa Lilian, July 26th. 1898.

Beloved, but very bad Papa,

I ask myself why you wrote to the poste restante on Sunday, when
I told you you could address your letters to me here? You had not
Mamma's presence to fear, or I should not have asked you to write to our
house. You might to know by this time that I am more than prudent.

I have not been to Paris for the last few days, and I did not suppose
I should hear from you at the Rue de Strasbourg. Hence my annoyance,
thinking you were neglecting me in such a brutal way.

I use the type-writer to-day, so as to punish you a little, and if I had
a little pride, I would leave you without news of me, as you do so con-
scientiously. But where you are concerned, I lose my wits.

Mamma went away this morning, as I told you. I am all alone here with my dogs, like a poor, little, wretched Cinderella. I have very frisky ideas, but I shall not tell you what they are, as you are not kind enough to me.

Soon I shall see you, I hope, my only love; and in spite of all, I send you a million caresses, each one more passionate and more voluptuous than the other.

I hang on your dear, adored lips,

LILY.

LILY TO JACKY.

Telegram, received July 28th. 1898.

Am dying to see you.

LILY.

LILY TO JACKY.

(Received July 29th. 1898.)

My only, best, sweetest love,

When a Papa does not do what his daughter asks, what happens? He receives unmerited reproaches. I begged you to write to me here and I naturally supposed that I should not have news of you at the post-office. Thus I was furious to find myself neglected and abandoned by you. That is the reason of my famous letter of Sunday which so displeased you.

I love you too much, and every little hitch puts me out. I fancied at once that you loved some other woman. There you see the jealous daughter appears again.

What a love you are to have sent me your photograph! There is only one fault; I can see too much of Smike and not enough of you.

Since yesterday, I kiss your dear face every moment and my happiness increases when I think that I shall soon be able to do it in reality. What a scrawl, you will say, adored master, but I am so unnerved that I cannot hold my pen.

Shall I come and meet you at the station when you arrive?

I am alone, I can do so easily.

I await your coming with something more than impatience, but nevertheless, do not be imprudent, and do not leave Lamalou too early if the doctor tells you to stop.

I suck you violently,

LILY.

LILY TO JACKY.

(Received July 31st. 1898.)

My own sweetest, loved Papa,

How happy I am; one more lonely day, and then I am to see you again. I am quite silly with joy. Will you just drop your daughter a line to let her know where and at what time you wish to see her on Monday?

I notice that you do not really love me quite as much as I should like to be loved, without any afterthought.

You seem to be ashamed of your Lily. What if someone you know should see me with you at the station? They would only think what a lucky man you are to have such a nice young girl's love. You may not think so, but so it is nevertheless.

You see, darling master, there are little things I cannot fail to notice, and sometimes I am afraid you simply mean to use me as a toy.

I hope my frankness will not sadden you again. Such is not my intention, on the contrary. But I love you truly and sincerely, so much so, that I would abandon all at a sign from you and for your sole pleasure.

Yes, in one word, mother and father, and everything and everybody.

I think that such entire love deserves in return true and sincere affection.

Your daughter desires you ardently and awaits Monday with the greatest impatience.

LILY.

P.-S.—I have done what my master ordered. From six o'clock last night until this morning, I did not pee, although I was dying to do so in the night. So I slept very badly. I also thought constantly about my dear little Papa, who was also thinking of me.

Lady Clara seemed to take a great interest in my liaison with Lily, and she had frequently written to Lamalou asking me for news of her. She was perfectly disinterested, as she had no Lesbian tastes, but she told me that the whole story pleased her greatly, and so I now and again gave her news of my "daughter."

I cannot do better than copy here a few notes that I jotted down about Lily, shortly after my return to Paris, having derived full benefit and relief from my course of baths.

Jacky to Clara.

(Notes on Lily.)

While I was at Lamalou, I tried to disgust Lily, as I was afraid she was getting too fond of me, but the worse I made myself out, the more she seemed to love me.

I told her I would discuss the marriage question when I met her, but not by letter, as things that sometimes look harsh in writing, pass easily in conversation.

I spoke against myself, about my age, my rheumatism and my big belly. She was pained thereat.

I wrote to her that I should like to have her naked under the table, as a footstool, while I sat and wrote. Also, that I should seat her on the bidet, and straddling across it, void my urine on her belly and "pussy." She likes these ideas.

She shall have a good talking to, when I see her. I will not scold by letter. I have no reproaches to make myself, as I never told her a lie or tried to mislead her. Is she madly in love with me, or is she scheming?

I would dearly like to take her maidenhead. But no, I must not ruin the poor lustful lassie. I will try to keep out of my Lily's body. I will not harm her.

I try to make Lily understand that the passions and the heart are two different things. She may be unfaithful perchance, but if she keeps a corner in her heart for me, I shall be satisfied.

She is not shocked when I try to bring her mind to grasp that she is absolutely my own slave, that she must obey my most voluptuous caprices, however vile they may be.

She writes so ardently about marrying me, etc., that I thought I would try to prevent her loving me too much, by telling her what a filthy brute I was, and laying stress on the fact that other men loved more decently than I did.

I stood confessed on my own showing as a despotic, tyrannical beast, gloating over her degradation and humiliation.

The more cynically and brutally I wrote, the better she liked it.

She is evidently fond of me and I must let things go on.

Does she think I am very rich?

She is very impatient, very excitable, and has got a hot temper. She has addressed reproaches to me, but I sincerely think she is slightly in the wrong. I have never lost my temper yet with her, but I treat her like a child, and she comes round again.

There was a slight misunderstanding about our correspondence and she wrote a nasty letter, giving me back my liberty, and saying she would never return to the Rue de Leipzig, as it was not good enough for her. I took no notice, but wrote quietly and reproachfully, and at last punished her for having written such a letter, by ordering her not to pee from seven o'clock at night until seven the next morning. She wrote saying she had obeyed me, and had passed a bad night.

I told her to come to the Rue de Leipzig on August 1st., as she was alone with her grandmother. I waited until 3:30. She never appeared. I went away, and did not return home until 6:50.

She turned up at 3:40, it appears, and sent me two telegrams. She was waiting at the Eastern railway station to see me.

I had dinner at seven instead. She wrote a rather furious letter, saying her Mamma would be back on Thursday.

LILIAN TO JACKY.

First telegram, received August 1st. 1898 about 4:30. P.M.

Will be Eastern railway station.

LILY.

Second telegram, received about 6:30. P.M.

Am waiting Eastern railway station.

LILY.

LILIAN TO JACKY.

Villa Lilian. August 2nd. 1898. 11 P.M.

What you could have done from 3 o'clock until 6:30, I really can't tell, and I will not even seek to know. That will always be a mystery for me, since you could only wait a little more than an hour, and yet you know I cannot always do what I wish.

In spite of my being alone at home, I still have to content my customers, and I am therefore late.

You lost something by not waiting a little longer, I assure you, for I was just ripe for a refined *gourmet* such as you are.

No matter, don't let us say any more about it, only Mamma will be back on Thursday, and therefore——

By losing patience sometimes, we lose many good things.

Lily is as vexed as she can be with her Papa and will not pardon him in a hurry.

I answered calmly and curtly, and gave her a *rendez-vous* for Wednesday, August 3rd.

LILIAN TO JACKY.

Telegram, received August 3rd. 1898.

Four o'clock. Usual place.

LILY.

Lily appeared, very pleased to see me, and very penitent, in spite of her peppery note, at the famous Rue de Leipzig, where she had said she would never come again.

She looked very sweet in my eyes, and was dressed in a charming, simple costume of *écru coutil*, fitting closely over her well-made buttocks. She was very proud of her bottom, and I have seen her tighten her skirt over it, and show it to her stepfather, when her Mamma had left her with him and me, saying she was Venus Callipyge.

Lily pretended to be cross, but I bluntly told her what a little fool she was. She had been an hour late on the preceding occasion and if any one ought to have lost their temper it should have been me and not her. She was perfectly ridiculous, with her jealousy and irritation, and finally I forced her to humbly beg my pardon. Then we kissed, as lovers had never kissed before. I half undressed her, and partly for fun, partly in earnest, slapped her, and pinched her, and pulled the black fleece that shaded her sex, making her suffer just a little.

I told her to come to me on the day when she was late, with the ribbon fastened to the hair on her *mons Veneris*, and she was also to have a great desire to make water, as she was not to "make herself comfortable" from the hour of rising. All this foolery she had done, and that is what she meant when she had said that she was ripe for me. This time, she had done none of these things, as she was annoyed with me. So I slapped her face. I frequently did so. I loved to see the slight patch of colour follow the sting of my hand upon her cheek. After each smarting blow, I saw the light of lust in her eyes, and her ghoulish mouth cupped my lips, as if to thank me for the exquisite joy my chastisement aroused within her. I recurred to the idea of her being my footstool, and I threw her roughly on to her knees in front of me, as I sat on the sofa. Taking her head in my two hands, I pressed her laughing face between my trousered thighs and rubbed her nose and mouth brutally against the cloth, through which the eager staff seemed trying to escape. Then I let her drop full length on the carpet, lying on her back, her skirts all turned up, and disordered; her drawers open. I kicked her with my booted feet, and turned her over with the toe of my boots, gently trampling on her naked belly. Lying thus at my mercy, she giggled, purred, and cooed, like a naked, happy baby after its bath. In the romp, some hairpins and combs had fallen from her luxuriant tresses, and gathering them up, I stabbed her thighs with the fine points, until she begged for mercy.

Then I pulled her up and made her take off my Russian leather lace-up boots, ordering her to kiss the soles and uppers. She did all I told her, and was happy to obey. Then I made her undress me, and she awkwardly performed the duties of a valet. Each garment, as she took it off, I ordered her to take across the room, hang it up, and return to me.

I commanded her to unbotton my trousers, fish out my member, and go on her knees and suck it. She was quite unabashed and would not have the curtains drawn. In the open daylight, we went naked to the bed. At the foot of it was the mirror of the wardrobe, and to her astonishment there was a looking-glass in the ceiling of the couch. We both sated our sight with the view of both our bodies writhing on the bed, madly kissing and feeling each other, enjoying the sensation of the absolute contact of our sensual skins.

I asked her if she wanted to be licked, but she preferred me to masturbate her.

I did so, and when she had convulsively joined her thighs in the delicious agony of the spending spasm, and recovered from the shock, I laid upon her. I got the tip of my weapon between the moist lips of her toy.

She said, as she always did:

"It does hurt so! Oh, you hurt me!"

And then she exclaimed:

"How nice it would be if it did not hurt!"

I then obliged her to lick my testicles and my thighs, and lifting my legs high up in the air, I told her and taught her that infamous, entrancing caress, called: *feuille de rose*, when the tongue, made as pointed as possible, penetrates the anus. She was quite docile and performed her strange task in a most charming manner.

Then she sucked me, and I spent freely in her delicious mouth, keeping her head in my hands, until I was quite soft again. Without an effort, she swallowed every drop, and when I left her lips, the urethra was as dry as if I had never emitted. She dearly loved sucking, and called my virile organ her *poupée*, her dolly.

I told her as she licked me, that I had still one or two more dirty little tricks to try with her.

I gave her two vilely obscene books to read, both on the same subject: the entire subjugation of a woman to man's cruelty and lust. They were: "The Convent School," and "Colonel Spanker's Lecture."

I told her that I meant to make her absolutely shameless, and utterly degraded, by the continual humiliations she would have to undergo when with me, and I explained that I gloried in making her do the most disgusting things. The more unutterably depraved I am, the more she likes it, and calls me her dirty Papa. She enjoyed being knocked about, shaken, and roughly handled by me.

When we were both naked, I made her lick me under the arms and suck my nipples. She demurred at sucking beneath my armpits, but I made her do it.

She liked the penetration of my ruthless fingers in her fundament, and I found that she had a growth of hair between the posteriors. As she gets older, she will be very hairy.

There was no question of money this time, her parents being away, and she informed me that her father and mother would leave her at home on the 20th., as they go to Germany, so probably I should see a little more of her.

My villanously lecherous brain now began to be excited by a dreadful idea. I dearly desired to give her up to Lord Fontarcy and Clara. In my presence, the couple could do as they chose with her. I tried to drive the dream away, but it kept returning daily and nightly. I thought it would be a fearful effort and a real ordeal for her, and the knowledge that I was corrupting the virgin who seemed to adore me excited and delighted me immensely.

I did not dare broach the subject. I thought over it, and in the meantime I remember that in all the letters I wrote to her, I tried to make myself out the most abandoned debauchee in the world.

6

O my love come nearer to Lilith
(Eden's bower's in flower)
In thy sweet folds bind me and bend me,
And let me feel the shape thou shalt lend me!
. . . .

What more prize than love to impel thee?
Grip and lip my limbs as I tell thee!

Dante G. Rossetti.

    And so I lay all night with him, but he . . . rose up and dressed him in the morning, and left me as innocent for him as I was the day I was born.
    I frequently lay with him, and he with me, and altho' all the familiarities between man and wife were common to us, yet he never once offered to go any farther, and he valued himself much upon it.

Daniel Defoe.

Lilian to Jacky.

Sonis-sur-Marne. August 7th. 1898.

My best beloved in the world,

Excuse me for not having answered your letter, and for using the type-writer to-day, but a mosquito has bitten my hand, and it is in such a state that I cannot use it.

I profit by a momentary absence of Papa to use the machine.

You are very impudent to send me such an awful caricature sketch of my very beautiful and very adored Blackamoor.

I think he is growing up nicely and I love him, so do not laugh in future at the way he carries his ears, or we shall not be friends at all.

I am sad at the thought of being so long without seeing you, for my parents do not start till the 20th. or later.

Waiting does not suit me, for as you know, patience and I have nothing in common. Besides, I want to see you. It is a bore to remain a fortnight or three weeks without giving a good kiss to one's Papa.

You warn me not to recriminate, but I can't help it. I must rebel against my destiny, and ask you to share my trouble.

I am off. Here comes Papa, and I won't have him question me about what I am writing.

To your dear lips, without forgetting my pretty beloved dolly.

LILY.

I think I had been writing some very erotic letters to Lily. I remember that I sent her an extract from a very obscene book, turning upon inhuman delights, entitled, "The Pleasures of Cruelty." (*See Appendix A.*)

I had also told her in my last letter, that she must remind me herself when she saw me again of all I had asked her to do and suffer for my sake. She was to say:

"Master, I have the ribbon ready for you to pull, and I am dying to make water, as I have not done so for many hours. May I do so now?"

There may have been other filthy things that she was to tell me and ask me to do to her, but I cannot now call to my mind all my extravagant exigencies.

LILIAN TO JACKY.

Sonis-sur-Marne. Sunday, August 21st. 1898.

My love,

I waited to be free to write to you, so as to be able to tell you: "Lily awaits a sign from her beloved master to run into his arms."

My parents are off at last. I am therefore left entirely to myself, and consequently when my darling little Papa wishes, his daughter, who is displeased with him, will come and tell him so with her own lips.

I will bring you myself the extracts you sent me, and in that way it will be easier for me to give you an account of my impressions. It will be sweeter to tell you all I feel, having my mouth glued to yours. and my cheek caressed by your beard, which is so silky.

I do not forget the orders in your last letter and I will remind you of all you desire.

A word from you, and I come to try and drive away a little of that sadness you feel.

Very softly, Lily imprints a long kiss on the end of her doll's nose, and pushes the point of her very indiscreet tongue where her Papa likes it to go.

LILIAN TO JACKY.

Telegram received at noon,
August 22nd. 1898.

Wednesday. Half-past two.

LILY.

LILIAN TO JACKY.

Telegram received 11 A.M.
Wednesday, August 24th. 1898.

Unwell. To-morrow, if you wish.

LILY.

LILIAN TO JACKY.

Undated. Received August 24th. 1898.

Lily is indisposed to-day, and if she is no better to-morrow, she will be obliged to put off the appointment.

In any case, if you do not receive a wire from me to-morrow morning, you can be at the usual place and I will come there.

Certainly, dear little father, I am grieved to have caused you pain, if only for an instant, but if however you had reflected a little, you would have found my silence quite natural.

Mamma is off on her pleasure trip, to a part of the world where it appears everybody is very elegant. As I look after her toilettes, and have to make her a lot of hats, I have not had a moment to myself, especially as she is not at all easy to please.

But I do not mind begging your pardon for faults, which exist in reality only in your imagination. There is only one terrible thing which you have probably put in your letter to frighten me: "I will punish you by not kissing you."

That I must resist with all my strength. I rebel. To be deprived of your mouth? I will never submit to that. I could not support such torture.

To-morrow then, my most severe master. I adore you.

AUGUST 26, 1898.

Lilian's father and mother had left her alone with a servant and her maternal grandmother. They had gone to Homburg. I was surprised to find that her periodical indisposition should be over by the 25th., when it generally made its appearance about the 27th., or 28th. Therefore, it must have begun on the 21st. And as she had not written to me between the 7th. and the 21st., I began to have shrewd suspicions that something was wrong.

I had got into my head that there was almost a complete understanding between her and her mother's lover. He had taken such great trouble to impress upon me that Lilian should on no account be allowed to get a glimpse at the "Horn Book" I had lent him, that I began to smell a rat. It was quite unnecessary to repeat that to me so often. Then again, she had written to me that she had not seen the book; that Papa kept it at his bureau and did not bring it home to Sonis. She had got that obscene dialogue too. I had sufficient knowledge of the secret monthly miseries of women to know that a virgin is generally pretty regular, but I was resolved to wait, watch, and not say anything. Lily was not communicative. There was nothing to be got out of her by a direct question; I must keep my ears open and see what she would let drop in her chatter.

I had a rod in pickle for her, however. Worse than a rod; in fact, a whip. I had ordered a strange instrument, which I am certain I invented myself, as I never saw it before or since. I called it the "whip-stick." Everyone knows what a swordstick is—a hollow walking-cane, in which is concealed a sharp blade or dagger. I had one made, but instead of containing a sword, it held nothing more deadly than a light lady's riding-whip, or whalebone switch. I could thus walk through Paris without exciting any notice. It was impossible for me to carry a whip in the town, and a very thin bamboo also looked ridiculous in the afternoon, in the hands of a portly, middle-aged gentleman in frockcoat and high hat.

Lily arrived; pretty, coquettish and very amiable. I scolded her for not having written to me for twelve days, but I did not touch upon the growing intimacy that I suspected between her, and he who stood in the light of a stepfather towards her.

I unscrewed the top of my stick and showed the whip that was hidden within. To try it, I made her lift up her skirts, and gave her one cut across her bottom over her half-open drawers. She uttered a shriek and writhed in real pain. I was surprised, but I found that using a riding-whip was quite different to a lithe stick or the hand. I soothed her and petted her, but tears were in her eyes, and she complained bitterly of the smart. I examined her bottom and found a long weal across her left buttock. What was worse, her drawers being open, the end of the lash had by some means curled itself right between the posteriors, and just above the pinky-brown orifice was a little cut. The skin was broken and there was one spot of blood, like a small ruby.

I did not think it advisable to let her know how cruel I had unwittingly been, but I glossed the matter over, and resolved to have a light touch in future with my whip. In fact, I never used it at all after this afternoon, when I was careful not to hurt her much. I afterwards gave it to Clara, who took it to London and delighted all her friends with it. She has it still, and it is one of her most valued possessions.

By aid of this whip, with which I carefully touched up Lilian over the back and the fat part of her arms, I got her by force to undress slowly before me, but before I had made her walk about the room with my hand clasping the two hairy lips of her second mouth.

When she was undressed, and I had feasted my eyes and lips on the neat little body I loved so well, and which excited me so strangely, I forced her to stand with her shift lifted up with both hands, as high as her neck. It was a pretty sight to see her thus exposed. She grumbled and laughed in one breath. She could hide nothing, but writhed about as she stood, as if by her serpentine movements she could conceal some parts of her frame from my lecherous gaze. If she tried to drop her chemise, I flourished my whip over her head and she took up her position again. As she stood there, bending down a little, as if by leaning her body over she could hide the fleece that cast a black shadow at the bottom of her maiden, flat belly, I slowly undressed, looking at her all the time, and walking round her as if she was a lay figure, and so heightening her confusion; which I thoroughly enjoyed.

Then I gave her my garments, shirt, etc., to go and hang up, and she knelt down and took off my boots.

She had tied the ribbon to the hairs of her mount and I amused myself by pulling it, in spite of her sharp little cries of pain.

On entering the room, she had reminded me of the ribbon and said she had a great desire to pee. I refused to let her do so for the moment.

Now, as we were both undressed, I told her she could empty her bladder, and although she wanted to very badly, she swore she could not void her urine if I looked at her while she did so.

I made her stand up, by threatening her with the whip, and felt her belly. It was quite hard and distended and I pressed my two first fingers into it on both sides, just above the thighs. She begged me to desist, saying that if I continued to press her navel and belly, she would be unable to keep from emptying herself any longer.

At last, by the aid of threats of the "whip-stick," and after a few mild touches with it, I succeeded in getting her on the vase, and her long pent-up urine trickled loudly into the pot, as I stood over her. She was crimson with shame, but nevertheless highly pleased and lustfully excited.

We then got on the bed, both completely naked, and after our usual kisses and close embraces, I ordered her to masturbate herself. This she absolutely refused to do, but I was obdurate. Again the whip was brought forward, and I kept it by my side on the bed. Finally, she reluctantly laid her hand between her thighs and began awkwardly and slowly, making out as if she hardly knew how. It was very pretty for me to see and feel her graceful body reclining across my thighs and watch the play of her features. She was cross and merry by turns, but lust soon overcame her, as the required result was brought about in the following way. She was willing to do what I wanted if I kept my hand on hers, and tickled her round about the tender spot, while she manipulated her rose-bud herself. By the united caress of her hand and mine, she soon emitted and then had a long bout of tongue and lip sucking.

I then got over her, pretending to penetrate her in the natural way, until we were both beside ourselves with desire. We were face to face, her thighs open and legs outstretched. My weapon was rubbing against the upper part of the openings of her furrow, our tongues joined, and the index of my right hand slowly penetrating her hot fundament.

Suddenly, she threw her arms around me and closing her thighs, pressed my organ between them, saying:

"It is nice like this!"

I pushed up and down in the imitation vulva thus formed, and rubbed against her pussy; she moved her bottom up to meet my strokes. Pleasure seized us both at the same moment; I felt the shudder of joy vibrate through her frame and I discharged copiously.

I turned over on to my back, and when we had recovered from the effects of our enervating sham fight, I showed her what a state her thighs were in, and her mount covered with my thick semen.

"Ah!" she exclaimed, in fright, her face and mouth distorted with fear. "Am I no longer a virgin?"

She seemed greatly alarmed, but I explained the difference between what we had done and genuine copulation. Reassured, she made me cuddle her tightly and fell asleep on my breast. I kept quiet so as not to awaken her and slept as well. When we both woke, it was six o'clock, and Lily had slobbered in her sleep on my hairy chest, like a little baby girl.

We had a long conversation, when she told me that she found the flagellation scene, between the father and daughter, which I had lent her to read "rather tame," and would have liked the couple to have enjoyed each other after the flogging, and she asked me if I had any new ideas of erotic slavery for her. I answered that I wanted to lick her private parts while she was bound down and her hands strapped together, and I promised to teach her a novel onanistic method. I would produce the spasm in her by tickling her clitoris with a camelhair paint brush, as I had written to her already from Lamalou.

All these lascivious projects she adored to talk over. I made her beg my pardon for not having written to me, and forced her to stand before me when she was dressed, holding up her clothes, showing both a front and back view, alternatively.

Her great dream was for me to be with her in her own bed at Sonis. I was to take the train on Saturday night, August 27th., at nine o'clock, the servant going to bed at that hour. Her old grandmother was silly, and incapable of seeing or hearing anything. My love would meet me, and we would go for a walk in the dark, as there was never a soul about at night in those parts. And then she would slip me into the house—the dogs all knew me, and would not bark—and I could take the latest train back, after we both thoroughly enjoyed ourselves.

I made her understand that although the newest way I had emitted with her between her thighs pleased me greatly, still I regretted her soft mouth.

"Rest a little," she said, "and I will suck you."

It was too late and I was exhausted. I did not tell her that I had passed the night with an expert Parisian matron. She recurred to the most infamous of kisses—*feuille de rose*—when her tongue had lovingly penetrated my anus, and confessed that she liked doing it.

I wanted to broach the question of meeting Lord Fontarcy and Clara, but could not summon up courage. I fancied it might be a hard nut to crack, and I determined to leave the difficult demand for another time.

There was also something else on the tip of my tongue, but it would not have been politic to mention it.

Her silence of a fortnight, followed by the change of date in her "monthlies," and the ready and expert way in which she clipped my swollen shaft between her thighs, made me certain that

Mr. Arvel had been playing with her before his departure. They had been reading "The Horn Book" together, and the incestuous Papa had clearly copied this artificial congress from the identical passage I had introduced into the text expressly for him and his daughter! Be that as it may, the coincidence was curious, and besides, this is a well-known form of pleasure, with all those who wish to emit with children.

I had not taught her this style of sensuality. She had learnt it recently, and had been up to all kinds of tricks, thus bringing on her menstrual flux in advance of the usual date. Virgins in fair health are very regular, but all women who abuse any kind of sensual pleasure find that their derangement is just as likely to be before its proper date as after. Very often, women suffer agonies of fright, because they are behind their time; and fancying themselves pregnant, take strange drugs, while this tardiness is only due to overindulgence in the delights of Venus.

AUGUST 27, 1898.

It seems but as yesterday that I arrived at Sonis-sur-Marne that hot summer's night, and saw my "daughter" waiting for me with her dogs. How happy was I to stroll with her, talk soft non-sense, and pet and kiss her in the dark, while she returned my caresses with passionate enjoyment, and I revelled in the knowledge that an hour later I should be naked in bed with her.

The time passed rapidly, and we returned to the villa, when I stepped gingerly within the gate and trod gently on the grass, while Lily walked noisily on the gravel path to hide the possible noise of my footsteps. She went indoors, but in obedience to her orders, I slipped up the staircase, on to the balcony which ran round the house. She had purposely left one of the windows of the best bedroom open, and I went in and sat down by the side of the parental bed, now without sheets or blankets, and I threw my hat, overcoat, and whip-stick upon it. The latter article I had no occasion to use.

I had not long to wait; Lilian came into her bedroom, and called me softly to her, through the curtained, open doorway which connected the two rooms.

Lily's bed was a pretty piece of modern furniture in Louis XVI style, with mirrored wardrobe to match. It was a gift of her stepfather, and was for her to take away when she got married.

I was happy to be in her room at night, and I kissed her pillow, trying to find the place where her head reposed, much to Lily's delighted amusement.

All was quiet. Granny was in bed on the second story, but Lily was vexed with her, as she was restless and disinclined to sleep. I hinted that another time, I would prepare a sleeping draught for the old lady.

I had brought with me a small strap, with which to fasten Lily's hands and a new paint brush to titillate her clitoris but I did not use either.

I was thirsty, but there was nothing to drink. Granny had the keys, and Lilly could not disturb her. She was thirsty too, .

"We have only our urine to drink!" I said jokingly.

"I will drink some of yours!" said Lily seriously, putting her face near mine, and there was an eager look in her eyes, as if she would have liked me to force her to do so.

There was no more shame between us. I undressed slowly and with nothing but a light singlet, went to bed, and laid fully exposed, while Lily quickly disrobed, and quietly used the night vase like a married woman.

She came to bed, and her capricious fancy had already caused her to divine what was passing in my mind, for she asked me how I should behave if I was really married to her.

I took her gently in my arms, and kissing her chastely, bade her "good night," and turned my back to her as if settling down to sleep, making a slight snoring noise.

Lily remained quiet an instant and then put her hand on my neck.

"Now, my dear, you must really let me go to sleep. You know I have to get up very early to-morrow morning, and I think it is most unreasonable to expect that your husband can be always caressing you. My dear wife, I beg you to put out the light and let us both rest."

Lily said nothing, but took hold of my member, and in a

few moments, she had got it as stiff as she wanted, and I turned toward her, and took her in my arms to enjoy the luscious intoxication of her melting mouth.

We showered on each other's bodies the most voluptuous caresses, and at last I pushed my Lily down in the bed, and she reclined between my legs; her cheek on my left thigh, I made her kiss and lick my member and also the dangling purse, and while she was gently sucking my testicles, I rubbed the stiffening rod against her face and nose. Then I took her by the nape of the neck and closing my thighs, kept her face imprisoned, pressed as hard as I could against my privates, even to suffocation, and then relaxing my pressure a little, I moved her head about in all directions, and I was really masturbating myself with her darling face. A little more and I should have spent madly, with her features pressed to me to receive the spurting semen, but I think the state I was in warned my artful virgin of the impending danger; so she slid away and took me in her arms.

She told me that she wanted to see me spend; she was mad with the idea of looking at her "dolly," as the seed spurted forth. I turned upon my back, and pillowing her head upon my breast, allowed her to enjoy her latest whim.

She worked me well with her nervous fingers, and never took her eyes off my organ, while I talked to her as lewdly as possible, telling her how dirty and vile she was, evidently much to her enjoyment, which rose to fever heat, as her wish was gratified by the full view of the gushing seed.

While maddened by the deliberate masturbation of my sweetheart, towards the end, I said that immediately the splash of semen should cease, she was to take my member in her mouth and suck it, so as to extract the last drops.

When I had spent furiously, I forgot my ravings during the moments of uncontrollable lust, and was quite surprised to find Lily slowly approach her lips to her poupée, and engulph it in her hot mouth, not at all disgusted to swallow the last big clot that was slowly exuding from the urethra. But the gland was so sensitive that I could not endure the delicate touch of her tongue, and I pushed her head away.

"Ah!" quoth Lily, "you did not think I should do it."

We rested a little, and then Lily put her hand on my privates again.

"I'm done now, my darling," said I, "you've thoroughly exhausted me."

"I'm so sorry," answered pouting Lily, "I don't like it when it is soft!"

"Like this, I'm not dangerous. You need not fear lest I take your maidenhead."

"Oh, my darling, you are never dangerous. I would trust my life in your dear hands. You are so delicate in all you say and do. It is so strange to me to see how you always act with us all; as my parents are so coarse and vulgar."

I offered now to make her happy, in any way she liked. She refused to be sucked and preferred me to masturbate her. I did so, and I think she cared for my fingers more than anything. I made her lay hands on herself, but she soon drew her own digits away and left me to finish her.

I was very thirsty, and she went on a filibustering expedition and managed to find a bottle of Vichy water, which she poured out, and brought to me with many a sweet word and caress.

Then she settled down between my legs, and supporting herself on her elbow began to talk.

She looked most beautiful at that moment, as I gazed upon her face with partial eyes. The yellow light of the candle suited her Spanish complexion, and her liquid, magical eyes sparkled as she gazed at me, getting excited as she spoke, and her splendid black hair flowed over her naked shoulders, for she slept nightly in summer, as she did then, with simply a day chemise.

This picture has remained in my mind, for I loved her then or rather I might have loved her, if she had shown some slight womanly tenderness, but she made me very unhappy, although I hid my feelings, by calmly unfolding a mad plan.

She wanted to go into business in Paris, in a small apartment and hinted that I was to take it for her, and I suppose furnish it. I was to be allowed to visit her there, whenever I chose, and she would have a little kitchen and cook for me. I could come and have meals with her, and we would dine together quite naked.

I hinted that I did not see how she could manage this at all, but she got out of temper because I disagreed with her. So I held my tongue and listened to her, half asleep, as her ceaseless chatter went in at one ear and out at the other.

I kept on admiring her, trying to impress her image on my poor brain, softened by the boiling baths of the previous month, as I felt inwardly, although I tried to drive away the sad thought, that she only cared for me because she fancied I should be able to give her money, and I was forced to say to myself that I should not have many nights with her.

I asked her to get my watch out of my waistcoat, knowing that it was now close upon midnight, and the last train went shortly afterwards.

And indeed, if I remember rightly, for all this took place two years ago and I have seen many women since, I got up to use the chamber, and was about to dress, when she told me that she intended all along for me to stop with her, as she was dying for me to remain one whole night by her side.

After a few moments' hesitation, I accepted, and came to her again, when, after a long kiss, we fell asleep in each other's arms.

It was about five o'clock, when Lily slowly woke me with the touch of her cunning fingers, searching for her plaything, which she found in the desired state, and she placed it between her thighs, turning her back to me, and inviting me by her lascivious movements, to push and move in this artificial coition.

I got very lustful, and found that these artful tricks by repetition produced a nervous effect that was far from pleasant, and I knew at last that if I slept with her again I should become brutal and try to violate her.

I kept these thoughts to myself, but in my mad rage, I grasped her tightly, and shook her roughly and brutally.

"You can hurt me if you like, master. I love you when you are just a little rough; but what have I done to displease?"

Her soft tones brought me to my senses. I did not know what to answer.

"It is hot and dry between your thighs. Make me wet."

"I have lots of moisture for you," said she with a laugh, and putting her fingers to her tight slit, she wetted them with the moisture of her "pussy," put some on my stiff anatomy, and rubbed the inside of her own thighs. I put my hand to her gap, and found she was indeed quite wet.

Then I turned her over and got atop of her, and she imprisoned me between her thighs, as she had done a couple of days previously.

I leant upon my elbows so as not to press her little body.

"No, no!" she cried, "let me feel your weight upon me. I like it. Lie upon me. Crush me beneath you!"

I let myself go and pressed her beneath the entire weight of my heavy frame, as I frantically pushed up and down, my organ in prison between her thighs, rubbing among her hairs, and against her clitoris.

I soon spent, and my wife of one night clasped me tightly to her, her tongue in my mouth, as I felt that unmistakable thrill, or shudder, go through her frame, which women, with all their cunning, have as yet not been able to imitate entirely.

The wish to be crushed by the weight of a man's heavy body in bed; the repeated tricky, teazing, thigh-clipping to imitate the real thing, convinced me that other hands and other male organs had been in contact with Lily Arvel's body.

I then arose, and took my leave of Miss Arvel. Charlotte was coming the next day (Sunday), to stop with her, and I was to come down again on Wednesday, the 31st., and pass another whole night with her.

She led me to the window of her mother's bedroom, and I stepped out on to the balcony, while, half-naked, she hid behind the shutter.

I crawled softly down and stepped lightly across the grass. It was half-past five, and broad daylight. I was bound to think that I was doing a very dangerous thing for Lilian's reputation, as the villa was surrounded by other houses, and some neighbour might find it strange to see a man unknown to the locality, creep stealthily out at that early hour.

At the corner of the road, not a stone's throw from the house, was a wineshop, and a girl belonging to the establishment stood at the door. She eyed me curiously.

Again I saw more danger for my Lily, and I went up to Paris reflecting on all these things in the train.

I wrote to Miss Arvel that day, and explained my fears to her, suggesting that on Wednesday, I had better leave her at midnight and take the last train. In the darkness, at night, there would be no danger of my compromising her.

I did not tell other reasons that made me disinclined to go to her bed again; the fear lest I try to make her mine by force, and the growing, uneasy feeling of repulsion that her broad, mercenary hints were beginning to cause in me.

Was I a fool?

7

... Would you not swear,
All you that see her, that she were a maid,
By these exterior shows?
. . . .

Yet a virgin, a most unspotted Lily....

SHAKESPEARE.

Lilian's plans for the future seemed to me impracticable, even if I had had the necessary available capital to set her up as a milliner. It must not be forgotten that I still had onerous duties to perform with regard to my poor Lily at home, whose life hung upon a thread, being no wife to me, and I began to suspect vaguely that Mr. Arvel and Adèle must have instilled strange ideas into their girl's head, as she appeared to weave all her schemes without showing any fear of her Pa and Ma. Did it mean that they would shut their eyes to any intrigues with a moneyed lover, or had her father taken such liberties with her that she felt she could brave him? Or a mere declaration of passion on his part just now would have been sufficient to show her the power she had over him. These and similar thoughts occupied my mind as I received the following:

LILIAN TO JACKY.

Sonis-sur-Marne, August 31st. 1898.

As ever, you are right, and I bow down to your experience and wisdom that I do not possess. It is even preferable that you do not come down on Wednesday evening as we had arranged. I will go with Granny to the *fête*. That will make me forget my great disappointment a little, for I felt much joy at the idea of having you again with me for one whole night.

Do not say, my adored one, that I am never contented, but I wish to arrange things with you once for all.

The life I lead at present is absolutely intolerable. I can only see you now and again and then always running and hiding like a thief, while my dream would be to have you often all to myself and only for me. This dream can be realised in two ways. Here is the first:

We must take a small apartment in Paris: three rooms and a kitchen. I should go and live there in the manner I told you, that is to say with the full consent of my parents to carry on my trade. Thus I should be entirely free; you could come and breakfast and dine with me as often as you chose and I should have you nearly every day. This thought drives me crazy with delight. And you, adored master?

Now for the second plan:

You would take a shop to sell the perfumes you make so well. Naturally, you would want a young girl used to commercial ways and at the same time pleasing to look at, as a saleswoman. I should be that young girl and I can assure you that the business would flourish. In this wise also I could see you as often as we could wish. As you see, two methods offer themselves to us at this moment. You must choose one at once, as later on perhaps we may not have the same opportunity. I await a word from you giving me your decision. If you prefer the apartment, I can start off at once to hunt for one.

Tell me also what day I can see you in Paris, as you can no longer come here?

I think of your dear lips,

LILY.

I had been showing Lilian some specimens of perfumery I had made, and had manufactured expressly for her a highly concentrated preparation of musk, as she was fond of violent scents. My chemical studies had of late led me in that direction. She saw money to be made with these odorous extracts. She was fond of money.

I answered, giving an appointment at the usual place, Rue de Leipzig. I also informed her that she had a wrong idea of life and life's duties, which I would explain more fully by word of mouth.

LILIAN TO JACKY.

Sonis-sur-Marne, September 1st. 1898.

If you have not understood my letter it is because you do not want to, for it was quite explicit enough. I cannot see either how the perspective of being able to see me as often as you wish could make you unhappy. I cannot make you out at all. I will not go to the Rue de Leipzig any more.

Come here in preference one evening, if you have anything to say to me.

And I thought my letter would please you. I am quite perplexed.

She who loves you too much,

LILY.

My reply stated that I considered her very silly, very disobedient and very hard to get on with, but nevertheless I was ready to take the train about nine P.M. on Saturday, Sunday, or Monday night, to talk matters over, if she would kindly choose one of those evenings and let me know in time. I heard no more of her until getting home to dinner at 6:30 P.M. on Sunday, when I found this wire:

LILIAN TO JACKY.

Telegram. 4 P.M. September 4th. 1898.

Can you come at once?

LILY.

The telegram had been at my dwelling since half-past four. I had some guests to dinner and could not leave them. I had waited for a letter until Sunday morning, before inviting them, and I felt angry to think that Lilian should expect me to be literally at her beck and call. I wrote at once that I could not run about to odd appointments at uncertain times at my age. I could not be her puppet. That she knew I took my meals with my family, and owed a slight amount of politeness to my near relations and others who were ready to dine with me at prearranged fixed hours, etc. That I had kept open three nights for her and she had not answered me properly nor given me due notice. In fact, she was not acting in a straightforward manner and I was disgusted.

This elicited the following epistle, which is ironical, to say the least:

LILIAN TO JACKY.

Sonis-sur-Marne, September 5th. 1898.

As ever you are right, and I agree with you that you should not be a puppet, especially at your age. I do not wish to disgust you entirely and if I have done so already, I beg you to excuse me, for I did not mean to, I assure you.

You require a calm and tranquil life and I can only do one thing —trouble your existence.

I humbly beg your pardon for my rudeness, since you say I am impolite.

LILY.

JACKY TO LILIAN.

Paris, September 6th. 1898.

When one loves anybody it is always nicer to answer letters as quickly as possible. That is what I do this day in reply to your few lines received last night, though perhaps you did not expect me to write?

You ask my pardon? I bear no malice, I am not angry. The way you act has not failed to grieve me momentarily. That is all. Let us say no more about it. I have made up my mind for the worst.

But I forgive you willingly and from the bottom of my heart. And I find that this exchange of bitter-sweet letters is an essentially stupid thing. It is ridiculous to go in for essays of literary style instead of seeing each other and explaining matters. I accuse myself of this fault and this shall be my last letter.

Your conduct has greatly wounded me. I pity you sincerely, as I fully believe what I have often told you: that you are in a great measure a victim to your nerves.

Being so, you prepare for yourself a life of sad agitation for almost always, people like yourself possess the peculiar gift of rendering profoundly unhappy those they love the most.

JACKY.

ERIC ARVEL TO JACKY.

Sonis-sur-Marne, September 9th. 1898.

My dear Jacky,

We are just returned from the land of "wurst," and are anxious to know how it has fared with you at the place where you consented to bury yourself to get rid of every ache and pain to which you had to make so many concessions. I have to thank you for the manner in which, notwithstanding your absence, you have kept me supplied with papers, and no doubt when I get up to Paris to-morrow I shall find a lot awaiting me, as we have been away a little over three weeks. The garden has suffered considerably during our absence, from the dogs, but they are all looking well, so I suppose we must not complain. Lili is still on heat, she seems never to be off now. Blackamoor is, as you may imagine, very miserable at being compelled to play the part assigned to Abelard.

When shall we see you? It is so dreadfully warm that we are on the verge of starvation, as we can get nothing tender to eat unless we take to boiled meats.

I suppose your family are all enjoying themselves away from Paris? When you write, please remember me to everybody.

All here send their kindest regards and best wishes, in which I most cordially join, remaining ever,

Yours faithfully,
ERIC ARVEL.

ERIC ARVEL TO JACKY.

Sonis-sur-Marne, 16th. September, 1898.

My dear Jacky,

I was pleased to see you had returned home, but we all regret to find that you have joined the "Tiny-Tiny" division. I want to see you and have a chat with you, but this week I was unable to name a day having all my accounts to make out, as well as to prepare a long series of articles on the gold mines.

Name your own day this coming week, and come and tell us all your adventures by flood and field since we last saw you.

Believe me to remain, cordially and faithfully yours,

ERIC ARVEL.

ERIC ARVEL TO JACKY.

Sonis-sur-Marne, 18th. September, 1898.

My dear Jacky,

I am very glad to find that you are coming down on Wednesday. We will keep to the "Tiny-Tiny" principles as far as possible, and you can do as you say, put on your oldest and shabbiest "dog-trousers," as long as you will let the bow-wows do as they like with you. I have managed to instil a certain amount of respect into them as far as I am personally concerned, but I have nevertheless had to copy your example and wear a "dog-costume."

Come down early, but if you want me to tell you the *mot de la fin*, do not increase the many obligations under which you have placed the ladies by bringing anything down with you.

Yours very truly,
ERIC ARVEL.

SEPTEMBER 21, 1898.

Lord Fontarcy and Lady Clara had passed through Paris and intended to return towards the end of the month. They were very excited at the idea I had formed to introduce them to Lilian Arvel. I think Clara did not much care for her own sex, but she had some notion that Raoul would be a nice acquaintance for her, especially as her master would not be jealous.

I have said that I would paint myself in my true colours, and I must boldly confess that recently I had imagined a horrible project for my own sensual delectation. I tried to drive it from my mind, but it would keep returning in spite of all my efforts. I wanted to see my Lilian in the arms of another. I desired to give her over to the tender mercies of my two friends, I being present, and the salacious picture of this abandoned outrage excited my dormant desire to a point bordering on madness.

So I repaired to the hospitable Villa Lilian, determined to force my love to accept and play a part in this *partie carrée*.

I began to think also that Papa and Mamma had some slight inkling that we were lovers, and no doubt they thought me much richer than I was.

I was well received as usual, and I noticed that Papa was more tender than ever with his stepdaughter. She seemed to encourage him. I purposely refrained from paying any attention to my host's growing passion for the girl, as I was bent on the sole object of procuring her for my vile purpose. I gloated over this species of cold-blooded rape I was preparing.

The dogs were very troublesome, above all Lili, who Black-amoor, her son, was trying to get at all day.

Papa enjoyed this struggle of canine lust and I suddenly sur-mised that I saw a lurid glare of incestuous thought light up his ordinarily cloudy gaze.

The in-breeding craze, condemned by all true fanciers, seemed to agree with his passion for his mistress's daughter.

I must not omit a little circumstance that confirmed my views on this subject.

Three months before, Lili, the original bitch I had given them, had been on heat and by the neglect of a servant, said Mr. Arvel, the enormous Bordeaux watch-dog had managed to cover the poor little animal. No one had seen the act committed and yet it was known to them all. Two months later, she had a litter of mongrel pups, which were dragged into the world by Adèle, and the poor mother was only just saved from death by tender nursing. Such a thing had never happened to me with all my dogs. I had always studiously avoided any *mésalliance*. I was inwardly disgusted. They had risked the bitch's life by their carelessness and worse than all, pretty Lili, after suffering in vain, was spoilt for breeding purposes.

And then the horrible thought crossed my brain that Eric Arvel, in some wild fit of bestiality, had allowed the hulking hound to crush into the poor creature. He had perhaps, Nero-like, enjoyed the cruel sight of the disproportionate impregnation and in company of Lilian—who knows?

I feel these reflexions to be insane, but I have sworn to sketch myself as I was and am. I wallowed in a slough of lechery in this house of lies and lust.

Before lunch, I had a long talk with Lilian and told her that her plans were impossible. What would Papa and Mamma say? She could not answer, or rather I guessed she dared not. She replied that I was no doubt tired of her, as I had written that she disgusted me.

I drew her to me and boxed her ears. She laughed and purred, as she always did when I struck her, and she was happy, as her olive cheeks reddened beneath the loving smart of my hand. But I kissed her tenderly and told her that she was silly. I was not disgusted with her physically. She was the most charming creature a man could desire between the sheets, but as a woman trying to get on in life, I considered she was entirely lacking in common sense.

At this, she seemed contented and we went in to lunch. The day passed off as usual at Sonis. Pa quarrelled with Ma, and then romped with Lilian, and she lovingly caressed him, and I kissed her in corners whenever we could get alone together.

Raoul's name cropped up and I heard that he had received a summons to join a regiment of the line in November, to accomplish his period of military service as a Frenchman. Three years form the maximum, but he, as a son of a widow, would only pass one year under the tricolour flag. Mr. Arvel explained that this was one of the reasons why he had waited to marry his mistress. When the boy had accomplished his twelve months of military training he intended to lead Adèle to the altar.

Raoul's mother evidently adored him and she consulted me openly at dinner on a very delicate question. The lad was earning a good living at the wine-merchants in London and the heads of the firm had taken a great liking to him. They were very much annoyed to find that they were to be deprived of his services during a whole year and had coolly advised him to remain in England and become a deserter. Both Lilian and Adèle seemed to take this as a matter of course.

To my great wonder, my host did not join in the debate. His

face seemed a blank and I could see that he was perfectly indifferent as to whether the son of his mistress and the brother of her daughter, for whom, I intuitively felt, he nourished a passionate desire, was disgraced for life or not. The two women seemed to have no opinion on the matter.

My feelings were aroused to see the future of an intelligent youth thus liable to be inevitably and irretrievably spoilt, and although I did not know him, I spoke up boldly and excitedly, and pointed out the folly of allowing him to be thus ruined, banished, and jeered at all his life as a cowardly malingerer, for the sake of one short year's penance in a blue coat and red trousers.

To retrace my pleadings would be an insult to my reader's intelligence; suffice it to say that the ladies listened attentively and I won them over to the cause of right and reason.

Adèle seemed so struck by my remarks that she hoped I would soon meet Raoul and continue my good advice to him personally, for her sake. All this was in front of Arvel who never moved. He only grunted with hidden rage.

It was easy for me to divine that he hated Raoul as much as he evidently loved Lilian, and was, I presumed, jealous of the brother. He did not care if Raoul became that shameful wreck, a deserter, or not; but would rather have seen him disgraced than otherwise. Strange anomaly! if he desired the sister, who was perhaps his mistress already, for aught I knew. Inwardly he would perhaps have preferred Raoul to become an exile, so as not to be troubled with his presence in France.

I am proud to think now that I saved the lad from disgrace, as I am certain that if I had advised them to let Raoul evade his military obligation, they would have listened to me; and his mother's lover would not have lifted up a finger to save him, but would have chuckled to see him fall. Adèle was too fond of her son, and he stood between his two loves as well as being between him and Lilian in some mysterious way I could not fathom at that moment.

Just before dinner, I had an opportunity of being alone with Lilian, and I proposed to her to lunch with two friends of mine from England, a lady and gentleman. I did not give their names.

She began by refusing, but I pressed the point, saying that I had promised already. She quite understood that she was to be a voluptuous toy for all of us to play with, and I could see she liked the idea, though she pretended not to. She said she would join us at the meal, but not do anything that was indecent. I retorted that it was then no use coming. She was to let me do what I liked with her and give her over to both my friends, unreservedly for their lust.

"No!"

"Is it really: 'No'?"

"You will see!"

"I want a definite answer. Will you let us do whatever we like with you? After lunch we may perhaps all be naked. Say yes or no without prevarication."

"Well then, yes!" she exclaimed, with a frown, as the affirmation came snappishly and unwillingly from her lustful lips.

Papa told me he had read "The Horn Book," and liked it immensely. He asked me for some more, principally works on flagellation, and I promised to send him a parcel of books on that subject. I did so the next day.

Just before I left, Papa brought me "The Horn Book," carefully wrapped up for me to take away.

This work was to have remained hidden at his bureau in Paris. I now find it at his house!

Mamma had gone to bed, I was alone with the father and daughter. Quite unnecessarily, Lilian put on an air of candour and said very slowly, with an emphasis on each word:

"What-is-that-book-Papa-you-are-giving-back-to-Mr.-S...?"

She spoke deliberately, looking steadfastly at Mr. Arvel the while. He seemed confused and did not answer.

"Is it 'Guinea Gold,' by Christie Murray? I have read that. It is very good," she continued.

I changed the subject, but I felt quite certain by her artificial tone and by the stupor depicted on Papa's face at her audacity that they had perused the voluptuous volume together. They were an incestuous couple, I could have sworn it!

They accompanied me to the station and on the way I lagged

behind and passed the parcel containing the book to Lilian. She was wearing a short tartan cloth cape, as the evening was chilly, so she slipped it under her arm. She was supposed not to have read it.

Now this was the first edition of "The Horn Book," and as such was issued in large octavo size, printed on thick paper, and made up into a parcel, formed quite a bulky packet. On their way back to the house, Papa must have noticed that she held something hidden under her scanty mantle, and he could not have failed to see that when I shook hands with them on the railway platform I no longer held the parcel, and the pockets of the scanty covert-coat I was wearing were empty.

I was firmly convinced of their complete complicity and resolved to keep a sharp eye on them, but to say nothing about my suspicions to Lilian at present. She, however, had tried to put me off the scent by complaining that Mr. Arvel did not like her brother, and she added that her stepfather's temper was unbearable.

"Did you notice his horrible finger stumps? Does he not bite his nails dreadfully? Are they not awful?" she added, with an expression of disgust.

I supposed this was only her low cunning to make me believe that she did not care for him physically. When we were all three together, in the absence of her mother, she would pat him, and admire his prominent paunch, saying that she liked fine stout men. He would never answer, nor even smile, but a dull, blank look overspread his gloomy features. He loved her ardently.

LILIAN TO JACKY.

Sonis-sur-Marne, September 26th. 1898.

My own dear Master,

Of course I shall be delighted to be introduced to your friends on Wednesday. The only drawback is the finding of an excuse. As you can very well imagine, I cannot go and lunch out without a plausible pretext. And I can only see this way. Write me a letter supposed to come from that famous Madame Muller, Rue Lafayette. Although she does not pay her debts, she is our mutual friend, as thanks to her we passed two delicious afternoons.

You must sign Helena Muller, for such is the name of that amiable lady. This is about what you ought to write. She has returned to Paris, and according to her promise, she wishes to give me something off the amount she still owes me, and as I have been kind enough to wait patiently so long, she begs me to come and lunch with her on Wednesday, when she has a friend passing the day at her house, who may perhaps become a good customer for me. Arrange all this according to your idea, for I do not know how to twist these little lies about, while you do so beautifully!

Thank you, my cherished little father, but my eye is not better. I hope, however, that it will be cured on Wednesday, for I am truly an ugly duckling with my swollen eyelid. I go to London probably next week, so that I am impatient to see you, as I shall remain absent about a fortnight.

I will do anything you desire Wednesday, as long as I can passionately suck my dolly. It is such a time since I have had that happiness, that I promise myself to exhaust it completely.

A kiss on the end of its pink nose,

LILY.

SEPTEMBER 28, 1898.

Lilian's slight stye was nearly gone when she came to the place of appointment I had given her, and it did not mar her appearance. I had written a letter in a disguised hand, purporting to come from Madame Helena Muller, and I appraised Lord Fontarcy and Clara, who were now in Paris, of my success in overcoming Lily's slight scruples.

Clara had had great hopes of being able to get Raoul for an hour or two in London during the next month, as I told her that Lily would be there with her handsome brother and Charlotte, as the annual commercial round of visits was to be made by the two girls. I had great misgivings on that head, as Lilian seemed to be of such a jealous nature that she would not allow Raoul to form any new female acquaintances if she could help it. He, too, was madly in love with Charlotte and Lily made out to me that she did not want her brother to know the little tricks she got up to with me. She alluded to Charlotte now, not as Lolotte, but as Charlot. When I enquired the reason of her name being used in a masculine fashion, she made no reply. My salacious, suspicious mind immediately evolved the idea of some Lesbian amusements between the two girls. I knew that Charlotte slept in Lily's bed when she visited Sonis, when Papa was absent. She had been there just after I had passed the night with my sweetheart. I supposed that Raoul, Lilian and Charlotte had all played "mothers and fathers" with each other when they were in London, and perhaps Papa had participated too. This would account for his great hatred towards the lad, now that he was affianced to Charlotte, and Arvel also roundly abused his stepson's betrothed and called her a whore to me, but permitted her to frequent Lilian! Such inconsistencies on the part of a staid man of the world of 60 years of age require little or no comment on my part. I could plainly see that the more I advanced into the secrets of this strange family, the more vice I discovered. But what cared I as long as I fancied that Lilian loved me?

The *partie carrée* was to take place in a hotel-restaurant, which is a very useful kind of establishment for lovers and all amorous couples.

In these places, where the business of a hotel is carried on jointly with that of a public restaurant, some of the private dining-rooms are fitted up with capacious beds, and on opening a desk or a mirrored cupboard, there is to be found every convenience for the toilette and a plentiful supply of clean linen. There is always a table laid out for meals; the desired electric light, and the proprietor and waiters evince no surprise if several people order a repast and stop many hours afterwards, leaving the bed and bedding in a state of disorder. Nor do they trouble about their paying guests in any way. A man may occupy the room with one or more women. Or several men with only one woman, and I have no doubt that the same reception would await parties of men together and women without men. In fact, I knew one Parisian gentleman whose peculiar pleasure was to take his mistress to dinner at one of these restaurants, and when the coffee was served, invite the waiter to violate his companion in front of him, while he enjoyed his post-prandial cigar.

I had arranged the meeting in one of the quiet squares near

the Trocadero, and after Lily had arrived and immediately made the conquest of my friends, we trotted to the convenient hostelry, which is situated about three hundred yards from the triumphal arch of the Etoile.

We were soon installed, and a good fire was lighted, for the day was cold, but Clara objected to the first room we inspected, because there was a bed there. And this English lady positively blushed. She was at present, not up to our Continental standard, although kind and charming. So we gave way to her prudery and chose a snug room with a large divan. One reason for her coldness on this occasion was explained by her informing us that her monthly "turn" had begun that very morning. Lord Fontarcy also said that he was worn-out as he had been "going it" lately with his mistress. They had been visiting the secret haunts of Parisian pleasure together, and while we ate, they gaily told us some of their adventures. Under the influence of the meal, all barriers of restraint were soon broken down, and the dessert was not on table before I had kissed Lady Clara and Lily's lips were eagerly glued to those of my old friend.

Then she glanced archly across the table at me and whispered: "Dirty Papa!"

But she enjoyed the situation. Her eyes glittered, and she passed her tongue over her carmine lips, like a cat in front of a milk jug.

We talked of her brother. She was careful not to destroy Lady Clara's hopes and promised to look up Lord Fontarcy herself during her stay in London and dine with him one evening.

When the coffee and liqueurs were served and the waiter had left us, I rose and bolted the door. Cigars were lit, and Lilian puffed away at a little cigarette, after having in obedience to my orders, bitten the end off my Havannah. Lord Fontarcy was seated at the head of the table and I faced him. On his left, on the divan, came Lilian, with Clara next to her, and consequently on my right.

Mutual caressing and kissing was the order of the day, but poor little blonde Clara was not at her ease. The experience was new to her. She was, I felt, very loving when alone with a man she liked, but venereal sport in common was seemingly out of her line. It must be remembered too that she was bandaged up to a certain extent.

Lilian soon rose from table, although she was now on the best of terms with his lordship, they having been whispering and kissing together, and came to where I was sitting. I drew her on my knee and after she had given me her warm lips, I told my friends what pretty drawers she wore, and boldly pulled up her skirts; all of us had a full view of her dainty knickers and black stockings.

The sight was such a pretty one that Fontarcy was soon forced to draw nearer and he took a chair in front of me and began to place his hands on her knees and thighs.

I explained that as Lilian wore her beautiful drawers in the French style, it was very easy for her to slip them off her stays, to which they were fastened. She did so at once and returned to her seat on my lap. I raised her petticoats again and placed my hand on her hot slit.

I had ordered her to fasten the famous little pink ribbon on the hair of her mount before she left home, and there I found it. She whispered in my ear, as she pretended to kiss me, to take it off, as she did not want her new friends to know about it. I got rid of it with the dexterity of a professional juggler. I have it still and treasure it exceedingly, as it is about all I have got to remember her by.

I have let the cat out of the bag. Yes, my story will have a sad ending.

Lord Fontarcy was not slow in placing his fingers near mine, but Lily demurred: a mere formality.

"Sit quiet, and let us have our own way with you! If you resist, I'll kill you, my pretty daughter!"

Undismayed by my threat, she kissed me.

"I love to degrade and humiliate my love," I exclaimed aloud. "One of these days I mean to have her violated by a woman."

Now, our four hands wandered all over her buttocks, thighs, and even dared to approach her mossy mount and moist cleft. In fact, she got quite confused at a little game I invented on the spur of the moment. I made her try and guess which of our hands was on a certain part of the body. She was never right, and when I said:

"It is I who am feeling your bottom and not my friend," she would refuse to believe me and we chopped and changed about so quickly that she gave up trying to find out who held the fort in front, or the secret passage behind. It was no wonder that she could not guess correctly, as our mauling had already began to act upon her senses and her eyes softened, while her head fell upon my shoulder.

I drew back my chair a little and while we were indulging in a long and passionate embrace, Lord Fontarcy dropped on his knees and pushed his head under her petticoats.

What he did, I leave the reader to guess. I could not see him, but I heard the "cluck, cluck," of his eager working tongue. It must have been a great treat to Lilian, if I may judge by her passionate utterances and the manner in which the whole of her mouth engulphed mine, while she thrust her hot tongue as far down as she could, and plunged and writhed in a paroxysm of passion.

Clara sat by with her lovely blue eyes wide open. This was all new to her.

I brought Lily to her and opened the front of her bodice, showing the Englishwoman the pretty French corset. She explained that she wore a pair of London-made stays, and unfastening her dress, showed us her high white corsets, which crushed and flattened her sweet, plump breasts, instead of simply supporting them and throwing them forward as in the Gallic style. I felt her warm bosom and kissed her neck and rosy nipples, making Lilian do the same, while she sucked my sweetheart's baby breasts. But my lady was very cold, and as far as the two women were concerned, my little experiment was a failure.

Lilian now paired off with Fontarcy, and I embraced Clara and talked to her, trying to find out for her amusement some kiss that she might not know. She was an adept at the art of osculation, until I proceeded to show her the ball-room kiss.

This, I explained, was performed in the following manner: the lady is in a low-necked dress, her arms bare. She bends up one arm, and her lover's tongue tries to insert itself in the fold of the forearm at the elbow joint. This is also a promise of minette. Clara was obliged to confess that I had taught her something she did not know.

I now turned to Lilian, and made her undress completely, even to making her take off her shift, and she stood before us with only her shoes and stockings on, and her beautiful black tresses hanging down to her waist. My friends admired her slight, well-built frame, and taking her arm, I walked her about the room. Then I posed her in various attitudes, and a pretty little statuette she made too. I next forced her to put her stays on over her naked body, and she turned round and gave us the view of her rounded posteriors. We admired her legs and Clara showed hers. They were splendidly shaped and Lilian praised and envied them. Her own, she said, were too thin. Clara was thus half-undressed, but she was very shy, as she sat in pleasant disorder, on the divan, never having left her seat.

"Isn't my Lily a naughty girl?" I said to my friend.

"Indeed she is," replied Fontarcy, "she ought to have her bottom slapped."

"And so she shall!"

I caught hold of her and slapped her face. Then I kissed her, and threw her face downwards on the couch, holding her firmly by her small waist, her bottom being higher than her head.

My lord approached, and boldly rained a storm of blows on both the rounded cheeks, spanking her with both hands at the same time. Lily never moved; she groaned a little, but I held her tightly and bade her lie still. I now begin to strike at her backside with all the strength of my palms and her flesh soon became crimson.

Fontarcy returned to the charge and smacked her vigorously. While he did so, my right hand kept her tightly pinned to the divan, and I slowly inserted my left middle finger in her fundament, until its whole length disappeared entirely within her tight little hole.

Clara was gazing at us with hushed curiosity.

"Look," said I, "I have got my finger right into her."

"Where?" asked my lady. "In front?"

"No!" I told her, laughingly. "In the wrong hole!"

We now let Lilian get up and she sat down and took breath.

She did not complain of her smarting bottom, nor of my digital sodomy.

I told Clara she was a virgin and Lady Fontarcy was quite astonished.

"Do you mean to tell me that he has never been up you?"

"Never," said Lilian.

"Why?" asked the simple-minded British lady, turning towards me.

"Because I did not wish to harm her. She will get married one day and her husband will have her maidenhead. Her Mamma has told her that men can easily perceive if their bride is a virgin or not."

"Nonsense," chimed in Lord Fontarcy. "Look here, Lily, don't you believe such a fairy tale. Lots of women get married and their husbands think they have got a maid, although the blushing bride has had many lovers. If the girl clips her thighs together and makes a great fuss, the man can't tell, especially as the wish is father to the thought, and he is full of infatuation, love and champagne. Of course, I speak of a real disinterested greenhorn who imagines he has got an angel. He is easy to work on. The other kind of bridegroom you need not bother about, as he is mating for money or some other unscrupulous motive and therefore does not care if he finds the little bit of skin there or not. So, Lily, there are only two kinds of husbands on a first night: those who do not know, and those who knowing are indifferent. The lady hides a bloodstained napkin or towel in the bed. In the morning, the new recruit of the universal regiment of cuckolds finds the crimsoned linen, thinks his wife has used it in the small hours, and is perfectly satisfied."

I was now mad with lust and taking out my swollen member I forced Lilian to play with it. She made me get up and go a few steps away from Lord and Lady Fontarcy, saying in a whisper:

"Don't let her see it! She will want it! It is mine! She must not see it! She must not have it!"

I threw her on the ground. She rose to her knees, and I stood up before her, my trousers open and my red rod exposed. She quickly hid it in her mouth, throwing her black hair forward to screen my sexual organ and testicles from the gaze of my friends.

This was not fair for the aristocratic couple, as I wanted them to see the operation, so moving away from her mad mouth, I sat on a chair near Clara, and motioning Lilian to kneel down between my legs, I took her head in my hands and made her suck me.

"Go on!" I said roughly to her, and withdrawing for a second, I struck her brutally on the face with my enraged staff, knowing full well how she liked being treated roughly and voluptuously. I was mad with desire. And I lost sight of the spectators as my head fell back, and I enjoyed the burning, moist mouth of my beloved Lilian and the eager, vivid touch of her electric tongue.

Lord Fontarcy had seated himself on the floor, and holding Lilian closely embraced, he kissed her cheek, licked her ears, and whispered as she sucked me:

"Suck him well! Make him spend! He'll soon come in your mouth! Swallow it all!"

His brazen talk infuriated her to madness, her lips worked convulsively and her tongue twisted itself all round my throbbing tool, as her pretty head moved quickly up and down.

I was not long approaching the crisis, and a great gush of semen burst from me. With many a throb, I lost all notion of where I was, but I felt thick clots of viscous sperm leave my delighted mark of manhood and disappear down her throat.

She then lifted up her head, much to Clara's surprise. Never had she performed her task so well. There was not a drop left in my canal and all had been swallowed with rare completeness.

Clara was still astounded to think I had been Lilian's lover just upon ten months and had never had connection with her. She seemed to doubt her virginity, and I think Lord Fontarcy was incredulous too.

"But I am a virgin!" exclaimed the naked Lily.

"Let us see," said Fontarcy.

"But you'll hurt me," answered my girl.

After a little trouble, Lilian took her seat just in front of the window and opened her legs.

Lord Fontarcy went on his knees before her and delicately taking the hairy, outer lips of her private parts in each hand, began to open them gently.

"You do hurt me," Lily complained.

My lord was bent on carrying out his investigation and I must confess that I was nothing loth. I lit a cigar and sat down in front of her.

"Now, Lily," he said, "open your legs wide and pull your lips aside yourself."

She did so, stretching herself open as she sat on the edge of a light cane chair, and Fontarcy carefully opened the little inner lips as far as he could. We had a full view of the pretty, rose-pink interior.

"Yes, she is certainly a virgin," said my lord, gloating over the view, while Lilian, her thighs well thrown back and holding her plump hairy lips apart herself, allows us to examine her carefully and quite complacently, as if proud of this parade of her maiden charms.

"Come, Clara, and look!"

Clara drew near and in the full light from the window gazed for a few seconds at the open cockleshell.

"Yes," she said, slowly and seriously, "I think she is a virgin!"

"Think indeed! I'm sure she is! See, here are the sweet inner lips, the clitoris above, and the vaginal passage is quite closed up!"

I took a long look at Lilian's vulvary vestibule and could see the hymen or membrane, the edges of which, facing each other, made a slight projection of a deep, violet-red tint, resembling in shape a half-moon or a rudimentary letter S.

We were all satisfied that Lilian's vulva was innocent of the penetration of the penis and this searching examination put an end to the miniature orgie.

We each rearranged our dress and tried to look like sober citizens once more. Lilian was soon dressed and her hair tidied up, after a visit to the mysterious regions of the ladies' cloakroom.

The evening was fine, and proceeding to a first class café, we took tea outside.

I conversed with my friend and the two women chatted together. At first, they talked toilettes and then their voices fell to a whisper. Evidently we men were being dissected by our two charmers in true feminine style.

We then parted, Lilian promising to look up her new friends in London shortly, and I walked with my mistress to the railway station, as we both felt a wish to take the air and stretch our legs, though Lilian's had been stretched enough already.

We talked merrily and lovingly together. Lily had enjoyed herself, but she said she would have liked better to have spent the afternoon alone with me. She did not care for Clara; women were nothing to her, but I fancied she was not displeased with Fontarcy. She told me that he wanted to see her alone without me. I told her I was not jealous, as I had just proved that fact beyond dispute and that I should be very pleased if she went to him when she was in England, during the month of October. Probably she was trying to teaze me or to find out what I really thought. She also essayed a true feminine trick upon me, as she declared that Clara had asked what I intended to do for my Lily in the future, and what was to be her social position by reason of my connection with her. I felt perfectly sure that Fontarcy's companion had never said anything of the kind, but that Lilian made use of her name in order to tell me things about herself that she dared not ask me boldly and frankly. I evaded these burning topics, and diplomatically fencing, we at last reached the Gare de l'Est.

In the station, Lilian asked me if I had the money to give her.

"What money?" was my surprised enquiry.

"You know I dare not go home to Mamma without giving her what Madame Muller has supposed to have paid me to-day."

"I am hard up, I have nothing!"

"What a fearful position you have put me in! Mother is already suspicious. She will go mad and drive Papa mad against me."

"But you can say you have got an order for some new hats That will keep them quiet."

"And when the new hats are not paid for?"

"Then you'll say they do not suit, or so on. In time it will all be forgotten."

"No, it will not. If I had known, I would not have come. This is dreadful for me!"

"Do you mean to say you have not got fifty francs you can show as if you had received it and then put it back again? Do you really tell me that all your accounts are so closely examined by your parents? I could not guess that you really are absolutely forced to bring home a few louis. It seems very strange to me that you can't get out of this somehow without me giving you money."

"No! no! I feel that I should like to run away and not go home at all. And it is so late too! What shall I say? What can I do? If I only knew somebody near here I would go and borrow it. It is dreadful!"

She seemed very much annoyed and her features were distorted with rage and disappointment. I felt disgusted with her and myself. I really did not think she would have been so hard upon me. I was far from being at my ease and she did not spare me, but reproached me bitterly. The hour grew near for the departure of her train. She bid me good bye icily and I told her to write to me from London. She turned from me without a word.

And I went away to see my poor suffering Lilian, at my little apartment, and soon forgot mercenary Mademoiselle Arvel as I cast up my accounts and reckoned what money I should require for the coming winter: coals, wood, medecines and all the incidental heavy expenses of a little household where there is a confirmed invalid. The fifteenth of October, the French rent-day, was approaching with giant strides, and I had hardly enough to make both ends meet. Poverty and passion do not go together, and when misery knocks at the door, Cupid flies out of the window.

LILIAN TO JACKY.

Sonis-sur-Marne, Thursday. (September 29th. 1898.)

Dearest Papa,

I am still stunned by last night's storm. It is impossible for me to tell you all the disagreeable things that were said to me, for I should want tremendous space to write it all to you.

I only succeeded in calming Mamma by telling her that my famous customer was going to send me at least a hundred francs by post tomorrow or the next day.

So therefore I come to ask you to make a great effort to procure that sum between this and then. As I know you are not well off just now, I will arrange matters so as to give it back to you on my return from London, but I beg you not to leave me in this trouble which has come upon me.

I count absolutely upon you for this, the first service I ask you to do me, and I know you will not leave me in such a predicament. As in every other matter I have confidence in you.

I await an answer as soon as it is possible for you. I hope to see you soon, my darling little father.

I send you all the kisses that I should have given you yesterday had we been alone.

Your slave who adores you,
LILY.

LILIAN TO JACKY.

(Undated. Received September 30th. 1898.)

My beloved little Papa,

A word in haste to tell you that Mamma said this morning that if I did not have fresh news and receive the promised money, she would accompany me to-morrow to Madame Muller's and show her that she must not make fools of people in this manner.

I tried to point out to her that I should then lose the new customer that had been introduced to me. She replied that under no pretext would she allow me to work for anybody presented by this creature. What steps ought I to take? If you do not send me to-morrow what I have asked you for, I think the best thing will be for me to confess all; that will perhaps prevent a scandalous exposure. I cannot let her discover that I pretended having received money from that woman.

I pray you, answer me quickly. I leave for London on Tuesday or Wednesday only.

I love you, notwithstanding all the sufferings I endure through you for the last two days.

My lips on your dear mouth,
LILY.

In reply to these two short, threatening notes, I sent on October 1st., a letter of excuses purporting to come from Madame Helena Muller, and enclosing a fifty-franc note. I received no acknowledgement, nor did I hear from Lilian.

8

And thou art old; thy hairs are hoary grey,
As thou wouldst save thyself from death and hell,
Pity thy daughter; give her to some friend
In marriage; so that she may tempt thee not
To hatred,—or worse thoughts, if worse there be.

SHELLEY.

DAUGHTER. . . . To marry him is hopeless
      To be his whore is witless.

BEN JONSON.

Wear this jewel for my sake, 'tis my picture;
Refuse it not; it hath no tongue to vex you.

SHAKESPEARE.

I passed a terrible month of October. As usual, every winter, my poor homely Lily was very ill. More new doctors, more demands on my half-empty purse, and to make matters worse, her temper, under the influence of her terrible, relentless malady, grew unbearable. She was jealous and querulous, and I always had to give in, as the slightest emotion might have proved fatal.

Miss Arvel had not acknowledged the receipt of the money I had sent her at the beginning of the month nor given any signs of her existence. I supposed she had gone to London, as she had told me, but I was not certain. Anyhow, she had not written and I did not know her address.

Lord Fontarcy asked me once or twice in his letters about her, as he and Clara expected her visit, she having promised to look them up if she went to England. But I could tell him nothing. Indeed, it was I who asked him for news of her.

He replied that she had not turned up, despite her promise, although she had his address. He could not understand her conduct, or perhaps he did not like to speak against her to me. All he wrote were these words: "Strange girl!" And Clara, discreetly, said nothing.

It was very odd that in the preceding year, when in London in the autumn, she had written to me, but had forgotten (?) to give me her address. Here again, she is silent. Evidently, I was not to know where my love was in the habit of stopping in London, when she was there with Charlotte and Raoul; and Papa, if in England, visiting the two girls daily. Did they think that I might take it into my head to cross the Channel? That contingency did not suit the party, or I should have been approached on the subject during the summer. I was not wanted when they were in England.

My demi-vierge was a puzzle to me just then. She had been a real enigma. I was very sorry I could not have her more often. She excited me dreadfully, as she never failed to do, whenever I involuntarily conjured up her image in my daydreams of lust. On the other hand, I was glad, as I could do nothing for her.

She wanted money and that money I had not got. Perhaps, thought I, my little lunch has caused a revulsion of feeling. I should have had very slight regret if she was disgusted with me, as even that might have been to my future advantage. But my passions called for her. In a sensual way I yearned for her. My common sense told me it was better for both of us not to meet again.

Her stepfather always asked after me at the Bourse, where I did not go any more. I supposed he would invite me if it suited him. I foolishly worried myself very much about Lilian and as time went on and no news came, I was, I confess it, weak enough to drop her a few lines on the 30th. of October, signed: "Marie." I do not know now what I said, but I suppose I expressed my surprise at not having heard from her. In my erotic cecity, for I can call it naught else, I had quite forgotten her last note, wherein she threatened me that she would confess all to her mother, unless I sent her the money purporting to come from the imaginary Madame Muller.

Eric Arvel to Jacky.

Sonis-sur-Marne, 4th. November, 1898.

My dear Jacky,

When you know that I have had half-a-dozen painters in the house, several bricklayers and a carpenter and locksmith for the last three weeks, you will understand why I have remained so long without thanking you for the many hours of pleasant reading the books I returned to you afforded me. I wish that the feminine confessions had been written by a woman, but I suppose that the daughters of Eve can keep their secrets better than men, and if they do tell tales out of school, when among themselves, they never find them written down. Many thanks for the budget of papers and the two packets of photographic printing paper. I have just had a dark room built, and if I manage to pull through the winter I shall go in for photography as a paying amusement .

When will you come down and eat the "côtelette d'amitié"? What do you say to Tuesday next?

With every kind of wish for you and yours, and with united best wishes for yourself from the Villa Lilian, believe me to remain,

Cordially yours,
Eric Arvel.

Eric Arvel to Jacky.

Sonis-sur-Marne, November 8th. 1898.

My dear Jacky,

Many thanks for your letter. I was sorry you could not come to-day but as we always want to see you sans cérémonie tell me what day will suit you best during the week save Saturday or Sunday. We shall be at home all Friday and probably Thursday, although on the latter day, I should be forced to leave you at two o'clock to go to Paris, to do some work due to appear in a Berlin paper on Saturday.

I am grateful for the offer of more books and I do not refuse, but I am going to London some time next week and I could not leave them about during my absence, so I will ask you again on my return.

Hoping that everyone at your house is well and that you have picked up again, I remain with every good wish for you and yours,

Most cordially,
ERIC ARVEL.

NOVEMBER 11, 1898.

When I arrived at the suburban paradise to spend a happy day, I was introduced to Raoul, who I saw for the first time. He was a tall, handsome youth of 21, with fine eyes, a nice black moustache and a thick head of hair to match. He very much resembled Lilian, and had she been dressed as a man and her upper lip slightly blackened they would have been as like as two peas. He spoke English very well with a strong French accent, and I found him to be a very agreeable young fellow, but I had few opportunities of judging him. He seemed very fond of his sister and she had evidently some authority over him at that time. His mother simply adored him and spoilt him as much as her old lover would let her. He, I could not mistake it, positively loathed the very sight of the boy, who, in return, did not care a straw for him. Raoul had a sly look in his eye and when he smiled, his lips curled scornfully and sarcastically. Like his sister, he had an expressive mouth. He had a splendid set of teeth, but I was disgusted to see that they had been greatly neglected, being quite green with accumulation of tartar. I told Lilian about this, and she thanked me warmly. When I met him again, they looked clean and wholesome, as a man's mouth should, especially when lucky enough to have a good set of teeth. Arvel was no father to him and his mother did not know. She was cunning, and sufficiently artful to pamper her old lover's stomach and put up with his tempers, but her intelligence was not above that of an ordinary domestic servant.

Raoul was in France for a year, and he was off to join a regiment of the line on the 15th. He was to be stationed at Belfort.

I talked to him and put him at his ease as much as I could, for Lilian's sake, and to my surprise, I saw that he had no idea of how to behave towards the officers who would command him, nor of the obligations and discipline of life in barracks. Arvel hardly spoke to him except to sneer visibly whenever he opened his mouth, and only Lilian's warning cough and intercession between him and Mamma kept him from quarrelling with everybody. Lilian was a power now in the household, I could see.

The house had been thoroughly done up and painted. I was shown the dark room, a very useful construction, near the garden gate, fitted with every convenience for Mr. Arvel's new hobby. He explained to me that he saw a future in taking photographs and writing articles round them for the illustrated newspapers, as that was now a new fashion in journalism. He had visited some old castles in Normandy already last month with a splendid detective camera he showed me. His negatives and the letterpress had been well received and an engagement on a newly started newspaper had followed. I knew a little about photography and gave him a few hints for which he was grateful.

Lilian was as cold as ice to me all day. She kept away from me in her workshop and I spent my time mostly with Papa, who talked against his stepson. According to him, he was a lazy, good-for-nothing fellow, fond of gadding about at nights, a silly fool to be betrothed to Charlotte—who was a little whore, though Lilian's friend—and utterly incapable. Luckily for Raoul, he said, his employers had taken a foolish fancy to him. His mother could see no faults in him and he had even got on the right side of Lilian. I tried to pour oil on the troubled waters, but nothing I said could stop my host growling when he felt inclined to growl.

Then I tried to interest the youth and draw him out, and Lilian would flit about a little in the background, with a cloud on her brow and two black crescents under her eyes. A neighbour, I think it was the wife of the village baker and pastrycook, came to see my little milliner and she had foolishly brought her black poodle with her, although she knew that the Arvel dogs were rather savage and jealous. The Bordeaux hound rushed at the intruder and began to worry him, and Blackamoor and the other dogs also attacked the poor little beast. Lilian, shrieking, appeared to get the big dog off, and everybody galloped to the scene of the affray. Eventually, all was made right, and the poodle, barring a little bit of flesh nipped off his loins, was none the worse for his encounter. But Lilian burst into a fit of hysterical weeping and though I tried to whisper a few words of comfort in her ear, she turned roughly away from me without speaking. What had I done to merit such rudeness from her?

Papa had engaged a waggonette and we were all to be driven a few miles off to the establishment of a horticulturist to buy fruit trees for an orchard and kitchen-garden, to be inaugurated next spring in the newly acquired ground.

We were all ready to start, but Lilian sent word she would not come, pretexting a lot of work, although Mamma asserted it would do her good. Lilian was far from well, she said, she had no appetite, did not sleep, and suffered from headache. So we started off without her, Raoul joining the coachman on the box.

As we jolted along, Madame Arvel told me what she evidently thought was greatly to her son's credit, as showing his love for his sister.

He was fearfully upset at seeing the dogfight, and witnessing the outburst of tears of Mademoiselle, and his anxiety grew into positive uneasy fear when his mother told him that it might be serious for his sister, as she was very unwell that day. Mamma chuckled at the brother's solicitude for the girl during her catamenial flow. I thought about the indelicacy of discussing such topics between mother, brother and sister, not to mention the master of the house and lastly myself.

So I sat to a-thinking as I felt awfully bored, listening and forcing myself to answer the commonplaces of Ma and Pa, and now and then my ears were delighted with fragmentary echoes of Raoul's remarks to the coachman. His every sentence began with the same words:

"In England we do so-and-so!"

My thoughts went back to the date of Lilian's menstruation. It generally began on the 27th. or 28th. In August, it was all over by the 25th., and in September also, as she had lunched with Lord and Lady Fontarcy on the 28th. of that month and now we were at the 11th. of a fresh period of thirty days, and she was menstruating freely. She was suffering from anæmia or chlorosis, I could plainly diagnose, though my medical knowledge was slight and empirical, and in such a state, sexual excitement and masturbation, alone or in company, would produce irregularity of her periodical loss of blood. She had been to London with Charlotte and had returned with her and Raoul. I did not know when she had left, nor how long she had been back. What had she been doing at the West End? How had they been living? Had she joined her handsome brother and Lolotte between the sheets? Was her friend in the lace trade a little Lesbian? Here was an explanation of Arvel's jealousy and hatred of the lad. Suppose that Lilian loved Raoul too well? Had they ever played carnally together as children, perhaps to amuse Arvel . . . perhaps at his instigation? That would be quite enough to make him jealous now that he loved Lilian, I imagined, not like a child, whose half-innocent caresses had warmed his blood before he joined Adèle in bed, but like a woman ripening gradually for sensual service at his fireside.

Time would show, I said to myself, and I drove those thoughts from me and wondered, poor fool that I was then, what Lilian meant by sulking with her wretched old Jacky!

Mamma and Papa bought about five hundred francs' worth of trees. Adèle was mad on gardening just then. She thought she could manage to have fruit enough to go into business the next year. I chatted with them all, and tried to be friendly with the brother.

I saw nothing of my charmer until a few moments before dinner, when we were all in the drawing-room. She arrived, nicely tidied up, with a dash of powder on her dark complexion. She immediately went to her Papa and sat on the arm of his chair, after having patted his face and told him how well he looked. She had a box of fancy note-paper in her hand and told me it was to write to her most intimate friends with.

"I am going to write some letters now," she said saucily. "When I don't care for the people, I send them type-written notes on Pa's business paper. Eh, Papa?"

He did not answer. He never responded to her advances or to her caresses before me. Whenever she rubbed against him, or tickled him, or caressed him in any way, his face grew dull; he frowned, and lost all expression. He loved her and a caress from the loved one was evidently a serious thing for him.

"You should never write letters. Never confess, never write and never reply. Such are the instructions of an old lawyer, a friend of mine."

And so we fenced for a quarter of an hour, Lily chaffing me to please her Pa, I supposed. She admired his clean-shaven chin and cheeks, and coolly told me that she hated men with hair on their faces. I wore my entire natural beard.

Then I was alone with her for a few moments just before we sat down to dinner. I took her in my arms. She struggled and got away. I slapped her face smartly, but she did not take it as usual, and complained I hurt her and was too brutal.

"Look how you have brought the blood into my cheeks, everybody will see."

She was very pale and my slap had caused a patch of crimson to overspread one cheek. This was a sure sign of poverty of the blood and deficient circulation. I asked her if she was cold. She shivered and said she was always chilly. I told her she ought to wear woollen stockings. She showed me her feet. She wore worsted socks under her black thread stockings. Here was every sign of anæmia and I inwardly thought that she must also suffer from that disagreeable affliction, vulgarly called the "whites." That would account for her occasional coyness with me, and also for her lack of sensual excitement the winter before. Anæmic girls are no use in winter; the circulation of the blood is deficient, and there is a discharge from the vagina generally accompanying the menses. At that time, if any attempt is made to worship at the altar of Venus or practise masturbation, there are ovarian pains and stomach cramps, such as Lilian complained about.

I need not say that I kept all these remarks to myself and being very much in love, I no doubt looked and behaved like a spoony swain, although I tried as I always did to be very gay and make everybody laugh, even if the joke was at my expense.

During the meal, Lilian thawed a little and slipped her foot under mine, letting it remain there all the time.

The Dreyfus affair came on the *tapis*. As was his wont, Arvel stuck up boldly for the heads of the French army. I ventured to say that whatever had occurred, there was no doubt that the alleged traitor had been illegally condemned, as pressure had been brought to bear on his judges in the council chamber by showing them secret documents, of which the prisoner and his lawyer ignored the existence, against all ideas of justice and fair play.

"But suppose they could not show them?" said Arvel.

At this answer, which I leave to my readers to appreciate, I could do no more than give up talking about the matter and I dropped the subject.

Raoul joined in, saying that he had only read English newspapers and knew very little about the case, and Adèle called across the table to me:

"Is he innocent?"

"Yes," I retorted.

"Then why don't they deliberate (sic) him?"

"They will in time," I answered, and Arvel shrugged his shoulders and talked a lot of nonsense about the luck of Dreyfus in being judged by his brother-officers and what more could any man want?—he added.

I did not reply I amused myself looking at Lilian, who gazed on her Pa with undisguised admiration. Her eyes were fixed on his and her half-open mouth drank in every word he let fall. Once during the dinner, she touched my hand with hers. Usually when I dined at Sonis, she never forgot to peel and prepare some fruit for me. This night I was neglected. I remember too that the conversation turned—as it always did at Sonis—on some indecency, either in a Parisian newspaper or at a theatre, and Papa denounced the immorality of the Parisians.

"Londoners are no better!" blurted out Lilian, in a passion, "how about the massage establishments?"

I noted this peculiar remark and saw Papa drop his beak into his plate. When Lily was flooding, Lilian's temper was bad.

Mamma was at the head of the table. On her right, was Papa alone. On her left, Raoul was seated, and next to him Lilian. I was at the bottom of the table, facing Mamma, but luckily there was a big lamp in the middle and I could hardly see her.

I suppose Papa was thinking whether Lilian's "tootsies" were on mine or not, as there was a slight scuffle under the hospitable board and Papa called out to his daughter:

"Hullo! scraggy longshanks, where have your feet got to? Can't you tuck 'em under your chair?"

"Oh! its no use you trying to *faire le pied* with me, you know!"

This is a slang expression, and may be translated as "playing the foot game," *i.e.* lovers' wireless telegraphy by means of sly mutual pressures of the lower extremities.

Still more indications for me of the emancipation of my sweetheart. But I was too much concerned with my own troubles to bother about Lilian and her mother's old lover just then.

Having silenced her amorous Papa, she rose and said she was going to take the dogs out with her brother. To my surprise, she turned to me, and asked if I would accompany them and smoke, and digest my dinner. Of course I accepted, and all three, without counting the canine pets, we went out along the road. It was a fine night with a bright moon. Raoul was not troublesome. He knew the part he had to play, and walked on in front teazing Blackamoor, leaving Lilian and me practically alone together.

I broke out at once:

"What is the matter with you?"

"I am very vexed. You left me in the lurch, and so I resolved to try and forget you. That is why I did not write from London as I had promised, nor did I go to see your friends. I asked you to do me a slight favour and you abandoned me entirely in the hour of need."

"But, my darling, I sent you a note purporting to come from Madame Muller, containing fifty francs."

"*I never received that letter!*"

"Good God! It's true I never registered it! This is horrible. In spite of all I may say, you will always have an afterthought that I have invented this lie to save fifty francs! How could it have been lost? Letters rarely go astray like this."

"Oh! the postmen are such thieves down here!"

"I sent it. I forget what day it was, but I'll look up my diary when I get home. I am stunned. What fearful ill-luck! Why should just this very letter be lost when so many others I have written have always reached you safely?"

I could not say very much more, I had not much time, as we were due to get back to the house for my train and I was all abroad. I must have looked as stupid as I felt. It was a hard case for me and incidentally for my friends, Lord Fontarcy and Clara. I was very unlucky, that was certain.

Resuming my talk, I said to Lilian:

"As you did not get the fifty francs, how did you manage?"

"My mother went to Normandy with Pa to do some photography and write about some châteaux, and I told her in a letter that I had received some money from Madame Muller."

"But when she came back, did she not ask to see the cash? You say she sees and knows everything?"

"Yes, but I told her I had used it to pay a bill that was due."

If I had recovered from this crushing blow, I might have continued by wanting to know whether she had seen the bill and if I could be allowed to see it too, but I frankly confess that I could not reason properly at that moment. I could only keep thinking how unfortunate I was. Nevertheless, it slowly dawned upon me that Lilian was awfully mercenary, and I think my love for her began to shrink a trifle. She went on to complain that Papa had found a post-card in one of the books I had lent him. It was from my mistress's dressmaker, speaking about a price to be paid for embroidering a jacket. Mademoiselle was evidently jealous of her or pretended to be so, and she plainly said that a man who could spend such sums on fashionable attire, and holding the great position I did in Paris, should have been more liberal with her, who had done all I asked her, and she thought I was rather tightfisted and a scurvy fellow (pignouf).

I must have been looking very miserable up to this and I lifted up my face to hers in the moonlight.

I was choking with rage, disgust, and surprise. I was completely taken aback and could not find a word to say:

"Oh, Lilian!" was all I could gasp out.

I think she must have seen something in my face that frightened her, or perhaps she thought she had gone far enough. She put her arm through mine and told me that it did not much matter:

"I am very unhappy! We were so miserable in London, were we not, Raoul?"

And she called him to create a diversion.

"I was in bed each night at ten o'clock. We went to no theatres or music halls. We had no money. All three of us, Lolotte, Raoul, and myself would dine at a foreign restaurant, and fagged out, retire to rest."

Heaven knows how much of this was true. I could not analyse her talk then.

We returned home, and at the gate, Raoul asked me if I was going to sleep at their place.

Lilian chimed in gracefully:

"Oh no! We are too poor and common for him!"

And she bounced past us. After having bid Pa and Ma good night, and thanked them for their kind reception, etc., Raoul and Lilian escorted me to the station.

The brother obligingly disappeared in the trees and she gave me her mouth, and put her hand to see if my manly organ responded to the cunning thrust of her tongue between my lips, as it always had done. Satisfied with her examination, she became somewhat mollified.

But there was a barrier between us. I felt a strange uneasiness, and I really do think that this was the turning-point of my *liaison* with Lilian. From that moment my feelings underwent a change. I could not see for myself just then, but light did come and I was saved, as the reader will see.

She asked after Lord Fontarcy. I told her how he had called her, "a strange girl."

She said she did not like the couple, though she could at a pinch have put up with Fontarcy himself. She told me frankly that her brother would never have consented to go and see Clara, as he was madly, sentimentally in love with Charlotte, who had been three weeks in London with her. He was fully resolved to marry his mistress, although she was about three years his senior. And Lilian added that she was tired out, unhappy and felt very ill.

"You require care, Lily. Your health is not good. You are anæmic!"

At these words, which I had let drop harmlessly enough, Lilian started as if I had shot her.

"Anæmic? I? Anæmic!" she shrieked out, and her face was all black, and her mouth twisted awry. She was in a fit of mad passion.

"I don't know what you mean. You've given yourself away fairly this time! You think you are talking to somebody else. You're quite mistaken, my dear fellow!"

I was surprised at this outbreak, but was cool enough in spite of my trouble to divine that if there was one thing Lilian hated more than another it was the truth.

I had pity on her too, because at that moment I still loved her in my vile, salacious way and my bowels yearned for her. I had not yet had time to think over the events of the day. But I knew enough of women to see that she was under the neurotic influence of difficult menstruation and as such must be spared for the nonce.

I do not remember if I spoke about seeing her again or not, or whether we made any plans for the future. I know I alluded to my beard. She shrugged her shoulders and told me that she was only running me down to please Papa and divert his suspicions, if he had any.

I never spoke of him nor of the numerous signs of illicit intercourse between them. I wanted to hold my tongue and learn more.

I told her I would write and I asked her to make a few discreet enquiries at the post-office at Sonis.

She did not reply, but with a cordial "adieu," Raoul and her saw me into the train and we parted good friends; not lovers, only friends.

I went back to Paris and dreamt that I was on my honeymoon with Lilian Arvel and that I was alone in a railway carriage with her, her skirts thrown up and my hands on her naked thighs.

I looked up my diary and found that I had posted the fifty-franc note on the first of October.

I composed a letter for Lily. I wanted to write a beautiful letter to her. I desired to make all my next letters kind and delicate, so that they should exactly delineate my thoughts and my state of mind as I wrote them. I kept altering a comma here, a word there, and often changed the order of sentences. This did not change the sense, but I flattered my wretched self that I made my prose lighter and clearer, with more tenderness, more kindness, more passionate love. Alas, poor Jacky!

JACKY TO LILIAN.

Paris, November 12th. 1898.

My dear Lilian,

As soon as I got home last night, I quickly looked at my diary and I find I sent the bank-note on Saturday, October 1st. The letter ought to have been delivered on Sunday morning, the 2nd.

In spite of all, I am as if stunned by a blow from a club, proving such atrocious ill-luck that I can hardly realise the fact of it being precisely that one particular letter which should have been lost or stolen.

What a misfortune for me and naturally for you too!

I have always tried to be so careful, to protect you, who I had so much joy in imagining to be my daughter; so that for once, neglecting prudence, I find myself in a pitiful position, for what causes me enormous grief, of which you cannot form the slightest idea, is that you have no longer confidence in me.

I am sad, weary, disgusted with life and all its defeats, illnesses and wounds. One has so little happiness in this world, and such, . . . oh! such trouble!

But you are young and you cannot understand at all what I feel. In a few short years, when you will have been able to appreciate life better; when you will have seen other things and other men, then you will think of me and render me justice. To-day, I hope for nothing.

I pray you, excuse the serious tone of this letter of complaint. There is nothing so silly as a man who groans and laments, but if I go mad with rage in front of this paper; if I choke in my throat as if I were about to be weak enough to weep, it is because I think that you have attributed to me: lies, villany and meanness. You have believed that my soul was base and paltry, as vilely low as that of a huckstering shopkeeper! But enough; perhaps I ought not to send you this sad scrawl?

Let me conclude with an effort to be gayer. I dreamt of you all night. Irony of the fates . . . we were on our honeymoon! I had just married you!

This was an effect of cerebral impression, caused by my conversation with you in the station, the railway ride, etc.

I thank you for your kiss, for your slight caress.

Do not forget to tell your brother, as I can see that he does not have all necessary advice given him, to cease having a will of his own directly he enters the barracks, and never to answer a superior even if a hundred times in the right. Let him become a machine—if I may venture to say so—and not a man.

Make him wear flannel, and woollen socks. It is impossible to walk with cotton hose; he would soon get blistered and bleeding feet.

Tell him also never to say: "In England we do this or that." He will find such conduct more prudent—at least for the moment.

He loves you well, that I saw. He will listen to this advice coming from you. Make out as if these were your own ideas.

And I love you also.

J. S.

LILIAN TO JACKY.

(No date or place.) Received November 15th. 1898.

My little Father,

I will not let you have a moment of sadness through any fault of mine, so I come quickly to tell you that I have no longer the least doubt about you, for a man who can have the kindliness and the delicacy to be able to understand all you have understood, cannot be base one instant.

Therefore all is forgotten and I am once more your loving "daughter."

I wish to believe that the wretched month I have just passed was only a nightmare, a bad dream.

I have suffered greatly. I found myself so lonely, so neglected. But all this is quite finished, is it not?

My brother left yesterday by the midnight train. I gave him all your advice and I thank you a thousand times.

Yes, you have guessed rightly. I love him very much. He is so gentle, so good, and then he loves me fondly too.

If you have dreamt truly when you supposed we were on our wedding trip, how proud and happy I should be; and I am certain that you would regret nothing, for I would make you so happy that the horrible sentence you write to me in your good letter would never enter your mind.

You are sad, fatigued, tired of life, say you? That is because you have no tie to make existence a pleasure. But if you had a good little wife, very loving, full of care for you; a pretty little household:—"home,"—in all the true sense of the word, your ideas would be quite different. And you have only a word to say to possess all this. Do not suppose that I speak lightly. I have reflected seriously and I am convinced that we should be mutually happy. Do you think it is so very amusing for me to see you only during a few short moments, now and again, and always with a little apprehension? And it will always be the same if we continue like this —but I will no longer.

I kiss you madly as on certain days,

LILY.

JACKY TO LILIAN.

Paris, November 16th. 1898.

My darling daughter,

I must hold my pen tight to-day so that it shall not escape and bolt away across the paper to express to you all the sweet joy your delicious letter, which I received yesterday, has given me. I can only see one thing: you love me!

That letter is you: my Lily, my daughter, my slave, my love, all mine; your heart to excuse me, to console me, and your body a hundred times offered for my pleasure, my lust, my enjoyment . . . and a little for yours, by the sole fact of the pleasure you bestow. For I often remarked that you found your pleasure in provoking mine. I would ask you: "What do you want now?" And you would answer: "You!"

When you are near me, you feel that movement which opens the sources of pleasure in your inmost being. I am proud to have been the first who produced in you that effect, and you always experience it when I am by your side; when I rub against you; when I look at you. I remember the first time I came to this conclusion; we were in that café where we drank some champagne. You looked at me, your nostrils quivered; you were spending and yet our conversation was commonplace. You were near me and you loved me as you loved me to-day. I never have understood your love and your passion better.

You talk of "certain days" and of your mad caresses.

Impudent girl! Do you wish to awaken in me all my lust, and excite and provoke all my desires—all the yearning I have for you? You make me remember my imaginations of slavery. I wish to call to you to come to my arms. I wish to command you to run to me, to execute all the voluptuousness of which I dream when my thoughts wander towards you —as it happens too often.

I have still a little virgin paint-brush in a corner of a drawer, wrapped in tissue paper. I would also teach you the bicycle race, when your saddle would be my mouth and face, and the handle-bar the head of the bed, or you could turn round and. . . . Will you, say Lily, my little incestuous daughter? . . .

But I stop and read over what I have just written. I ought not write thus to you. I am mad. So much the worse for me! . . . I send you my incoherent thoughts. Excuse me. I will try to be more cold and reasonable.

My dream, which was delicious, for you gave me your mouth in the railway carriage, and then your thighs and the rest, is impossible to realise for reasons which I will give you some day by word of mouth. It would be too long and useless to tell all here. I must be brutally frank and say that I can give you nothing that you deserve. You have come too late in my life. I am unfortunate—not by your fault, I hasten to say— and if I could have foreseen that our love would have become what it is to-day, I think I should have fled. Besides, you must remember how long I resisted? Yet I regret nothing, I shall always have the remembrance of the exquisite joys given and taken. But there is no future for us. All you write to me is just and sensible and when you say, "you will not continue like that," I have only to bow my head. I have nothing to say. You are right.

I ought to have been stronger and not have succumbed, but your eyes were too beautiful; your lips, rosy and moist, too sweet; your passion caused mine to grow. I took you and chanced it. It was so lovely. I say I took you. I do not say I hold you now, and yet you are mine, despite that I love you too religiously to profit by your delicious weakness and make you a woman. That word "religiously" may not match the rest of my letter, but you will understand what I mean—what passes through my brain. And if I am forced to disappear to-morrow from your life, even by your orders, you will always be mine for your whole life, in spite of yourself, free or married, by the sheer strength of the feelings I excite in you. Therefore; fly from me, for I have nothing to offer you but a little sensual pleasure and that is not enough. Leave me alone with my wasted life. It will be better for both of us.

This letter is vague. Will you be able to make head or tail of it? What is the "horrible sentence" of my poor letter? Have I said anything horrible to you . . . whose soul I martyrise?

Have you never guessed how I always struggled against your fascination? How many times have I regretted a night I refused at Sonis—do you recollect? I feared to compromise you. Yet had I been more selfish? That lost night! . . . what a fool I was!

You told me: "I often go to Paris now." Is that true, or only to teaze me? You often liked to vex me by telling me little things which were not true, to laugh at my amazement afterwards.

Can I see you? anywhere you like . . . to talk to you an hour or less, between two trains . . . if it is true that you often come to Paris. I ask nothing of you. I no longer speak as master. I am a wretch and a coward!

I have nothing of you as a *souvenir*, not even your photograph. Your letters are not mine, but your property. I want to give them back to you. I have nothing but a little bit of pink ribbon.

J. S.

The foregoing letter I have copied from some rough notes which I happened to keep. I think I wrote more than what is set down here. I alluded to my age and said that marriage was impossible between a man of 46 and a girl of 22. I also concluded very erotically, asking her to meet me at night in the darkness of the country lanes at Sonis, while her Pa was in London during the remainder of the month.

The general effect of my letter was to show her that I could not possibly carry on our connection any more, as I could see that she wanted something advantageous—money or marriage; and infatuated though I was, it slowly dawned upon me that Miss Arvel did not want Jacky, if Jacky was poor. At the same time, I was careful not to blame her in any way, but heaped reproaches on my own head.

I had no answer. I did not expect she would reply when I wrote. I bore up manfully against the blow, for which however, I was slightly prepared by her silence during the preceding month, and, being so much troubled in every way in Paris, I began to get used to the buffetings of the world. One wound more or less, what does it matter when you are fighting, and getting the worst of every round?

She could only have written in one way and that would have

been to say: "I want to see you at once," and she should have appeared and cried in my arms and proved her love for me in a thousand pretty ways. Luckily for me, she did nothing of the sort. She was not one of the crying kind, being too selfish and hard-hearted. She never wept for me.

I think as far as a man can judge himself, that I really felt an immense love for her, of an intensely sensual kind at that moment. I will not tell what thoughts filled my racked brain at this juncture, but had she sought me out, she might have done what she liked with me. But it must have been at once; every day took me farther from her. She did not know her power then, and I may as well say frankly that she never regained it. She did not really care for me, save as stepping-stone to get over part of the torrent of life dryshod.

On the 6th. of December, I received a small envelope, bearing the Sonis postmark. It contained a little portrait of Mademoiselle Arvel, about the size of a postage-stamp. This had been torn off her railway season ticket, which I suppose she was now renewing.

It was in answer to the last part of my letter of "adieu." I supposed that she wished to begin with me again, so I sent the following note which I candidly confess I wrote with great care and sincerity.

JACKY TO LILIAN.

Paris, December 7th. 1898.

My dear little Lilian,

I am very perplexed. I do not know if it will please you or not to receive a few lines from me, as I ignore what you may have thought of my last letter, written about the seventeenth of November.

As far as I can recollect . . . it is nearly a month ago! . . . and the time seems so long to me. . . . I wrote then a few sentences a little too lascivious. I do not ask you to excuse or to pardon me, for I sent that letter under the influence of a species of fever, combined with lust. And I am sure you have understood and if you are vexed with me it is not for that. Therefore I am going to be calm and reasonable, and as brief as possible. As you have not answered me, I think it may perhaps bore you to receive a letter from me, but I shall soon know that by this very simple sign: if you do not reply, that will mean that Miss Arvel informs me that my little daughter is dead. Indeed, when the 26th. of November passed without news of her, my heart went into mourning. It is true that I am so unhappy, covered with so many wounds, so to speak, that a new grief, a fresh wound, cannot increase my sufferings much. For me only the worst happens.

See what a wretched position I am in, in front of you. If I complain, that will seem to you perhaps ridiculous on the part of a man. If I show temper, you will say I am spiteful because you will not see or write to me. If I sulk and do not write to you, you will think (and rightly too), that we ought to be at least polite and always answer a note, especially when corresponding with those we love and esteem. But it is all over between us two. Our love has gone with the summer sun, with all that was joy and pleasure. Now the cold winds blow. All is frozen. Winter is here.

Let me get done: the real motive of my letter . . . which is probably tiresome for you . . . is to thank you a thousand times for having sent me the portrait of my little daughter, so adored, so desired, who will never come to my arms again, since she is no more. I can see her prettier than on that photograph, because I love to remember her features when she smiled, her mouth half open, her lips all moist, and her beautiful Spanish eyes lighted up and sparkling, laughing. Then she was truly beautiful. Poor child! I loved her well.

It is a good and charming movement coming from the bottom of your little heart that has made you send me that portrait, and I recognise your usual kindness.

I dare not ask you news of your health, nor of your brother, nor of Blackamoor, because I do not want you to think that I use tricky means to drag a few lines out of you.

I ask for nothing; I want nothing of you out of pity or charity.

I think I have already told you (an old foreign snob like me has the privilege of repeating himself a little), that I detested the idea of two persons who love each other, or who have loved, doing composition, or sending ironical letters, making bitter-sweet sentences, etc. If I write to you it is purely and simply without any after-thought to have the pleasure of chatting with you from afar.

A strange idea has just come into my brain . . . (you know my peculiar imagination? All this pleased you once. Why have you changed? Mystery!—which I shall try to clear up.)

"Mademoiselle Arvel had a little sister, Lily, who loved me. She is dead. I called her my daughter. When poor Lily died, her big sister, who knew of our *liaison*, found a photograph of her, and sent it to me. She died towards the end of September."

I assure you I loved her well.

J. S.

My bookselling friend in Rotterdam was evidently pleased with my efforts in correcting "The Horn Book," for he now took the liberty of sending me another long and very obscene manuscript to correct and send through the press for him.

It was called, "The Double Life of Cuthbert Cockerton," and strange to say, was principally about incestuous love between a father and daughter.

This book necessitated a lot of correction, and Vanderpunk insisted upon me adding a few words to the preface, and I did so, with the thought of my love Lily, now dead to me, running through my poor brain. (*See Appendix B.*)

END OF VOLUME I

II

1

Amour, fléau du monde, exécrable folie;
. . . .
Si jamais, par les yeux d'une femme sans cœur,
Tu peux m'entrer au ventre et m'empoisonner l'âme,
Ainsi que d'une plaie on arrache une lame,
Plutôt que comme un lâche on me voie en souffrir,
Je t'en arracherai, quand j'en devrais mourir.
                                    ALFRED DE MUSSET.

I have already said that my health had been bad, and that I had great difficulty in getting over my sharp attack of rheumatism of the spring. The treatment at Lamalou had pulled me down exceedingly and after the course of baths of boiling water, I returned to Paris in a state of mental and bodily fatigue.

That is why I had fallen an easy prey to Lilian, and I had not struggled against the fearful longing I felt for her; nor had I troubled to reason with myself. My brain was dulled. In September, I had enjoyed long bicycle rides in the country, and I now began to experience the benefit of the waters I had taken. I was light and gay, without a pain, and my sweet invalid companion also had a brief respite, in this gloomy fag-end of November and beginning of December.

I carried on now a pretty intrigue with a new flame, and the

179

lady in question was such a curious person that I think she deserves to be lightly sketched in this my little book, which, started in summer, sylvan retirement, as a rapid review of a love-affair, is fast growing into a stout work of salacious confessions.

THE STORY OF A SLAVE.

I dined at the house of a French friend, a married man. I was introduced to a lady, who I had never seen in that house before. She was rather goodlooking, but a trifle too stout, of Oriental style, like a fine, fat Jewess. She was about thirty, and had two children. Her husband was a manufacturer, and lived in the north of France. She was alone in Paris for a few days, I forget now for what reason. Louise, as I shall call her, seemed to like to laugh and joke with me, and sat down to the piano, and played for me and to me. She was a splendid performer and was very well educated. The little party broke up early, and as Madame Louise made out that she was not at her ease in Paris alone at night, I offered to be her cavalier and take her home to her hotel. I was accepted, and we left together. We were soon friends, and I prevailed upon her to walk with me instead of riding, and by dint of persuasion, got her to go to a *café* with me.

She talked of her home in the country and of the difficulty of getting good servants. I told her jokingly to whip them to make them obedient and that many women, whether domestics or ladies, liked to be chastised. It was a lucky hit of mine, as she would not let the subject of flagellation drop, and after a little fencing, I elicited from her that she dreamt daily and nightly of the joy of being a slave to a man she would love. Louise would never have gone so far if she did not want me to make love to her, and at last she promised to meet me in Paris the next afternoon.

Then she really became my chattel, a most docile toy, and she came to Paris every month or so, and scarcely ever failed to meet me. I hear from her now occasionally, and our adventures together would make a most entertaining volume. But I have only introduced her here, to give the translation of some of her letters, which will enable the reader to guess what Louise wanted, and which

I knew well how to manage. I need only add that she was perfectly disinterested, and it may be guessed that this peculiar passion cannot exist among professional beauties.

Master,

The day after I became your slave I wrote you a letter of twelve pages, telling you of my dreams of mad torture, which I made as I desired you to be a thousand times more cruel than you were with me.

Then I reflected, and tried to forget you, and never more return to this kind of voluptuousness. I burnt the letter, and I hoped that you would never write to me; that I might be strong.

But I cannot. I return to you. Do with my body as you will, but my dream is that you should only see in me a slave and naught else; that is to say a creature who you will always cause to suffer cruelly.

I see you now, as in a vision; your eyes with the same expression they had in the cab, forcing me to look at you; telling me so, roughly.

And then, when I come to Paris, you must not receive me in such a rich apartment—for a slave, the vilest place is too good—but at an ordinary hotel. Then you will lunch—I could get to you about eleven o'clock —and I would look on without eating, happy to accept on my knees what you would please to throw me.

You could exact anything from me, forcing me to reply at each command: "Yes, master!"

I must never be allowed to answer in any other manner, and if I forget myself, you will box my ears with great force. You will force me to caress you with my arms bound behind my back, and if I lick you awkwardly, you will flog me on any part of my body; and never, never will you allow me to show any other expression on my features but that of the most absolute tenderness and submission.

Afterwards, you will cause me to approach you, and look, by violently stretching open the lips of my private parts, if I desire you. Should I be wet, you will make me cross my legs, and brutally you will force your fist between my thighs. You will pull my hairs, force me to show you the sign of my sex, and if I am pouring with liquid lust, you will cut me with a riding whip. You will make me wash myself again with the water containing the lump of ice, and you will dip a towel in the frozen liquid and put it on my loins, so as to annihilate my desire.

Should you wish to ejaculate in my mouth, when you are in the bed, you will put me on my knees over you, my back towards you. Thus you will have the pleasure of pinching me, of biting me, or of lashing me, while I shall have your divine instrument in my mouth.

And if I am exhausted by unslacked lust, you will only give way to me when I have begged and prayed for coition, and you will possess me with my arms bound, tortured by a cruel belt that will compress my waist.

You will force your fingers into my slit, which will be thirsting to be filled up by you, and you will command me to fix my eyes upon yours, and with your other hand, you will pinch me, prick me, and scratch me with a needle, for the pleasure of seeing me suffer. I would that you were very, very cruel. Perhaps I shall be free one day next week. I will get to Paris in the morning and go back at six o'clock.

I await your orders, master, and on my knees, I kiss your feet.

Your submissive and devoted slave,

LOUISE.

To-day I desire you madly, and your cruel eyes. Oh! to look at them on my knees, to see them plunged into mine, to feel your hands enter pitilessly into my flesh, hurting and bruising me; brutally taking hold of my leg, dragging down my stockings, and watching your joy increasing, as the needle's point sinks into my quivering body. At each painful stab, I would say: "Thank you, master!"

Oh! to be knocked about, pinched, humiliated and degraded; to see you smile cruelly at my sufferings and kiss you all over, while I should be dying with discomfort in the instruments of torture you showed me; to suffer for you, master,—oh! how I desire you!

I can no longer support the thoughts of you! If you were here I would prostrate myself at your feet and pray you to make me enjoy.

Oh! I will be continent, I promise you; I will do nothing alone. I will wait. I have no will but yours. You forbid masturbation; I will obey. It does me good to write you my insensate longings.

Make me suffer, even from afar. Send me something that I can wear next my skin that will hurt me.

Oh! for my mouth on your naked body, to kiss your feet, and let my tongue touch everywhere! I am mad with lust. My throat is dry, my heart beats and I am all wet. How I long for you! Pardon me, do, my master; I will be so submissive, so tender with you, so obedient to make you forget all my shortcomings. Write to me soon, I supplicate you.

With humility, I lie at your feet, you can walk on me. And I shall still say: "Thank you!" I kiss the darling feet that stamp upon me, and also your dear hands that hurt me.

I kiss your whole body, my respected master. Oh! if I could always be frightened of you, as I was the other day beneath the gaze of your cruel eyes.

I want to be frightened of you always; you must be wicked and cruel; your only joy must be to make me suffer without ceasing.

You must make me come myself as you order me on my knees, to receive a flogging, if you so desire it.

I am your thing, your bitch, your submissive slave.

LOUISE.

You must do what you told me on my next visit to Paris: put me on my knees before you, my eyes turned to yours; the vase beneath my chin, and splash my face, my lips, my cheeks, with your hot urine, amusing yourself all the time by hurting me, and always exacting a tender and submissive look in my eyes.

It is so difficult for me to support your gaze, when it is hard and cruel, as it was last night beneath the glare of the electricity.

I wish to see your small hand gently prick my flesh with your scarf pin; and revel in your awful joy, as you see my blood, and then force me to pour vinegar upon the wound.

You will allow me, will you not, master, to suffer through you, and for you?

Pardon me for having tried to escape from your influence. I come back to you, more tender, more humble, more submissive than before. Do to me whatever you please.

You will see, master, all my efforts to satisfy you, so that your joy may be complete so that you may permit me to kiss your hand. The traces of your hands are still on my flesh, my arm is still black and blue.

Pardon me my bad writing. Next time, I will strive to make my writing more legible, but to-day I am too nervous, I hunger too much for you.

If you wish it, if it will please you that I read the books you told me about, I will do so with joy. But I should wish that all you do be for your desire and your caprice, and not to be agreeable to me.

The only reward of a slave is that her loved and respected master should find her worthy to suffer for him and for his pleasure.

I will try also not to think of myself when I talk to you. I will only think of making your pleasure slow and perfect.

I will try and support pain with a tender and submissive look, and my face shall show pleasure whatever I feel, so as to please you, and not have the hard and sulky expression, for which you so rightly whipped my bottom the other day.

You should be still more exacting; very severe, very cruel, to form me for your taste, and make me sweetly tender, docile, and obedient, punishing me each time I give way to my lust; and driving it out of my frame by dint of suffering.

Let me only think of you; only dream of you; let me only look at you; let my eyes, like those of a fawning, loving cur, never leave your eyes; let them never look elsewhere; nothing should make them turn away from you, when I am in your dear presence.

I am very sensitive about the hair. You must order me to let it down, and then comb it out, pulling it roughly, until the tears come in my eyes, and if I weep, punish me for my silly sensibility. You will do that, will you not? I wish to suffer for you, my desired master.

Have you not dreamt worse sufferings than these?

If so, will you kindly tell me of them, so that I may think of the suffering in reserve for me, and get my mind used to fresh divine torture.

Do not forget your little riding-whip. Shall I bring one myself?

If I had my own way, this letter would never be done, but it would end by wearying you. I finish here regretfully. To write to you is a great joy for me.

I place my head beneath your feet, which I feel on my face, crushing my cheeks with your boot heels. I feel your hand twisting and tearing my flesh; then you pinch me. I feel your hand smartly slapping both cheeks, while I am on my knees, my arms strapped tightly behind me. I feel the stinging lash of your whip cutting into my flesh at long intervals, so as to make your pleasure last longer, and tears roll down my cheeks, in spite of all my efforts, as, to punish me for loving you too much, you tear off the hair that hides my sex. Each time I must say to you: "Thank you, master!" If I forget, your dear hand shall slap my face, as hard as it can strike, and always my eyes are fixed on yours: softly, tenderly, and submissively. I am your enduring obedient slave,

LOUISE.

This new passion did not prevent me nursing my poor Lily at home, and working at my chemical inventions, while I took as much exercise as I could in the open air. I seemed to get younger and gayer, as I would leave my bed as early as possible, and stride merrily along, drunk with the lightness of the pure morning air, my good old Smike careering joyfully round me.

Good health means gaiety, and my greatest trouble was the beggarly lightness of my banking account, now that my poor invalid seemed a trifle better.

Now and again, I thought of the Lily of Sonis, and I felt that there was something very strange in her conduct.

I had said in my last letter to her that I would try to elucidate the mystery, and having, as I expected, no answer, I began to ask myself what steps I ought to take to unravel the puzzle. All my old powers of reasoning, that I thought I had left for ever in my bed of pain, came gradually back to me, and I saw that Mademoiselle Arvel had no real tenderness for me.

I had never read her letters over again, although I had often said to myself that I would do so. I had them all, as I have given them here, dated, and tied up in a bundle.

One afternoon, my new mistress, Louise, failed to keep an appointment, and having a moment to myself, I got the packet of Lilian's letters out of a drawer of my desk, and read them all carefully through, one by one.

Then I began to vaguely sketch in my mind all the little criticisms that I have spread over these pages, and I found the explanation of many things she had said to me and which I had let pass at the time.

When she told me that rigmarole story about the fifty francs, supposed to have come from Madame Muller, and how she wrote to her Mamma in Normandy, that she had got some money, and had paid a bill with it, without showing any papers to her vigilant parent, I had smelt a rat. But I was so stupid in my blind passion, that my suspicions did not take a proper shape, until I reflected upon the letter of the 26th. of April, wherein she said that she had written to me on her return to Paris from the South, and that the letter had been probably mislaid.

I jumped to the conclusion that when she denied having received the unregistered missive, containing the fifty-franc note, she was telling a deliberate lie.

When she came to lunch with Lord Fontarcy and myself in Paris, she expected more than she got. She evidently hoped for some present from my friend. When I sent the money, torn from me by a threat, she was disgusted at the smallness of the sum, and never acknowledged it, nor wrote to me from London.

Then, when I dropped her a line five weeks afterwards, which was weak on my part, she got me invited to Sonis, and to excuse her fault, she worked the missing letter dodge again.

Two missing letters in ten months! She lied.

When I first made love to her and offered her caresses without danger of pregnancy, she answered that she would want "something else," i.e. money.

After our first meeting in November, 1897, when she left me at the railway station, I noticed her uneasy look. She was thinking of the five pounds she said she had lost in London, and was no doubt saying to herself: "Is he not going to give me something?"

Laugh at me, kind reader, if it so please you, but at that time I should not have dared to have offered her money.

When I write and tell her my grief at being suspected of paltry mendacity, she replies immediately that she is ready to marry me. She would have no hesitation in linking her existence to a blackguard who would lie to a woman for two sovereigns.

I could only find one excuse for her. She suffers from anæmia or chlorosis. There is evidently psychopathic deterioration, and she is a neurotic subject.

Masturbation and unnatural practices before the age of puberty have produced neurasthenia with its attendant symptoms. It is a clear case of hysteria.

No doubt she had been often received in her mother's bed, and Arvel had played with her as a mere child. The mother shut her eyes to his behaviour, finding that his passion for her daughter kept him at home.

She cooked for him, and allowed her girl to romp with him. Here is the explanation of the door of communication being taken down between the two rooms.

Raoul has also had funny little games with his sister. As children, Arvel encouraged them. Now that Lilian is a woman, he becomes jealous of the lad. They were not always well off, and pigged together in one small lodging. And Charlotte, who sleeps with both sister and brother in turn? When they are all three in London, what barriers of shame can exist between them? and, to cap all, when Papa is in England with both girls and no mother by, what goes on then?

No wonder Mamma was jealous of her daughter at the beginning of the summer.

And Lilian's lie to me is easy to explain. On the eleventh of November she is in the heighth of her flow. She has a fit of weeping, a mental and emotional sign of irritability and instability, impairing her integrity, and rendering an unbalanced individual like this morbid girl, capable of any villany while in such an emotional state.

If she were still a virgin, she would not be long before she got penetrated by the male, and perhaps the work was being done as I wrote these lines, at the end of November, 1898.

All the best and most sacred part of my love was gone. Lust alone remained. The idea of her being the mistress of her mother's old lover still excited me. I bow my head, as I confess that the thought of this loathsome *liaison* stirred up my secret erotic longings, even as the plan of the visit to a brothel might inflame a man of tranquil spirit. He knows that he is going there to choose a mercenary, common female who will give him an imitation of love for a few coins. It is disgusting, and he is well aware of it, but he goes there all the same. He is sensually excited and that is enough for him.

So I felt with regard to Lily, but I was saved, as I began to judge her, and what was better, I judged myself.

I felt strong, and proof against her wiles, or any future lies, for what harm can come to a man from wicked, womanly intrigues, when he despises himself and has no vanity for the sirens to play upon?

But I never forgot this particular lie of Lilian's. I may pardon her perhaps some day, for who and what am I, that I should refuse to forgive a neurasthenic woman? but forget it—never!

Immediately before and immediately after the advent of her "courses," her sentiment of actual desire would doubtless increase, as she had caused me to be invited just on the day when she was menstruating. She was no longer unwell on the 25th. or 27th., but had jumped to the middle of the month.

Last year, I had sent Papa and Mamma a parcel of smoked fish. On the 8th. of December 1898, I repeated my little attention, and on the 12th., the post brought me this note, which is dated the 10th., and bears the postmark of the following day.

LILIAN TO JACKY.

Sonis-sur-Marne, December 10th. 1898.

My dear M. S . . . ,

We have just received a parcel of delicious fish. Naturally, we suppose that it is you, who according to your charming custom, have had that delicate attention, for nobody but you could show himself so amiable in everything.

Mamma begs me to be her interpreter with you, so as to thank you, and charges me to tell you that she would have been very happy to have you for lunch and dinner, but she will not bore you beyond measure with the society of two women, knowing well that it is preferable that Papa should be there to receive you better. Therefore, we put off the pleasure of having you amongst us until the return of Papa.

Mamma joins me in begging you to accept the assurance of our sincere friendship,

LILIAN ARVEL.

Here is news of her during menstruation, or when she is due; a sure sign of nervous, psychic trouble, for this note came exactly a month after her last "turn."

I did not write, as it would have been uncalled for, and I heard nothing of Lilian until the morning of Boxing Day.

LILIAN TO JACKY.

Sonis-sur-Marne, December 25th. 1898.

Dear Mr. S . . . ,

We hope you have spent a Merry Christmas and that the New Year may bring with it the realisation of your wishes.

We have Monsieur and Madame Poqui, "local residents," to dine with us to-morrow, Monday night. They are very simple people. The lady is an excellent pianist. Will you come down in the afternoon to go for a walk and dine with us? There will be no ceremony or dress. "Dog clothes" allowed.

Papa brought you over some tobacco and a thousand matches.

With every good wish, believe me to remain,

Yours very sincerely,
LOUISE ARVEL.

DECEMBER 26, 1898.

According to French custom, I was bound at this festive time of year to give presents down at the Villa Lilian, where I had partaken of so many meals, so I bought for Mamma: a jar, or tea-caddy, of Dresden porcelain, with a silver-gilt screw top, filled with tea, and for Lilian: a small, ancient looking-glass, or hand mirror, with solid silver frame and handle, of the Louis XV. epoch.

I went in answer to the invitation, carrying with me the presents, which comprised both Christmas and New Year's obligations.

I was affectionately greeted by Mamma, and Lilian soon appeared, called down by her parent to receive her present.

She was very pleased to see me, I was sure of it, as I watched her narrowly. She had taken a little trouble with her toilette, and her face was thickly powdered, while she had reddened her lips. This was new to me.

She looked older and bolder, but as I greeted her, she seemed very confused and turned red and white by turns. Her hands trembled a little. She did not speak very plainly, being all of a heap, and in her excitement, she said:

"What a long time it is since we have seen you! You never honour us with your presence now."

"I come when I am invited! Here is a little friend I have brought you."

"I want no little friends!"

"But this is a friend who will always tell you the truth, after a few moments' reflection. As I know you love truth, and detest lies —here is a mirror for you! And I wish you a happy new year!"

She reciprocated my wishes, and was delighted with my gift. But she said very little, and the more gay and lively I was, the duller she became.

I went for a walk with the father. When I returned, she fetched me, pretexting that she wanted me to come and help her to get linen out for the dinner-table from Mamma's cupboard in the best bedroom, and we were alone.

I was indifferent. I kept a watch on myself and found I did not have the same desire that I formerly felt whenever I was near her, breathing the same atmosphere.

Seeing me so nonchalant, she began to show a little temper, and in return to some cool remark of mine, made use of a very coarse exclamation, amounting to: "I don't care a damn!"

I replied that I had nothing to say in answer to such talk, and to annoy me, and probably excite my jealousy, she told me that she had a customer who was going to give her a ring.

"A customer, eh?" I replied. "Male or female?"

"A lady, of course! Customers often give presents. Lolotte had one given to her."

"I know such things are often done in the Rue de la Paix, but then the girls who get the presents are forced to suck the ladies who are so generous, or let themselves be licked and played with."

"You are a most awful, dirty man, and very impudent to talk to me like this!"

"What does it matter? You have nothing in common with me any more."

"Of course I have not! But I have got a new sweetheart!"

She paused for a reply. None came. I laughed.

"He is an officer—a lieutenant. And through him I shall get favours for my brother. My sweet officer has given me a silver châtelaine."

I congratulated her warmly, and with genuine pleasure. I really did not care for anything she might say to me, true or untrue. Did she think she could arouse the jealousy of the man who had himself handed her naked body over to his friend? Yes, I suppose so. I knew there were men who did not mind infidelities as long as they were committed in their presence. Otherwise, they were jealous. I use the word advisedly, as I can find no other under my pen. I, luckily, had no such mixed feelings. Before abandoning her to Fontarcy, I had put a severe question to myself: "Will you be jealous later? If so, beware, Jacky, of the green-eyed monster."

I answered the small voice of my conscience, as follows:

"Lilian is ambitious and mercenary. She had been perverted before you knew her. Nothing can save her. So amuse yourself with her as long as she lets you, without fear or remorse. She is a perfect toy, for a debauchee like yourself. All you can ask is that she should act honestly with you."

Finding I was not to be drawn out and that nothing she said had the slightest effect on me, she got a little more calm and a trifle kinder, and before going downstairs to the dining-room to lay the cloth with the linen she had got out, I asked her to kiss me. She refused, and then, grave for the first time, I told her I should never ask her again. So she gave me her mouth.

We had some more skirmishing talk in the dining-room, and I told her that it was no use to be so nasty-tempered, as I knew she could not live without me.

Here she pretended to turn up the lamp, and hid her face from me, not answering. I now noticed that whenever she was in a quandary as to what to reply to me, she said nothing. I always interpreted her silence as a hit for me.

"Somebody has been putting me away with you? Perhaps Charlotte has been speaking against me?"

"Oh no, the poor girl!" she replied.

I found that she was redolent with a very powerful, pungent scent, in which musk predominated. In answer to whether it was any of my making, she refused to give me satisfaction, but I at last elicited that it was a mixture of "Le Jardin de Mon Curé" and "ambre." The first-named coming from an expensive house in Paris, I guessed that her new lover or lovers had given it to her.

And as I watched her in the strong light of the two large petroleum lamps lit for dinner, she seemed greatly altered. She was a trifle stouter; her glance was more audacious; she was more womanly. I had not seen her for six weeks, and I could have sworn a great change had taken place.

I went to the cellar with her father, as he was in some difficulty with a padlock below, and wanted me to help him. As I was
going down, she called out in French:

"Mr. S . . . , do you like going down to the cellar?"

Now this was a bawdy slang term for the lingual caress, as applied to a woman's private parts. "Going down to her": under her
petticoats, or beneath the bedclothes. A similar phrase is: "doing
the little photographer," in allusion to the disappearance of an
operator's head under the black cloth of the camera. Recently the
young men of Paris call it, "going down to the cream shop."

I was so astonished at hearing her say this quite loudly before
her stepfather, that I could only turn round and stand stock-still on
the steps, looking up at her, as I gasped out: "No!"

When I returned, I asked if she knew the meaning of what
she had said.

"Of course I do!"

"Who taught you that? You never learnt it from me?"

"Never mind who it was!"

"Does he do it nicely?"

"Beautifully!"

"Then you are no longer a virgin?"

She fired up at this. The blue-black cloud overspread her features, and she looked ghastly through her powder.

"You are an insolent fellow. I certainly am, just the same as
ever!"

Poor Lilian, I am afraid, betrayed herself by the expression of
temper that always showed in her face when I was right. I felt certain that she was no longer a maid.

"Does your Papa know the meaning of what you said?" I
continued.

"If he does, he will never dream I do. That is why I said it."
And to change the conversation: "Do you know I am not going to
Nice this year but shall remain here alone with Granny? Pa and
Ma leave on the tenth of January."

I now began to use the same tactics as she did. When embarrassed, I found it easy not to speak, and so I let the statement of
her being alone at home go by, without the observations that she
doubtless thought it would bring forth.

After some more desultory chaff, she asked me:

"Do you want to sit next to me at dinner?"

"No!" I replied coolly.

But she placed me next to her all the same, and I told her during the soup to put her foot on mine and keep it there. She did so, and seemed pleased, merry, and happy to be with me.

The table was a square one, and we sat at the end, where there was just room for two. She was on my right. On her right was Papa. Whenever she could, she caught hold of my hand and made motions imitating the act of masturbation on my fingers, and I tried to follow her example by copying the same caress on her palm or between her digits. I was perfectly certain that Mr. Arvel saw part of our play. She was very excited and knocked my glass over.

She could not finish all her plum-pudding, and for fear of her mother, who had made it, asked her father to change plates with her. He refused, and finally I took her plate and finished her slice, under her father's eyes. In fact, we behaved like lovers, quite openly.

During the meal, Papa got into a towering rage with the servants, and bawled out his remonstrances in a strident voice, as he half rose from his chair, as if he would leave his place to go to them.

Lilian rose too, and placing her hand on his portly paunch, said to him in English:

"Don't be silly, darling!"

I thought this rather strange, as she had never addressed him in this way before me, especially as Mamma, so jealous, I was led to believe, knew what "darling" meant. I kept this to myself for many months.

Lilian distributed little bits of holly, fixing one in my button-hole herself, to bring luck during the next year. The withered remains of my sprig are stuck in an ornament on my mantelpiece.

As I write, I look up and see it, just upon a year afterwards. I have had no luck these twelve months. So I rise and throw the darkened, prickly leaves, and discoloured stalk and berries in the fire. They curl up and turn black, even as Lily's lips, when I aroused her anger; and then they disappear, even as Lily's lips.

After everyone has their holly, I produce a branch of mistletoe, and whisper to Lilian that I am going to kiss every woman at the table. I knew this coarse, commercial traveller's joke would be properly appreciated at Sonis.

Lily flies into a towering rage again, and under her breath tells me that if I kiss her mother, she will never speak to me again in her life. Strange jealousy! I do not insist. I did not wish to kiss her old grandmother, nor her Mamma, nor the lady guest.

During dessert, when she condescends to prepare me an orange, she again tries to make me jealous, by telling me that she had been a great deal to Paris lately, and had been to some theatres. I took all she said quite coolly and told her one or two plays I had seen. Then I asked her what pieces she had witnessed, but she dropped that subject quickly. I did not believe her. Her little trick was to try and invent stories that she thought would teaze and annoy me, and above all excite my jealousy.

I felt quite a different man with her. I was entirely at my ease and watched her well, listening calmly to all her statements. I had great command over myself now, and I could divine all her deceit, and began at last to study and know her, even as I knew myself. Analysis, alas! is death to sentiment.

When the guests were gone, she asked me to go out alone with her and the dogs. Her parents consented. This was absolutely the first time that she had left the villa alone with me at night. She spoke up boldly too, as if mistress of the house. I noticed all these changes, and made up my mind to get to the bottom of all the hidden vice of the villa, if I could. This resolution excited me strangely. I felt like a kind of sensual Sherlock Holmes.

We went out, and I walked with her in the lonely, frosty roads.

"Put your arm round me. And now hold me tight. Feel my back and shoulders. Pinch my arms. Take me. Be nice and rough."

I obeyed her behests and she pressed herself against me, cooing and purring, as in the old days. But I did not have the old sensation of pleasure. I felt some slight upheaval of my innate salacious being, but not as I once did. And a great feeling of bitterness came over me, as I thought of the lie of the lost letter, and what trouble I had had to gather the money together to keep my poor invalid in comfort in Paris, and how this black, lascivious lass had treated me for the last three months.

Lilian now broke the silence, by using the little phrase with which she had so often teazed me when we were together:

"You hurt me!"

"I adore hurting you. But if I hurt you, take it in your hand yourself, and stop it if it goes in too far."

She rubbed against me like a cat, with a little mewing laugh at this recollection.

The more caressing she got, the more my bitterness increased, and I spoke out, surprised at the sound of my own voice, hoarse with suppressed rage, which she did not guess at, astonished at the courage I had to talk so plainly. A few months ago, I should never have dared to be so veracious and categorical, whatever she might have done.

JACKY. But why do you treat me so strangely? Why didn't you write to me, or try to see me. You do not love me. No power on earth can stop a woman communicating with the man she really loves. Why even your fraternal love is stronger than the feeling you have for me. What could prevent you seeing or writing to your brother?

LILIAN. Oh, I don't care for him.

JACKY. Then who do you love? No one? (No answer.) It is true you never said outright to me: "I love you!"

LILIAN But the other woman has everything, and I have nothing.

JACKY. Don't talk about her, please. She is very ill. Her heart is touched. She may live perhaps only a few months, perhaps years, no one can tell. But she is always suffering and sometimes—as you want me to tell you everything—her limbs are swollen until they are as big as yonder post. Do you want any more details? (No answer.) Do you want me to leave her?

LILIAN. No, it is your duty to look after her. You have had her youth, as you would have mine.

An answer was on my lips. I could have asked her what she was doing with her youth, and to whom she had given her flower. I could have demanded details, concerning the mystery of her life, and what strange feeling of misplaced pride had caused her to give way to the senile passion of her mother's old love? But I resolved not to touch upon that topic as yet. I studiously avoided alluding to Mr. Arvel any more. I had something else to tell her before that. I was sensible enough to know that I should have had no satisfaction, but on the contrary, she would have been on her guard against me, and perhaps warned Papa that I was too far-seeing. More evidence was what I wanted, and I resolved to wait for it. I did not care if what I was going to say would widen the breach between us for ever. I was quite prepared for her to tell me that all was over between us, and I behaved and spoke as a man would when seeking the rupture of a *liaison*.

JACKY. I want to say something to you. I wish to speak plainly, and you must promise me that whatever I may say you will not be offended. And after all, if you are, what matters it? I shall then only be in the same position as I was this morning. In spite of all you have ever said or written to me, you do not love me. All you care for is money; the money you think I ought to give you. Whether I have got it or not, does not matter to you. You are mercenary. I told you I had nothing but my love, and that was clearly not enough for you, and so you never answered my last letters, proving that you did not want to see me, without I gave you money.

LILIAN. You only wrote a lot of foolishness. And if I did not write, it was because you told me not to.

JACKY. That is a lie! I said: "If you do not write, I shall know you have had enough of me." Read my letters again. And even if I had said so, I am going to be fool enough to tell you what you ought to have written—if you really loved me: "I want to see you. I don't care what you have written. Come to me, for I want to see you soon. Be of good heart, for I love you."

LILIAN. But you want everything and give nothing in return. I am not mercenary.

JACKY. That is not true. You are. I'll prove it. I could not fathom your conduct up to now, but I have just done so. Listen to me. I am not intelligent—

LILIAN. Yes, you are.

JACKY. No, I am not. I am slow at seeing things, but I remember, and think them over, and put two and two together; and by analysis and deduction I find out the truth, even as I have now got the key to your mysterious conduct of the past month. I know you now. That is why I brought you a looking-glass. I can see all, as though in a mirror. Every move you make has a motive of venality.

LILIAN. (*Quite off her balance now.*) You don't understand! You have wrong ideas of me! You are strange! You are unjust!

JACKY. Then tell me what you want. (*No answer.*) You would not come to Paris where we used to go any more. Shall I take a furnished apartment at about a hundred and fifty francs a month?

LILIAN. No.

JACKY. Will you come if I promise you five louis for every visit to me in Paris?

(*Here she did a thing I had never noticed in a woman before. She turned away from me and twisted her body as if I had a whip in my hand, writhing as if I had struck her.*)

LILIAN. Oh! no! no! I don't want that!

JACKY. Then tell me what you are driving at. Marriage? That you've asked me for twice. I'm 46, going on for 47. In four or five years I shall be used up, good for nothing. You'll be in your prime, and I shall be done for, perhaps a querulous, rheumatic invalid. I am a prisoner. Can't you see that? You should be kind to a man in prison.

LILIAN. All men are free, or should make themselves so. You have no consideration for me or my feelings.

JACKY. Untrue again. Whatever I may be, I have been loyal to you. You made the first advances. I have not seduced you. You set your cap at me. Is that a lie? (*No answer.*) You know that I should never have dared to take a liberty with the daughter of the house, where I was a guest, unless I had plainly seen that she wanted me. I have long since proved to you that I desired you two years before you thought of me, and I kept my lust hidden. Had I been the traitor you try to make me out, this is what I could have done, and take heed of what I am going to say, as it applies to all men. (*I caught hold of her by the arm and tried to see her face, but she kept her features averted from my searching gaze and bent her head upon her breast. To make her hear me, I had to bend my head too.*) This will be useful to you: beware of men who promise much. Let me suppose that this summer I had promised you all kinds of things for the end of the year—marriage, money, and God knows what! Then I could have said: "Now let me have you entirely." Believing in me as you do, and though you often lie to me you know I have always been truthful to you, have I not?

LILIAN. Yes.

JACKY. Well, I could have taken your maidenhead, perhaps got you in the family way, and gone away laughing at you and all your people. (*There was no reply to this. She bent her head still more, and dragged herself away from me, writhing strangely as she spoke.*)

LILIAN. But this is my position. I am a milliner. It is supposed down here that I am carrying on this trade merely as a pleasant occupation until I get married. I have talent and taste. I know I have. Here I hardly make headway. I can't get workgirls or fresh customers. I have to give a hundred francs a month to Father for my keep. (*The last time she told me this, the sum was a hundred and fifty. And Papa had just told me in the afternoon that he had given her a purse with silver mounts and five louis in it for a Christmas present. This did not look as if she was paying for her board now, whatever she may have done up to this winter. The word "darling" would not be so lovingly applied to a grasping Papa.*) He gives Mother only a hundred francs a week to keep house. It is not enough for five mouths and all the dogs. Besides, he is a great glutton and wants everything of the finest and well served. He does not care a straw for me or my future. I know I please men generally and I could marry to-morrow if I liked (?), but I could never act the part of a loving wife to a man I did not care about. My stomach rises at the very thought. I want to go and live in Paris, and start a millinery business in a little apartment of my own. My parents won't help me. When I came to Paris this summer to you, and brought back the money you gave me, supposed to be the bad debt coming in from Madame Muller, they received me with open arms, and asked no questions. But when I returned from you and your English friends empty-handed, there was an awful row, and Mother was going herself with me to see the lady I was supposed to have spent the day with.

JACKY. Which reminds me that I thoroughly believe you had that letter of mine with the money in it, but being angry at having to worry me for it, and thinking too that it was not enough, you never acknowledged it. Later, when I asked you about it, to get out of it all, you denied having received the letter. That was a lie.

She did not seem astonished at this accusation, but looked quite dazed and replied softly: "What ugly ideas you have of me!"

JACKY. But you can't go and live alone in Paris. You might perhaps carry on a business, if you were to go home and sleep at your mother's every night, but otherwise your reputation would be damned. People would talk, and ask your concierge, and he would say that you were all alone, and that there was an Englishman who often came and stopped late, and so on.

LILIAN. But I know a girl who is in business all alone, and no one speaks against her. I could not go backwards and forwards, as the work must be ready for the girls at seven A.M., and sometimes they work until eleven at night. You don't or won't understand me.

JACKY. All this sounds very fantastical to me. I don't understand it at all. And I can do nothing for you in this matter. I have nothing for you. It is all too strange.

LILIAN. It is you who are strange and unjust. I am very unhappy at vegetating down here and I worry and fret when I think of you!

JACKY. (*With surprise.*) What! Poor little Lily, does she really think about me sometimes?

LILIAN. I shall be in Paris to-morrow evening at five P.M. I have to see a customer. I have many customers in Paris now.

This was a lie to teaze me and make me jealous, and to confirm my opinion, I try the following proposition:

"I will come and meet you at the station."

LILIAN. (*Quickly.*) Suppose you do? How much better off will you be? What good will that do you?

JACKY. No good at all, but I should see you for a few minutes. As you don't care about it, I will not trouble you.

We were now home again, and nothing more definite had been said. I bade good bye to her mother, who gave me a lump of pudding to take away, and Lilian and her father accompanied me to the station. Mademoiselle was very quiet, and looked embarrassed, but caressed me furtively on the way. My plain words had evidently been a surprise for her. It was half-past twelve; time for the last train.

I can see myself now standing on top of the steep steps that led to the bridge conducting to the up platform. Papa and his Lilian looking up at me, as I wave my hand to them. She gazes at me with a look of wonder and puzzled wistfulness in her large eyes. I turn away with a feeling of pity and sadness for her. She does not know me, and does not possess any delicate feelings, and the advice that her Papa will give her will never be conducive to her benefit.

I returned home with the impression that she would no longer have any wish to see me again. I was glad I had found the courage to speak plainly. How many men would have dared to tell a woman they desired anything that might cause them to lose her? I supposed she would send for me, if she wanted me, and if she did not, so much the better for me; it would be a worry the less, for considering the slight amount of sensual satisfaction I got at rare intervals, it was not worth while associating with the semi-incestuous couple.

I had to write to Papa the next day about a bitch he had ready to whelp—more in-breeding!—and to send to his *bureau*, in the Rue Vissot, a box of writing-paper for Lilian, which I had promised her as far back as the famous 11th. of November, but which I could not get from the maker. I had two boxes made. One was for my Lilian at home. It was fancy dark blue note, with the name of Lilian in the corner, embossed in white.

Mr. Arvel knew about the paper and I think he knew a little more.

I determined I would not make the slightest move towards her.

My lady readers will be very angry with me, and tell me I expected too much, having been cruel, really quite too awfully cruel, morally, to a poor little girl, whose only crime was that she wanted to get on in the world, and how could she do that, unless she got somebody to help her—lover or husband?

To which I reply that had Miss Arvel been a poor little milliner, living alone in one small room, working truly for her daily bread, depending on the caprice of her employers, I should have befriended her to the utmost, and moved heaven and earth to make her comfortable. But she had a good home, and everything she wanted, with parents, who whatever their vices, did all they could to sweeten her life, and at any rate kept her off the streets.

I was to be the victim, it seemed. What beasts men are! There was my poor dying companion at home ready to deprive herself of the common necessaries of life if I so willed it; ready to do without her doctors and medecines—unfortunately useless—if my purse was empty, and I was neglecting her, and fencing with this little viper, a living lie, and bad all through, from her tapering heels to the ends of her black tresses.

I ought to have behaved with the same dignity as the year before, when I refused to go to their Christmas dinner, for what had I gleaned? That she was certainly no longer a virgin, and had become her "Papa's" plaything. In answer to my accusation of venality, she simply replied by a description of her commercial projects. There was not a word of womanly tenderness; being so taken by surprise, she had no time to invent any story. For a year, she had the reins loose on her neck. I suddenly woke up, and blurted out my real idea of her disposition. What a surprise it must have been for her!

Like many women of strong passions I have met, she is perfectly hysterical and readily anxious to try all kinds of strange joys, but they never have any idea of truth, or what is right or wrong, or of the flight of time. Everything is muddled in their brain, and they are only fit to be enjoyed, and avoided as much as possible out of bed, or they would lead you to hell. This theory explains her strange proposals: marriage, and going into business with me, etc.

I sent her the box of pretty writing-paper on the 30th. of December. I wrote inside the lid: "1899. A Happy New Year! Never answer any letters."

The same evening, I received a New Year's card, representing a sailor in a boat, with "1899" painted on the bow. In the distance, a brig is rapidly sinking, a perfect wreck, but flying a flag, whereon is inscribed: "1898." In the boat is a large bouquet of lilies. Underneath the picture are the words: "A Good and Happy New Year!" and my charmer had enclosed her father's card, and written thereon, with her own fair hand: "With Mr., Mrs., and Miss Arvel's best wishes."

I really think they would have allowed me to set the girl up in business, or marry her, or anything, as long as there was money hanging to it. I think they would have sold her to me, or shut their eyes, if she was a rich man's mistress. Anything for money. My eyes being open, I found all this very curious and amusing.

2

Even as a botanist only wants one leaf to determine the family to which a plant belongs, even as Cuvier would reconstruct an animal of which he had only a few bones, we can deduce the knowledge of the man in whom we have remarked one single trait of character, especially if the act be a trifling one.

Indeed, for important things, people take precautions, while in trifles, they act according to their natures, without taking the trouble to dissimulate.

SCHOPENHAUER.

ERIC ARVEL TO JACKY.

Sonis-sur-Marne, January 6th. 1899.

My dear Jacky,

Many thanks for your letter, and for all the good wishes it contained. They are heartily reciprocated for you and yours.

We had a funny commencement to our New Year. At about three in the morning, we were woke by our unruly Bordeaux hound, who barked without ceasing. I went downstairs, and found that he had wanted to give us notice that the little bitch put into the warm kitchen with him in a box of her own, had given birth to a litter of puppies to the credit of Blackamoor, who is unmistakably represented. There were six puppies, three of each—one male and one female—the very image of their father The latter pup is dead, but the male remains. The five which live are white, save one—the colour and marking of your Smike— and likely as a female to make a good match for him. Will you come down and see them on Sunday, taking breakfast with us?

Yours very truly,
ERIC ARVEL.

I began the New Year under the impression that Lilian Arvel would cease all communication with me after my frankly brutal speech of Boxing night, and would naturally, or rather, unnaturally, in this case, wean her father from me, as I was more and more convinced that she was the real mistress of the house.

I suppose I must have acknowledged the New Year's card, by a polite note of seasonable greetings, as the above letter shows, and I was quite surprised to guess by what I read that I was still in Lilian's good graces. Had she not told her Pa? or did they still think I was only an old miser; or at any rate, that I had enough for what they wanted, if I would only loosen my purse strings?

It mattered very little to me now. I looked upon the couple as a pleasing puzzle for my concupiscent curiosity to play with, and I resolved to follow up my quarry. I had nothing to lose. My great love was well-nigh dead. The lust still remained, although less. But I felt towards Lilian as a man feels towards any woman who pleases him; he desires her caresses, if he can get them, and if he cannot, he carries his manly cargo into another port.

I noted the success of the in-breeding mania. Here was a daughter of my Smike, covered by her father, and accidentally (?) coupled with her own brother, who is of course by her sire. To crown all, my genial friend wants Smike, the original Adam of the lot, to "line" one of the latest products of this incited canine incest.

It could not but desire to see what fresh developments awaited me out of such strange material as was to be found at the Villa Lilian.

I got the letter on Saturday morning, the 7th. of January. I could not accede to their demand and go to them the next day, Sunday; the weekly day of recreation being sacred to my invalid companion, since I had left her bed about a year ago. And I was agreeably flattered to be invited on a Sunday to Sonis, as I knew that was the day when Lilian was entirely at liberty, the little workshop being shut.

I made up my mind to go at once and surprise them, as I knew they would be off to Nice in a few days. So I took the train after lunch and found no one at home, but Mamma and the puppies. The latter were really very fine, and I urged the old lady to keep them, until they were two months old, and then sell them.

One looked exceptionally good, as far as I could judge from a six day pup, and I was told that Lilian had said she intended to bring it up for Jacky. They were her litter, said Ma, and if they were sold, the money would be for her. My silly heart beat a trifle faster at this. So Lilian was not vexed. She rather admired my frankness, I guessed, and I felt certain she had some sort of respect for me and was fond of me in her own peculiar, hysterical way. I resolved in future not to spare her, but to treat her coolly and tell her, as near as possible, what I thought of her. If she liked to keep on with me, she could, but I did not want to play the languishing lover.

Lilian was in Paris, at her Father's bureau, helping him with some type-writing, which had to be done before his departure. It was arranged that Adèle was to go and fetch her daughter to do some shopping that afternoon. Would I go up to Paris with her? I agreed and we went together. Mamma's conversation was all about Lilian and what a good, obedient girl she was; a splendid housewife, and domesticated. She spoke of her as if she was blest with every virtue.

I tried to draw her out about the affection of Mr. Arvel for Lily, but she refused to follow me on that delicate ground, and I was too cautious to press it. Her talk was that of an old bawd, and I imagined that they all still had designs on Jacky. Mamma was very cunning. Under a veil of hearty maternal affection, she hid a deep, designing nature, and was difficult to get at.

I let her run on, agreeing politely with all she said, and cudgel my brains as I will, I cannot remember much of her conversation. It could not have been very important.

We soon arrived at the Rue Vissot, which is a few minutes

walk from the Eastern railway station, and found Lilian and her stepfather installed in the one room, which formed his Paris *bureau.*

At the type-writer sat Lilian, bolt upright, visibly ill at her ease, and at her side, Papa, quite surprised to see me walk in with his mistress.

To my mind, they looked as if they had been indulging in an eager discussion, or making love. There was some heavily-written manuscript in front of them, but the last lines had been dry some time.

I explained my visit to Sonis, by saying that I was not free next day, having to go and fetch my bicycle, which I had left in the country, on the Orléans line, and could not lunch with them, but I had taken the liberty to run down and view the pups before the departure of the family for Nice.

I thanked Lilian in suitable terms for her offer of the pup, which I accepted, and she was very cold and over polite. I was the same. I exaggerated my tone and watched Pa and Ma. They did not seem surprised, and according to their custom, they never interfered when Lily and I were talking.

I was invited to dinner. I hesitated, and then turning suddenly round to my sulky love, I boldly said to her:

"Shall I?"

She started with surprise at being thus audaciously consulted in the presence of her father and mother, and visibly embarrassed, replied:

"Certainly—that is, if you like!"

So I accepted, and from that moment, I treated her purposely before her parents as if she was no longer the daughter of the house, but something higher—or shall we say—lower? And I was familiar in my talk with her. More like a son-in-law, but these shades of conduct were thrown away on the people of Sonis. They did not know; did not understand; and did not care. Or perchance, they pretended not to notice? But I was greatly amused and delighted to find that I had regained such complete mastery over my own passion.

Lily and her mother went off to make their purchases, and it was arranged that I should pass the afternoon with Papa, and go down to Sonis with him at dinner-time.

He rapidly finished his work and to pass the time, began to show me some private photographs. My readers will guess what they were.

"You see I keep them carefully locked up. I am so frightened lest Lilian might see them."

I chuckled inwardly at this ever-recurring phrase. It was perfectly useless and in very bad taste to always try and impress upon me that she was so innocent and had never seen anything obscene. She was in her twenty-third year now, it must be remembered. It was unnecessary, I take it, to mention a daughter's name, while showing obscene photographs or books. Is it not perfectly well understood that a father, tutor, stepfather, or guardian would keep such things out of the sight and reach of young people? Why this exaggerated declaration of virtue? Then he got out a framed photograph of a Japanese beauty, and told me for the third or fourth time all about her. The story was briefly that when in Japan, he had a native girl on hire as his mistress. Here she was photographed with him. Again he told me how careful he was to hide and lock up this little picture, but when he spoke of his wife finding it, I saw he was frightened of her. She was truly, madly jealous, or had made him believe so.

I think I pitied the poor old chap a little that day. He was a slave to all his grosser passions. The soft blandishments of Lily and the excesses of the table—these were his delights. The two women had got him firmly fixed between them.

I felt certain, as he unrolled the very ordinary tale of his Japanese amours, that Lily had heard it too from his lips. He told the same stories always over and over again, and knew nothing of the world, as it moved daily. His brain had stopped ten years ago, and in a garrulous, purposeless way, he would talk to me of people we had known about that time, and so will you and I, reader; so will we babble on, when we get to live over threescore, and continue to indulge in wine, women, alcohol, and tobacco, until we are *sans* eyes, *sans* teeth, *sans* penis, *sans* everything.

We went to the station eventually, having first locked up the photographs, with great fuss and luxury of precaution, and got into a wrong train, which took us right on to Meaux. It was Papa's fault, and he was in a fearful funk. I noticed curiously enough that he dared not stop out after a certain hour, and he was dreadfully exercised lest the ladies should have arrived before us. Luckily, we caught a train back quickly enough, and there was not much time lost. We raced to the house, as fast as Papa could shuffle, for I noticed that during the repose of the winter, the pleasures of gastronomy had rendered him quite obese, and to his gasping relief, found that the entrancing fascination of the Louvre and the Bon Marché had made the ladies late. We were home first, but they soon arrived.

Lily did not come near me. I stopped with Pa; he showed me a small smoker's table, garnished with tobacco jar, ash-tray, cigar-cutter, etc., that his two women had bought for him. He added that he hated receiving presents from them. He told me he had given Lily a purse with money in it, but he did not speak of any gift he had made to his wife. He took me upstairs to wash my hands. The bedrooms were no longer on the first floor.

It was too cold, I was told, and the second story was now used nightly, as there were three rooms, opening one into the other. The doors were left open, it appears, and one portable stove kept them all warm. One bedroom was occupied by Pa and Ma, another by Lilian, and the third by Granny, who was installed there, ready to take charge of the house when Mr. and Mrs. Arvel had left for the Riviera.

He pointed to one bed and I saw an expression in his face and a light in his eye that I had never seen before, as he said to me, with a devilish grin, and his mouth full of saliva:

"That's where Scraggy sleeps!"

And he stroked the pillow with an affectionate gesture of his stubby, nailless fingers. Then he showed me a suit of pyjamas on his bed, and told me that Lilian had made them for him.

The dinner passed off without notable incidents, but afterwards Lilian calmly asked me to go out with her and the dogs, in the dark, leaving Pa and Ma at home. It seemed to be a recognised thing now, that I could walk out with her at night. No doubt Mamma knew I could not hurt her now.

I must confess, with due shame, that I have no particular recollection of our chat, although it ought to have been important
enough after what had passed at our last meeting.

My impression is that I waited to hear Lilian complain of having been accused of lying venality by me, and that she never alluded to anything, but seemed to want me to forget everything and
start afresh. So I was bound to think that I had guessed aright;
should I be forced to despise her now?

All I can find in my scribbling diary is one word: "Reconciliation." So we must have patched up a peace somehow or the other.
Lily went so far as to repeat that she had tried to forget me and
could not. She also said that the old couple, who had dined with
us on the 26th. of December, had put me down as her fiancé. This
was certainly one of Lily's little crammers to see what I would say,
and she had placed her own thoughts, words, and ideas in the
mouths of these strangers.

"I suppose, one day when I get down here, I shall be introduced to some nice young man, and Mamma will say: 'Mr. S . . . ,
allow me,—Mr. So-and-so,—Lilian's betrothed!'"

"Oh! that will never happen," she exclaimed, adding a peculiar
half-sigh, half-groan, that I was fated to hear twice more later on,
and which seemed to be the strongest expression of anguish to
which she could give vent.

She told me that she was not going to Nice. That was no lie,
at all events, and she said she would try and manage to see me
while she was alone at the villa with her Granny. She was very im-
pressive in informing me that she could not get to Paris without
good and valid reasons, but I did not grumble about that. I knew
she could do pretty much as she liked. I let her chatter as she chose,
and was careful not to commit myself in any way. She could have
no suspicion of what I thought. I almost lost my presence of mind,
however, when she told me that she had broken off the marriage
between Charlotte and Raoul. She said that they did not meet any
more. How she managed it, she would not tell. I dared not press
the point, but the sister slept with the lad's mistress and they were
still friends, but Lolotte was not to see Adèle's son any more. What
did it all mean? I jumped to the conclusion that Papa was now
fairly ensconced in Lilian's heart and bed, and together they had

jockeyed Raoul's sweetheart. Mamma spoke about the rupture of the marriage and hinted that Charlotte had too many lovers. Wicked Lily had betrayed her brother's betrothed, but was artful enough to still be friends with her. No wonder she called Charlotte a little goose.

Lilian was not well. She looked pale, worn, and worried. A doctor had been consulted, and she was taking cod-liver oil. I had guessed aright about her anæmia in November, but I held my tongue now, and did not recur to her fit of blind rage, when I had dared to say she was poor-blooded. I would not quarrel any more with her.

Lilian kissed me rapturously and promised to write to me soon.

"Not at all," I answered, "I want to see you as soon as possible."

"No, no; you must wait."

"Then you don't love me. All right, darling, let all be over between us."

"Oh! no, do not say that," and she showed great concern and alarm, as she always did when I spoke of a real farewell.

"When do your parents leave?" I asked.

"On Tuesday, the tenth."

"Then I shall take the nine o'clock train on Tuesday night. You can bring the dogs out at a quarter past nine, and I'll walk about the Avenue de la Gare up to the Place d'Armes, until I see you."

"Perhaps I'll come and perhaps I shan't."

"I'll bring you a pretty book I want you to read. It is all about cruelty, with pictures."

"Oh! I should like that!"

"And it is in French too. I have never lent you a French book yet. Now perhaps, you will come out to get the volume, which is quite decent and proper, and meant for young girls at school."

She laughed, and gave me her luscious mouth, as we finished our little walk. I wished her parents: bon voyage, and promised to keep Papa supplied with papers during his absence. Mamma said Lilian had such a lot of work to do that she could not go with them, which was a great pity.

I did not believe Mamma. They were leaving Lilian at home for a purpose. What was it? Was it for me? I began to think I was not of much importance. She had other lovers—real ones—who she did not want to stay away from, for interested motives. Or did Mamma, now knowing Lilian was on an equality with her, refuse to travel in her company? These were the little mysteries I never was able to solve, with many more, which I hope will not bother the reader as much as they did me. I rather liked getting on the track of this series of traps and pitfalls. I felt my sense of penetration growing very acute, and was as pleased as the schoolboy who deciphers a rebus, knowing that the year before, I had been totally unable to reason as I could then.

JANUARY 10, 1899.

I popped the first volume of the original edition of *Justine et Juliette* (by the notorious Marquis de Sade, in 10 parts, with 101 engravings,) in my pocket, and at 9 P.M., well wrapped up, with a good cigar in my mouth, I took the train to Sonis. I was scarcely out of the station when I met my charmer, who I noticed, without saying anything, had freshened herself up, and put on a very nice hat and cloak.

Lily began her old trick of trying to teaze me by asking me ironically why I took the trouble to come down and leave my warm fireside. She also made a fuss when I wished to kiss her. So I retorted, and told her that I found she lacked all true feminine tenderness and pleasing politeness.

"I do not mean the ordinary politeness of society, which is a kind of light varnish which cracks and peels off at the slightest scratch, but true politeness of the heart; that which is to be found in worldly manifestations, as well as in sentiment; and in sensual affairs, just the same as in social associations."

Lilian said I was too serious.

"And I find you are not serious enough. You must not think I only want your body. I am very fond of you; fonder than you think. I can have lots of women's bodies. I want something more, and that is why I am here. But I shall not get what I desire at

Sonis. Here I find only falsity, trickery and little villanies. And you are such an awful liar too!"

"I'll not have you call me a liar. I am not a liar!"

I begged her pardon ironically and asked her how she had got on with her lovers during the last three months.

"I have no lovers," she answered snappishly, "I have had a letter from Gaston and that's all."

"What did he say?"

"Oh! a lot of filth," she replied contemptuously.

"Do you mean to tell me that you have been twelve weeks without spending?"

There was no answer.

"I really thought you had somebody who had cut me out. Let me see, there's the lieutenant. And you have been all this time without a man's member to play with?"

"No, I haven't!" She was getting angry now.

"How many have you had?"

"Fifteen!" she exclaimed, in a nervous, staccato manner. The words came through her teeth, when she was in a passion, as if clicking automatically from a talking machine.

"A good many! And I had hoped to see you married shortly. I should have liked to have left you with a good husband."

"Who would have me without a dowry? And then we never see anybody down here. You are the only person we invite. But I have told you I could not play a part, or imitate with a man the love I did not feel."

"You want a man who you could love as you do your Papa. Oh! not me—Mr. Arvel, I mean." I paused for a reply. None came. "You do love him. How beautifully you made him that suit of flannel pyjamas. Did you really cut it out yourself?"

"Of course I did."

"You are very clever. You can make dresses, hats, and cook. I noticed how well the trousers were made. They were really trousers and not loose pyjamas. Did you take the measure of the trousers yourself?" She was silent. "How nice! I wish you would do that for me. I should like to feel your fingers fumbling with the tape between my legs."

"You are always the same; quite obscene."

"True, I am an obscene devil. I am a sadistic wretch. A disciple of the Marquis de Sade, whose masterpiece I am going to lend you to read. I have brought you the first volume. I glory in my shame, because women love us; we are dirty beasts, expert in every vile caress. We leave aside all mawkish sentiments. No birds, and flowers, and soft music with us. Am I not right, my darling daughter? Answer me, my child!"

"I'll not have you call me your daughter, nor your child. I do not like those terms of affection now. And I will not be your slave either. All that is over. I won't call you Papa any more!"

She said this rapidly and with genuine accents of rage. I drew my own inference from this strange outburst. Of late Papa had been using these words to her, and in my mouth they jarred on her nerves.

A strange thrill stirred me. I had frequently told her to seduce Arvel, so as to be mistress of the house, and I felt sure the thing was always in the mind of the stepfather. She had laughed at my vile imagination, as she called it. Had I been the indirect means of this guilty understanding? Had I driven her into his arms, only to lose her myself through my own bad advice? If so, I deserved my fate.

But no, the true reason why I had often persuaded her to give way to him, was because I always saw that it was bound to happen, even if the act had not been really consummated during the past winter; during the long evenings beneath the lamp, when Mamma had gone up to bed early, soon after dinner, leaving Pa and Lilian alone together. To sum up: I should think he had always had his hands under her petticoats, more or less, from childhood and her final fall would be insensible.

"I'll be your mistress, but not your slave, nor your daughter," she continued.

"Whatever you like, Lily, as long as you tell me that you love me. You do love me, do you not?"

"Of course I do!"

"Then say so. You have never said to me: 'I love you!' "

"I love you! I love you! I love you!" She said this with the same nervous clenching of the teeth. It was an effort for her, under a feeling of annoyance, to be forced to utter these words which she did not feel.

Decidedly, she did not care for me, and she started off once more to talk about her millinery business and how she wished to open in Paris. Each time I met her and heard her speak, I noticed more and more the emptiness of her heart. I allowed her to continue her discourse unchecked, and she always returned to a series of vague complaints, when she would make out that we could be much happier and see each other more often, if I could help her by finding a small capital. The more she asked, the more quiet and calm I became. I pointed out the folly of her projects. I also added that I had no money and without beating about the bush, informed her that I was heavily in debt as well.

"Really now? You have debts? Dear me!" she exclaimed, with surprise. "How unlucky we both are! And I am not at all well. Papa has made me some quinine wine, as I have been ordered it."

I asked her how he did it. She informed me that he put sulfate of quinine in sherry. I ventured to disagree with this formula, and told her that I thought the bark properly macerated in old Malaga would be better and she asked me to make some for her. I promised I would. She thanked me, and we talked about books. She alluded to "Flossie" which I had lent her in the summer, and believed it was incredible that a girl of fifteen, such as Flossie was, should have experienced pleasure at her age, in using her maiden mouth to quench men's lusts. And an English girl too! that was quite impossible.

I did not dispute, although I knew from experience that directly the crisis of puberty is past, a girl is ready for anything, if of warm temperament.

I asked her if Raoul was much cut up about breaking off his engagement. She answered in the negative and told me that he had written to her, and had finished up his letter by saying: "I kiss your sweet lips!"

"I sent it to Papa to let him see what Raoul had written to me," Lilian went on to say, "and told him not to let Mamma know. And of course, the first thing he did, was to translate this compliment to her and we have both got into an awful row. Papa is vexed with Raoul, and Ma is in a temper with me."

Now I could see more than ever why Papa was jealous of his stepson. Always shadowy signs of incest with Lily; and half-truths!

I verified the story of the purse with a fiver in it, given by Papa. I had greatly changed my estimate of Lily's veracity. I now did not believe one single word she might say.

I pressed her to come to me in Paris. She swore she could not get out. Granny had orders to telegraph to Nice, if she absented herself without a plausible excuse! This was an awful lie. She did not wish to get into bed with me. Had she wanted me, she would have arranged to meet me somewhere or somehow. Or more likely she was expecting me to offer her money. I did not push the point. What was the use? I had no money to spare, and if I had I do not think I should have given it. Any fool can buy women.

Without me asking her, she told me that it was not possible to get me into the house at night, as Granny and her slept in two rooms, with the doors open, so as to let the heat of the stove into both, and she would try and arrange something else for me, if she could. "But there is the dining-room," I asked. "The stove is perpetually alight in it?"

By this time we had reached the house and stood beneath a gas-lamp in front of the gate. Lilian put on an air of innocent candour, and said slowly, like a child repeating something learnt by heart:

"What can we do in a dining-room?"

"Nothing," I answered, roughly.

My face must have betrayed me. In my disgust, I forgot myself, and lost all control over my features. My mask dropped off. She kissed me warmly.

"You are all topsy-turvy. What is the matter with you?"

I did not answer.

"Well, good night," said Lilian.

"Good night, and adieu!" I angrily replied, turning on my heel and striding off to the station.

I was very vexed at the moment. But it soon wore off, as I could see through her so well. She was very coquettish and wicked, but shallow and superficial. Her great trick was to "work up" her man by all kinds of artifices and carefully watch the effect produced on him. If she found she had gone too far, she would come back with a kiss and a caress, until the next manœuvre, and so on *ad libitum*, as long as the amorous male would stand it. Is this the way cunning courtesans wheedle money out of men? Do their votaries offer gold to induce the intriguing female to put an end to their torment? I suppose so. It simply disgusted me. I had no experience with wicked women. And I found out why. I had never stopped long enough with a thoroughly bad, scheming woman. When such a one would start her tricks, I saw through her, and was off and away. Why did I have so much patience with my black magpie, Lilian? I cannot tell. I was never her dupe long, if ever I was at all. I suppose I had felt a great lust for her ever since four years ago, and this would take a little while to get out of the system. But I was gradually sickening. She was always begging. I must have been mad up to then. I wanted to be loved for myself alone, at the age of 47. Perhaps I was like a woman and my change of life was acting on my brain? I had only been the half-lover of a quarter-virgin, so there was nothing much to regret. After all, it was better that she should have treated me badly for the last two or three months. A few words of tenderness, one leap of her heart, if she possessed one, towards mine, and I should have continued to live in the belief of her love for me.

You have nothing to complain of, Jacky, I soliloquised, you have had a year's amusement with this trifling intrigue. Twelve months illusion: is not that enormous in the ordinary sadness of life?

And so saying, I put out my lamp and settled to sleep.

LILIAN TO JACKY.

(No date or place.) Received January 12th. 1899.

Dear naughty darling,

Here is what I wish to propose to you: if next Sunday you have nothing better to do, you can come here directly after lunch, under the pretext of asking me for one of the little dogs and you can choose it. We can then go and have a nice walk, both of us, or stay at home, as you choose, and you shall stop and have tea with your

LILY

JACKY TO LILIAN.

Paris, January 12, 1899.

Little Lily,

Your proposal is adorable; to pass a whole afternoon with you would be true happiness for me. And then I feel that I possess your thoughts and I see that you try to please me. I am very grateful.

Unfortunately, we do not live like characters in a novel and have to go through life in quite another way. We must show that we possess common sense and a practical spirit.

What would your parents say when they heard that I visited their house while they were absent and that I had passed several hours with you?

Reflect a little, and you will understand, I am sure, without wanting me to explain myself more fully.

If you desire more ample explanations on this subject, I am quite at your disposal, without any hidden thoughts, quite frankly, and in platonic fashion. To prove my good faith, I will take the nine o'clock train any evening you may point out, Friday, Saturday, or following days, no matter how the weather is, and I will only stop with you the necessary time to demonstrate to you the impossibility of your amiable project.

To sum up: visiting Mademoiselle alone with her Grandmother, in the absence of her parents, would be rude and incorrect, calculated to make them uneasy, and sufficing to close their house against me for ever.

Don't be wicked, jealous, nor in a temper.

Yours always, even in spite of yourself,

JACKY.

LILIAN TO JACKY.

(No date or place.) Received January 13th. 1899.

Having been brought up like an English girl, I am consequently more practical than romantic, and if I proposed to you to come here Sunday, under the pretext that I gave you, it is only after having carefully reflected on the consequences, and knowing all the ideas that my parents might form on that head. I was absolutely convinced of the solidity of my proposal.

You will not profit by my good intentions in your favour? Very well then—do as you like.

You cannot, however, prevent me from remarking that you are never free for me on a Sunday. You probably have to occupy yourself with your bicycle, as on Sunday last.

I am not wicked, nor jealous, nor out of temper. I only note simple facts.

(Unsigned.)

JACKY TO LILIAN.

Paris, Saturday, January 14th. 1899.

Dear Lily,

All last night and this morning I have reflected on the letter received yesterday evening. I can only repeat that I feel sincere gratitude for your good intention which delights me, but your starting-point is false. The more I think about it, the less I understand.

The aversion I have for the exchange of sour letters and which I have often expressed to you, grows stronger than ever, therefore I will be truly brief.

Since nearly three months, I suffer, I think, as much as a man can possibly suffer morally.

A new subject of discord now springs up between us.

This is atrocious!

JACKY.

She did not write, and I am ashamed to say that two days afterwards, I sent her the following letter:

JACKY TO LILIAN.

Paris, January 16, 1899.

My dear Lily,

You are vexed with me because I think that I ought not to enter your father's house when he is away. Do you not understand that?

I think that if I saw you I should find arguments to convince you, for the last letter that you wrote proves that you are very intelligent.

I have an immense desire to see you. It is a great joy for me to be at your side.

That is why I hasten to send you these few lines to tell you that I shall come to Sonis to-morrow, Tuesday night, by the nine o'clock train, and I will stroll about until ten.

If you can't or won't see me, you need but send me a wire, as follows: "Do not come."

I could have waited a few days before writing to you, but I do not wish you to believe me capable of sulking, or of watching to see who will come round first. Those are little, vulgar, stupid, mean artifices which are repugnant to me.

I love you and would like to see you to tell you so, and force you to say to me, your lips against mine, like the other night: "I love you, I love you, I love you!"

I come to you loyally, sincerely and frankly, without beating about the bush; without chicanery; ready to answer all your objections and to plead my cause with you, without lying, showing myself to you as I am. So much the worse for me if you will no longer love me. I shall always love you, good or bad, dead or alive, even if I may be forced to think no more of you as a mistress.

At all hazards, I shall put the second volume of that little book for young people in my pocket. If you do not want it, you will return me the first volume and all will be at an end.

Do not fear that you will meet a silly, whining lover, groaning, and scolding. To-morrow evening you will simply see your dirty Papa, and quickly you will offer him your pretty mouth, saying: "Good evening, Jacky!"

And we will begin to quarrel if you will.

But I want to see you.

JACKY.

A few months ago, I should have written, like the saucy wretch that I am: "Lily, don't forget to tie on your little pink ribbon." Now I no longer ask for anything.

JANUARY 17, 1899.

Lilian had invited me openly to spend Sunday with her in the absence of her parents. I refuse and she is vexed with me. What is the reason of this seeming imprudence? She is hand in glove with her Papa, and is now his mistress. Or she wishes to compromise us both. They must all have had a very mean idea of my intelligence to think I could not see through them.

These were my reflexions, as full of curiosity, a curiosity which bid fair to conquer my lust, I took the train after dinner. It was a dull and showery night, and with the fear of rheumatism still upon me, I put on my box-cloth overcoat and a pair of thick shooting-boots.

Lilian was already out on the warpath, received me as usual with tantalizing remarks, and showed great jealousy. My refusal to pass Sunday with her touched her to the quick, and I was obliged to tell her that I always spent the weekly day of rest with my poor invalid mistress. She retorted that I did not love her much, or else I would not mind a quarrel at my home for her sake. I tried to make her more reasonable, but all my trouble was in vain. I allowed that she should feel some pain at my apparent devotion to my mistress, although I made her understand that the doctors forbade her all excitement or worry, but I could not see why she should draw me on to behave so indelicately towards her stepfather. Here I watched her closely, as I said:

"I will not come openly to the villa, when the master of the house is away. I have behaved dishonestly enough as it is. Do you think it is the action of an honourable man to carry on an intrigue with the daughter of the house where he has been received with such confidence?"

I paused for a reply. None came. I continued:

"If your Papa was to know what I have done with you, he would be justified in kicking me all round Sonis, and I should have nothing to say."

She never answered me, and my heart leapt in my breast as I now knew perfectly well that Pa, Ma and Lilian formed an infamous Trinity of which I was to be a victim.

My home thrust caused her to hurriedly change the subject, and she talked of "Justine." She had read the first volume and I had the second in my pocket for her. It had created a great impression on her. The parts that pleased her most were those where there were men and women together.

"Oh! that book!" she exclaimed, "I have not slept for reading it. I roll about my bed, and bite my pillow, and I am forced to relieve myself with my finger. I could not help it. And then it is in French too. The other books I have of you are in English. I will return them to you to-night. This is the first French one I have read. I am going to be very good to you to-night. I will take you into the house. I have arranged with Granny by telling her that I am going to sit up and write some letters. She knows I received one from Papa to-day. By the way, I want you to do something for me in Paris. I do not want to go up to-morrow, as I have such a lot of work. I have got a lot of commissions from Papa."

And she drew out a type-written letter. I stepped back, out of delicacy, but she said I might take the letter, and read it, and keep it to do all that he requested. I did so, and at that moment had no idea of writing our story, or I should have copied the conclusion of the paternal missive. In guarded terms, Papa alluded to her health and begged her to take great care of herself. He said that she could count upon his great affection, and wished her to think of him as he was always thinking of her bodily health and her future welfare. It was not the letter of a guardian, but that of a lover.

Then we had our usual little quarrels. I was always reproaching her for her caprices and hard-heartedness, and she was ever jealous of my mistress, and hinted that I ought to work harder and try and make some money.

Then she would press closer to me, and make me kiss her and feel her all over, outside her clothes. I had a gold pin in my scarf, and as our conversation touched upon the pleasures of cruelty, I amused myself by slightly pricking her arms and thighs, as the sharp point was strong enough to penetrate her clothes, and she did not seem at all averse to this insane diversion.

I asked her why she was always so wicked to me in winter time. Last year she would hardly see me, and now again it was the same. I compared her to a dormouse, but she could only laugh, and as usual I had no satisfaction. I ventured to say that perhaps she had some animosity towards me for having given her over to Lord Fontarcy. But she scouted the idea and said she had enjoyed herself enormously.

I wanted to know her impression while being flagellated and sodomised by my finger before witnesses.

"I had a feeling of disgust to think that Clara was there, looking at me. I would do anything you might possibly think of with men, but I loathe women. I would not mind being alone with ten men."

"I love to degrade and humiliate you for my sensual pleasure, and there are lots of things I should like to do to you and with you. But I would not exercise real cruelty. I should always tell you beforehand what I was going to do, and if approved of by you, if you think you would like it, we could try it."

"I'll never come with you again if there are to be women present."

"Then if I asked you to join me alone with another woman?"

"I could not. I should refuse. I should be sick, or have a nervous attack. I hate women. If you and your friend want to amuse yourselves with women, don't invite me, but get some other girl that day."

"I will never ask you to meet a woman, as I quite understand that tastes differ. I, too, find no pleasure with my own sex, but I can quite understand that other men might."

"You are tolerant and are large-minded. I like you for that. I should be very pleased to meet Fontarcy again with you, but without Clara. It would be beautiful to be alone with you two. He likes me too."

"How do you know? You never saw his member. It is likely enough he never got an erection with you."

"Yes, he did. When I was being sucked, I saw it sticking out. It was stiff against my leg."

"That was while he was licking you."

"He never licked me. You did. But I saw his big, stiff machine."

Here were two hallucinations, or falsehoods. My readers will remember that Lord Fontarcy had produced her orgasm with his tongue, and not I, and I knew perfectly well that he did not open his trousers that day. I have since submitted this to him, and he agrees that Lily was mistaken. I take it that she was thinking of someone else.

"I am pleased you like all my mad imaginations," said I to Lily. "When Lord Fontarcy returns to Paris, if you could get out, no doubt he would be delighted to see you. I don't know anybody else well enough to offer you, as it is a ticklish thing to propose. All men do not understand such things. There is no danger with my friend. He lives in England and does not even know your name."

I asked her why she had never looked him up in London and she replied that she was frightened of her brother. She said she kept him in entire ignorance.

"And now," whispered Lily, nestling up to me, "tell me something nice and horrible, that you would like to do to me."

"I should like to have you naked—"

"Always naked!" she interrupted, with a sneer.

"Yes, for this diversion, most certainly, and then strap a broad leather belt round your loins as tight as you could bear it, so that you would not only be very uncomfortable, but I should enjoy the sight of your small pulled-in waist, and your bottom which would swell out bigger than ever in consequence."

She kissed me most voluptuously and asked me for some more "dreams" of mine.

"You are my slave, and you stand upright in front of me, not necessarily naked this time. Your legs are close together and with the same belt, I strap your thighs together, just above the knee, as tightly as I can. Then I would force my hand through your thighs just under your pussy, from the front, and then from behind, under your bottom, and the brutal passage of my hand would hurt you a little, but you would have pleasure, as I would tickle your slit. I should enjoy the delight of power and domination, without speaking of the soft contact of your skin, and the captivating manner in which my hand would be imprisoned between your thighs. And you would be ashamed to be thus exposed and humiliated. The combination of two such opposite sensations would be very pleasant indeed."

"Oh, I should like that!"

"I promise you we will do it. You always did enjoy being badly treated by me."

"Oh! I like all you do!"

"There are men who enjoy being ill-treated too."

"Yes, I know. One of my best customers, who lives down here, Madame Rosenblatt, married to a German Jew, has got a lover, as her husband don't give her enough money for her dress. Her friend possesses that mania. He has got a German grammar and studies it. He is about 40 years of age. He has a small apartment in Paris and he goes there first and begins to learn his lessons. Madame Rosenblatt soon appears and pretends to be in an awful passion with him. She boxes his ears, and makes him kneel down and say his verbs. Whether he knows them or not, he has to take down his breeches, and she beats him well. After that, he gets into bed with her and enjoys her. His birthday is soon due, and his mistress is going to give him a present: a little silk cushion for him to kneel on. I am making it and she is paying me well for it."

"Has she never asked you to see her pupil, or have you never evinced any curiosity to view this strange correction?"

"Oh, no! But she wanted me to go with her one day. She told me he would like to be whipped and humiliated in front of a strange young woman, but I shall not go. I would not do such a thing.".

I am obliged to confess that this story excited me very much, and although I had never allowed a woman to domineer over me as yet, I almost thought that I should have no objection to play the unruly pupil, if the governess pleased me, just to see how it felt.

I held strong suspicions that Lily had seen this pupil-lover, and that the cushion would be paid for by the man himself.

I still continued to be as dumb as a fish, or I should never have heard or learnt anything.

According to Lily's calculations, Granny and the servant were now in bed and fast asleep, and it was safe for me to follow her into the house, I did so, stepping cautiously on the grass, so as not to let my footsteps be heard on the gravel, as I had done in August. It was raining hard. A pace or two to the right, and I was in the dark room, and waited there while Lily went to see if the coast was clear. She soon returned and taking me by the hand, guided me into the warm dining-room, where we sat down on a little sofa under the window.

I took her in my arms and embraced her with great tenderness, beginning to put my hand under her clothes. She repulsed me, and told me that she did not see why she should give way to me, as I showed no desire to do anything whatsoever to content her.

"When you try to please me you shall have all you want, but until then: nothing, nothing, nothing!"

I immediately withdrew my hand from her calves—she had not let me get any higher—and releasing her waist as well, I drew myself entirely away from her.

"I guess what you are up to. These are the tantalizing tricks of a coquette. Possibly Madame Rosenblatt"—I did not dare say Papa and Mamma—"has given you advice how to behave with me. I can hear her saying to you: 'Never give way to men too readily, or they will think nothing of you. Hold the carrot in front of the donkey's nose, but don't let the animal touch it until he obeys you. Keep the chaps away from you and they will run after you all the more!' I understand all your ways."

And I got up as if to go.

"Come and sit down by me," she said, as she looked at me strangely, with a wondering look in her eyes, astonished at being read so easily, "and I'll be good to you. You know I like you so much, that really I don't know what I am about when you are near me."

And she threw herself upon me, and kissed me as she had never kissed me before, begging me to suck her lips and tongue, and caress her in return.

She ruthlessly thrust my fumbling fingers from her, and told me she was "unwell." Her monthly courses were now on.

I at once made a little mental calculation. She had begun her menstruation on the 11th. of November, that was the last date I had been able to note and she was therefore due again on the 12th. of December, or thereabouts. Here we were at the 17th. of January. Why so late? Now I understood Papa's letter regarding her health. No doubt there was the fear of being in the family way. Had he drugged her before his departure? Or was the old witch of a grandmother dosing her with her secret decoctions of herbs, so as to bring on her tardy "menses"? Is that why she is friends with me again? If she found herself really *enceinte*, did she intend to give way to me entirely, and declare all her trouble as of my making? There was some deep scheme, which I never got to the bottom of.

She took me in her arms and pillowed my head on her breast, as she sat at the end of the sofa, and her audacious hand pressed my stiff dagger outside my trousers. She pinched it.

"Do I hurt you, Jacky?"

"No!"

"And now," pressing it with all her strength.

"No! I like that!"

"It does hurt, but you won't say so. I'll try again," and she gripped the acorn top through the cloth.

"Ah! now you hurt me! But I like the pain coming from you, Lily!"

It was cosy in the pretty little room, and I was very comfortable in Lily's embrace! my head almost underneath her arm; my delighted nostrils enjoying the odour of her armpits; the true coppery, wild-beast fragrance of a brunette, who, during her menstrual period, puts no water on her body.

She now began to undo my trousers. I put out my hand to help her.

"No! Let me do it. I like to arrange it my way."

She unbuttoned the breeches, and drew out the little gentleman, who was as pleased as Punch to show himself and stood up bravely.

"Ah! here is my *poupée!* I love to see it and play with it! Are you happy, Jacky?"

"Yes, Lilian. I am so pleased to be caressed by you. I like you to see me thus, all shamelessly exposed to your gaze. Kiss me! Now look at it! Keep your eyes on it!"

She gently moved her hand up and down the shaft. She was more expert than when she had masturbated me in August.

"I want to see more of you," she said, and I opened my trousers as fully as I could, letting them down a little, and pulling out the testicles. These she caressed as well and passed her hand even lower down, tickling the neutral zone between the scrotum and the fundament. And then she closed her hand, manipulated me furiously for a few seconds, and when I moved convulsively, feeling that I was about to spend, she suddenly stopped.

"Why do you cease, darling?"

"I don't want to make you enjoy too soon. I am trying to make the pleasure last as long as I can!"

Lily had been taking lessons, I saw plainly.

"Well, do what you like with me. But don't hurt me. Would you like to hurt me? Or violate me, perhaps?"

"Oh no, dearest."

"I should like to be quite naked with you, all dressed as you are!"

She moulded my testicles, never taking her eyes from my weapon, and then once more firmly grasped it with her left hand, supporting me against her breast with her right arm.

For a little while longer, she continued her play, shaking it violently in her soft hand, and gradually going slower until her fingers became motionless. A wee caress of the wrinkled purse, an exploration of the perineum, and then back to the principal actor, who, no longer able to restrain himself, burst in delicious agony and sent a gush of semen on to my belly, followed by several thick clots, much to Lily's delight, as I distinctly felt a thrill run through her frame, the unmistakable shudder of voluptuous pleasure, that I knew so well.

"Why! You've come too, Lily!" I exclaimed, in delighted rapture, as soon as I regained my senses.

"Yes! How do you know?"

"I felt you spend!"

She was still under the influence of the feeling the onanistic play had excited in her, and she threw herself furiously upon me, and taking my head in her hands, thrust her mad tongue down my throat, and sucked my lips until she took my breath away.

She was a real woman at that moment of her life, inasmuch as she adored the male, with the true evidence of the force of his desire pointing to heaven and would have let a man do anything to her, and she would have done anything to his body.

She rose and fetched a clean dish-cloth from the adjoining kitchen, as she said she did not dare go upstairs to get a towel. She carefully wiped away all traces of the recent spermatic eruption, and we settled down for a talk, after she had got me some brandy and water.

She looked over the second volume of "Justine," and enjoyed the pictures. A little packet was ready for me, containing the first volume, and also "Flossie," "The Yellow Room," "Colonel Spanker's Lecture," "The Horn Book," and "The Convent School."

And then we spoke of marriage, and I talked about her virginity, narrowly watching her expressive face the while. I told her that our voluptuous games were all very well in their way, but if I lived beneath the same roof with her for a few days, I should most surely have complete connection.

"Indeed," I added, "you Lily would ask me yourself to make you a woman."

I saw again the troubled, puzzled look come into her eyes; there was an expression of pain in her face and she leant her cheek on her clenched hand, which was tightly clasped.

"Should I? Tell me more, Jacky. Talk to me. I like to hear you."

I told her how delicious the nuptial tie must be, when both man and wife really love each other, when there is no disgust, no repugnance. On the other hand, how horrible for a girl to be thrown into the arms of a brutal male, who violates her on the first night, and perhaps makes her hate the approach of a man ever afterwards.

"Yes, that must be horrible!"

A change came over her. She looked angry, worried, pained, and disgusted, and seemed full of regret. A confession was trembling on her lips. She looked at me with melting eyes, and then they flashed fire. As I spoke, she seemed angry with herself and with me. A pause, a sigh, and she regained her self-possession, entrusted me with Papa's commissions in Paris and gave me the money to get them done. She lost her temper, and began worrying me about the plan to spend Sunday with her. I refused once more, and complained vaguely of her conduct towards me during the past winter and how unreasonable she was even now.

"Would you have sent for me, if I had not written my last letter?"

She was turning over the pages of "Justine" as I spoke, and she looked up at me with a wondering, wandering look in her fine brown eyes, and these words dropped languidly from her fevered lips, tired by a long series of wet kisses:

"I don't know!"

"I read you so well. I know how bad you are, and yet I am here. It is a great struggle between this—" I touched my penis,— "and this—" I placed my hand to my forehead.

"But how about that?" and she put her hand on my heart.

"Never mind that, I won't tell you anything more. I'll say nothing."

"I suppose you think I am not worthy to listen to you? Or perhaps that I cannot understand?"

"Perhaps. Anyhow, you will find out one day how I loved you, and later on I shall have my revenge. Oh! not as you think; I shall never harm you. Other men will avenge me. When you shall have been jeered at, mocked, and sullied; forced to smile, when some syphilitic wretch shall have made you sick with his pestilential breath; crushed beneath the weight of a monster, covered perchance with eczema; sweating; stinking; you will retch with disgust, and between two fits of vomiting, softly in the night, you'll cry bitter tears, and despite yourself, my name will come from your lips, yet burning from the pressure of the hated mouth. You will call for me: 'Jacky! Jacky!' And he will not be there!"

"But I shall never have anything to do with monsters, so that can't happen to me!"

I looked at the clock. I just had time to catch the last train.

"Oh! of course, there you are looking at the time. You are tired of me already."

I sat down again and listened as she told me to see about some seats for the Opéra Comique, the new building which had only been inaugurated in December. She wished to go with her first workwoman, I think. I departed, and lamp in hand, she opened the door to me, but could come no farther, as a perfect storm of wind and rain was now raging.

"I shall look forward to your visit on Sunday."

"Not Sunday, please, Lily."

"Yes, or you will see how angry I shall be."

"Not Sunday, my darling."

"Yes! Yes! Yes!"

The glow of the lamp showed me her black and sullen, frowning face, as she closed the door angrily. Through the blinding rain, I ran to the station. The last train had left, just five minutes before and I was stranded about ten miles from Paris.

I turned back and tried two infamous inns, to see if I could get a bed for the night. The first one never answered, and at the second, a ferocious dog drove me away.

It was no use lamenting. I had half a mind to return to the villa, but I was fearful lest Lilian should be unable to hear me, or that I might wake the servant, or Granny; so I started to walk. The ten or eleven miles did not frighten me, but the road was far from being safe. To be stabbed, or thrown into a river or a canal, for a few pounds, is not very nice. I thought of this, as I stumbled along all in the dark, my little parcel of books in my hand, and Lily's money in my pocket. I lost my way, regained it, slipped and fell in the mud, and as I picked myself up, saw a carriage approaching. I had walked two or three miles. I asked for a lift to Paris. Luckily for me, it was an empty brougham going to Pantin only. I arranged to give the man five francs, and I jumped in and found a rug on the seat. I lit a cigar and made myself comfortable until I got to Pantin. The rain had ceased. I paid the man and gaily tramped through the silent streets.

Before getting into bed at about three in the morning, I opened the parcel and looked through the books. In "Flossie" and "The Yellow Room," I found several heavy, black thumbmarks. Papa, beyond a doubt, had read these volumes with Lily.

I laughed grimly to myself as I jumped into bed, and with a loud and merry: "Good night, Lily!" addressed to my solitary pillow, I turned on my side and was soon snoring. But at half-past eight, I was up and dressed, and with my faithful comrade Smike, was soon at the bedside of my sweet, suffering, unsuspicious mistress.

3

How now, how now? how go maidenheads? Here,
you maid?

SHAKESPEARE.

... what opinion he must have of my modesty, that
he could suppose, I should so much as entertain a thought
of lying with two brothers?

DANIEL DEFOE.

LILIAN TO JACKY.

Thursday. (January 19th. 1899.)

My very own Jacky,

Are you? No, you are not. You do not love your little girl as she
ought to be loved.

I almost had an idea of what would happen to you Thursday night,
and I waited a good long time before going up to my room, supposing
that if you had missed the train, you would have thought of returning
here. I am truly sorry at what happened to you, without nevertheless being able to pardon you the affront you put upon me after all for next
Sunday.

No, you are not a man, as you fear a few moments of bad temper or
a scolding, for that is the only reason that prevents you coming on Sun-

231

day. I can plainly see that I shall never occupy anything else but the second place in everything and every way.

I thank you extremely for all the commissions which you have done deliciously well, therefore I will abuse your kindness and ask you to be so kind as to go to the Opéra Comique when you receive this note, and take the eight-franc seats you mention for Saturday evening.

We will settle up Sunday if I see you, or by letter if you do not come. I count upon your amiability for these tickets. Can you send them to me by post?

You will lose if you don't come. You would find something good, for I feel inclined for a little naughtiness. Those who wish to profit therefrom, please take notice!

I love you too much and I am unhappy.

LILY.

JANUARY 23, 1899.

I had executed all the commissions entrusted to me by Arvel's daughter, and had been able to obtain for her, or rather for her father, a very large percentage, such as he would probably not have succeeded in getting. And by the manner in which the little piece of business was done, he must have known that I had managed it. The seats for the theatre, I also bought, and sent by registered letter, to avoid the accident (?) of the preceding October, and I also wanted her to feel that I had never forgotten the lost bank-note. She was so careful not to allude to this when she saw me, that she no doubt felt the implied reproach. I have no recollection how I answered her last letter, but I think I sent her a statement of accounts, and once more impressed upon her that it was impossible for me to leave Paris on a Sunday. I added that I should come down to Sonis on Monday night, the 23rd. of January, by the usual train, with all the receipts for her Papa, and another volume of "Justine," ready in an envelope, and if I did not see her, I should slip everything in the letterbox of her villa, and return the way I had come.

So I went accordingly, and found my Lilian strolling in the dark with her dogs. To my great surprise, she was extremely gracious, and had evidently given up as a bad job all idea of trying

o drag me away from my dominical duties. She had enjoyed herself very much at the opera, having gone with one of her workgirls.
I replied that I had intended to go myself and see her at the play, and
she said I ought to have done so. I could not very well answer that
perhaps she had not gone with the girl, or that if she had, the latter
might have told her parents that I was there. All this proved the
hidden complicity of both mother and father, and had I opened
my mouth on this topic, it would have lead to useless quarrels.

I told her during our walk that Lord Fontarcy was shortly
coming to Paris again, and very probably he would show a desire
to see her once more.

"You would have to be very kind to him this time, especially
as Clara would not be there. You could not refuse giving him
pleasure with your mouth, the same as you like to do with me."

"Oh no, I could never do that to *him!* I would use my hand,
but nothing else. I have no idea of disgust with you. I would do
anything for you!"

"We will see later how far your devotion will take you. I shall
feel great excitement in forcing you into the arms of my friend,
and I am sorry I do not know anybody else I can trust. You can
have no idea how pleased I am to think that you love me well
enough to prostitute yourself for my pleasure."

"Yes, I do love you and all your ideas."

She said this in a low voice, under the influence of an inward
wave of voluptuousness, for I must not forget to remind the reader
that our conversations, during these nocturnal rambles, were
carried on to a running accompaniment of the most lewd kisses and
reciprocal gropings and touchings.

"I have the vilest ideas with regard to you," I continued,
"there is nothing revolting, degrading, or horrible between man
and woman, but what I should like you to execute with me, and
I will eventually force you to say that I have become a vile, repugnant brute in your eyes."

"Never, never! You don't know what you say. Have I not told
you over and over again that everything you do in regard to the
pleasures of love is perfection, and just what I like? I have enormous delight with you."

"I am afraid you would refuse many things when it came to a pinch. Look at all the horrors described in the book you are reading, and which no one should ever know you have perused. By the way, I have brought you down another volume. Well, you have noticed how the poor martyred heroine, Justine, is forced to go with nearly all her persecutors to the water-closet, and wait until they have evacuated, to cleanse their fundaments with her tongue. Would you do that with me?"

The answer came quickly, without hesitation:

"Certainly, I would! I'll go to the closet with you. But I won't let you go with me."

I now made her tell me the story of Gaston's attempted rape in the train again, and I could not help excusing him. She agreed with me that she had done wrong to lead him on, having never granted him the least favour, but now, knowing what she did about men and their desires, she would never have let him kiss her and play with her, to such an extent, if she had no intention of giving way.

This talk and a lot more of the same kind, that I cannot now remember, had made both of us most fearfully excited, and we must have formed a strange picture, if anyone had met us, on the dark road. Lily's hat was all awry, her hair disarranged, and her face, neck, and throat glistened with the saliva my delighted tongue had deposited on her warm flesh. We held each other closely embraced, and her arms must have been black and blue from the way I had pinched her, always much to her delight.

I desired her greatly that evening, and in my pocket was a leather belt, which I had bought that day, as I had hoped my wayward girl might take me into her house again. Of course, I did not tell her of my peculiar purchase.

I had noticed that she was much stouter, as I held her in my arms, and I told her so. She agreed that there was a slight increase of fat.

"That is because you are no longer a virgin," I explained.

"What makes you say that? I am a virgin, I assure you."

"You seem strangely altered in many little ways," I answered, "and your entire bearing, which last year was that of a young girl, is now to my idea more like that of a married woman."

She laughed. I continued:

"I can soon see if you are a virgin or not."

"How?"

"I have only to insert my finger gently, if you will let me."

"Certainly, I will. Why not?"

"Why not indeed? Come along, put your foot up!"

"What do you mean?" she asked, feigning surprise.

"You have only to place one of your little tootsies on yonder bench and I shall be able to tell you in a jiffey."

She laughed and began to walk a little bit faster, getting away from the bench, and complaining that she was afraid some one might see us. Why had she not found that out before? The silly girl was utterly mistaken in me, and believed she could make me digest the most transparent falsehoods. As I walked by her side, silent for a moment, I could not help asking myself if the game I was playing was worth the candle? Should I not do better to leave her alone entirely to rot in peace, entrenched in her laager of lies, with her mother's lover? The thought of the old gentleman made me inclined to take up my position again, as I wanted to be certain of what was at present mere conjecture. And I was very curious to see what would be Lily's next manoeuvre. Why did she so wish to keep up the fable of her virginity? I had told her scores of times that she could do as she liked with her body. I was not jealous, nor did I expect fidelity; all I desired was a little love now and again, if she cared to grant it to me, and when she told me to leave her, I would do so without a word, and keep all my suffering to myself. This evidently did not suit her, as she must have wanted me to be jealous, so as to have some feeling to work on. At present, I was impregnable. I waited for her to speak, and as I thought, she tried to punish me for my suspicions anent her maidenhead, by trying to arouse my jealousy—which did not exist.

She had been invited to dine out the evening before (Sunday), by Madame Rosenblatt and her sister, together with some gentlemen friends; cousins, brothers-in-law, or what not. If memory serves me rightly, one of them was an officer. I candidly confess that I do not recollect the story properly, as it was rather muddled. In plain words, it was a lie. The only thing that was true, was that she had had what is vulgarly called a jolly good spree, and had

dined in a private room with a merry party. I only asked her quit
coolly how she managed to elude the vigilance (?) of the sill
old grandmother. She replied that Madame Rosenblatt had sen
her a false telegram, inviting her to dine with her at her house
The dinner had taken place at the Hôtel-Restaurant Narkola
which I knew from experience to afford bedroom accommodation
as well as meals. She had been so jolly, and drank so much wine
that she had lost a silver purse which hung on the silver châtelaine
I never saw. She pretended to be very much put out about thi
loss, as she was frightened that her Mamma would notice it and
ask her awkward questions. There were twenty francs in the purse
too. I replied that there was a slight balance due to me on the
commissions I had executed for her father, and I should be pleased
to offer her that, and shortly I would give her a new silver purse
although it might not match the one that was gone.

"Oh! that would not matter, but I dare say you think I have
told you this story to make you give me something."

"You should not say that. I only know that you say you have
lost a purse with money in it. You therefore need not repay me
for the two seats I got for the Opéra Comique, nor shall I claim
of you the little sum due to me on your Pa's account. As for the
purse—"

"Never mind about that. I thank you for the seats, but I am
afraid you will think I expected you pay for them."

"I do not think anything. I only know that it gives me great
pleasure to make you the smallest present in the world and you
know very well that it would be impossible for me to accept money
from you for theatre tickets."

She thanked me briefly, and looked up to me with surprise
and timidity, as if trying to read me and utterly failing to do so.

I inwardly resolved never to allow her or her people to penetrate my thoughts. The only way was to change my conduct and
humour every time I saw them or the daughter. I had no chance
at Sonis unless I became a perfect comedian, or walked off altogether.

So I entered on my part at once, instead of showing my
suspicions about her virginity, or the absurdity of the story of her
dinner with Madame Rosenblatt. I was very gay, respectful and

nder, during the finish of our long walk and we reached the door
f the house. I gave her the accounts and receipts for her Papa and
nother volume of "Justine." I returned her the letter from Nice,
ut I kept the type-written envelope, on which was her name and
ddress. Without asking her to let me into the house, I made as if
) go, holding out my hand to say good bye. She broached the
ibject herself.

"I can't take you into the villa to-night, as Granny won't let
ne sit up. Even now, she is waiting for me to come to bed, and I
hall be scolded for stopping out so late. There is another thing
)o, that I hardly like to tell you. I am unwell again. I thought it
vas all over and now I have got what is almost a *perte*, or flooding,
vhich fatigues me very much."

"Anyhow you are not *enceinte!*"

"How amusing you are!" she replied, laughing.

"Poor little girl! I suppose you must suffer too from the
whites'?"

"How strange you should have guessed that!" She spoke with
eigned astonishment.

"I had some *fleurs blanches* for the first time in my life last
Saturday. How ought I to cure them?"

"You must see a doctor and take a course of tonics, and some
ron and quinine. I will make you some quinine wine. You should
use a syringe with some astringent for the 'whites.' "

"You know I can't take injections!"

This was playing the game rather too strong, but I withheld a
bitter laugh, as I bade her a loving farewell and saw her go into
the house.

This had been an evening of revelations for me. Papa had left
her at home to bring on her periodical flow by hook or by crook,
and permission was granted to go with the paying friends and
lovers at the accommodating Hôtel-Restaurant Narkola, where I
could play the spy the next day if I wanted to know about the
banquet. And there was the repeated lie of the maidenhead! Lily
little knew that in habitual liars, persistent, obstinate denegation
is equivalent in many cases to an avowal.

I stopped short in my stride on the way to the station, and
although it was a frosty night, a heavy sweat broke out upon my

brow, as I thought of what might have been. Up to last October I was deeply struck with Miss Arvel, and had I been rich enough I do not know where my weakness might have taken me. To think that I might have given my name to her, introduced her into my family, and one day found old Eric in my bed! My marriage would have broken the heart of my poor, sweet, devoted invalid at home. I should have pensioned her off, and sent her to some warm climate—had I been rich. Other men have put away wives and mistresses after years and years of cohabitation; why should not I have done the same—had I been rich? I could have refused nothing to Lilian Arvel, or her parents, and so should never have allowed myself time to analyse their motives—had I been rich.

And I wonder what the few passengers waiting on the platform of the station of Sonis that wintry night, thought of a mad Englishman, who suddenly lifted his head out of the depths of the broad, warm collar of his fur-lined pelisse, and, taking his pipe from between his lips, shrieked aloud:

"Thank God, I'm poor!"

I should not have been human if I had not been extremely annoyed at Lilian's conduct towards me. I was wounded in every way, and I felt there was a lack of confidence; she would tell me nothing of her inmost feelings. I was to be an ordinary victim to her wiles, and this being entirely repugnant to me, I resolved to let her run loose. I was getting tired of her tricky ways.

These thoughts crowded into my brain, as on the 24th. of January, I started making her some quinine wine. It was a great success and I manufactured several quarts, which met with the approval of everybody at the villa, as I gave them to her later on.

Lord Fontarcy now reappeared in Paris, and the day after I had made the first lot of wine, we had a quiet bit of luncheon together all alone, as Clara had not accompanied him this time. Naturally, after we had discussed serious matters, the talk reverted to Lilian, and in as few words as possible I stated the case, without seeking to spare my own poor self. His face showed great preoccupation and I could see that he was in point of fact, quite disgusted with her.

"Why can't she be frank and good to you quite simply, or lse let you go in peace and never see you again?"

This was a plain, Anglo-Saxon way of putting things which a voman like Lilian was totally incapable of understanding, and had he been as he wished, this story would never have been written. asked him if he cared to see her, adding that I knew she would e glad to join us in a little orgie, but he declined, and in a few autiously worded sentences, led me to understand that he did not pprove of her conduct in general, and having no faith or condence in her, preferred to have nothing to do with her. He was, think, vexed at her having broken her promise to Clara and him oncerning the proposed visit to his place in London, being very ensitive on all such simple points of honour, if I may be permitted o use such a term here. What pleased me most about my good old riend was, that although inwardly disgusted with Lilian's stupid ame of hide and seek, he studiously avoided saying anything that might have construed as being against her. But I read his kindly houghts:

"She is fooling thee, but that is your own lookout; if you like her alculating, capricious ways, who shall gainsay thee, surely not I, y friend? But I will have nothing to do with her. She is too dishonest for me, and I fear her, and all such scheming maidens after her kind."

All the above he did not say, but I knew him well enough, after a friendship of twenty years, to be able to know exactly his great horror of deliberately wicked women.

On leaving him late in the afternoon, I stopped mechanically in front of a jeweller's shop, and my eye fell upon a row of silver purses. I remembered how Lilian had told me that she had lost hers from off her châtelaine, and I resolved to buy her one, and send it to her as a present, which would signify: "Good bye, sweetheart, good bye!"

I chose a pretty purse, with a separation in the middle to divide the gold from the silver, and going into the nearest postoffice, I sent her a letter-card, couched, as well as I can recollect, in the following terms:

JACKY TO LILIAN.

Thursday, January 26th. 1899.

Little jade,

I have just had lunch with Fontarcy, who desires to be remembered to you. I have bought you a silver purse, with a separation.

"Purse—separation." How do those words strike you?

I will send it to you shortly, and also your quinine wine, which will be ready in ten days.

I hate you!

"PIGNOUF."

This short and rude note brought the following answer:

LILIAN TO JACKY.

No date or place. (Received January 28, 1899.)

For supreme elegance and refinement, commend me to the signature, with which you have embellished the note received last night. Nevertheless, I prefer the name, which I often catch myself murmuring under my breath; the name which for me possesses infinite sweetness— Jacky—and I assure you I will never answer any letter signed otherwise.

"Pignouf," signifies a mean cad. You are one perhaps, but I would pray you to forbear carrying your love of truth so far as to use that highly decorative-word as a nom de plume.

I am in bed just now. There is no danger, but I suffer greatly. I will tell you all about it when I see you.

Amuse yourself well with your friend; but do not renew the little orgie of last year with anybody else but me. I shall know it; and I assure you that all would be finished for ever between us. On that subject, I do not possess your lofty and liberal ideas.

Give Lord Fontarcy a nice long kiss from little Lily. Tell him I should love to see him and that I hope to very soon. Is he quite well and happy? I really believe I am in love with him. Are you jealous, my poor, darling Papa? I am afraid your daughter is very naughty. She feels so anyhow.

Thank you for the quinine and also for the purse; how kind you are to have thought of that!

Your little puppy, Pip, grows more and more handsome every day.

He is the pick of the litter. He has got a funny, little, twisted tail; quite wonderful, but not as beautiful in my idea as that of Jacky. I speak to him of his future master, and he is very satisfied with his fate. But will he always remain with you, or share the life of all your others? This last idea does not please me at all.

As for me, I do not hate you—I adore you!

LILY.

JACKY TO LILIAN.

Paris, January 30, 1899.

My little Lily,

I need not explain to you the sweet joy that your last letter, received Saturday morning, has given me, since you wrote it with the firm intention to please me. That I perceive and feel completely. What has often vexed me was to see that you knew well how to make me love you when you chose, but you did not always choose.

If you would only use the tenth part of your malicious and natural cunning to bestow upon me a little of the inexhaustible kindness which is to be found, it is said, at the bottom of every woman's heart, how happy you would make me, by bringing a trifle of happiness into my life, which, already so sad, was about to become more desolate without you. For when I sent you that letter-card last Thursday, I was firmly resolved to break with you. Perhaps, as you are very intelligent, you read between the lines of silly and low joking, and, understanding my thoughts, you have had a leap of love towards me, and you wrote to me to console me and stop me in time. Is that right? No matter; the essential is that you wrote me the most beautiful letter I have received from you up to the present, I think, although you have sent me some very nice ones—especially those of Lamalou.

After leaving Lord F. . . , I saw some silver purses, and the idea struck me to buy one for you and make you a "good-bye" present. I love you too much to endure any longer your treatment of the last few months. Hideous nightmare! If you had been indifferent to me, I should not have noticed it. But the rôle of the suffering sweetheart, groaning, whimpering, swearing, supplicating, afflicted with the epistolary dysentery of unhappy lovers, juggling with the words: "sadness—wounded pride—broken heart," and other commonplace phrases, is not in my repertory. I saw myself continually the toy of a little shrew, with a heart of stone, wicked, teazing and bad-tempered, to say the least. It was too much. It was sickening, and I did not want to return to my vomit.

I wished never to see you more, and I had the intention to put off all invitations by pretexting a voyage. Two such refusals and I should never have been invited again. I should have passed for a boor, and should have felt great grief, but not much more than this winter; and time, I hope, would have closed my wound.

Am I right or wrong, my little daughter? Heaven only knows! But such was my firm intention. Ask Fontarcy.

Is he your new sweetheart? And Gaston, what will he say? How sweet you are! Oh, you are a real woman! What makes me split my sides, is that you take upon yourself the right to make me a cuckold before my eyes, or behind my back, and I must say nothing, and never stray from the path of virtue? Where is the little slave of bygone days? She has broken her chains.

But I will be avenged, and this is how: you say you want to renew the little saturnalia of last autumn? I am willing, but I condemn you to execute such horrors with your new lover, that you will be disgusted with him for ever. That will be your punishment.

I begin to see now what you like, and perhaps I may be able to satisfy you in a terribly exquisite and perverse way. But it is a very delicate matter. I must talk to you quietly about it. I am accomplishing a work of seduction just now for your future enjoyment.

And you, love, work for me. Think of everything that might please me in your house at Sonis, and out of doors when you can venture to escape.

Seriously, I should like to have news of your health. Are you perhaps more ill than you like to tell me? I am very uneasy about it. You do not say what it is, but I guess. I have already guessed lots of things about you! I have to—you are so wanting in frankness.

Poor little puppy Pip! You are very amiable! Only think, he was about to become an orphan; what an escape—and for me too—and for Lily too!

What you say about the name of Jacky delights me and tickles me agreeably. What happiness if, when I see you, you were to be as in your letter. You ought to—but no, I am not going to tell you what you ought to do to make me love you. If you have naught that is good in your soul for me, say so and let me go!

JACKY.

LILIAN TO JACKY.

Tuesday. (January 31st. 1899.)

Can you come to-morrow night by the nine o'clock train? I shall expect you and do my very best to secure an hour's *tête-à-tête* in the nasty little dining-room you know.

Is Lord Fontarcy still in Paris?

My parents will be back Saturday.

Kiss and love,

LILY.

As I went to keep the above alluring appointment, I reflected on the mind and character of my charmer and the result was far from being complimentary to her. I was surprised to find that she had answered a letter, where I had the sinister audacity to say that "I did not wish to return to my vomit!" I was opening my eyes at last, and I did not care if she were to be offended with me or not. Still I could not have very deep love for a woman to write to her as I had just done.

Where she made her great mistake, as a trifler with men, and I beg my lady readers to make a note of this, was in not knowing her customers. She used the same bait for all her fish. It was easier for her, but such proceedings savour of narrow-mindedness. A woman is clever who alters her tactics with every lover. A true huntsman uses a different cartridge for each variety of game. Had I desired the complete favours of this hysterical, selfish creature, I should have had to pay a fearful price. And, in return for all my sacrifices, I must have suffered in the terrible bondage that would have held me—a sensitive man—tightly tied, by the links of my own lusts, to this fearful example of a wickedly neurotic female, without reason, without shame, without the slightest particle of self-respect. I was vile enough, in all conscience, and I have little right to judge her, but I had no wish to torture her; I wanted a little love, if it suited her to love me, and that was all. She could do whatever she liked, and enjoy a crowd of miscellaneous lovers, as long as she behaved honestly to me, and when she had enough of me, she was to say so, and I would walk out of her life without a murmur. But this was too simple and sincere for her. There was no money in this, nor any hold on a man. I was not jealous, I had never asked for her virginity. How could such a man be "worked"? It will also be noticed that I asked her in my letter to think of all that might please her in her house. I meant that she was to try and make her Papa like me exceedingly, so as to invite me often, and she accepted all my sly innuendoes on this subject as a matter of course. I wondered too why she called her dining-room: "nasty"? I had never said so, but it must have been because Papa had possessed her in that room, in the evening after dinner, when Mamma had gone up to bed. I also thought, as I sat in the train, that the principal reason for her kind invitation, was because I was bringing a little silver purse.

She was waiting for me with her dogs as I came out of the station, and greeted me kindly, affectionately, and with much rapid gossip, so as to prevent me recurring to the harsh part of my letter. I was quite satisfied to have produced my slight effect; I knew—alas!—that all my remonstrances would be soon forgotten.

After a short walk, she told me to keep a sharp eye on the dining-room wondow, which faced the road. When I saw the light go out, it would mean that she had gone upstairs with her lamp to Granny and would see that all was quiet for the night. I was to go for a little stroll, and when I saw the light reappear, come softly into the house, as that would mean she was back in the dining-room again, waiting for me, and supposed to be writing letters. Everything was arranged as she told me, and twenty minutes later, I was in her arms. She had nothing on but a dove-coloured dressing-gown, of some soft material, over her chemise, petticoat and drawers.

After a passionate bout of kissing, she sat on my knee and chatted gaily, and I frankly confess that I forgot all her wretched shilly-shallying in the joy of holding her loved form clasped in my arms.

Why she had been ill in bed was this: she had suffered agonies through toothache and after trying all the domestic remedies of her grandmother, and obtaining no relief, had fled to Paris alone, and rushed to a Dental Institute. There, a young dentist told her she had a very bad abscess of the gums and declared it must be operated at once. On her affirming that she feared suffering, he offered to administer some gas and produce insensibility. To this she had consented.

"Were you not frightened? He might have taken liberties with you and perhaps violated you? Had you no fear, as you say you were all alone with him?"

I watched her narrowly as I said this. She answered me coolly that she had no fear on that head, and I felt more certain than ever that I was right in thinking that her maidenhead had disappeared in October or November.

Duly put to sleep, she remembered nothing more, until she found herself half-undressed and quite dazed, with several windows open, and a crowd of people round her. It appears that the young doctor had administered an overdose, and as an older man, who was now in the room, told her, her life had been in danger. She had been accompanied to the railway station and was now, although out of bed, still under the care of a doctor.

I told her that she ought to have telegraphed for me, but I did not say how I felt inclined to disbelieve her entirely. Her troubles, to my thinking, might be connected with her womb, and I was afraid that the visit to a dentist meant some uterine exploration. There may have been an abcess as well, and I felt a movement of horror, as I thought of a contaminating contact. It is only just to say that these disgusting thoughts came into my mind later. Everything seemed to conspire against Lily, and drive me slowly from her: her own conduct and the dread secrets of her prostituted frame.

The operation had taken place during the past week, and Charlotte had spent Sunday with her, sleeping at Sonis, before the return of Lily's parents. While Lilian talked to me, I had my hand on her naked thighs, and toyed with the luxuriant growth of hair on her mount.

"Charlotte did like that to me the other night as I was falling off to sleep,—just the same as you are doing to me now."

"Did you spend with her finger?"

"Certainly not," answered Lily, indignantly, "I turned over, pushed her hand away, and went to sleep."

I have often noticed that if a woman is allowed to talk without being contradicted, she will tell a series of half-truths, relating to what occupies her mind at the time, and an attentive listener is thus often put on the track of secrets he would not otherwise be able to get at. Many men also possess this same grave defect, and lack the retentive power which should prevent them making the slightest allusion to anything they may wish to hide. So I gathered that Charlotte and Lily had plenty of tribadic fun together.

Still I kept my own counsel, and by laughing and joking, contrived to produce upon her the impression I wanted; that I was a love-sick loon, desiring her madly, full of strange sensual longings, and ready to believe anything she might tell me.

I now began to get rather lecherous and excited, having her half-naked body on my knee, and I made her stand up, while my hands wandered all over her lithe frame. She still kept up a slight show of resistance and I felt greatly irritated and lewd, as I knew that my angel was merely shamming, being by this time expert at every caress. But I played my part, and enjoyed the idea of passing for a fool, especially as I knew that all my sayings and doings would be reported to Papa and Mamma on their return. I opened her peignoir and was astonished to find that she had grown much fatter in every way and I told her what I thought. She agreed with me, but did not seem to suspect that I noticed she was now a woman. All her girlishness was gone.

As she stood in front of me, I took off her petticoat, and she, in obedience to my wishes, at once dropped her drawers and was naked, with the exception of her loose robe, chemise, shoes, and stockings. I will not weary my reader with an account of my ecstatic caresses, lickings, and feeling of that serpentine body I loved so well, and which I had not seen naked for four months, but I must describe how I fulfilled a strange longing I had felt for some time past.

I had in my pocket the leather belt of which I have already spoken, and she graciously permitted me to clasp it round her naked waist.

I drew it in as far as it would go, and unluckily found I had forgotten my penknife, or I would have made some fresh holes, to tighten it still more, as my idea was to hurt her a little. It excited my passion to a great extent to imagine that a woman could endure a little suffering for my sake. The circumference of her naked waist was about twenty inches, and I could have easily have gained a couple more had I persevered. She complained in a sweet way that she was not at her ease, and that she did not look pretty, as her little belly jutted out in front by the pressure of the girdle. Paying no heed to her peevish complaints, I drew another strap from my pocket, and fastened her legs securely together just above the knee.

Then I forced a passage through her legs from the front, and thoroughly enjoyed the sensation of roughly pushing my hand between her smooth thighs thus drawn together. She seemed to enjoy the fun, especially as I did not forget to caress her clitoris, ever moist, on the way. Now I altered my tactics, and keeping my right hand forced against her slit, my left tried to effect a passage through the strapped thighs from behind.

Directly I began to push my hand under her bottom, she gradually let herself fall to the ground, and with many a contortion, managed to dislodge my fingers. She swore I tickled her to such an extent that she could not bear it. I desisted, having long since made up my mind that I would allow myself to be made a fool of, until I should tire of the rôle of victim, and so I released her legs, but left the belt still round her waist. I then asked her what I should do to her, and she asked me to provoke her orgasm with my tongue and quickly installed herself upon the little sofa for that purpose. I was in a good humour and smiled to myself, as I thought what splendid control I had over my passions. Here was a woman, who swore continually that she adored me, exercising all her cunning to keep up the pretence of her virginity, and trying all she could do to present only a front view of her secret charms. She willingly stood up naked before me, but when I approached her from behind, when my fingers could have so easily slipped into an excited vagina, she artfully wriggled away. I ought perhaps have spoken, but I was curious to see what she meant, and where she was going. Did she know, poor fool that she was?

She reclined upon the couch, and I was soon on my knees, my tongue sucking and licking all her body, from her breasts to her knees.

I was very excited, albeit I never lost my presence of mind with her, and I told her I loved to lick her all over and I felt certain that at some time or another I had kissed every part of her body, except her feet.

"Oh! you kissed and licked my feet too once!" she exclaimed.

"Did I? When was that, darling?" I knew perfectly well that I had never done so to her.

"In August, when you slept all night with me."

What strange illusions, and what a quantity of lovers she must have had to so mix up their caresses! I grunted an answer that might have meant anything, as my mouth and tongue were busy at work upon her lively clitoris; and I found, being perfectly cool and collected, that her private parts were quite different beneath my lips, being fatter and more open, and my tongue seemed to slip more easily within and penetrate further. I now began to caress her with my hands, while I continued sucking her in the most artistic and elaborate way I could, and I tried to get hold of her two hairy lips and under pretence of caressing her, force a finger within. But she was too artful for me and taking my hands in hers, drew them away. She seemed to enjoy my efforts to please her, and kept me between her legs so hard at work, that I lost all desire and got quite tired. I remember now how I thought of Charlotte, and guessed she had pumped my Lilian dry on Sunday, and Monday morning too, and I grasped the difficulty of my task with Lilian, having to fight against Papa, Lolotte and her other lovers.

And so I sucked and sucked, my penis rising and falling, according as my thoughts led me, but Lilian laid with closed eyes, enjoying the sensation caused by my industrious tongue.

Now and then, she would murmur: "Enough! Enough!" and then, of course, I went on more ardently than ever. But the best of everything must come to an end and she at last pushed me away, I must have been at least an hour between her thighs, which I consider a record time for such a young woman.

She lay panting; breathing heavily, her eyes half-closed, her legs outstretched; all in voluptuous disorder, her shift rucked up to her navel and wide open in front, showing the ruby nipples on her baby breasts.

"Now I am going to see if you are still a virgin, as you agreed to let me do."

"All right," she said, dreamily, raising herself a little, "how will you do it?"

"With my finger," and I went to work and just placed my index at the entrance of her grotto. She started and drew herself up, out of my reach.

"Oh, it is so tender and sensitive so soon after spending!"

Here was yet another proof of the wrecked virginity, but I took not the slightest notice. I found this useless fencing very curious, but I wanted to ejaculate also and therefore resolved not to quarrel. I drew near to her head, as she reclined lazily on the couch, and I rubbed my weapon and my testicles all over her face for a few minutes, revelling in the fascinating contact.

"I shall spend on your face, dear."

"Oh, don't do that!" she cried out in alarm.

"Well then, take me in your mouth."

"I can't, I am still sore about the gums."

She was so indolent, tired, and worn, that I could see she was quite out of sorts, and would have thought it fine fun to let me depart as I had come. But I induced her royal highness to take it in her hand, and she gripped it tightly and manipulated it cleverly enough as I stood by the side of the sofa, my breeches down; while she still lay in the same position.

"Let me see it," she said, turning her face towards its scarlet head.

I was getting near the crisis now, under the influence of her soft hand, and I held her head up and said to her:

"Look at it! Keep your eyes on it!"

She fixed her gaze upon it for a second, and then turned her eyes away and released her hold. A tired expression came over her face; she had spent her fill and wished me to finish quickly, or not at all. How selfish she was! How she loved me!

"How shall I spend?"

"With my hand! Make haste!" And she accelerated her masturbating movements.

"Let me spend on you!" I exclaimed, panting with suppressed desire.

She laughed, but opened her peignoir and pulled up her chemise, exposing herself completely, as she guessed my wish. She gripped my bursting rod fast, and shaking it violently to and fro, I felt the most torturing pleasure as the floodgates opened, and the seed flew in the air, to my great delight and relief. She held the red knob well over her belly, but her grasp was so convulsive that the liquor escaped with difficulty and in tiny spurts and clots. As she felt the hot drops fall rapidly, one by one, on her hairy mount and stomach, she uttered a little cry of surprise and dismay at the fall of each one:

"Oh! Oh! Oh! What a lot! Will you never be done?"

At last the shower ceased, and she let go my dart. As I recovered my self-possession, I could not help smiling as I noticed that her black bush was covered with little spots of spending, as if snow had fallen. There was some too on her smooth belly and the edges of her dressing-gown were also soiled. It is astonishing how the seminal spurt goes far, and lands in all sorts of holes and corners, when allowed to escape in the open.

She arose with a sigh of relief and asked if she might take off her belt. I released her and gloated over the red marks its pressure had left upon her skin.

And now we sat down and talked awhile, as she lazily turned over the pages of "Justine," and explained to me what awful pleasure that infamous book had given her. She loved the disgusting pictures too, with which this terrible work is adorned. One character amused her greatly. She spoke quite seriously about it and I could see that this was a deep impression. I allude to Dorothée, or Madame d'Estreval, who appears in the third volume, possessing a clitoris three inches long. It was this malformation that had greatly excited the libertine imagination of my sphinx-like mistress.

Having spent, she once more began to worry about me and

show signs of jealousy, which increased as I told her that I was obliged to go to London shortly for a few days on a matter of business. Indeed, it was a wild-goose chase after some money that was owed me, and which I saw a chance of getting, if I went myself. At this tale, her temper increased, and I pulled out my little parcel, containing the silver purse, which she was artful enough not to have alluded to as yet, although she was no doubt waiting for it.

"Here it is," I said, "and I had a good mind to throw it in your face and say 'good bye' for ever, if you had not sent me that nice letter."

"It is a very pretty purse," she said, dreamily, but evading a direct reply.

"What a bad temper you are always in, directly you have spent!" I replied.

"And before, as well!"

"Yes, my darling, you are always out of sorts. You have got a devil's temper, you little whore!"

This was the first time I had ever dared to use such a word to her, or indeed to any woman. To my great surprise, she did not mind. I think she rather liked it; I was coming down to her level, she thought.

"If I am a whore, pray, sir, what are you?"

"A maquereau! Your Papa-maquereau!"

She started and looked at me strangely, as I had never spoken to her like this before, and I wondered at my own boldness, which arose from the flight of my illusions.

In obedience to her request, I explained to her what I meant when I said in my letter that I was preparing something new and terribly perverse for her special delectation. Knowing, or rather guessing, that she would like to renew the little orgie we had enjoyed with Lord Fontarcy; that is to say, allowing her to be with another man in my company, I had been casting about to find that second person, and, to attain my object, had begun to throw out hints to a gentleman in whom I had entire confidence, and whom I saw every day. Lilian was very eager to know who, and I did not teaze her long. The man in question was my own brother, who I was trying to seduce for her, without telling him who she really was. This vile scheme delighted Lily, and excited her greatly. She urged me on my work to debauch my brother's brain for her, and there is no doubt that the idea of belonging to two brothers acted in a powerfully lascivious way upon her seething, salacious imagination.

Promising to do my best, I took a tender leave of her, and told her I would write, as soon as I knew when I left for certain and where I stopped in London. She allowed me to write openly to her from England, although my letters would bear the British stamps and postmarks, showing a difference to the preceding year, when I was not allowed to correspond direct from Lamalou. And perhaps the parents always knew all along?

4

My journey to London became inevitable and I thought there
was a chance for me to put my hand on a large sum of money. I
dropped a line to Lily on February 4, and left the next day.

LILIAN TO JACKY.

Monday. (February 6, 1899.)

My adored Jacky,

I am not going to do like you—write without scolding. I must absolutely scold you. You went off to London without warning me of your
exact departure, and without asking me if I would like to go with you. I
would most certainly have gone if you had asked me, and how happy we

253

should have been and how I could have been "naughty" at my ease, without any fear, or afterthought.

You never imagine any combination which would allow us to be together. It seems to me that if I were a man and as much in love as you pretend to be, I should surely find some scheme, and be happy for a few days at least, at any cost. Life is so short that we must be truly in the wrong not to take a little pleasure when we can.

My parents have returned, and it will be no longer easy for me to get out now, otherwise I should have had much pleasure in lunching or dining with you and Lord Fontarcy, if that would please you.

Frankly, this is what I think, as you know well that I cannot love him, since I am silly enough to be madly gone on you. Nevertheless, if it amuses you, you can tell his lordship that I have a great passion for him. He will believe it or not; it will not matter in the least. Above all, no debauchery in London, if you please.

This is what I beg you to bring me from London: a husband, or a *miché sérieux*, of sufficiently refined taste to appreciate a good *taille de plume*,* etc. If you wish to please Mamma, bring her a little tea. I suppose I do right to tell you everything frankly. Need I stand on any ceremony with my dirty Papa? I am no longer your slave, I am your mistress, and I shall punish you on your return as you deserve. I desire a letter of you from London. You can write in perfect safety.

Au revoir, beloved Jacky, my dear love, my sweet little husband. My mouth is better, but Pussy frets after her little dolly. Good luck, sweetheart, and come back soon. Thanks for the quinine.

A most voluptuous kiss from

LILY.

P.S.—If you can imagine a combination, we can lunch and pass the afternoon together on your return. Another kiss.

---

* Literally: "the cutting of a pen." A universal slang term among French-speaking people, signifying labial pollution, as performed on the male. Derived from schoolboy vernacular, as when a pen or pencil is cut into a point, it is generally twisted round in the mouth before using. In all schools, there are a few boys who lend their lips for the accommodation of their comrades, and the expressions: "Shall I cut your pen?" or "Cut my pen!" are well understood, when preceding the buccal onanism. The collegians made use of their erotic argot beyond the walls of the universities, and added a new expression to the language.

My sweet Lily, as can be seen by the above letter, was now perfectly emancipated, and Papa and Mamma must have been quite au courant. She spoke freely about going away alone on a journey with me, and told me to get tea for her mother, besides writing boldly to her house.

My journey to London turned out an utter failure, and I told Lilian as much when I answered her at length by return of post. All her "combinations" simply meant payments, and it seemed to me that her parents, finding that her maidenhead was gone, given to Papa or a stranger, allowed her to have a few subscribers, on condition that she brought home some money every time she went out.

I told her that I could offer her a nice lunch, with lots of love and nothing else, but she could come out on a Friday, which was a day of mortification, and then all would be well. That I often thought of her in London, and imagined her running about with her madcap, lustful friend, Charlotte, to all the fashionable massage shops. I said that I did not expect an answer, as I knew the fate reserved by women for men who were "stone-broke." I added that she could understand my letters much better now, as her mind was more developed and she was more open in every way. Also, that I had focussed the X-rays upon her and now saw through her plainly. I said I was off again, back to Paris on the ninth.

ERIC ARVEL TO JACKY.

Sonis-sur-Marne, February 11th. 1899.

My dear Jacky,

I have been endowed with a fair share of laziness. Of this you must be convinced, since I have not written to you. I have been "going to" every day, but the sun in the South is so intimately connected with dolce far niente, that my good intentions have only added to the paved surface of another place. I must thank you very much indeed for your weekly instalment of papers, the last of which enabled me to return home without experiencing the tedium of the journey. I must confess a weakness in favour of "Pearson's," "Tit-Bits," and "Answers." The pups are in splendid condition, and Lilian is anxious to receive her first instalment as a breeder.

When will you come down and see the dogs, so as to advise about the advertisement, putting us on a par with the dukes and princes who ask the public if they want to "buy a dawg." How would Monday do for you? Lilian takes a holiday and would be free. With kindest regards to all at home, believe me to remain,

Yours very truly,
ERIC ARVEL.

MONDAY, FEBRUARY 13, 1899.

I was very pleased to visit the Arvel family again, but had I not still had some lingering lust for the daughter-mistress of the house, I ought to have broken off the connection there and then. The girl told me plainly enough that she wanted to be paid to come out to lunch, and when I coolly replied that I had no money for her, does not take the trouble to answer my letter, but gets me invited instead to come and see her at her house, and makes Papa write the letter and mention her name twice in it.

I arrived with all my little presents, as usual, and was cordially received, especially by Mamma, who was delighted with her tea, and was not surprised to find that I should bring her from London just the very thing she wanted!

Lilian was very gay and sprightly. She was dressed more coquettishly and with greater care than formerly, and her lips were artificially reddened, without counting a new beauty-spot on her cheek, made with a careful application of a caustic pencil. Liberal use had been made of her special musky mixture, and she perfumed the whole house with the delirious odour that now evaporated slowly from her redolent skin, puffing up mixed with her natural armpit scent. In fact, all her maiden grace had departed and she looked like a brazen strumpet. She spoke up boldly, and her mother seemed quite subdued now, albeit on good terms with her, but I may say at once, to save me alluding to it too often, that her behaviour with her Papa was perfectly free and outrageous, and she never left him a moment's peace. I could see he greatly enjoyed what appeared to me to be her complete seduction of him, and I, to my shame, am obliged to confess that her coquetry with the old man, had a most libidinous effect upon me, and I was in a fever of lust every time she mauled, and patted, and petted him in my presence. I think he liked to be cajoled in front of me. Very likely it excited him to think I was jealous, and no doubt Lilian had not yet told him that Jacky positively liked her to have as many men as it might suit her to enjoy.

Raoul was there, and he seemed to be getting on very well at Belfort, never having been punished yet. Papa was just as furious against him. They were at daggers drawn, and I was perfectly certain that if the elder man so hated him, there were some reasons connected with jealousy of the sister, for I could find no other cause for this bitter feeling against the lad.

Lilian had got into her head that she should go up to Paris with her brother the next day, and join in the riotous fun of the boulevards, watching the maskers, and revelling in confetti-throwing. She made out that her parents would not let her go alone with Raoul, and so she asked me at table if I would take care of her, and meet her and her brother in Paris, to spend the afternoon with them. Of course, I accepted, and after strong opposition by both Papa and Mamma, the motion was carried.

I did not get to speak privately with Lilian until after lunch, when she was in her workshop. Before I had hardly time to open my mouth, she exclaimed that all was false that I had written from London. I suppose she meant that I was wrong to throw doubts on her virginity, or dare to imagine that she knocked about London "on the loose," with Charlotte. And then she made herself so agreeable to me that I fell under the charm once more, as she informed me that she had been earnestly endeavouring to force her father to invite me often and to be great friends with me, so that we could meet more often. She also told me how I was to behave with her Mamma; how I was to praise all her cooking, and above all interest myself in the welfare of her son, who the old lady adored. Lilian was so good and kind and earnest that I forgot all my grievances, and gaily accepted the situation, which seemed as if I was to be the accomplice of Papa and Lilian. This crapulous alliance suited my debauched nature, and I took the liberty to add:

"I am a virgin as far as my own sex is concerned, but if your

Papa likes to violate me, he can do so. Anything to be near you!"

To my surprise, Lilian took this vile proposal as a matter of course, and coolly replied with a little laugh:

"No! No! I know he would not like that, and I should not care about it either!"

We then went for a walk in the garden, accompanied by her brother, and as ever, she began to teaze me. What it was about, I cannot now remember, but I told her that I could not put up with wickedness from her. Then, suddenly changing her tone, she swore she was not going to alter her nature for love of me. I replied that even in that case, I should find consolation, as if she was very bad to me, I should have less regrets when the end should come, as it surely would if she did not amend her ways with Jacky. At this, as whenever I spoke of leaving her, she came round again, and in the sweetest way in the world, promised that in future she would always be good to me. I was infinitely delighted at this kind word from her, and running to the new white wall near us, I took out a pencil and wrote up the date: February 13, 1899.

We had no more words that day, with the exception that I had occasion to tell her that I knew she sometimes said she had not received letters when she had, and that the trick of *billets doux* going astray was a very old one and quite worn out. She only laughed slyly at this, and did not mind it at all. And we were all very happy together. I had never been treated so kindly by them. Papa called me his dear Jacky, and affectionately tapped me on the shoulders, asking my advice on photography, with which he was very much taken up just then, and Lilian came and praised me as much as she could in front of him, saying how useful I should be to her fond Papa, and he proposed that I should become an effectual aid. He suggested that when there were great fêtes in Paris: reviews, state funerals and so on, he and I should go together with his fine detective camera. After taking as many views as possible, I was to start away to Sonis with the plates, and develop them rapidly, while he stopped in Paris to write the letterpress. As soon as I could manage, I was to return to Paris with the negatives finished, and manuscript and photographs could thus be sent off to London by the night mail, and in case of need I would take everything over myself. To do all this, it was necessary that I should learn the management of all his apparatus, and the recipes of his developers, etc., and so it was agreed that I was to come to the house much more often. I was swimming in an ocean of delight, and at each project for my collaboration with Papa, my Lilian appeared with a cunning smile on her rose-pomaded lips, and a sideglance at me, as if to say: "See what I am doing for you!" In the evening, she told me plainly that she was working her Papa in an underhand way for me, and in time I should be his secretary, if I liked. Even the mother took me on one side while I was busy at the south side of the garden with some printing frames, for we were hard at work already on some views of Sonis and the house and garden, and told me that her husband had too much to do and that he ought to have somebody to help him in his writing. I replied that I had some small amount of literary talent, and should be glad to do anything he wished, and she gravely said that I should have to work with him. Can it now be wondered that I fully believed all this, and felt grateful to Lilian, as this was her doing, and all for love of me? Disinterested love too, for she knew by this time how poor I was.

The kindness of the Arvel family and the sweet solicitude of Lilian extended all through the month of February, and I mention this fact, so as not to keep recurring to her parents' goodness or her caresses, as she never passed me without a gentle touch of her fairy hand, or she would give me a luscious kiss if there was no one in sight.

I believe the afternoon was rainy, for we passed much of our time in the drawing-room: Lilian, Raoul, and I. Papa was busy doing some press work and was shut up in his little library. Lily was very gay, and so was I. We frolicked and belaboured the piano in turn, laughing and singing like so many children. I was struck by the great love shown towards her brother by Lilian, now that for the first time I saw them together for a few hours. She would ask him to kiss her, and throw her arms round his neck, while their lips would meet in a long embrace, and Lily would heave a deep sigh of satisfaction and exclaim: "O-h-h-h, sweetheart!" I loved to see this voluptuous play between brother and sister, which confirmed all my suspicions, and the mere sight of their gambolling together in such a lewd way, quite unbefitting their consanguinity, caused me to have violent erections as I sat with them. The same madly voluptuous feeling would also overcome me when she approached her Papa, so the reader must not be astonished when I tell him that all my old desire for Lilian had returned and was stronger than ever from this moment. I think any man would have felt much the same in my place. I was in a delicious daydream of lust as I danced and waltzed with Lily that afternoon, and she gave her brother and myself a private view of some high-kicking, which was simply remarkable for a liberal display of black stockings and frilled drawers of more sober style than those she wore when she came to me in Paris. Whenever she lifted her leg, I did not fail to notice that she half turned her back to me, and Raoul had a full view of the mysteries of her *lingerie*, while I only saw as far as her garters. The whole concluded with a rapturous bout of osculation, as Lily threw herself on her handsome brother, and I sat by in an armchair, possibly looking as silly as any man must, when his virility threatens to continually burst through the cloth of his nether garments.

During our play, Lily spoke of tuition in dancing, and our talk drifted into speaking about lessons in deportment. Merrily taking up the suggestion, she put me through a kind of fantastical drill of her own, and made me sit down, remain motionless, with my legs apart, or joined together, and I had the greatest trouble to hide my lump of manhood from the brother's gaze, though perhaps he saw it all the same.

I am not ashamed to say that the idea of being ordered about by Lilian excited me to boiling point, and for the first time in my life I began to realise that there was really a bewitching kind of lascivious joy in becoming the slave of the woman we love, and I could now understand what was meant by Masochism.

Everybody seemed happy in that house, and the only blot upon the picture was the backbiting of Papa with regard to Raoul.

Lilian was anxious to sell her litter of pups, so I arranged to put an advertisement in a Parisian "dog paper" as soon as possible, and Papa declared that all the proceeds were to go to the fair daughter of the house.

Mamma was very gracious to me, and went so far as to consult me on the menus of the future meals I was to take at their hospitable dwelling. I begged her to be less generous in future, and not to put three rich dishes on the table at every déjeuner, as she had been in the habit of doing, but to treat me as a real member of the family, and cater for me in more sober style. She agreed, and bidding me good night, left with Raoul, going up to Paris to see Cyrano de Bergerac; Mamma was right glad to go abroad with her handsome son, who had really improved through his military training, and looked very well in his French military uniform, although it is not very pretty.

I was in the seventh heaven of delight, and saw a great erotic future before me at Lilian's house, being pleasantly aroused from my day-dream by Lilian whispering to me:

"By and bye, ask me before Papa to put on my Japanese dress!"

Before I had time to reflect, I heard her call over the top of the staircase:

"Papa! I am going to dine with Mr. S . . . , as a Japanese girl!"

He pretended to be annoyed, and said it was not comme il faut, and her mother would be vexed, but I, of course, smoothed him down, and said I had asked her, adding that we were in the thick of the carnival, and therefore a pretty disguise might be tolerated. He gave way, and I soon afterwards met Lilian on the stairs, coming out of her bedroom in full Japanese array, looking the very portrait of a fashionable "geisha." Her robe was adorned with large scarlet flowers and set off her dark complexion to great advantage. The loose gown was largely open in front, cut in V-shape, and I could not resist thrusting my hand into her corsage, but she rudely repulsed me, with an air of defiance. Lilian was full of these whimsical changes of mood. I let the matter pass, and complimented her on her beautiful appearance; for in truth, she looked weirdly fascinating.

She told us that she had had great difficulty in finding the key that fitted her Mamma's wardrobe, so as to get out her costume, and shortly afterwards, we sat down to dinner: Papa, Lilian, Granny, and myself. The old woman does not count in this narrative.

Lily took her Mamma's place at the head of the table, with Papa on her right; I facing him, and the grandmother at the end. I merely mention this meal to note that Lilian frequently placed her feet on mine, with many a loving pressure, and towards the end of the meal, I distinctly noticed that at one moment, withdrawing her feet, she made a decided lurch of her body towards Papa, and must have touched his boot. I saw the well-known change come over his face: a look of dumb bewilderment, which left his features without any expression, as he dropped his head in his plate, and insolent triumph lit up the bold countenance of his mistress's offspring.

After dinner the table was laid out with supper for Mamma and her boy, when they should return from the theatre, and Papa and I were seated on a broad divan, in the little vestibule giving on to the dining-room, and which was used as a kind of smoking corner. Granny had disappeared, and Lilian came and threw herself languidly on the sofa, pressed close against Papa, and placing her half-bared arm on his shoulder, she lightly caressed his shaven cheek with her fingers. He did not respond to her blandishments, but the same silly, dazed look came into his eyes and his lower jaw dropped. How ugly we are, when we are sensually excited!

Lilian said she was happy to be nice and quiet with her dear old Papa, and I asked her as usual when we three were alone together, when she was going to be married.

"Never!" she exclaimed, "I am going to be an old maid and stop with my poor dear old Papa and take care of him."

"And quite right too!" I heartily answered as I always did when this was said.

I was in the same state of sensual longing as before dinner, and I am sorry to say that my recollection of our conversation is slightly dim and confused. Lilian did most of the talk, and I kept the ball rolling as well as I could. I was panting with lust, and Papa seemed as if under the influence of some pleasant drug. Lilian was the embodied type of the bold, black temptress, as exemplified in modern cheap fiction, and I am certain now that she was quite cool, and revelled in the idea of sitting between her two elderly lovers, perhaps laughing in her sleeve at both of us.

Our broken chatter, as we smoked lazily, drifted to Papa's recollections of his travel in Japan, and he told us how the ladies of that sweet land of immodesty wore their light flowing garments and what they carried beneath them. This was an opportunity for Lilian to tell us that she had no stays or drawers on, and she rose, tightened her dress around her, and then turned about with her draperies pulled tight over her large and well-shaped posteriors. Humming a scrap of a tune, she waltzed in front of us two men, and after a few steps, again took her place next to Papa, patting and caressing him as before.

The conversation still turned upon the delights of Japan, and Papa said with a sly laugh, that he had been very dull all alone in that faraway country.

Lilian looked at me across her Papa and put out her tongue, not as a saucy girl might, but with a salacious wriggle of its rosy point, worthy of an experienced courtesan. I did not respond, as I was frightened lest Arvel might see me.

"If you were so virtuous in Japan, what is the meaning of that photograph at your bureau?" And Lily assumed her most innocent air, as she put this ticklish question.

I was delighted, as I always was when I found I had guessed aright, as I had done in January. There was an awkward pause, but I tried to save the situation by saying:

"The possession of photographs of women means nothing. I can buy pictures of actresses in Paris, but it does not follow that I know the ladies."

Papa seemed really confused and to teaze him, I suppose, or to excite him before me, Lily said:

"Oh, but the photograph I mean is not the portrait of a woman alone!"

Papa did the best thing he could do under the circumstances: he got up and left us, and as he rose, Lilian put her thumb to her nose, and "took a sight" at him, much to my inward disgust, as I felt sure she would also turn me into ridicule with him whenever she could, and such low cunning did not please me.

"Take care what you do. He might see you, as when you showed me your pretty tongue just now," I whispered to her.

"Oh, he is so short-sighted!" was her sneering rejoinder.

"I see you know all about his adventures in Japan!" I exclaimed.

She looked at me with well-acted astonishment.

"I don't know what you mean!" was her icy retort, and she leant across the still warm empty place, marked by the deep impression of her stepfather's body, and gave me a most luscious kiss, interrupted by the return of Mr. Arvel. He sat down again between us, and once more Lily's hand tickled and caressed him.

It was getting late, and I began to talk about departing, and looked round for my coat, and some newspapers I had in my pockets.

"I want 'Le Journal;' I used it to wrap round the bottle of quinine I brought. There is a story in it that I have not quite finished. It is very good."

"I've read it," said Lily, quickly, a smile playing on her lips.

"What is it?" said Papa, with a slight yawn.

I did not answer. I felt embarrassed and I wanted to hear what Lily would say. She looked saucily at me, and thus I was forced to break a nasty pause.

"It is about a father and daughter—"

"Oh, yes!" Lily interrupted me. "A father marries his own daughter!" And she looked at me with audacity, as she moved her fingers slowly on her Pa's cheek. I could not meet her glance, and I am certain that she was the coolest of the three of us. I felt most terribly lustful and would have given much to have taken her in my arms at that moment. To hide my voluptuous emotion, I busied myself in collecting my newspapers, gloves, hat and stick, etc.

The story, *Le Lien Factice*, is to be found in "Le Journal" of February 13, 1899, and relates how an old gentleman marries a young girl, and on the wedding-night, respectfully informs her that he is her father, having been her mother's lover, and he gives her proofs in her mother's handwriting. The girl's legal father had always been jealous of him, and had made the daughter unhappy besides, so, fearful lest he should be forced to quarrel with the widower, and therefore never see his daughter again, he had resolved to marry her. But he only wishes to make her happy, swears he will respect her, and as soon as she finds a lover, divorce from her, to let her marry the man of her choice.

"Let us hope that we may not find him too soon, Father!" exclaims the girl, and the story ends with that remark, leaving the readers to guess what they like as a conclusion.

Papa now made as if he was very fatigued and could not rise from the divan, and Lilian told him not to move and she would go and get him some matches he required to relight his pipe. She got up, and passed her hand lightly over his large stomach, her favourite caress to him; but this time her right palm descended swiftly, rapidly, and gently, and as she rose, her fingers passed over his private parts, which were distinctly to be seen, forming a vast protuberance in his trousers, which were tight and of a very light colour.

This was done quickly, her hand trailing behind her, on getting slowly up from the sofa, as if it was an accident.

I was glad she went out of the room at once, without turning round, as I felt an extraordinary wave of lust pass through me and I went red and white by turns. I knew I should have had the greatest pleasure in the world if I could have seen them in bed together, and I had an intuitive feeling that my presence excited Papa, and he would have allowed me to join him with Lily, if she chose.

She now returned, having renewed the powder and lip-paint, and told me it was time for my train. Evidently she wanted to get rid of me, to have a long series of caresses before Mamma returned, so she told Papa to get up.

He made out as before, laughingly, that he was too tired to move, and so Lily took hold of his left hand to pull him off the couch. He being too heavy, she could not move him and asked me to help her. I did so, by grasping his right hand, and together we dragged him to his feet. This was nothing, but after an evening passed in the society of the semi-incestuous couple, the touch of his warm and moist palm had a most peculiar effect upon me. My flesh had never been in contact with his, save in the hurried conventional grip, and the knowledge that Lily held one hand I the other, all three knowing our mutual relationships, irritated my desire to a most fearful extent. I was very thankful to my charmer for her efforts in my favour, as I thought she was endeavouring to do her best to let me into the secret of her *liaison* with the master of the house.

My brain was in such a whirl of lust from this day forward that I am sure I missed several signs and incidents that might have shown Eric Arvel and Adèle's daughter in closer connection perhaps, but I think anybody will now be satisfied that Papa and Lily were lovers.

My passions were excited immensely, and cudgel my brains as I will, I cannot call to mind whether the couple accompanied me to the station or not.

If this story was a novel, it would now be my duty to say that I was hurried out of the house and left to go to the train alone, and then I should say that I climbed over the wall, and creeping up to the window, saw Papa and the Japanese beauty joined in the closest copulation.

In the excitement of desire, and while emitting freely, as only heroines of bawdy books can, she cries out: "Oh, if Jacky were only with us, Papa!" At these words, I jump through the window, and am naked at once! We join in triple voluptuousness; we are surprised by the return of Mamma and Raoul, and they are also introduced into the tableau.

Unfortunately, this is a true story, and I remember now that Papa saw me to the station alone, while Lilian went probably up to bed to get undressed and wait for him to return, while I went quietly to Paris by the train.

What is perfectly sure, however, is that the continual state of erection I had been in all day, without satisfaction, left me with excruciating pains in my testicles, and I made up my mind not to let the presence of Lily and her sly caresses have such an effect on me in future.

On arriving at the Eastern railway station, I met Adèle and her soldier son going to take the train home, and I stopped and chatted with them for a few moments.

The spirit of mischief moved me to tell Mamma in a careless way that she would find her daughter at home in Japanese costume, and I added that Lilian had had hard work to find the key to get out the dress.

"Dear me!" replied Madame Arvel, innocently "I've got my key in my pocket. Lilian has her own costume in her bedroom wardrobe."

After hearty thanks for their cordial reception they went to their train, and I departed thinking over Lily's fib, which was to hide the fact that the Japanese dinner disguise was a pre-arranged project between her and Papa.

SHROVE TUESDAY, 1899.

Lord Fontarcy was on a flying visit to Paris alone, and we breakfasted together, while I excused myself for leaving him at two o'clock, as I told him that I had to meet Lilian and her brother and join the confetti fight. I asked him to come with me and told him how he could make use of the occasion to worm himself into Raoul's good graces and get him for Clara. He refused, as he did not see the fun of waiting until Raoul had finished his year of military service in September. Nor would he accompany me to see Lily, and I saw that my good old friend did not like her at all and appeared frightened of her and all her family. Without knowing the secret of Lilian's life, which discovery I kept to myself, his experience in matters of this kind, greater than mine, led him to go so far as to utter the sinister word, "blackmail," but I laughed at his well-meant warning and told him that I knew how to take care of myself.

I did not tell him that I knew how Lily, who had undoubtedly had some kind of carnal pleasure with her brother, was too jealous to let him make the acquaintance of Fontarcy and his wife. That was why she had broken off his engagement with Charlotte, meaning to keep him for herself.

He left me, and I went to the place of appointment, arranged with my Lily of Sonis, which was at the corner of the Place de l'Opéra, near the Café de la Guerre.

I was frightened I might miss her, as the crowd had already begun to thicken, and the tiny atoms of coloured paper were flying thickly, as the gay Parisians threw them into each other's faces, with many a merry laugh.

Lily now appeared, prettily dressed as usual, and powdered, scented, with her reddened lips, according to her latest fancy. Raoul had not arrived yet. She told me he had taken an earlier or later train, I forget which, as I was under the charm, and thought only of the happiness I felt at spending a whole afternoon with her. I suppose her brother had gone to see Charlotte, but it is of very little account.

Lily scolded me, as her Papa, she said, had informed her that I was not energetic, and did not try to get on in the world. As long as I could find time to get out with my dog, Smike, that was all I wanted, she said.

I told her of a certain number of projects I had formed and she gravely approved of them, but I could not help saying that I was unaware such interest was taken in me at the villa.

"Oh! we often speak of Jacky and we want you to get on. I do all I can for you with Papa and Mamma, as I am really very fond of you."

"Excepting in the winter."

"You must not complain, as Gaston, poor fellow, ran after me for years, and I never granted him *that!*" She clicked her thumb-nail against her teeth in true Parisian style.

During the conversation, we were walking round the Opéra, until at last I took her into the Café de la Guerre, and we sat down and had a glass of champagne, her beloved beverage, keeping our eyes on the door, so as not to miss her brother.

She now made me a kind of declaration of love and completed my sense of sensual intoxication, by telling me how she loved me and how she had tried to struggle against her inclination, but unable to forget me, she had now made up her mind to throw all scruples to the winds and let herself be mine without restraint, enjoy herself with me and see as much of me as she could. Life was too short to deprive oneself of love! Did I not believe her? Was she not doing all she could for me at Sonis?

"Doubtless you love me a little. If not, I should not be here to-day, as there is nothing to make you seek me out, unless you choose, but you are very ambitious and in your wordliness, lose all tender feelings. I know you would like me to be better off and join me in business if possible. But what would Papa and Mamma say to you being in partnership with me, or if I provided a sum of money to start you as a bonnet-builder in Paris, could I afford it?"

I never got an answer when I introduced her parents' names into the debate, and I judged it to be more prudent not to allude to Papa, or the fun on the divan of the preceding evening. Nor did I tell her that Fontarcy was in Paris. We drifted on to other subjects, and I repeated what I had always said and believed, that the only future for a woman in France was the married state, and that if I had always been fool enough to respect her, it was because I saw her with a loving husband in all my dreams of her future. I thought it best not to allude to the least thing that might hurt her feelings.

"You will pass happy nights in the arms of a husband, and will soon forget Jacky, his filthy caresses and his mad ideas of whips and belts. Don't forget, Lily, that husbands enjoy their wives in very sober fashion, without any fancy flourishes."

"Then I should not like it!" she exclaimed, with a disdainful toss of her pretty head.

Raoul now appeared on the scene and joined us in a glass of champagne; Lily told me I was to spend all day with them and return to dinner in their company at the villa, but I demurred, saying that I had already been there the day before, and such behaviour would savour intrusion. Lily told me to have confidence in her and not to prevent her bringing about our mutual happiness in her own way. I accepted, thinking *in petto*, she was the mistress of the house.

Raoul and his sister whispered together, and begging to be excused, both of them went off to see somebody, who was employed at the American bar, which is in another part of the building, and it struck me that Lily was well-known in the establishment. I knew it was frequented by many officers. She returned soon, with Raoul, giggling and whispering foolishly with him, and we began to talk about starting on our tour down the boulevards, to join in the paper war, which had already waxed fast and furious. Lily boldly said before her brother that she wanted to do a little "pee" first, and we waited until she came back, with a fresh dab of powder on the end of her insolent nose.

After loading ourselves with bags of confetti, we were soon lost in the fray, and I cannot now remember how much we used, but none of the ladies on the boulevards that day were more audacious than Lily. She attacked all good-looking young men, fighting till vanquished and surrounded, as she always was, by a crowd of lusty males, who, under pretence of covering her with confetti, popped their fingers down her neck, or pinched her posteriors. I am sure she liked the rough horseplay, although she would break away from her tormentors and throw herself in my arms, hiding her head in my breast, which ostrich-like proceeding dispersed the attacking party, and she drew breath until the next onslaught. I noticed that she rushed at all soldiers in uniform, especially young and handsome officers, and boldly making a stand in front of them, defied them, as it were, to mortal combat, and my suspicious mind, remembering her talk of Boxing-night, immediately gave her an officer as a lover.

The battle continued without interruption until nearly six o'clock, with only one or two interruptions, when seeking the shelter of a doorway, we extracted tiny fragments of paper from Lily's beautiful eyes.

I fully entered into the fun of the riotous public romp, and we gradually got away from the best part of the boulevards. As dusk came on, liberty degenerated into licence, and I amused myself by making Lily a little jealous by the sight of my vile behaviour to ladies in the crowd. I approached them with hands outstretched, as if to throw confetti, but I only put exploring digits down their necks, or even went to the extent of pressing their breasts, when the bust of an unknown beauty looked tempting. It was a rare treat to mark their cry of stupefaction, at being so imprudently outraged by a stranger, and before they could recover, I was off, seeking fresh game.

Tired out, dusty and with her luxuriant locks full of bits of coloured paper, Lily cried, "Enough!" and we made the best of our way to the Eastern railway station, where having a little time to spare, I treated the two young people to refreshment and supplied Raoul with cigars.

In due time we reached Sonis, Lily being very tender in the train, and Raoul turning out a model of discretion.

I found Papa reading some of my magazines and whether I was expected by him I know not; but Mamma had not been warned, as I caught her on my arrival in the kitchen, superintending the preparation of the dinner, and attired in a dirty old dressing-gown.

Everything passed off very agreeably, and everybody treated me with the utmost cordiality, while Lilian insisted on putting on her Japanese costume once more, and I made my appearance in the dining-room attired as a Jap as well, Lily having fished out for me a man's oriental gown, in which I looked as ridiculous as possible. Mamma set her face against Lily's masquerade, and said it was not convenable, especially before me.

At dinner, Lilian was seated next to her Papa. I was at the lower end of the table, on Lily's right, and she pulled her clothes halfway up her leg, and threw one over mine, keeping it there during the whole of the meal, without attempting any disguise.

After dinner, all the womenfolk went away with Raoul to prepare for his departure, as he had to return to his regiment by a late train that night, and a large basket of eatables was got ready for him.

During this time, I sat and smoked a pipe with Papa, and his talk as usual took an obscene turn. I promised to bring him a small parcel of books from my little collection, and mentioned "The Romance of Lust."

At this moment, he got up to fetch an ash-tray, and turned his back to the door, at which Lily appeared, and looking at me, without uttering a word, threw up her clothes, completely exposing her legs encased in black stockings, and her drawers, which, half-open in front—purposely, no doubt—showed a portion of the liberal growth of black hair which hid the mark of her sex. Papa turned round,—she was gone!

Resuming our confab, Papa asked me what "The Romance of Lust" was about, and I told him a few of the leading incidents, as far as I could remember. He expressed surprise, and I answered him very slowly and deliberately:

"I am never surprised at anything where passion is concerned!"

He did not reply, but I saw the same dull, blank expression

that always spread over his face when nonplussed, and neither of us spoke for a few seconds, until Papa rose, and making some excuse, left me alone.

Raoul now took an affectionate leave of his Mamma and Granny, who idolized him, and Lily, covering up her Japanese costume with an ample waterproof, accompanied Raoul and me to the station, Papa following us.

On the way, she told me that she had arranged for me to be invited on Friday, to have a long day's work at photography with Papa, and suddenly in a mock whisper, said, lovingly:

"I am going to tell you a secret!"

"Proceed, your story interests me!"

"You are a dirty pig!"

"That is no secret!"

"No, but this is: I love you, just because you are an adorable dirty pig. I should hate a man, if he was not horribly naughty, as you are!"

When we reached the platform, she managed to get me into a dark corner and give me one of those delirious, long, wet kisses which she knew how to make thoroughly enjoyable. It was only interrupted by the appearance of Papa, and if I did not know he was short-sighted, I should have thought he saw us.

"Papa! Mr. S . . . has been telling me about a book on photography he has got for you!"

Papa did not reply, but only grunted, and Lily continued, with a merry twinkle in her eye:

"Oh, Papa, he is such an awfully naughty man, and so vicious!"

There was another awkward pause, until I laughed, and made some joke or the other, and we all said good bye, but not until Papa had forced me to accept an invitation to spend the day of Friday and have a long spell of photography.

The dog Pip was mine now. I took it to Paris either Shrove Tuesday, or the day before, as near as I can now remember, and Lily seemed very affected at parting with the pretty little animal she had brought up with so much care for Jacky.

I concluded this eventful day for me, by a long conversation in the train with Raoul, when I tried all I knew to give him good advice, so that he should not get into any scrapes at Belfort, and seemed sensible and grateful for my counsel. I could not have said much more had he been my son, as I had been led to believe that Mr. Arvel never took the trouble to speak to him at all.

He went to catch his train to the eastern frontier, and I returned home in a state of wild delight, quite under the spell, and thoroughly convinced that Lily loved me and was duping her satyr Papa for and with me, or else he allowed her to have me as a lover. I did not take much trouble to fathom the arrangement exactly, as I was quite content to let things be as they were and trust to Lily.

FRIDAY, FEBRUARY 17, 1899.

Laden, as usual, with quinine wine, perfumery, books and papers for Papa, and a volume of "Justine" for Lily, I was again punctual at the train, but I anticipated a good scolding from the young lady, with whom I was over head and heels in love, having quite forgotten all her past whimsical treachery and deceit in favour of the lascivious sweetness of her present attitude towards me, as she seemed to allow me to become a sharer in the secret of the passion of her stepfather; and it appeared as if I should at some near period be admitted to their sports, a consummation I am abandoned enough to confess I prayed for with all my heart.

I had shown the pretty Pip to a veterinary surgeon, who was a good friend of mine and my mistress, and he, after extolling its beauty, declared it was afflicted with a shortness of breath, which would render its bringing-up very difficult, if not impossible. My poor Lily, who was passing through a most trying recrudesence of her old rheumatic symptoms, resolved to forgo the pleasure of keeping the little animal, especially as we had three dogs already, my particular Smike and two others; and only dog-fanciers know the trouble it takes to bring up a dog from puppyhood, Pip being, as it will be remembered, only six weeks old. So my devoted invalid covered him up in one of the little woollen shawls she knitted herself, and cried over him as she put him in my arms.

Upon the servant opening the gate of the Villa Lilian, I dropped Pip on to his paws, and he was right glad to scamper to his mother, who was disporting herself in the garden, with the four other puppies of the litter, his brothers and sisters.

I went to Papa's study and gave him a parcel of books, including the four volumes of "The Romance of Lust." I had also brought down for him, the copy of the first obscene work I had ever lent his daughter:—"The Yellow Room"—and to give it to him, I moved towards the window, under which stood a little table. I called to him to come and see this book, which I made as if I had forgotten. As I had shown him each of the others, he had made some remark on each, facetious or otherwise, and as he came towards the light, I put the book on the table and stepped back a pace or two, so that I have a good view of his face in the full noonday sun, and he could not see me. He took up the little volume, and bending down, slowly opened its pages, holding it close to his eyes, as shortsighted people do. All expression left his face; he knit his brows, opened his mouth, and did not speak for a second or two, as, visibly embarrassed, he slowly turned over the pages.

Then he closed it, without a word, and asked me to come out for a stroll, while the lunch was being prepared. I followed him, highly delighted at the success of my ruse, as I was now perfectly convinced that Lily and he had read my bawdy books together. I may say at once, that he afterwards returned me the volume without saying a word in favour of the work, or against it.

I noted that Lily never took me to help her to lay the cloth any more, but she asked me to accompany her in longish walks on all kinds of pretexts, such as doing commissions in the village, taking out the dogs, going to the post-office, etc., and Mamma beamed on us both. She had got the habit of retiring to rest immediately after dinner, leaving Lily with her Papa, and they were supposed to retire about midnight. Papa never got up before nine or ten o'clock, and Lily brought him his breakfast in bed. She was not in good health and took drops of nux vomica before meals to give her an appetite. She looked far from well, in spite of her coquettish toilettes, and rose lip-salve and face-powder, without counting her grain de beauté, which I could see was carefully renewed.

At the midday meal, she was in a towering rage with me for having brought back Pip, and her face was perfectly hideous, all dark and scowling, with blue lips, as was her wont when out of temper. I gave my motives, and said that I had braved her anger, sooner than sell the pup, which I could easily have done, or given it away and told some lie to her. She refused to listen to my reasons, and it was only when her mother took my part, and told her not to be rude to me, that she gave way and came back to her usual manner.

The advertisement for the sale of the dogs had appeared the day before for the first time, and they were delighted at my effort to put a few pounds in Lily's pocket. So much so, that she and her mother had ordered an ice-pudding for lunch for my special benefit.

All went merrily as a marriage bell, and Lily, alone with me, asked for news of the gentleman I had promised to seduce for her. I told her frankly that I had proposed to my brother to join me in a miniature orgie, saying that I would introduce him to a little brunette, but, of course, without telling him her name at present. After accepting in a half-hearted way, he had cried off when I asked him to tell me the day he would be ready, and I apologised to her for raising false hopes. It was not my fault if my brother was inclined to be a little sentimental and averse to sleeping with women who had been with me. Lily heaved a sigh of regret. The idea of being in the arms of a brother of mine had excited her greatly. I spoke of her plan to get to London in my company, but she did not seem to think there was anything out of the way in coming to England alone with me. It could be done by her making out that the employers of Charlotte would be supposed to send her to London on business, paying her expenses and giving four pounds a week, during her stay. There was no occasion to write any forged letters, or do anything except send her a first-class return ticket; her parents would believe her, whatever she might say. Now was the time to go, as she could say she was wanted for the fashions of the coming summer. I added that on the morning of her departure I could be at the Northern railway station, as if I were going to London alone, and affecting surprise, offer to chaperon her as far as Charing Cross. Lily could not guess that this was a little trap of mine to see if her Pa and Ma knew of our intrigue, and she agreed that my plan was perfectly feasible, always providing she came home after a fortnight or so with a ten-pound note of her own at least. I told her I would see about it and perhaps in a few days, I might be able to afford it. But inwardly I am forced to declare that I could only think of a certain poor ailing woman in Paris, and there were old bills owing to doctors, a long score at a chemist's and other little odds and ends.

Lily was very excited at the thought of being alone with me for a week or so, and I told her that she would have to be my slave, and we both got ourselves into an awful state of lust by imagining what we would do together. I remember she took such a fancy to a couple of very nasty fancies of mine that she made me repeat them.

At the word of command every morning, she was to rise, and stripping naked, seat herself on a toilet pail, after having prepared a tooth-tumbler, with tepid water and dentifrice. I would then rise and clean my teeth, expectorating on her body, she allowing me to rinse out my mouth and empty my throat all over her, so that the liquid would fall upon her and trickle down her breasts and belly, dripping into the receptacle. Then she would become the living chamber utensil of her beloved master—"a thing you often said you would do and never did"—she added regretfully, and I saw that she really enjoyed these filthy projects. She would then have to soap me in my bath and assist at my toilet, and when completed, Lily having put on my boots, etc., I would go out and leave her to get dressed herself.

The rest of the day passed off in the ordinary way; Papa and I were in the dark-room most of the time and even after dinner. Lily would escape from her workshop whenever she could, and come and pay us a visit. Then I would get a long kiss, and half of her wicked tongue would disappear down my throat, which I vastly enjoyed, although I knew I should pay for my fun in the evening, by testicular pains.

Mamma was rather against the photographing craze, as Papa passed too much time in the little house, which was very damp and cold, and he had taken Lily to assist him—I pricked up my ears at this—and the two had spent the whole of one evening shut up alone together, in the famous dark-room.

It was indeed very cold, despite the large petroleum lamp that was burning, most of the printing being done by artificial light, and being in there after dinner, Lily appeared, saying her hands were cold, and boldly stuck one paw into Papa's trouser pocket, while with the other hand stretched out behind her, she caught hold of my member. I immediately unbuttoned myself. She slid her hand inside, and gently tickled the top. She thus had one hand in her Papa's trouser pocket and the other was feeling me.

"Your hands are not cold," grunted Papa, with the dull, serious face of the lewdly excited man, that I now knew so well.

"But suppose I like to say they are?"

Finding now that Lily was always putting her hand between my legs, whenever we were in the dark-room with Papa, I never went to Sonis any more, without arranging my drawers in such a manner that my organ was at liberty, and I only had to undo two buttons to have it ready for her hand. Many a time, Papa would be developing, mixing, explaining, and I was not learning anything, but was caressing Lily; and she kept her hand on my naked weapon behind Papa's back and sometimes we were all three entirely in the dark, when a plate was being developed.

Just before dinner was served, Lily said that I ought to sleep at Sonis one or two nights now and again. I answered that I should be delighted to do so, that very night if she liked, but I should have to be up very early so as to see my mistress in the morning, as was my habit.

"I hate her! I hate her!" she cried, clenching her little fists.

I paid no attention to these ravings, but waited patiently until the storm subsided, and then I asked her if it would do any good for me to sleep at the house.

"You would not come to my room in the night?" I said, dubiously.

"Yes, I would. I would manage to worm myself in to you!"

I asked her how it would be for me to have a false attack of giddiness after dinner, which I could ascribe afterwards to indigestion, and I showed her exactly how I would act as a man utterly unable to stand upright without assistance. It was arranged that I should play that part, and she added that Mamma would never let me go to Paris in such an apparent state of weakness. Having arrranged with her not to laugh while I was acting, as I knew in that case I should laugh too, she left me and we dined shortly afterwards. But the first moment she could find to speak privately to me directly the dinner was over, she told me not to attempt my scheme of sham illness, as I looked too well and jolly after the meal. I did as she told me, but I still think that she consulted Papa and it was by his orders that she changed her mind.

I have no recollection of anything more particular taking place that day, but I find by a note in my diary that I was again a guest at the Villa Lilian on:

FEBRUARY 21, 1899.

Instead of taking a train at ten o'clock, as I usually did, I could not get to the station except for the 11:30, and while quietly seated in my compartment, I saw Lily running up and down the platform, peeping into every carriage. She was looking for me, hoping that I had taken the same train as she had. She had been up to Paris to go to market and was returning with her purchases, being accompanied by one of her workgirls. We carried on our conversation in English, and we spoke of a letter I had written her, wherein I had informed her that "all the schemes on which I had built to be able to take her to London, had fallen through, and I was very unhappy, but nevertheless I counted on the love of the daughter of the Mikado, and hoped she would intercede for me with the great chief and master of the house, over whom she possessed such *extraordinary influence.*" I wished her to understand that I knew all that was going on between her mother's lover and herself, but that I was not jealous and could perfectly understand that a man could fall in love with a young girl, with whom he was in daily contact, especially as she resembled her mother in several little ways. Here was a man of strong animal instincts, linked to a vulgar, jealous woman, albeit devoted to him as the breadwinner, and I should think, incapable of disinterested affection. To keep him at home, she would voluntarily shut her eyes to any commerce he might have with Lily and the task would be easier if they had already, both of them, been too free with her as a child. Lilian never took offense at this moment when I recurred to the understanding that existed evidently between Mr. Arvel and herself, while I made my allusions in a most respectful manner and never let myself be betrayed into speaking against him, although Lily always alluded to him with a show of contempt, and I sometimes pitied him as whatever his faults, he slaved and worked for these two women, who after all only formed his little harem. He did sleep with the girl, but was it real incest? Was he her real father, or not? The idea could only be loathsome to the lascivious lass, but as long as she herself felt no disgust at the approach of the man whose lips had pressed her mother's for twenty years, and who had dandled her on his knee and brought her up, who had a right to feel indignant? She was a woman of strong passions, and if she was to become a whore, what mattered if the little man who was her natural guardian possessed her or not? As far as I was concerned, I was rather pleased to think that now she ran no risk of being driven to ordinary professional prostitution.

Lily was very lively and full of fun, and she got quite spoony over a handsome young officer who was seated in front of us, and who really looked very smart in his cavalry uniform. She turned red and white by turns as she furtively admired him and I chaffed her about her adoration for the military.

An exalted personage had just died in France, and all sorts of strange rumors were floating about concerning his death, as it was currently reported that he had died suddenly in a woman's arms, or rather had succumbed to the caresses of a complaisant mistress. He had died in erotic delirium, and this end, more frequent than many people might think, was only remarkable by reason of the great positions the unfortunate victim to his passions had occupied during his lifetime. His age was about 60, and I told Lily the peculiar story of his last moments and how he had while unconscious continually called upon his numerous concubines by name and cursed his weak organ of virility, because it refused to respond to the call of lust.

On arriving at Sonis, I went for a walk with Papa, and I recited to him the wonderful end of the great statesman. I looked at him out of the corner of my eye as I walked and talked with him on the pleasant country road, and I soon saw the dull, sullen look steal over his face again as I broached erotic subjects, which I saw interested him deeply, and now I was almost certain that I could produce that expression on his features whenever I chose.

Elated with the sense of my power of reading the thoughts of Lily's Papa, I took the liberty of asking him if it was true what I had heard concerning the genital strength of men of sixty years of age, more or less. I explained that it appeared to be a most unfortunate state of things when the desire of venereal diversion, centered in the brain, persisted years after the seminal flow had ceased, and I opined that it must be terrible for an old man to be tortured by lewd imaginations without having the natural means to gratify them, when driven by erotic dreams into a woman's arms. It was a fearful ending for a man to finish up like a mad eunuch. He pooh-poohed my theory, which I submitted to him with the greatest deference, as I always treated him with respect and politeness, and told me that desire ceased always when the virile power was dead, and though I did not believe him, I agreed with him all the same. I always enjoyed the suburban skill of the narrow-minded dwellers in villadom, as they possessed a wonderful knack of settling the most difficult problems in a moment. They always knew everything, and arranged political and social complications with a rapid coolness that would have seemed conceited in a Cavour. And they did not want a fine library, a staff of secretaries or a lot of expensive maps; they settled things offhand in a tramcar or a railway carriage.

I envied such men as these, and Mr. Arvel was of the same kidney, for they made life easy for themselves by the adoption of certain easy formulæ which did away at once with all useless discussions. With some, all women were prostitutes; another camp swore females were angels. It was the same with everything else: religion, the army, and the benighted inhabitants of any other nation. Their petty view of things in general betraying limited intelligence only inspired me with a desire to leave their society at once, but their principal fault was that, in their great desire to show their knowledge and talk at all hazards, they thought nothing of confiding to utter strangers the secrets of their wives' wombs, their daughters' constipation, and all possible sexual troubles. Arvel's pleasure was to talk against everybody, and he did not spare Lilian, her brother, or his wife.

But we were all very happy in spite of his grumbling and there was joy in the house of Arvel, and money too. All kinds of goods kept continually arriving from the big shops and stores of London and Paris during this month, and Arvel pulled out handfuls of gold to pay the bills. The garden too cost a lot of money, without counting the photographic requisites and the painting and decorating of the new part of the house, which was never done with and was sufficiently comfortable.

During the breakfast, which was most generously served, in spite of Mamma's promises of moderation, Lily's health was the topic discussed and Papa announced his intention of taking her away on a journey to give her a little change of air. Mamma did not object and Lily said nothing. I opened my ears as wide as I could, and as I was always ready in that house to agree with everybody, gravely said that it was the very best thing that could be done for the health of Mademoiselle. Papa mentioned the name of a seaport town and asked me what I thought of it. I replied that I did not think she would care much about the sea at this time of year and that there was not much to be seen in a small French port at any time. So Papa suggested Brussels or Berlin, and after a little conversation it was decided that Lily was to visit Brussels, where she had never been. It was on the tip of my tongue to ask Mamma if she was going too, but I thought better of it, and indeed the sprightly Lilian left me no time for reflexion, but kept me thoroughly enchanted with the frequency of her most audacious caresses and never passed her good Papa without touching and tickling him too.

I told her how excited I had been to see her in Japanese costume and asked if she could not manage, as she knew how to make a dress, to knock up a very low body and come to dinner one night in this very *décolleté* bodice, which I wanted to be quite low under the arms, so as to show the arm-pits, and was to be cut in the same V-shape as the Japanese costume, both front and back, as that shape suited her thin figure admirably. She replied that she dared not attempt such a thing, as Mamma had scolded her dreadfully about the Japanese disguise, and as for fancy dresses, at that moment: "she wasn't taking any!" I loved to hear her speak in English slang with her French accent.

We had a very nice long walk that afternoon together and she enchanted me by giving me a little present as a surprise. This was quite spontaneous, and formed the first and last present she ever gave me. And it was simply a little sachet about two inches square, of white silk, embroidered with the initials of our two Christian names. It smelt strongly of Lilian's aromatic scent, but the curious part of the matter was that she told me she kept the wadding it contained for two nights inside her virgin (?) furrow, in order that I should always be under the charm of the *odor di femina* which I loved so well, especially when I knew it was Lilian's. In spite of my blind lust for her, I am sorry to say that I did not believe her; I could not see Lily sleeping two nights with a little bit of wool inside her crack, for anybody. Still I was very pleased to think she should take the trouble to invent such a pretty lie for me, as the intention to make me happy was clearly there. I discovered that she carried her hatred of sentimentality so far as to be very delighted when I called her by the most opprobrious epithets and as I applied them to her, she would purr and lick her lips in a transport of delight, and rubbing herself against me, make me repeat the words: *salope*, *putain*, *vache*, etc., over and over again.

She also asked for more erotic dreams of cruelty and told me she kept most preciously the strap and the paint-brush I had left behind me at the end of August, when I had slept all night with her. I told her how I should like to spread-eagle her by tying her to the end of a bedstead, her arms and legs stretched out, forming with her body a kind of a Maltese cross, but she pulled a long face whenever I spoke of any position or diversion of passion which would force her to open her legs. I was more than ever sure that her little bird had flown, but I put on a most innocent air and asked her if she was not afraid to trust herself so much alone with me, because I might throw her down and violate her and I could do it easily here at Sonis, as she dare not cry out or make a movement that would disturb her dress.

"You need not take all that trouble, as I am keeping it for Jacky!"

I was so astounded at the coolness of her reply that I was suffocated for the moment, and she profited by my stupefaction to run on and tell me what happiness it would be for her to go on a journey with me to London and sleep with me several nights. I gathered from that proposition that she wanted to keep me from her until she could get me into a bed at night, and then she would make me believe I had seduced her. I was careful not to say too much, or she would have flown into a temper, been on her guard and I should never have known anything.

The same fun went on as before in the dark-room just as before dinner, and once being alone with Papa, he asked me if the authorities still allowed bawdy-houses to be carried on. I replied in the affirmative, and no more was said about the matter, but I thought it was just on the cards that Papa wanted to take Lily with him to one of those hospitable homes of free love.

Lily reappeared and put a stop to our conversation and we soon had to go in to dinner, for which we were late, much to Mamma's disgust, and we were treated to a long lecture from her as she pretended to make out that this photography was a folly and would never bring in a penny, while he and Lily would catch their death of rheumatism, if they passed their evenings in the damp little hut together as they were now doing nightly. This diatribe did not prevent Lily from following me to the tiny studio when I had to go in the middle of the dinner, or a plate would have been spoilt. We had a good bout of lip and tongue sucking and she put her fingers in the front of my trousers for a second, and then we returned through the dark garden as if nothing had occurred. Lily's lips were all chapped and feverish and she kept putting on the pink pomade. Both Papa and myself must have been licking her delicious lips this month, as they had never been licked before.

After dinner, Lily and I were quickly in the drawing-room, as Mamma had stopped all photography for the night, and getting rid of Granny, we kissed and caressed each other to such an extent that I begged her to finish me with her hand, or I should go mad. "What, really? You will enjoy in your trousers? You must not do that!"

Granny now returned, and speaking to me, drove my unsatisfied lust from my mind for a time, and then the pains came on again. I sat by her side as she tried to knock a tune out of the piano, but as her Papa said, "she couldn't play for nuts."

I talked to her in English and told her how I was suffering from what was called a "suppressed horn" and that I wished she had made me spend in my breeches just then. She said that would be disgusting. I retorted that there was nothing to be disgusted with when it is a man we are supposed to love, and she was very happy to have me tell her that if ever she slept with me again, she would have to lick my feet and under my arms, without counting other peculiar and strongly smelling parts of a man's body, at six o'clock in the morning, when all is hot and redolent of a rutting male. She agreed, and all was arranged in her mind to try and come to the station with me and masturbate me in a secluded spot, but nothing came of it. I think she played a deep part, promising me anything, and praising all I suggested, but I could not take any notice of what she said. I always guessed she would cry off at the last moment, and despite my great desire, I never believed much of all the stuff she told me, though at this moment I was ever head over heels in love with her.

Now came Papa to interrupt us, and he carefully installed his portly figure on an armchair, while Lily, as if obeying a sudden impulse, left the piano abruptly and took a footstool, which she placed at Papa's feet and then sat on it, pushing herself hard against his legs, as I could plainly see. Papa always maintained a dignified silence when Lily approached him in loving style before me. Mamma joined us and there was no peace until I had promised to come and spend the day on Monday, 27th. of February, as Raoul was to be there, having a holiday on account of the funeral of the illustrious personage I have referred to, and there was also to be present, a German friend of Mr. Arvel, of the Berlin financial papers.

FEBRUARY 27, 1899.

I started from Paris with a novel for Lilian, called *L'Anneau*, as the subject treated of a young girl who falls in love, but her sweetheart fights shy of her because she is a virgin. So she throws herself in the arms of a cool, debauched rake, who is quite surprised to find she is a maid, but he violates her speedily and, fearful of the responsibility, never sees her again, but the man for whom she has done this also discards her. Another lover now comes after her, but he is sentimental and proposes marriage. She accepts, hiding from him the fact that she is no longer intact. Through the boasting indiscretion of her seducer, as I call him out of politeness, the would-be bridegroom finds out her deceit and reproaches her bitterly. The curiosity of the novel is in the up-to-date manner in which it concludes. In the old sentimental days of my youth, the author would have rushed to suicide as a wind-up; here the young man takes the heroine to be his mistress and we leave him buttoning the girl's boots after a scene of sensuality in the middle of the day. I also kept Lilian supplied with the volumes of "Justine," and Papa and lynx-eyed Mamma must surely have seen the volumes sticking out of my pockets.

And another peculiar circumstance took place that very day. The advertisement about the dogs brought a number of answers and I may say at once that two were eventually sold for fifty francs each, out of the five that formed the litter; and all kinds of applicants wrote to ask about the pups. Mamma showed a post-card where most peculiar details were asked, the writer thinking that these were pedigree dogs, whose sire had won prizes at shows, etc. I told her to answer and say she did not know anything about pedigrees, but the dogs could be seen at any time.

"Sign your letter with a woman's name, and then you need not bother to give particulars. Any name will do,—Marguerite, Antoinette—"

"Or Justine!" exclaimed Mamma, interrupting me, while her

beautiful black eyes pierced me through and through, as she tried to see what effect her bold mention of that name would have upon me. I was taken aback and staggered for a second, but I made no sign. Mamma and I were alone at the time, or else she would not have been so bold. I debated with myself whether I should tell Lilian or not, and after reflection decided to keep this queer answer of Mamma to myself for the nonce. It was a useful bit of information anyhow, as it enabled me to see that the mother was an accomplice to Lilian's goings on, and as the afternoon grew towards a close, another incident confirmed my theory and this time it was of much greater importance.

We were all in the dining-room. I think the five o'clock tea was being drunk, or had been served, when a ring was heard at the gate of the villa. It was a gentleman who had come to see the puppies, from the advertisement in the newspaper. Whenever anybody called, Lilian always rushed to the garden to see who it was, and evinced great curiosity and a wish to show herself, and Arvel generally followed suit, as he also liked to know what was going on. But this time the couple never moved, and Papa told me to go after his wife, who was already in the garden, and explain about the dogs to the gentleman. I went, wondering at the attitude of Lily and her Papa, who were standing up side by side, their backs to the *buffet*, and both looking embarrassed and uneasy. Lilian held her head down, and Papa looked quite shame-faced and also seemed to be studying the pattern of the carpet. The visitor was an officer in the French army, and he gave his name and address, which I carefully noted, and he also mentioned that of another officer, his friend, an amateur of the canine race, who I knew by reputation as an *habitué* of the Café de la Guerre, where he used to have his letters addressed. The visitor was a fine, tall, gentlemanly, handsome fellow, about 35 years of age, with blue eyes and a large fair moustache, but with no beard. I was very glad to note this little detail, as I knew Lilian liked shaven chins, and I wore all my beard, as I have already stated. He seemed very quiet and subdued in his manner, and was visibly either ill at ease, or very shy and nervous by nature. He asked a few unimportant questions about the little dogs and Mamma drew him away to see the rest of them and their father and mother, in another part of the garden. I turned back to the house out of discretion. As I went strolling along, I saw the officer striding towards the gate, followed by Mamma, who had to trot to keep up with him. He was very tall, and little, paunchy Mamma was running by his side, talking earnestly and looking up at him, like a street-walker soliciting an unwilling stranger. She followed him out of the gate, and I went back into the dining-room, where I found Lilian and her Papa, who had not moved from their straitened position against the buffet.

Raoul, who was at home that day, on a special holiday on account of the funeral I have mentioned, now came running in to the dining-room and announced that Mamma had made a present of a pup to the officer, although he had not seemed surprised at first being asked sixty francs for the one he had chosen. Everybody seemed astonished except Lilian, who asked me what I thought. I answered that I could not understand it at all. I could not tell Lilian that I fancied he was her adorer, and that she was giving each of her lovers a pup, as I was to have had one. Papa, coarsely, as was his wont, said that if he had been a man and such a thing had happened to him, he would have thought that the woman who gave the animal, to him a perfect stranger, wanted him to sleep with her. Mamma took me on one side and in a greatly excited state, her voice, quite hoarse, and her lips white and trembling, excused herself to me, saying that she had done this to curry favour for her son. This was laughed at later by Raoul, who explained that he was in another part of France, and naturally this officer could do nothing for him. Altogether each one acted his or her part splendidly, including myself, who listened and looked at each and every one, saying never a word, nor betraying myself in any way. This is the man who took her virginity in November, I expect, and accounts for the story of the lieutenant, the silver *châtelaine*, and the late newly-developed love for officers in general. I kept my own counsel.

The German friend arrived after breakfast, but left before the officer came, I think, although he has but the place of a lay-figure in this story.

Papa had fainted away as from giddiness on Saturday and Sunday and was far from well.

After lunch he had a slight fit of vertigo and it was all he could do to keep on his legs. I offered to stop with him, but he refused and went to lie down, while Lilian, who I watched narrowly, never turned a hair. She seemed very hard-hearted, for although he was nothing to me, I suffered to see my big, strong friend grow white, and stagger like a drunken man, but the boy and girl were unmoved; and as it had been decided that Raoul, Lily, and I were to go out on bicycles, we did so, leaving Papa with his wife and Granny.

I must not forget that I had borrowed a Kodak and took everybody's portrait, but most of my films were monopolised by Lilian, and I got her in all sorts of positions, with her dogs and without, and I experienced sweet lustful emotion in ordering her to turn and twist in front of the lens, and make her pose in a variety of attitudes, merely so as to have the pleasure of commanding her to stand in such and such a way. She obeyed me with docility and was kind, loving, and tender to me all day, looking very bewitching both in front of my camera with her big, red, burning lips, and afterwards during our pleasant ride, in a bicycle costume, with a divided skirt.

When we returned from our ride, Papa was better, and I tried to diagnose his illness and reckoned it up as the result of a long winter's indulgence in the pleasures of the table, with no exercise; and living in a confined atmosphere, breathing the poisonous emanations of a slow-combustion stove in his sleeping apartment. There were the remains of the old mysterious illness of years ago and I began to ask myself if he were not syphilitic perhaps, but all this was in a very crude state in my brain at that moment, as my faculties were dulled by Lily's blandishments. Papa recovered enough to come and take some photographs of Lily with Raoul and me, and I tried to get Lily with her head pillowed on the broad breast of her handsome brother in uniform.

We dined late and Lily was seated next to me. She pulled her clothes up so as to expose her naked left thigh and signed to me to touch it. She remained like this all through the dinner, and I felt her thighs when I chose and when I could, without counting touches of her hands, and pressures of her feet. Add to this the kisses of the whole day and I think I had nothing to complain of.

The German friend had been invited to come and lunch on the first of March and go out for a bicycle ride afterwards with Miss Arvel, and I was told to come too. I consented, nothing loth, and returned to Paris with Lily's kisses wet on my lips and thoroughly convinced that despite Lilian's many lovers she still kept a corner in her heart for me. And I was ready to forget and forgive all, Papa and the others, past, present and future, if black Miss Arvel would keep her word with me.

MARCH 1st. 1899.

Papa had experienced difficulty in getting the requisite poisonous chemicals used in photography and I brought him what he wanted, some cyanide of potassium and bichloride of mercury, one ounce of each, together with some other trifles, measuring weights, samples of photographic papers and so on, to make myself agreeable to him, and I had, for the last year, taken subscriptions to the papers he liked and which I found inexpressibly silly: "Answers," "Tit-bits," "Pearson's Weekly," and a more serious publication, "Photography."

Soon after my arrival, and the most flattering welcome, Lily, who was ready dressed for the bicycle, gave me back the novel, *L'Anneau*, and when I asked her how she liked it, merely nodded her head, and ran away, leaving me alone. I had made a hit then? Something in that book had touched her to the quick. What was it? Had the man to whom she had given her virginity last winter left her after the sacrifice, or was she disinclined to talk about the rupture of the hymen? Should I ever know? What an amusing game of hide and seek she was playing, and what was her motive, if indeed she had one at all?

The Berlin gentleman I had already seen came to breakfast, and he spoke German nearly all the time with Papa, while Lily and I had it all to ourselves at the end of the table and a very pleasant meal it was, my lustful charmer being as amiable as it was possible to be.

In the middle of the repast, the wine ran short. Lily was sent to the cellar, and asked me to accompany her, which I did with delight, and we sucked each other's lips and tongue with rapture, Lily telling me to follow her into the dark-room immediately after breakfast, as she wanted to show me something there. We left Papa eagerly discussing the Dreyfus case in German, and as usual he was all in favour of the generals, as was the Teutonic guest. I had refused to join in the discussion, although Mamma, knowing my opinions, tried to get me to talk on the subject by telling the stranger that I held contrary views to his! I preferred to slip away with Lilian and we were no sooner inside the little cabin than after a long sweet kiss from her fevered lips, she plainly informed me that she wanted me to give her pleasure with my finger as she felt very "naughty." Nothing loth, I put my hand up her clothes, as she stood up, leaning against the sink, and my finger immediately touched the spot. I was very surprised to see her start and draw back, with a rapid movement, dislodging my hand completely. I saw at once what had happened. She knew, of course, that she was no longer a virgin, but her great preoccupation was to make me still believe in her virtue. In her excitement, she had presented herself in quite an easy position, the knees half-bent, eager to be manipulated, and I, full of lust and luncheon, had pushed my finger in too far, as I could tell by the soft warmth and moisture. I asked why she drew away from my touch.

"Oh, that is nothing. Don't be offended! Surely you can excuse an instinctive movement of shame?"

I was too clever, and at the same time too excited myself, to do anything but agree with her, and I was content to do my best to bring about the crisis, as she stood bolt upright now, her thighs pressed together. After the usual expressions of pleasure, she suddenly broke away from me, exclaiming that she had spent, and I said to myself that she had been remarkably quick about it. She now made a dive for my neglected organ, which she found quite ready to her hand, as it was all prepared, sticking out of the drawers, as I have explained. She caressed it a little, telling me to keep a sharp eye for fear any of the workgirls should come along, and bending down, took it in her hot mouth, rolling her agile tongue round its swollen head. She had not been sucking me for two seconds, when she got uneasy, and left off. I begged her to continue and finish me, as she stood by my side laughing and looking, and admiring my sign of virility, and she bent down again, once more popping it into the velvety seclusion of her warm mouth. But directly she felt that I was about to ejaculate, she left off suddenly, exclaimed that she heard footsteps, and fled rapidly from the tiny building, leaving me all alone with my stiff rod sticking up out of my trousers. The disappointment was so great that my erection soon passed off, and I was too much in love with the coquette to feel any anger with her.

With the same sensation of stupid passion, which is pleasing in its way, I started on my ride, with Lily and the German. Miss Arvel showed us the road, and she agreed to pilot us to a kind of tea-garden, about ten or twelve miles off. The German was not troublesome; he walked Miss Arvel's bicycle up all the steep-hills, and there are many along the Marne, while we lagged behind and talked. I saw Lily did not want to work too hard, so as not to perspire, or tumble her hair. She wore a veil too, and was powdered, perfumed, and her lips well reddened, albeit they were swollen. Our conversation was very lewd. I showed her a lusty beggar on the road and admiring his rustic beauty, asked her if she would like to see his staff of life, adding that he would very likely show it for a few coppers.

"He would show it me for nothing," said Lily, with a merry laugh. "Charlotte would go and ask him, if she were here." And with a change of tone: "I can rub my little button in this divided dress, as I walk along," and the German being a long way off, she made all the requisite movements as far as I could see, and after a time announced that she had finished. I need not repeat how I talked to her; my readers will guess the state I was in.

"You don't think I've come like this?"

"Yes, I do! I know you are so awfully lewd. But soon you will be able to enjoy yourself immensely when you will be travelling alone with your Papa."

She feigned surprise and pretended not to know what I was talking about, but I saw she was not offended with my allusions to her Papa's love for her.

"You are going away on a nice little journey all alone with your Papa who loves you dearly, and you are very fond of him, which is not to be wondered at, as he adores you. It is a real honeymoon. Do not think I am jealous. I have noticed his love for you for a long time. It reminds me of a beautiful novel I have got, and which I must lend you, all about a father and daughter who go away together for a pleasure trip."

"Do you think that a daughter cannot misconduct herself with her Papa without travelling with him?"

"You are quite right, but it is much nicer to be entirely alone with the man one loves, amid fresh scenes."

She did not answer me, but laughed the matter off and changed the conversation. I think I chaffed her a little more that day, when the hazards of our ride brought us near to each other, out of hearing of the German gentleman, and she took it all in very good part, as if I was alluding to any ordinary flirtation. I am bold enough to say that she was proud to have made the conquest of her mother's old lover. What amused me most was the part played by the woman who was known as Mrs. Arvel. Did she know? As a jealous woman of ordinary intelligence in sexual matters, she must by this time have an inkling of what was going on, if she had not connived at it already by her policy of the open (bedroom) door. That was the one blot on the salacious picture, to my thinking, for having long since made up my mind that Lilian was one of those women of passion who were destined to have many lovers, a fact that excited my passions more than anything, it was a matter of perfect indifference to me who the man was, and how many we were to share her affection. I did not know whether to feel pity or disgust, when I thought of Lilian's mother. The latter sentiment carried the day, and I put her down as a selfish, calculating woman, who had given up her girl to serve her own ends. I felt a trifle horrified at that idea. All women have been tempted in their lives. Some fall, some few resist temptation, generally for the sake of the children, when there are any; and many a time I have seen and heard mothers, sometimes in a low station of life, shudder and weep at the idea that the little one, who had clung to their breast when an infant, and who they had seen grow up from an unsteady, tiny toddler to a graceful girl, might one day despise and blush for the woman who had carried her nine weary months in her womb, and whose lilliputian feet had kicked ever so gently within, as if to say: "Mummy, I am here!" How then can a woman who has ever "felt life," as it is called, in that way, prostitute her child surpasses even my understanding, all debauched and besmirched as I am. No, there was no excuse for Adèle; any woman is free to dispose of her own body, but not to debauch her children, her own flesh and blood. It is quite bad enough when they "go wrong" themselves. Lily's mother could not plead ignorance, as she had lived among harlots all her life and knew what went on behind the scenes in Paris and London.

I did not say very much more to Mademoiselle Arvel than is set down here. I, like all love-sick men, was afraid to put her out of temper, an easy task with wilful Lily, and I possessed a sentiment of delicacy with regard to her which was perfectly ridiculous. I hinted that she had done well to accept her Papa's love, and thus become the true mistress of the house. Her brow grew dark and serious as I spoke and she dropped into a brown study. To prevent her being too sad, I joked, and begged her not to forget poor Jacky, when she became "queen of the harem," and she allowed me to make all these silly quips and jokes. If I had not seen with my own eyes the recent passion of Papa and Lilian's seduction of him, my conversations with her would have sufficed to fix her guilt, as no girl, however debased, could have supported the strain of my lewd talk if there had not been something between them; something more than mere playing and romping.

Laughing gaily, we reached the garden and the inn to which it belonged. I called for a bottle of champagne which we soon finished, and Lily had her full share of her favourite wine.

We returned, and were late getting home at dark, Lilian having slipped us on the road and we two old fools lost our way. We had no lights and I was riding a hired machine, without a break, down steep hills in the dark. We struck the town at last, and I use the term advisedly, as I got my front wheel into a tramway rail and came down elegantly. And my reader must remember that I was 47 years of age.

We got back to the Villa Lilian, and were received like two prodigal sons, or rather two gay, old prodigal fathers, and as I told the story of how Lily had left us in the lurch, her Papa whispered gently to me that she was "yappy"; *i.e.* mad. (London slang of the East End.)

Lilian wished to know what we were making a mystery about, and I told her. I tried to improvise a "Limerick," and began:

> "Miss Arvel was a pretty young Jappy,
> "Who her Pa said was perfectly 'yappy' ... "

And of course, I pretended to be unable to finish it.

Dinner was now served and Madame Arvel complained bitterly that she had prepared tea for all of us, including the gentleman from Berlin, and all the two big potfulls would be wasted.

"Not wasted, Mother," said Papa, with a saturnine grin, "it will do for Lilian!"

The remark being made in English, no one understood it but the speaker, Lilian and I, so Papa repeated it to Granny, laughing and chuckling to himself, as if he had made an excellent joke. I laughed inwardly, as by what he had said Papa had corroborated my suspicions extending over two months, concerning the virginity of his daughter. For the benefit of all young unmarried men, I must explain that tea is used as an astringent in cases of the "whites," the same as alum or walnut leaves, but such infusions are of no practical use, unless taken as an injection, and as injections cannot be taken by virgins, Papa was simply telling me that his bewitching Jappy was no longer a maid, and the tranquil way in which he said it, and the matter-of-fact manner in which Mamma, Granny, and Lily herself laughed at the witticism, proved that her maidenhead had gone some time back, sufficiently long enough ago for all her people to get used to her shame, if they knew what shame was.

I sat by as if I heard nothing, putting on the most innocent air I could assume, but nobody took any notice of me. No doubt, in years gone by I had let many strange remarks pass, without notice, so wrapped up was I in my love for Lilian, and they were all quite right to continue to treat me the same. I was not displeased at finding that I was supposed to be a fool, and I made up my mind to continue to play the part of one, which was the only chance I had of finding out the truth, without counting, and I hardly knew it myself then, I had a mortal dread of quarrelling with her I still foolishly called my Lily. So I suppose Papa thought Lilian had told me the truth, or that I had had connection with her, as he had, and she had not yet told him how I was a kind of a half-believer in her virginity.

When Papa had spoken, dinner was nearly over, and Lily jumped up and called me to come and help her to take the dogs out, and we promised to be back in time to say "good bye" to the German and accompany him to the station.

Lilian, finding that I had paid seemingly no attention to Papa's remark, made herself most agreeable to me, and I suspect the champagne and the day's outing had made her feel a wee bit jolly.

She told me point-blank that she wanted me badly and that she had formed a plan to get out on the day of Mi-Carême, which was Thursday, the 9th. of March, and spend the afternoon with me.

"What shall we do that day?" I asked, as I did not know but what I was wanted merely as an escort, as on Shrove Tuesday.

"Whatever you like, my darling, I shall be yours that day, and I will go anywhere and do anything you like."

I thanked her effusively, as I always was foolish enough to do every time she took it into her head to be like an ordinary tender woman to me, and our lips met in one of Lily's special, long, sucking kisses. There was not a soul to be seen, and we embraced and caressed each other madly; indeed I was rampant with lust, and made use of the most bawdy language, much to the wayward girl's apparent delight.

I cannot remember how it happened exactly, but I should fancy that I alluded to our masturbation of the morning.

"I owe you one!" said Lilly, "as you made me happy and I was too frightened to finish you, but I will now if you like!"

And before I knew where I was, I was walking along the

country road which led from the Villa Lilian to the Place d'Armes, with my person fully exposed, and Lilian gently manipulating me as I walked by her side. Whenever we caught sight of a rare passer-by, I drew my overcoat over my stiffened member, and Lily, with-drawing her fairy fingers, marched by my side like a nun going to chapel. Was it my fault or Lilian's that Papa's name was men-tioned? Lily always called him: "Mr. Arvel," when she spoke about him to me, and I talked once more about his love for her, she still pressing the sign of manhood in her warm hand, having taken off her glove for the purpose.

"It would be to your advantage to let him love you. Why don't you seduce him?"

"That would not be difficult!" was her swift rejoinder.

"I am a long time coming to-night," I said after a few moments' silence, during which I began to enjoy the touch of her clever hand on my private parts, for I could feel she was rapidly becoming an expert. "I suppose Papa is not so long coming as me?" I asked this question in a most quiet, offhand way.

"Oh, he is much longer than you," she replied quite naturally.

"How do you do it?" I answered, "with your hand or your mouth? Which does he like best?"

I thought I was getting on finely and had I had a proper reply this book would never have seen the light. Another moment per-haps, and I shall know all and as I spend she will confess her im-posture. But I had no experience with wicked women, as Lily dropped my weapon, which was about to go off, and ran away from me across the road. Like a fool; like a man burning to emit, I went after her, my miserable weapon sticking out in front of me at half-cock.

"What's the matter, Lily?"

"How dare you speak to me like that?"

That is what she said, or words to that effect, as she saw she had been too far. I only knew one thing at that moment; I wanted to spend, any way she liked, so I put my pride in my pocket, especially as I did not care whether Papa used her as a toy or not, if she would toy with me. I begged her pardon, making a very pretty little speech all about people who love each other never sulking or quarrelling together, but making the necessary complaint at once, and after discussing matters, the one in the wrong should freely beg the other's pardon and all be cleared up at once. Entirely mollified, my queen deigned to take me in her soft palm once more and kissed my lips, complaining how chapped and feverish her own were, while she continued to rub my stiff shaft.

We were standing on the pavement against the railings of a beautiful villa, and I told Lily that she was behaving like a common woman who made men spend in holes and corners at night time for a few pence.

"A common low prostitute that a man can do anything with, not like you, a wretched little cow . . . quicker now with your hand . . . who does not love me in spite of all she says!'

"Oh, don't say that! I do love you and would do anything for you!"

"Faster, love . . . faster, little whore!"

"Oh yes, I am your little whore!"

"And you would do anything for me? Anything, no matter how dirty or disgusting?"

"Anything, as long as it is you!"

"I take you at your word! I have a little biscuit in my pocket and when I have come, I will moisten it with my spendings and you will eat it!"

"Certainly, my darling, and I am ready to do anything else you may ask me!"

"All this time she kept on with her movements to make me enjoy, and I was so greatly excited that I knew I should be a little longer than usual in attaining the height of pleasure. It was a cold night; I was tired from my ride, and the champagne and the wine and liqueurs I had drunk had got into my head, for I am a water-drinker. I wanted to be finished before anybody came along the road to interrupt us, so I called out to Lilian:

"Faster, go faster still—and grip me tight! So! Hold it as tight as you can!"

"I can't press it tighter! I can't go faster! Oh, my wrist aches! I can't keep on! I shall let you go!"

"Beware if you do, little whore! I'll pay you well!! I'll give you a franc, two francs, if you do as I tell you!" She redoubled her efforts. "Now, I'm coming!"

Lilian shrieked, as if frightened, but she had sufficient *sang-froid* to direct the jet through the railings of the garden, against which we were standing, and I lost my head in the delicious agony of this onanistic diversion in the open air.

I took the biscuit and with it wiped away the drop that remained at the urethra, walking after my sweetheart, who had moved on a pace or two. I offered it to her. She refused to keep her word, as I thought, and I was in no way disappointed. I knew my own mania, common to many other men, if they would only confess it. It is that of imagining all kinds of horrors, or impossible tricks and schemes of lust when they are under the influence of extreme sexual excitement, but once they have discharged their elixir, all is generally forgotten. Women know this, and promise anything to the male while he is in this state. Beware then, my masculine readers, of what you tell your mistress during the long-drawn-out copulation of the morning, when, steadied by the work of the night before, the erection is constant, but the end is as yet far off. Ask your mistress at the moment to give up to you all her relations, masculine and feminine, to grant you the most filthy and unheard of favours. She will consent to all, and when you are satisfied, will laugh at your insensate longings. You, perchance, have betrayed your secrets, while talking as you lazily moved in and out of her hot gap, and now she knows that you want her sister, or would dearly love to have the little girl or boy who is asleep in the next room, in bed with you two. Perhaps the child you covet is of your own blood? So much the more voluptuous, but take heed of the awakening, when the delightful crisis is passed. Thus Lilian was debauched, I venture to think, when she came into the bed of her mother, between her and her lover, in the morning early.

I threw away the biscuit, laughing inwardly at my own folly, which I take a strange pleasure in unveiling here, and we began to turn towards her home.

She explained that she intended to go up to Paris on Thursday, the ninth of March, which was the day of Mi-Carême, under the pretext of visiting Charlotte, and her parents would let her, if she took her principal workwoman with her. She would leave her at the station, which would suit the girl too, and come to me, meeting the assistant in the evening to return home with her. I was delighted and thanked her a thousand times. Then she told me what to say to each of her parents in turn when I should see them at the station. I was to evince a lively interest in Raoul, and ask Mamma how I could send him some Eau de Cologne, since I myself had taught them that it was a sovereign remedy for tender feet. To Papa, I was to say that I hoped I should soon have the pleasure of a long, long day with him in his dark-room, without any gadding about, so as to become a real and efficient aid to him.

When we got to the station, the train had gone and the German too. We were both well scolded, and after due apologies on my part, I walked on with Mamma, as there was half-an-hour to wait for another train. I told her that I wished to send some Cologne water to her son, and she told me to arrange it with Lily, as Papa must not know, being too jealous of the lad.

During this, I watched Lily, who was eagerly and excitedly whispering to her Pa. Then I said good night to him as Lily moved away to let me recite my lesson, and he heard me out patiently. When I had finished, he frowned; and grunted, as was his habit, but never answered me at all. He was no dupe of our, or rather of Lily's petty intrigue, nor did he take the trouble to dissimulate.

After the usual effusive compliments at the end of such an amusing day, I took my departure, and went away to dream of the charming offer that my adored Lilian had made to me, all for love of me, for that glorious Thursday in eight days' time.

5

Virgin me no virgins!

. . . .
I must have you private—start not—I say, private;
If thou art my true daughter.

PHILIP MASSINGER.

Then, as to what she suffers from her father,
In all this there is much exaggeration.
Old men are testy, and will have their way.

SHELLEY.

LILIAN TO JACKY.

Sonis-sur-Marne. March 5, 1899.

My Jacky, who is mine alone,

My sweet dream for next Thursday, day of Mi-Carême, will not be
realised, as I start for Brussels, Tuesday morning. I am very much annoyed. I should also have liked to have seen you before my departure,
but in spite of all my insinuations, there has been no chance of arranging matters to have you invited. So I am in a rage, and I dare not insist
too much for fear of exciting suspicion, which must not arise at any cost.

To-morrow is Papa's birthday. Do not forget to telegraph your best
wishes on receipt of this note, which I write in haste, and in which I
make the most monstrous faults; but you will excuse me, will you not?

I must have a line from you before I start, Monday evening or Tuesday morning.

I leave you; I hear someone coming upstairs.

I kiss you where it will please you most. I love you,

LILY.

JACKY TO ERIC ARVEL. (Telegram.)

Paris, March 6, 1899.

Many happy returns of the day.

JACKY.

As it will be seen, I sent the wire of birthday congratulations to my old friend, and I was highly delighted to do so, because I had no idea when his birthday fell, or what was his exact age, but I took it as proof that Lily was still at work for me, and in reward for my absence of jealousy, was doing all she could for me to remain in the best books of her elderly lover, for there was now no possible doubt concerning the illicit intercourse of the semi-incestuous couple, and once more the knowledge that he also knew about me from Lilian—as he could not be such a blind fool as to have ignored our connection—brought a glorious thrill of lust through my veins, as I conjured up a lascivious future at the Villa Lilian.

In obedience to my charmer's commands, I sat down and wrote her at once the letter she had ordered, which, as well as I can recollect, for I kept no copy, may be summarized as follows:

I thanked her for thoughts of me. I excused her not keeping her appointment, as it was not her fault; I told her to enjoy herself in every way and not to fret about me. She need not even trouble to write, if she could not find an opportunity. What did I care for a letter or so, more or less, since she had told me how she loved me? I was proud to be one of her troupe of marionettes, which she manœuvred with such skill, and she was so clever, I opined, that I took the liberty of calling her Mademoiselle Bismarck; and did not forget to put in a good word for the health of Papa. I told her that I should love her without stupid jealousy, and added some guarded maxims about women employing their natural cunning, talents, and beauty to entrap men for their own ends. "Seduce and give way, but propose your conditions beforehand, and remain sovereign mistress." I told her that I had been thinking over what she had said about an instinctive movement of shame when I had touched her between the legs. I wished to cure her of that feeling, desiring her to be absolutely without shame with me, and utterly perverted, if she cared to please me. I intended to punish her for that recoil from my middle finger, by making her stand before me, and with her clothes well raised, open her drawers and masturbate herself thoroughly, remaining as long as possible in this humiliating position, until thoroughly cured of all false shame with me. I concluded with all kinds of good wishes for her health and enjoyment, and recommended her to go to the Wiertz Museum, and the Zoological Gardens at Antwerp.

LILIAN TO JACKY.

Hotel des Grands Fabricants. Lille, March 8, 1899.

My best beloved,

We left yesterday morning, or rather yesterday afternoon, at 1:15 for Lille. We arrived at 5:30, took a little walk, and then had dinner. Then we went to a concert, where we assisted at a two hours' procession of the most grotesquely ugly women it is possible to imagine. After that, we returned to go quietly to bed in a large double-bedded room, as they told us there were no rooms communicating.

This morning, Papa had gone to Roubaix to see a friend. As for me, I told him that I did not care to go, so as to be able to write to my Jacky, for perhaps I shall not be able to do so before my return.

Now I am going to write to you very frankly. You are not mistaken; Mr. A. loves me and without quite knowing it himself. Nevertheless, he is and always will be respectful towards me. To begin with, I love Mamma too much to let things be otherwise and I do not love him at all! And then the bare idea disgusts me deeply, and is repugnant. Therefore, in future, I shall keep a watch over my most trifling words, and my most innocent gestures, as far as he is concerned, for I will not encourage this idiotic passion.

My dear adored one, you who are my only love, I hope that you will be able to understand completely what I am going to say. I am very unhappy here. I suffer and I should like to be home again already; firstly, to see you, to feel that you were near me, and also that you might support me by your counsel. I want to open my heart to you more than I have done up to the present. I feel so lonely and so sad. Mamma does not love me as before, and yet she has nothing to reproach me with, and I love her dearly. Mr. A. is so wicked towards my brother, that the poor woman thinks she ought to love him doubly. Note that I am not jealous, I love my brother too well for that, but I suffer to feel myself neglected by Mamma and I am too proud to let her see it.

But I fatigue you with all my lamentations; how can I help it? It seems to me that you alone understand me.

Love me well and tenderly, my beloved Jacky, my adoration. I swear to you that I require all your love and that I am worthy of it. Never have I loved any man before you, and never has any other man touched me.

I detest Mr. A., for it seems to me that it is his fault if Mamma is so changed towards me.

You . . . I love,

LILY.

I am very good and shall always be so, where you are not concerned.

If ever I felt the lack of literary training, it is now. Oh! for the pen of a Thackeray, or the smallest modicum of his talent, to enable me to bring home to the reader in some slight degree the effect this letter had upon me. That it was entirely false from beginning to end, I was nearly inclined to believe; and although I did not mind her trying to conceal from me that she was now the official concubine of her mother's old lover, I felt a terrible pang of disgust and horror to think that Lily had pushed the deception so far as to try and render me unhappy and extort my pity by daring to say that she was suffering. I was always ready all my life to put myself in the wrong, so I confess I did for an instant have a little remorse, as I reproached myself for having given her bad advice. Had I debauched her? Had I ruined her young life? Had I, by my infamous training, nurtured those wrong ideas in her, which had driven her into the arms of a senile satyr, who had perhaps violated her, whipped her, kept her all night at work on his body, and disgusted her entirely? I got the letter in the evening. It was long; one of the longest letters I had ever had from her, and there was not an erasure in the whole of it. So, evidently, she had been at some pains to compose it and catch the post. She was fresh out of bed when she did so. I think the document may have been geniune up to a certain point, as far as the words "double-bedded room," and from there, all branches off confusedly, and she wanders and flounders about in her desperate attempts to hide the truth from me. And why write at all? Had I not told her a hundred times that I was not jealous and that she was free to dispose of her body as she listed? I wanted but a trifle of that love which she had always offered me herself from the onset, and as I have plainly stated in this wretched story, I never asked her for any favour that could possibly interfere with her young life, now devoted to the old man, who had shared her mother's bed for twenty years or more.

And why drag Adèle's jealousy into this pitiful writing, designed to trick and pain? She knew very well that her mother had naturally been jealous of her for years, and now she alone could form an idea how her mother looked and felt on the morning of her departure, and what she had said to her husband before God. There may have been some little disgust at the events of the night, although that is open to doubt, but any trace of physical repugnance would soon be gone after a nice *déjeûner*, when her Papa should return from Roubaix, if ever he went at all. Arvel's jealousy of Raoul I have already explained.

It is likely that the sexual act itself in its bare manifestation of penetration had no great charm for my ex-virgin, who cared much more for the preliminaries, and delicate caresses and attentions. Papa had probably never "had" her at his ease, nor quite freely, entirely naked in a bed in his arms; and the month of February had served as a sort of training for him, to get up his genital strength for this "honeymoon" trip. He was too fat and scant of breath, unable to stoop, and he would require time, warmth, and full commodity and space to enjoy a woman at his age.

It had long been arranged that she should give way to him. She had seduced him, partly from interested motives, partly through vice. She liked him; she was used to him. It was a great achievement for her to have triumphed over her mother, who in time would come round and accept the situation, if she had not done so already, and the two women would hold Papa between them and look after any money and property he might leave behind him when he died.

I took a great deal of trouble to try and analyse Lily's feelings from her horrible letter, with its depressing undercurrent of physical repulsion, showing the disillusion she experienced at the first night completely alone with him and at his mercy. In the morning, sick, tired, disgusted, full of regret and remorse; all her daydreams of tender voluptuousness rudely dispelled by the long and painful pushing efforts of the heavy-bodied and coarse stepfather, with his teazing semi-erections; ready to vomit; the cheap champagne, and bad drink and food of the provincial restaurant, and café-concert having produced their effect of nausea; her thoughts go out to me, and she starts a confession, which, like those of all hysterical females, is made up of equal parts of truth and lies. Lily is fearful lest I despise her; this tardy effort to stand well in my eyes is pitiful in the extreme, and to anyone unable to dissect the mobile brain of such abnormal creatures, the letter penned after this "first night" with Papa reads as the wailing cry of a violated, disappointed bride.

And perchance, all said and done, it may have been a vast and wicked hoax, arranged by the guilty pair to torture and trick a miserable lover, who must perforce, according to their petty ideas, be madly, wildly jealous, and at any rate, Lily, full of weak vanity, posing as a queen over men, and badly advised as usual by her Eric, would imagine that once a man has said, "I love you!" to a woman, he is her slave, bound by the chains of his passion, forged with his own hands, and therefore in a fit state to accept whatever stupid falsehoods his mistress would have him believe.

I am convinced that women are purely instinctive beings, inexplicable; continually changing and renewing their ideas and capable even—accidentally—of obstinate fidelity. They are to be pardoned or despised according to the degree of love we may feel for them. Arvel's mysterious daughter liked us both, but she wanted to keep her secret. Her treachery towards me and which she knew I had discovered, was a precise and plain fact which had upset her murky understanding.

She thought she was in duty bound to make me believe she had chosen between us two men, by saying that she must hate Arvel because she loved Jacky, not realising that I was quite ready to grasp the fact that a woman could be just as faithful to two men as to one.

LILIAN TO JACKY.

Hôtel des Trois Pigeons. Brussels, Wednesday, March 15th. 1899.

My love,

Just a word, in the greatest haste, to announce my return to you. We leave to-morrow, Thursday.

I am delighted, firstly because I hope to see you soon, and secondly, I am dreadfully bored here.

I must have a letter from you at Sonis for Friday, without fail.

To your dear lips,

LILY.

The foregoing was scribbled in pencil on the paper of the hotel, with its printed heading; the letter from Lille was also on the hotel paper, but in ink.

About this time, I had received news of Lady Clara, who was travelling in the south of France, and she never forgot to ask for news of Lilian. I had told as well as I dared that the course of my true love was far from running smoothly, and, without initiating her into the mystery of Lily's *liaison* with her Papa, I said enough to show her what a wicked little woman was my idol, and I told her that the history of Jacky and Lilian was as strange as a penny novelette.

"A novelette?" replied dear Clara, by return of post, "say rather a real three-volume novel! You write very nice letters, Jacky, why don't you put your adventures into a book?" I scouted the idea at first, but now smarting at the treachery of Lily, who was trying to turn me into a simple uxorious, paying customer of hers, I gradually got used to the thought of making the whole story of Lily, as far as I knew it, in book form. I counted my puppets. There were Papa, Mamma, Raoul, Charlotte, Lily and the author. A goodly troupe, by my faith! of which the first five formed as many links in a chain of vice; pleasant, alluring vice to a libertine like myself, but my gall was bursting to think that all was now changed, by reason of the news from Lilian. She had been talking to her Papa, and I was not to be admitted into the magic circle. The chain was stretched against me. Hence her change of attitude at present. I ought to have remembered that I was an Englishman, and have walked away quietly, without ever giving proofs of my existence down at Sonis, but long residence in France had made me as cunning as a monkey. I was tickled at the scheme of using my puppets to form a future novel, and I seemed to be doubling my personality, as I looked upon myself as an actor-author, playing the principal part in one of his own dramas. I wanted purely and simply to find out everything, with regard to Lilian, not for my own curiosity, but to be able later on to take her pretty head, and rub her sweet, pointed nose in her filth, shovelled up by her own hands. I knew perfectly well that Lilian was no longer a virgin, but up to now, I had pretended to believe her when she kept up the fiction to the contrary; I was fully convinced that she was the mistress of her mother's old lover. I wanted to show Lily that I knew all the lies she could invent; I should have the ferocious satisfaction of a Marquis de Sade, if I could only succeed in showing Miss Arvel that I saw through her, by placing before her eyes proofs of her own villany. How was that ambitious programme to be carried out?

It was a long time before I hit upon a scheme, or plan of campaign, which would enable me to show Lily and her parents, if necessary, that I not only knew, but possessed proofs, of three things: Lily's intimacy with Papa; the disappearance of her maidenhead; the evident complicity of all the inhabitants of the Villa Lilian to get money out of me, and let me have my sweetheart every day to myself if I would only "pay, pay, pay!"

How was I to go about my wild scheme? It did not come to

my mind all at once, but when it did creep into my brain, I fully grasped the idea, and it became an obsession, until I worked it out. To resume everything briefly, I intended to play "Hamlet" in private life, and pretend to go mad, if need be, to get Lily and any other inhabitants of her villa off their guard. Of course, should Lily prove true and tender to me, as she had promised before going to Brussels, I would drop my Shakespearean mask, and become my ordinary self once more. I knew I could hardly fail to succeed, as they were all so self-sufficient, that they would never dream that any man would sacrifice his own vanity, and coolly and calmly play the fool to try and find out a lying sweetheart's secrets.

To begin, I wrote the letter that Lily wanted to be at her house when she arrived home, and I kept a rough copy of it, which I am thus able to give here, and now all my love being well-nigh gone, and naught but a slight, forlorn hope of future lust remaining, I began to make notes and collect material for the volumes which are now in the hands of my patient reader.

Jacky to Lilian.

Paris, Thursday, March 16, 1899.

I love you, my Lily, and shall always love you whatever happens. I loved you first. I love you faithful or unfaithful, good or bad. Present or absent, I shall love you the same. You are my only love; the last love of my life.

Is not this the best answer I can give to your letter from Lille,—the cry of a troubled soul?

You can understand that I have great difficulty in composing this letter. I have so much to say to you; so many things which cannot be written, I think.

I have been truly full of anguish. I have worried my brain and passed through every kind of moral torture. I reproached myself many things, and felt remorse for certain advice I gave you. I accused myself of not having loved you as I ought to have done.

What greatly pained me was a sentence where you spoke of not being worthy of my love. But, little darling Lily, if one of us is unworthy, it is certainly not you.

You spoke of lamentations? I could complain all day, and I shall only be happy when I shall have seen you and consoled you. I will not let you suffer, darling.

The love I feel for you is quite devoid of all jealousy or mean afterthought. You have only to tell me, as you do now, that you love me and I shall be the happiest man in the world. I believe in you, because I feel that you adore me truly, and that you are always trying to find out how to give me pleasure. You are always thinking of me.

Certainly, I adore your caresses, your hands, your mouth and all your body—your childlike breast, your little black and pink thing, the other callipygean side, and your thighs, and all I have pressed, pinched, struck, felt, licked, sucked and moistened with my seed. But if you were to offer me all that, giving me to understand that you love me no more, that you give yourself to me solely for my pleasure,—I would refuse everything.

I appreciate with tender joy your true and entire love, with your heart coming at last to me with all your confidence. How good you are now! and I am worried, as I think that you have perhaps sacrificed yourself for your Jacky and I am responsible for the pain I cannot help seeing in your letter.

I must remind you that you promise me for the future absolute frankness; you pledge yourself to open your heart to me. You tell me that I alone understand you.

Then the mania I have for turning over every word you say in your letters, and for scrutinising and analysing all that comes from you does not displease you? Do I see clearly when I observe you, my angel?

There are moments when I curse my clairvoyance and I envy the grocer who is neither perverted nor vicious. But I have one consoling thought—if Jacky was not so *cochon*, you would not love him.

For the advice you ask, I am forced to tell you at once, until I can better make you understand my thoughts by word of mouth, that we should have no pride or haughtiness with our mother. You must absolutely go to her as if you were a little girl. Do you not know that we are always little children for our mothers? And a mother is never astonished to see her children come back to her at any age, as they used to do when they were ten years old.

Already a year ago you asked me the same thing, and my counsel was identical. The beginning of the reconciliation will be hard for you, perhaps, but you must persevere and make yourself caressing, tender and full of prayer to her. I cannot develop my idea more fully here.

This letter may seem to you stupid and incoherent. You must excuse the writer. I grope in the dark.

Since the 8th., I am as a madman. Only Smike understands me. The other day he did as follows for the first time in his life. We were alone. I felt all "topsy-turvy"—your word when you put on your air of innocence. Softly, he came to me and licked my face, my eyes. Then he left me, and went and laid down sadly.

Last Friday, at three o'clock in the morning, you were with me. I felt myself seized in a close embrace and a hand seemed to touch my face. In the trouble of the dream I said to myself: "Ah! 'tis Lily,—that is why Smike does not bark." I called you and woke bathed in sweat, crying out your name.

If I let you catch sight of a little corner of my heart, so sensitive when you are concerned, you must not think that I have become a poet since your departure. No, in spite of myself, I am always thinking of some delicious follies to execute with you, my adored little woman, and I have added a few holes to your leather girdle. You will give yourself freely up to this game of teazing pain and imitation of torture, will you not? I love it so much, because I know you give way for love of me.

I mean to inflict supreme shame upon you. I will have you in front of me in your drawers, and you shall come to me, opening them yourself, as I shall order you, and pushing away the chemise to show me your "pussy." I shall leave you thus for some minutes, happy at the slight humiliation you will undergo in exposing your nakedness yourself. Next, you will open your little slit yourself, with your two hands, so as to show me the inside quite fully. And I shall be quite naked, having undressed myself at once before you, so that you may judge yourself of the effect you produce upon me. It will be an extraordinary lewd delight for me to be naked as I was born, and keep you a little while with me, you being completely dressed.

I have developed the photographs I took of you and your brother, etc. There are only six good ones out of the twelve negatives. Bad work, that. But at last I have a photograph of you, taken by me, for me. I have half a mind not to show it to anyone, not even to you. It is indeed my Lily, who twisted and turned with such docility before me. I have the effrontery to adore you when you obey all my caprices at once.

One day in my life, I should like to have you quite humble and tender, saying: "Yes, Jacky,—if you wish it, Jacky,—certainly, Jacky, as long as it pleases you," etc. I should like to box your ears, and you say to me: "Thank you, Jacky." That is impossible; it is not in your nature.

I hope that the end of your journey was better than the commencement, and that your health has been good.

What would I not give for an hour or two of quiet chat with you! I will not read over these pages; if I do, I shall not have the courage to post them. But this will not prevent me when I see you, from treating you like the lowest woman in the world, and covering you with insults, as I call you by the filthiest and most infamous names,—since you have told me that to be insulted by Jacky makes you spend.

To both your wet mouths!

JACKY.

LILIAN TO JACKY.

Sonis-sur-Marne, March 18, 1899. My Birthday.

My own Jacky,

At last here I am back again, and I find your good, long letter. Have no fear about our correspondence, as never any of my letters are opened; you can therefore rest easy on that point. I was awfully bored during the whole week we remained in Brussels; in a word, this trip has been more of a task than a pleasure. I have many things to tell you, but I cannot describe them, as it is impossible to develop my thoughts on paper. So I shall do my best to have you invited.

I love you.

LILY.

P.S. Mind and amuse yourself well to-morrow, Sunday. I know that it is a day that you would not sacrifice and give up to me for anything in the world. This is a pity, as I shall be free to-morrow.

In my letter, to which this was an answer, I had put a postscript expressing fears lest my letters to her might fall into the hands of her parents, which was part of my scheme to prevent her thinking that I suspected her collusion with her Papa and Mamma.

What I had said in my long epistle had evidently worried her not a little, as I plainly let her see that I suspected something, and that I pitied her not a little for having been forced (?) to give way. And it was perfectly natural that I should sympathise with her, since she had apprised me of her suffering. My tenderness for her supposed trouble annoyed her, because she was lying. She tells me that she is going to get me invited to her home, and in her little, venomous P.S. teazes me for devoting my Sunday to the sick woman, as I had told her. I received Lily's note on Sunday morning early, as I was just rushing off to the country to spend the day with some relations of my poor mistress. I did not like them, but I went with the sick woman, who always thanked me for my slight sacrifice; she knew and appreciated it, as being done for her. So I sat down and nearly missed my train, in scribbling a hasty word to Lily, entirely forgetting in my temper the precious part I was playing, albeit it fitted itself in all the same. The evil intent was plain. She knew I was not free, so she said *she* was. She was also cognizant of the fact that at such short notice I could not come and storm her Villa, or telegraph boldly to her to meet me in Paris, in the face of her parents. I was very angry, and I told her, after the usual compliments for her birthday, of which I had hitherto ignored the date, of my rage, something after this style:

"Your P.S. was bad. I am deeply hurt. It is a useless, insulting sting. You are silly, and that makes me understand the word 'task' in your note. Beware then, lest you become too foolish; too kind; too good and easy with those who are not quite so loyal as Jacky. If you give them all the kindness that is so conspicuous by its absence in your P. S. you may just as well be dead. Do not be a slave, but try and make slaves; I will teach you how.

"Do you remember that night last winter when I missed the train, and I said to you: 'Some time in your young life you will be crushed beneath the rank, stinking, sweating body of some brutal monster? Then you will call out for your Jacky in the horror of the night; but he will not be there!' I did not think my prophecy would come true so soon, nor that I should be such a truthful soothsayer."

Next day I reflected how foolish I had been to write so harshly, just at this juncture when I wanted to get as near the truth as the Arvels would let me. But I soon found a means to repair my error and turn it to account, as the changes of mood that I was now going to simulate would make Lily and her father believe that I was going mad, and nothing is so flattering for a woman, as to suppose that she has such power over an infatuated male.

I am very intimate with a manufacturing jeweller, and to him I repaired without loss of time, and ordered, from my own design, a very pretty lady's ring, consisting of a turquoise, with a diamond on each side, and when made up, it formed a very handsome present.

I chose a turquoise, as that stone is symbolical of the month of November. Many of my readers may not know that there is a stone for each of the twelve signs of the Zodiac, and the last month but one in the year, governed by Sagittarius, has for gems, the blue stone I had chosen, and also the carbuncle, and in occultism they are lucky, and bring inheritances, gains, and fortune to the wearer. I chose the turquoise, because I had first had Lily in my arms in that foggy division of the calendar, and I had another reason, which the reader will see in due course, but I carefully refrained from letting her know, until it should suit my purpose to tell her.

After ordering the ring, I went to a post-office, and wrote a most designedly foolish letter to my own sweet Lily. I announced my present, and asked how I should offer it to her. Should I slip it into her hand on the quiet, or give it openly as coming from Mr. S . . . ? If she cared to say it came from a lady-customer, she could do so, as I did not wish to show off before her parents. It was quite enough for me to know that she had it from me. I said it was merely a trifle, but that I could not unfortunately afford to give her what she really ought to have.

I was very saucy to conclude with, saying that when I saw the word "birthday" on the top of her note, I immediately thought of a present for her, but I resolved not to give her anything, because of the insulting venom of her wicked P.S., and I think I added something about her want of delicacy at such a moment as the present, when her duty was to spare my feelings and be as considerate as I was. She knew that I was condemned to the weekly agony of a sickroom, and that if she loved me, she would write one word of regret, that little word the truly loving woman utters, when she hears the voice of her sweetheart change, as his eyes grow dim, and she hastens to cry to him: "You were wrong, dear, to say those cutting things to me, but I was wrong too. Let us forgive and make it up!" I added that she would never say those words, and I did not care if she did not. I was utterly indifferent and expected nothing but evil from her.

On Wednesday, 22nd. of March, I was confined to my room with a slight attack of influenza, the prevailing epidemic at that moment, and which I had caught from my poor mistress, who was always sure to become a victim to any contagion. Having nothing to do, I continued my work of posing as a mad lover by sending the following letter to Lily, which I devoutly hoped she would show to her Papa, and as I wrote it, I fancied I could see her running up the gravel path, after having taken her correspondence from the box, as I had seen her do, but this time, she would wave my letter over her head, exclaiming: "I've got him, Papa! I've got him!"

JACKY TO LILIAN.

Paris, Wednesday, March 22, 1899.

My nerves have been shattered these last few days for many reasons, but principally because you gave me to understand that you were unhappy, disappointed, and something had happened to cause you a great disillusion. I suffer too from pangs of remorse, as I think I am perhaps the cause.

I was about leaving for the country on Sunday, to put on a good face in front of people I loathe. The little bit of wickedness in your letter (which was otherwise delicious for me, although, poor little Lily, you still spoke of your misfortunes), fell exactly at the proper moment and on the right day to drive me beside myself.

It was stupid, for at an ordinary time, if I had been a little gay, I should not probably have paid much attention to it.

Therefore in my stupid rage, I answered too hastily, and in a coarse, cruel and impolite manner. I am not ashamed to confess that I bitterly regret all I said, especially as it is not my habit to write in such a manner, and above all to you, who I love more than anybody in the world.

Besides, I have not waited long to repair my wrong-doings, as my letter of Monday shows. Therein I offered you with a good heart a birthday present, proving that I tried all by myself, without waiting for a reproach from you, to mend my ridiculous ways, for which I blush.

You once said to me: "You don't know how I am worried and annoyed when I think of you!"

Fancy then, what I feel to-day, my adored Lily, and you will find a thousand excuses for me. I ask you simply to bring things back to the point they were at on Sunday morning. I ask you in the name of our love.

Oh! this correspondence, these sterile letters! I curse the deplorable facility for writing which I possess. It always makes me say something I should have left unsaid.

Here my rough notes break off abruptly, but, if my memory serves me rightly, I terminated by an abject apology, and declared that the fear of losing Lily had made me so ill that I could not sleep, and was obliged to take large doses of chloral, although I can truly say that I never was forced to fly to a narcotic in my life, and I added that if she would send a kind word by telegram on receipt of my letter, I felt almost sure I should regain my power of normal sleep. And I signed, "poor Jacky."

LILIAN TO JACKY. (*Telegram.*)

Sonis-sur-Marne. March 23, 1899, 9:50 A.M.

Sleep well, sweetheart.

LILIAN TO JACKY.

(No date or place.)
Postmark: Sonis-sur-Marne. March 23, 1899.

My very Own,

You had the scent of a detective to write to me yesterday, as I confess that I felt disposed to never more give you the slightest sign of life after your letter of Sunday.

Papa is in bed with the influenza, and I myself am only just a little better.

You are absolutely in the wrong and you do not understand what

I write to you concerning Mr. A. There is positively nothing and there will never be anything between us, but a great desire on his part, which manifests itself openly each time that he finds himself alone with me, which is horribly wearying in every way, and even rather more repugnant than anything else.

I suffer greatly from this state of things, but how can you fancy yourself responsible for it? It is no more your fault than it is mine, I suppose?

Thank you for the ring. I shall wear it with all the more happiness, knowing that it comes from you. It is preferable that it should be Mr. S . . . , who gives it me openly, as one of my lady customers is going to offer me one, and two would be too many.

You will soon be invited, but the indisposition of Papa alone puts off this happy moment.

I am impatient to see you, for we have a multitude of things to say to each other, and then I wish to see you for the sole pleasure of feeling that you are near me.

To your dear lips,

LILY.

The effect of my insane correspondence was now beginning to make itself felt; and my young lady was quite bereft of all prudence, or the atmosphere in which she lived had caused a total eclipse of all moral sense. Here was a young woman declaring coolly that her mother's old lover pursued her daily with his infamous passion; she living under the same roof as him, and this desire manifested itself openly whenever they were alone together. Which possibly meant that he opened his trousers whenever he caught her on the stairs, or coming out of the W.C. To write so coolly concerning a stepfather, with whom she had just travelled all alone, added to her letter from Lille, would, I thought, have been sufficient circumstantial evidence in a divorce-court, but I was still dissatisfied, and the more she tried to keep me off the track of her incestuous secret, the more I wanted to know.

Seriously speaking, no woman could live in the manner Lily wanted to make out to me. The loathsome disgust she would feel at the approach of the lips of her beloved mother's paramour, at the touch of his gouty, nailless hands fumbling round her petti-coats; could drive her to flight or suicide, if she really was the right-minded girl she now wished to make herself out to me. Where were the dreams of collaboration and photography with Papa? How about the appointment for the day of Mi-Carême? She talked vaguely of inviting me to her house, but there were no signs of sensual longing. The ring and my show of rage, followed by an unasked-for apology, had quite fogged Lily, and she took no trouble with me, thinking evidently that I was in a condition to di-gest the rawest falsehoods, and I could not divest myself of the notion that Papa was amusing himself by reading all my letters, and that he was now her lover, pander, and father-confessor rolled into one, so I locked myself up in my little den, and wrote the following extraordinary concoction destined to throw such a cloud of dust in their eyes, that in their vanity, she like all shallow, crafty, vain women believing that my love or passion for her was so great, that I could be easily rendered blind, and forget all teachings of experience and common sense; while Papa loving darkness, rather than light because his deeds were evil, kept advising her to stick to the lie she had written to me in that vile elucubration from Lille, which I am almost inclined to think was composed by the pair together, or at his dictation, over the *café complet* in the morning, in the double-bedded room. And why double-bedded? I had only Lily's word for that. Since she had been imprudent enough to write to me, probably because I expressly told her not to, on the printed paper of the hotel at Lille, what was there to prevent me taking the train and passing one night in the same hotel, perhaps in the same room? My lust was sufficiently cooled now to enable me to shrug my shoulders, as this thought came over me. And I am sorry to say, I declared that they were not worth the trouble, and I preferred to stop at home in Paris and nurse my influenza, which was troubling me considerably. Moral: Be careful how you use the hotel note-paper. A good plan is to write at a different hotel to that you are stopping at. You can always get a sheet of their paper for the trouble of taking a cup of coffee there, and if you know how to lie glibly, an answer can easily be received there too.

JACKY TO LILIAN.

Night of 24/25 March, 1899.

Little Lily darling,

So you have been ill? Influenza? You say that you are only just getting better?

I asked for news of your health in the long letter I wrote to you on your return. I hope that when you receive these lines you will be quite reinstated.

I am better. Sleep has come back to me, a little. Your good telegram, followed by a still better letter, comforted me and made things easier.

Then, darling, I felt myself loved by you. In 1897, you loved me only a little; in 1898, much more; and in 1899, you love me passionately. After my letter of Sunday, I might add not at all.

Frankly, that letter was too insulting. I still blush for shame of it. You have pardoned me, my love, because you are "crazy on Jacky." You said that yourself, when you called me your little husband. A wrong done to a woman we love is only inexcusable when she no longer loves us.

I still feel the desire to excuse myself. I detest narrow-minded, obstinate, pigheaded, vain people who think themselves degraded to have to say: "Pardon me, I am wrong."

I know some of the middle classes, decorated with the Legion of Honour, who would let themselves be cut into a thousand pieces sooner than retract anything they have once said. How stupid! I am vicious, perverted, depraved, my intelligence is below ordinary standards. I am a very ordinary faulty, vulgar man, but I try to be delicate in my sentiments and when I have to reproach myself for having done wrong, I candidly confess it. My loyal avowal is my best justification. I know the folly of mankind, and that the loving heart is often the prey of error or weakness. I shall always acknowledge my mistakes without false shame, pride, or obstinacy, but with sincere regret.

Charming Lily, who is about soon to call me to her side! I shall be able to touch you, to feel you near me, to enjoy your perfume, living flower that you are; read my pardon in your beautiful eyes, and depart with the satisfaction that I am still loved by you.

For the ring, spare me, I pray you, sweet love, the annoyance of having to give it to you, before everybody. Be ready and dressed, as soon as I come. I will give it to you when we are alone. Then you can run and show it to your parents, to know if you are allowed to accept it, etc. You know the old tune better than I. It is only a trifle, and for that reason will pass as swiftly as my tongue in your mouth. I am not rich enough to give you what you deserve. I only fear that by its style, by the stones I have chosen, it may not perhaps please you. And you are so good for me that you will always say it delights you exceedingly. I should like to put it on your finger myself. I would that it were never off your hand, that you wore it at night; especially at night.

I go mad when I sit down to write to you. It is true that I see you so seldom. My letter takes the place of a chat with you.

I feel my light, little, pointed, perfidious whore of a pen which would like to spring from my hand, not to be "cut," but to wander across the paper, and touch upon a burning topic to which you alluded in a bold, albeit delicate manner in your letter. And the inkstand is there gaping wide, full of treacherous blackness.

Permit me, sweet little baby, to wait until I see you to talk to you about it. I am afraid of myself and am frightened of my own literary dysentery, I feel that in a tête-à-tête with you I could risk saying almost anything, but written words seem often hard and wounding; that is why I leave a portion of your letter without an answer.

You write well, you say much in a few words, just enough. That is rare in a woman, but I have remarked—I have told you so—that you possessed a little of the resolution and the firmness of a determined man. I think I am more tender and sensitive than you. A man has never made you cry, I am sure, and never for me—but halt!—little, dirty prostitute of a pen!

I have some Eau de Cologne, a pint, prepared in a tin travelling bottle. It is what I promised your mother for Raoul. I must really bring it, or else your Mamma will think that I am one of those idiots who promise heaven and earth, and never mean to keep their word.

Shall I bring another volume of that romance of sanguinary pleasure? And now, enough! I have worried you sufficiently for this once.

To my dear lips, say you? Those are charming words, and I answer: Take them, my Lily, take the whole mouth of your

JACKY.

Although I tell you in my letter that I would not mention the burning subject you allude to in your note, I cannot prevent myself from saying that I sincerely pity your lover of Sonis. I judge him a little from myself. One vicious, depraved man is much alike to another. You love me and I live in the hope of some little compensations now and again, and yet I am very unhappy by the great longing I feel to have you all naked and palpitating in my embrace. How then must he suffer, from what you tell me? For he sees you daily, hourly, and there is no hope for him. Nothing for him. That must be Hell upon earth. I can understand his recent illness, his vertigo. I feel for him. I have known him over twenty years. He knew me as a youth. Now I like him more and my heart goes out towards him, as you make me realise his state of continual desire. Such is cruel suffering. In writing this, I have to make a great effort not to send you a lot of erotic stuff about the dreams of lust you cause me. I make myself ill with imagining all the things I could do with you. Alas! my poor dreams of voluptuousness are fated never to be realised.

When I write to you all these nice, lewd, mad tricks, my brain whirls round, and one of the four following disgusting things is sure to happen:

I.—I cannot sleep and if I slumber a little, I dream of you, and I ejaculate spasmodically in erotic nightmares, which fatigue and exhaust me physically and morally. Hence my nerves are unstrung by the cerebral masturbation of those erotic letters. I take chloral. I lose my temper and thus nearly lost you; to sum up: rank stupidity!

II.—Or I master myself, and then I have frightful pains in my testicles and lower down, in consequence of these erections and partial erections that I overcome and drive away. That is what happens to me when I return from Sonis after a long, but never too long, happy day, passed with Lily. These are particularly sharp pains, especially as they begin by sweet, slow enjoyment of a teazing kind, provoked by your delicious secret touches and your stolen kisses, my beloved.

III.—Or else, being alone by day and night, thinking of you in spite of myself, and of all I could do with you, my hand slides, without my knowing it, between my thighs and with a few movements of my wrist I discharge in my fingers. It is idiotic and sickens me as soon as the brief sensation of burning pleasure (?) is passed. Thus does one become disgusted with oneself. Once I spent in the train coming back from Sonis this winter, after you had said to me: "What can we do in a dining-room?"

Miserable mankind! What a dirty bundle of rags is our poor body, when excited by our sad monkey brain, boiling over with infamous lusts.

IV.—To conclude: the sole resource of salvation for he, who can still have an erection and emit, is to seek out natural, complaisant pleasure for cash on delivery, but I think that disgusts me as much as my hand. All my life I have hated mechanical delights. I never had any taste for the joys of love without some sympathy; if only for an hour; without a little reciprocal passion; or, let us say a small quantity of affectionate illusion on both sides, in default of true love.

What confessions! You will soon know the male in all his ugliness. Perhaps you will be disgusted with me?

If it pleases you to answer me in a few lines you will make me very happy. I chiefly beg news of your health, and of your Papa.

I should wish you to give serious attention to what I am going to tell you. When you announced your departure, you said to me: "I must have a letter Tuesday morning." Then, from Brussels you wrote: "I must," again. Those orders expressed by you gave me a new sensation, that I had never tasted or desired with any other woman up to now.

The first revealing shudder of this new form of passion which comes from you to me, because it is you, shook my frame when I was with you and your brother in the drawing-room, where, laughingly, you gave me a kind of little lesson of discipline. I have already spoken to you of the effect produced, as well as of the strange excitement caused in me by your recital of the tale of Madame Rosenblatt's pupil. You are cunning enough to guess the meaning of my new thoughts. If this is repugnant to you, if you think I am ridiculous in trying to see if we cannot both find a novel and real pleasure, I, being your slave in every way, in the true sense of the word, and you, by holding me beneath your severe yoke, to be punished when you shall judge that I deserve it,—I promise never to speak to you about it.

I must confess frankly that this desire, although a little vague at present, thrills me and makes me tremble deliciously. I am agitated voluptuously by a movement that I have never yet experienced until this day. I am quite overcome by this change which has taken place in my being.

It rests with you to do with your Jacky whatever pleases you in this direction, or to forbid him to have such ideas.

In either case, this is the only indication that I shall give you. To teach you your part practically would cool me completely. I could not do it; I should not have the courage; I give you the broad lines, hoping that as I dare to say that my *poupée* rises at that idea, you, as you say you love me, ought to be wet as you read these words.

I will not tender you the homage of my obedience, unless you also get a glimpse of a new incarnation of sweet, loving delights.

I offer you the virginity of my humiliation. I shall understand that you accept with transport the abandonment that Jacky makes to you of himself, and of his so-called manly rights, but I should also comprehend without surprise that you would perhaps like to remain as we are, instead of reversing our positions to see what would come of it.

I tell you also frankly that, although taken up by this strange longing, ever since the day I told you, it may happen that once tried I may be the first to mock at myself. That remains to be seen.

It is an experiment to be tried, if you smile favourably on my ideas. With my wide tolerance for every manifestation of sexual passion, whatever it may be, I should not be surprised either to see you accept with enthusiasm, or refuse with mirth. As you please, Lily. All you do is right.

I have faith in your imagination, if you accept the command of your lover as freely as he gives it.

In the meantime, whatever you decide, I give up to you the direction of our correspondence, and will only take the liberty to write to you when you desire a letter, telling me the day, etc., as you did when travelling.

I have serious reasons for asking you to accept the entire direction of our liaison in the future.

I feel that I want to believe in you, to see events with your eyes, and feel in everything as you do; as you shall kindly direct my mind, by your firm will.

You have seen, I confess it humbly, that I have dared to doubt your word, though plainly written, as I rebelled idiotically against you last Sunday, when I began to lose the faith I had in you. I actually dared to form absurd theories about your conduct, instead of dutifully, and religiously believing in you, as I had done up to the present.

Take me therefore quickly and knead my brain,—the unbelieving brain of a man madly fond of you,—as you will, so that I may look at things as you desire and direct. Let me only have the ideas that you may dictate to me. I want to believe in you blindly. You shall be my religion; my holy, persecuted virgin.

Save me from my thoughts, and come and direct my soul with my body for your caprices, for your wants.

I await the pleasure of your answer with anguish. My eyes will be dim as I shall open your letter, if you deign to write to me shortly, to signify my salvation to me, and the peace of my tortured heart brought to me by the blind worship I dedicate to you.

But directly I see that in your great kindness you accept to tutoyer me,—while I shall return to the true respectful formula I ought never have abandoned,—I shall know that I am at last worthy of being fashioned and moulded by you, as you may wish.

I hold at your disposal all straps, belts, pins, whips, and all instruments, which I confess, to my shame, I meant to use with Lily.

Your humble slave,

JACKY.

I felt sure that the foregoing letter would convince Lily that I was mad with uncontrollable lust for her, and I also wanted to know if her Papa saw my letters to her. That is why I had added the paragraph concerning the unfortunate lover. The only danger I ran was that Lilian should see through my artifices, and feign indignation at my bold insinuations. But no, I had had in my life a tremendous experience of liars, and I have found that habitual falsehood-mongers are exceedingly credulous themselves, and Lily and her father would be sure to fall into the trap I had set for them. That a man should so degrade himself as to boldly set himself down in writing as a convert to the doctrines of Sacher-Masoch, and parade his sexual inversion, proves that he is entirely under the charm of the enchantress, and by apparently throwing aside all vanity, I hoped to arouse all that of my infamous couple.

The girl would be proud to show her old man how desirable she must be to so fuddle my brain, and her elderly lover would be elated to know that he was making a fool of me.

How lucky it is that women are not truly intelligent. All they really have is their natural charm and the power to draw us in their net by reason of their possessing that which our genital instinct forces us to covet: the little, furry money-box. Put a coin in the slit, and the figure will work, but as our lust is soon satisfied: to keep us enthralled, women's cunning is called into play, and their principal weapons—lying and craft—are furbished up to supplement the influence produced by their beauty and our own infatuation. If, added to their sexual sorcery, they were able to get the true range and direct their fire; without exaggeration of mendacity and diabolically distorted fables, then would all men be slaves without exception.

In my case, Lily was so sharp in her jugglery, as witness her recent letters and principally the missive sent after the night at Lille, that she would never credit that I might fathom her deceit and take to sending Machiavelic manuscript as well.

The study of this strange creature became quite absorbing, and I left myself no rest. I thought about my old flame by day and by night. It was well I did so, as I suddenly remembered that I possessed a very old friend, who lived in Brussels, whither he had retired to end his days, after a long and brilliant career at the English bar. He had been a criminal lawyer, and his name, Augustus Mallandyne, was well-known in the divorce-court. He would seize the situation at once, so this was what I wrote to him.

JACKY TO AUGUSTUS MALLANDYNE.

Paris. Wednesday, March 29, 1899.

My dear Mr. Mallandyne,

I want you to do something for me, which is very easy, but it is confidential, delicate work, such as only a man of the world like yourself can undertake for another man of the world like myself. Please note my subtle flattery, as I purposely refrain from speaking of your legal talent.

And after all, if you do not like the job—why do not do it. But if you can, you will be rendering me an immense service, at no cost or trouble to yourself.

I have no time to-day to tell you all the ins and outs of the story, but I will, and you will be delighted, later on. It is a charming love affair, and if you can get the information I want, I may be very happy.

A lady and gentleman stopped at the Hôtel des Trois Pigeons, 255, Avenue des Haricots Blancs, Brussels, for about a week, leaving for Paris, I believe, on or about Tuesday, the 16th. inst.

Description of gentleman:

Tall, any age over 50, bald-headed, aquiline nose, wears a pince-nez, talks loudly, with an English accent, dresses carelessly. A fair moustache, no beard or whiskers. Big belly.

Description of lady:

Young, about 23 or 24, looks older. Very dark, lots of black hair, good figure, although very thin. Long nose, not pretty, but pleasant; fine Spanish eyes, swarthy complexion, nice teeth. Coquettishly dressed.

Would probably register under the name of Arvel. Try for this name first. If not Arvel, what name?

Did they travel as Mr. and Mrs.? Or as father and daughter? Or uncle and niece? Or what?

IMPORTANT—What rooms did they occupy? What numbers? Single bedded; double bedded; two rooms communicating; or two separate rooms?

Did they seem loving and happy? Was the girl sad or gay? Did they go out at night, or go to bed early?

I want you to go at once about this, as soon as you get my letter. I shall look for details by return and expect a letter Good Friday morning—if you are in Brussels.

If necessary, be generous to garçon d'hôtel or femme de chambre, and I will refund any pourboires you give. May I ask you also to send me back this letter? Not that I care much, but this is rather indiscreet what I am doing.

The whole story when I have heard from you. Be quick, and accept beforehand my heartfelt thanks.

JOHN S...

P.S. To make things easier, I enclose a photograph of the lady, I have just got hold of. You must hurry, please, as the photograph has got to be put back in its place before its loss is discovered. So please return it with information, if you don't mind undertaking it.

To avert suspicion, go gently to work like this at first:

See visitors' book. If you find:

Arvel, Miss and Mr.

or,

Arvel, Mr. and Mrs., with dates and numbers of rooms, or number of room,—say nothing, but remember the figures, and under pretext of choosing a room for a friend who is coming, go up and find out the sleeping accommodation of the rooms occupied during their stay by the Arvel couple. Because if they registered as Arvel, I shall not want you to show portrait, or get other details, unless the servants should gossip easily.

LILIAN TO JACKY.

No date or place. Received March 30th. 1899. Postmark:
Sonis-sur-Marne.

My own Slave,

It is an understood thing. All you propose in your letter pleases me enormously, with but one exception. I want you to still continue to tutoyer me.

Enclosed you will find an article on fashions that you must translate literally into English, and as soon as it is done send it me with a long letter.

You will be invited for Easter Tuesday, if you do well the little work I give you now.

LILY.

I want a very passionate letter.

This note contained a long article on ladies' fashions, cut from a Parisian daily paper, and I was highly pleased, as I saw my vicious scheme was working well. The translation was wanted by Papa, there could be no doubt about it, and the fact of asking for a lustful letter proved that my mad effusion had amused and perhaps excited the lecherous stepfather. It is always a bad sign when a woman asks a man to write letters in a given key, and nearly in every such case, someone is waiting to laugh at the writer. It may only be a female friend, but of a surety the confidential character of the correspondence is gone. It is no longer the frank communion of two hearts that beat as one; a third party has been invited. I could not refrain from heaving a deep sigh of regret, despite all my scepticism. Lily had betrayed and sold me to her mother's lover; my letters served to make me a laughing-stock in his eyes, and I shuddered to think what a fearful fate awaited me if I had been possessed of less knowledge of the wickedness of the world.

The more I found that I was right in my awful conjectures, the more I was devoured by the feverish desire to carry on my endeavours to the bitter end, and know the worst. It was only thus that I could cure myself of any love I might still feel for the traitress of the villa.

Spurred on by the spirit of deceit, I tackled the translation and got it done and posted the same day. I did not forget the letter of lust, and dashed it off so quickly that I had no time to make a copy. But I made a few notes next day, as I was still thinking, and the thought assumed firmer proportions every day, of writing my romance that was growing fast out of the festering soil of the garden at Sonis.

Some of the photographs I had taken last month were tolerably good; one, representing Lily lifting up her skirt just a little, and smiling saucily, I had printed several times, and a copy was enclosed in my letter to Mallandyne, to aid in identifying the pretty little tourist. Another showed her reclining on her brother's breast. He was standing up in uniform and his arm encircled his sister, whose eyes were half-closed, her lips parted; and there was a smile on her features that gave her the appearance of a woman in the act of enjoyment, and there is no doubt in my mind but what she did feel a secret titillation of the vulva at that moment. I had rendered an ordinary sheet of note-paper fit to receive the impression of the negative, and I printed her head and bust on it, temporarily arranging the plate so that no other details appeared.

My letter was not very good, consisting of four pages of erotic twaddle, relating to the cruelty of women. I was careful only to speak very vaguely and I did not give her any details of what could be done to a man who might be really fond of being whipped or ill-treated by one of the weaker sex. I knew Papa was fond of books on flagellation, but I did not see my way clear to give him examples of torture. I told Lily that she knew how disgusted I always was when I had to write lascivious letters, as the effort aroused my passions uselessly, which was my real opinion, and it was downright cruelty on her part to force me to write voluptuous manuscript, being unable to see her as I should wish. Not content with making me suffer morally, she now seemed resolved to try how to torture me physically, and I concluded by the narrative of a dream I was supposed to have had, when I saw Lily reclining on a sofa, and as far as I could judge, enjoying the caress of an eager tongue. She was spending, and some hidden power held me back, and prevented me from rushing to her, or calling out her name. Yes, she was spending, and he murmured: "Enough! Enough!" All my lust seethed up in me; I felt I must approach her, and making one mighty effort, I awoke! I rose from my bed, to refresh my burning mouth and wipe away the trace of this "wet dream." Before returning to my weary couch, I gathered together some sheets of paper on which I had been taking some rough notes, before falling to sleep, and Lily must judge of my surprise when I found impressed upon a fragment of white paper the beloved features of my sweetheart in the act of enjoyment. I had felt inwardly during the vision, that I longed to possess her portrait as she thus appeared, and now some mighty, supernatural power had caused the dream-face to leave its impression on a leaf from the note-book of her lover and victim. I terminated with the humble wish that one day I might perhaps be allowed to produce her orgasm with my tongue.

Generally, according to Lily's old directions, I always addressed my envelopes in my disguised female hand, and posted them at a post-office a little way away from my dwelling. This time I did not disguise my writing, and posted the bulky missive, so that it bore the postmark of an office in the very next street to where I lived. I need hardly add that this was never mentioned to me later, but I noted it silently for my own satisfaction.

AUGUSTUS MALLANDYNE TO JACKY. (*Telegram.*)

Brussels. Friday, March 31st. 1899.

Commission executed, writing.

AUGUSTUS MALLANDYNE TO JACKY.

Brussels. March 31st. 1899.

Dear S ...,

Yours to hand. I know the two Boomaens, Ghent people, brothers, who keep the Hôtel des Trois Pigeons. I saw the principal man. He very willingly gave me all particulars.

The couple took Room No. 4, composed of two rooms en suite, separated by a lobby, where you could hardly see. The front room, with

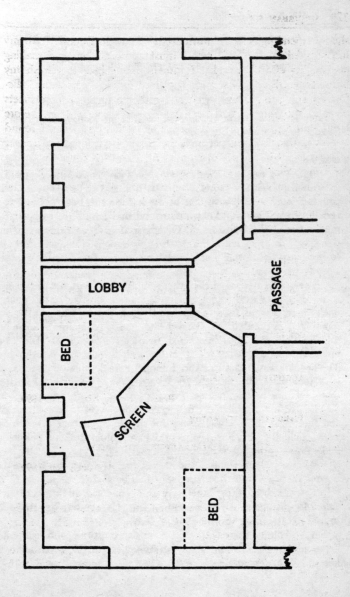

one or two windows, I forget now, but I think two, giving on the boulevard, is large, and with two beds.

Introduced the girl as daughter—several times—and also to gent in room when taken, who had not yet turned off. Boomaens tells me he would say, with pride: *Ma fille, monsieur!*

When the out-going lodger came down to the *bureau,* he said: "Funny father! I almost thought he wanted me to have his daughter. Seemed to be throwing her at my head!"

They had one room with a screen as shown by the drawing enclosed.

Out every evening, theatres, etc. Very gay, apparently happy. He recognised photo. They arrived on March 8, and registered as A . . . , *pere et fille.* A . . . has been here before and is a client of the hotel, to a certain extent. I am well known there and they have a great respect for me, as I send them customers. Of course, I gave no name as to my principal. Boomaens knows I am acting professionally. *He seemed quite to understand that the mutual relations of the two visitors were assumed.*

They could have used the other room if they liked, but they never touched it. They used to get up late. It appears somebody in the hotel, one or more persons, used to slip into the dark passage between the two rooms and pry and listen. They heard noises of romping, laughing, sounds of slapping, and smothered, inarticulate sounds, as plainly demonstrative as they were incompatible with the declared relationship. The bedding was always in a very tumbled state, leaving no doubt as to what took place. Also, towels, stains, etc. I fancy from what I elicited that something peculiar had been seen.

I dared not ask for more details, as it might get to my wife's ears, and she might think I was spying for myself, but it was plain, those walls, could they have spoken, would have unfolded a tale of lust as seldom reaches the public ear.

Why not come yourself and stop a few days with us as you did before? I'll take you to Boomaens. Shall all be glad to see you.

This is a cheap, quiet hotel, very well conducted, and quite respectable. My wife and a lady friend came there only a month ago, in order to take an early train, next morning, to Italy.

A . . . coming there with a little Parisian prostitute, and registering her as his daughter caused a sort of excitement in the hotel. She was known as *la petite femme.*

Boomaens said A . . . was in some way connected with the Stock Exchange. I am quite sure that Boomaens is not likely to commit any indiscretion. He took me upstairs on his own invitation and explained the arrangements of No. 4, about the best in the hotel, on first floor.

The visitors' book was blank as to departure but I would not, in fact could not, wait while he turned up his accounts. I had a heap of business to attend to, but I·managed your affair all the same.

I wired you this morning: "Commission executed, writing," which was intended to show you all was in train. Are you happy? Let her have it *hot*.

Yours truly,
A. M.

Very pleased to be of use to you—old friend!

I can find nothing better to write here than the well-known sentence: "Truth is stranger than fiction." Lilian and her mother's keeper had gone to a town together where lived my friend, who "understood things," and to whom I could write freely; and by a lucky chance, he happened to be on intimate terms with the proprietor of the hotel where they stopped. I am perfectly certain that many of my readers will smile increduously at what they will consider the artfulness of the author of this book, and the very strange coincidence which I point out will suffice to make them doubt my veracity, a contingency which I cannot prevent in the least.

I was satisfied with the result of my enquiry, which fitted in well with my suspicions, and I felt myself fully armed to meet my darling and see what would be her next move.

Is it not extraordinary that a man known to an innkeeper should register as *père et fille*, and remain from the 8th. to the 16th. in a double-bedded room? Apart from the question of vice, is it not madness? Sleep with your daughter or stepdaughter if you will, while on a trip, but is there not some other cleaner way of going about it for the sake of the young woman, whose reputation you are thus coolly damning, whose life you are wasting? As I write these lines, the hot blood rises to my face, I blush for shame to think that I should dare to judge this man; I, who had perhaps been as great an agent of corruption as he.

Arvel's behaviour in this instance was so monstrous that even Boomaens does not believe his companion can be his daughter, and Mallandyne, who is far from squeamish, has not guessed, and cannot guess at the truth. Perhaps that is why Arvel does it?—"If I do it openly, no one will believe it." Like the woman who goes up boldly to her husband and says: "Do you know, dear, that your friend has just had connection with me?" The newly made cuckold bursts out laughing at his wife's indecent fun, and the jesuitical adulteress joins in his mirth. Perhaps he tells the lover in covered terms of his wife's joke and they all roar together.

The great Mallandyne had returned me the photograph and my own letter, together with a sketch of the room at the Hôtel des Trois Pigeons, from which I have prepared the plan given in this volume.

If the reader has any doubts as to the fornication of Arvel and Lily, I must beg him or her to reflect a little on what a celebrated English judge, Mr. Barnes, said when directing the jury in the suit for divorce of Sprague v. Lihme, which was decided in the spring of 1899, in London. (*See Appendix C.*)

JACKY TO MALLANDYNE.

Paris, Monday, April 3, 1899.

My dear Mr. Mallandyne,

It is impossible for me unless I were to write eight pages, to thank you for the clever and prompt way in which you have behaved in rendering me this signal service.

It is strangely lucky that the only person I know in Brussels, should be the very one, almost the only one, who could see through things, and guess exactly what I wanted and do what was wanted. If you had read in a novel how a man possessed a friend in a strange city, who did for him what you have done, precisely when he required his aid, you would sneer at the barefaced lameness of the invention.

I remembered your many delightful stories of the law-courts and how you had taught me some of the tricks of spies and criminals, and that is why I took the great liberty of asking you to help me.

What I have done through you is not a very clean thing, I admit.

Spying is mean and I say so myself. My excuse: "All is fair in love and war."

I have no need to tell you the whole story. It would be too long and I see by your letter that you in your worldly wisdom have guessed everything.

No doubt we shall see each other before we die and have a nice, long "crack" together over a friendly glass. Then you will hear all. It is only of interest to me.

I don't think I shall give it to her "hot," though she deserves it; I shall tuck your information away in a pigeon-hole of my brain and await developments.

Perhaps one day, I shall ask her if she has ever read a novel by Conan Doyle, called: "The Sign of Four."

Thanks for your kind invitation, which I shall remind you of in July, if you are then in the Belgian capital and care to have me.

Please remember me to Mrs. Mallandyne.

With more thanks,

Yours very truly,
JOHN S . . .